DAGRIL'S LEGACY

DAGRIL'S LEGACY

ALVAH PHILLIPS

DAGRIL'S LEGACY

iUniverse books may be ordered through booksellers or by contacting:

iUniverse
1663 Liberty Drive
Bloomington, IN 47403
www.iuniverse.com
844-349-9409

ISBN: 978-1-6632-3996-9 (sc)
ISBN: 978-1-6632-3997-6 (e)

Library of Congress Control Number: 2022909148

Print information available on the last page.

iUniverse rev. date: 05/13/2022

CONTENTS

Prologue.. vii

Chapter 1   On the Hamen Starship................................... 1
Chapter 2   Explosion 6
Chapter 3   Going to Florence 13
Chapter 4   Florence 16
Chapter 5   The Banker's Party.. 18
Chapter 6   The Dark Cloud 22
Chapter 7   Buying the Dress Shop................................... 29
Chapter 8   Trouble at the Stable 34
Chapter 9   Everin and the Dress Shop 38
Chapter 10 The New Stable 49
Chapter 11 Doc..51
Chapter 12 The Dress Shop Windows............................... 55
Chapter 13 Riding Back to Florence................................. 59
Chapter 14 The Dress Shop Girls..................................... 64
Chapter 15 Lucca... 70
Chapter 16 Alerton Looks for a Farm............................... 77
Chapter 17 Moving Uriel 82
Chapter 18 The Bank... 89
Chapter 19 The Food... 92
Chapter 20 Setting a Date 96
Chapter 21 Uriel 100
Chapter 22 The Dress 104
Chapter 23 Jewels.. 106
Chapter 24 Wedding Day 110
Chapter 25 Christmas 114

Chapter 26 The Plague...116
Chapter 27 The Plague Strikes Home 119
Chapter 28 1477...128
Chapter 29 Dagril's Legacy 130
Chapter 30 July 28, 1914..134
Chapter 31 Steam Yacht...206
Chapter 32 Special Marine Aircraft...................................213
Chapter 33 Mingaladon, Burma...230
Chapter 34 Problem with Henri 234
Chapter 35 2014..251
Chapter 36 2017..277

PROLOGUE

IN AD 1347, A STARSHIP FROM A DISTANT WORLD WHERE THE PEOPLE, because of perfected DNA, lived exceptionally long lives was observing Earth for benign scientific purposes. When the starship exploded, two escape pods were launched.

One pod carried one Hamen on board, Dagril. It was overloaded with precious metals and jewels but for noble reasons. The load made the pod overheat, and Dagril perished on the way down. The second pod contained three Hamens, one female and two males. They knew they would be marooned on Earth for a minimum of forty Earth years. A distress signal would take twenty years to reach Hamen, and a rescue mission would take another twenty years to reach them.

They salvaged both pods and protected what they salvaged. They used the valuables they saved to make their fortunes. The three Hamen survivors were Everin, Alerton, and Metrool.

1

ON THE HAMEN STARSHIP

THE B CREW WERE IN THE DINING AREA, WHICH WAS DECORATED TO their taste and redecorated automatically. Everin entered the dining area and requested meal 359 from the automated meal creator.

Alerton, technically in command, said, "Everin, ever since you programmed that meal, you ask for it half the time."

Everin answered, "Strange. It's a copy of an Earth meal, but I find I enjoy it."

Rondal, a computer telescope tech, said, "Everin, how can you possibly eat that? It has a dead animal in it."

Everin replied, "You know better than that, Rondal. All our food is created by the computer from basic elements."

Rondal said, "The computer gives it the taste and texture of the real thing."

Dagril said, "Leave her alone. We are letting those beings kill and eat animals and kill and maim one another, and we do nothing about it. Now a disease is spreading across their world, killing untold thousands."

Metrool, a technician, said, "I have shown you the history tapes. Every time we try to help a society advance, things go wrong—sometimes terribly wrong."

Arrista, one of the official historians on board, said, "We have interfered before on this very planet."

Dagril said, "We have? When?"

1

"Well, as most of you know, two small colonies of us settled on this planet forty thousand Earth years ago."

Metrool asked, "Were there two or three?"

Arrista said, "We are not sure."

Everin asked, "What happened to them?"

"Well, you know our home planet, Hamen, was attacked by the Lucians at that time. We would have given them gold, but they wanted to annihilate us and have the whole golden planet. It was total war, and we barely survived. It was three thousand Earth years before we could rebuild Hamen to a level where we could build starships. Then we came back."

Metrool said, "Well, Arrista, don't leave us hanging. What did they find?"

"Nothing—or almost nothing."

Metrool said, "I don't like the sound of that. What do you mean 'almost nothing'?"

"They found nothing physical, but they found traces of our DNA in the earthlings."

Dagril asked, "How is that possible?"

Arrista said, "Quite simple. Some interbred, and the others died off from natural or unnatural causes."

Everin, who was medically trained but not a practicing doctor, as the medical robot did that job, said, "You mean earthlings and Hamens can interbreed?"

Tekril, a scientist, said, "That's disgusting—mixing purified, DNA-corrected blood with these animals."

Arrista said, "Well, a hundred thousand years ago, we weren't DNA-corrected, and we were a lot like these animals."

Tekril said, "Yes, we were undeveloped, but we were never like these people."

"Well, about one thousand three hundred seventy Earth years ago, there were some in our governing body who felt that part of this planet's problems were caused by those colonies and that our DNA interfered with their natural progression."

"Well, they did nothing about it."

"Oh, but they did. They sent a secret mission to Earth to try to put the planet back on its correct historical track."

Everin interrupted. "Well, did it work? Tell us about this secret mission."

Arrista said, "I can't; it's totally unrecorded. I was told this story by an old historian who had heard it from another historian."

Metrool asked, "Then why do you put any faith in it?"

"When I heard this story, it intrigued me because of a peacemaker legend I had heard. So I began to make discreet inquiries about it."

Dagril said, "Then tell us what you found out."

Arrista said, "I didn't find out anything, but the Controller sent his personal envoy to talk to me. They told me the mission was just a legend but let me know in no uncertain terms that I was not to ask about it anymore."

Tekril said, "The Controller's personal envoy? He isn't seen in public, and he came to you to shut you down?"

Arrista said, "Yes, but as he walked to his floater, he turned around and said, 'It worked.' Then he was gone."

"Dassrilla," Tekril said, muttering a cuss word. "Then there really was a mission."

Arrista said, "I don't know for sure, but I truly believe there was, and yes, I believe it worked too."

Metrool said, "How can you say that? What evidence do you have?"

"I have observed that since the time of that legendary mission, there are groups of people who put society's welfare ahead of their own."

Alerton said, "Weren't there always a few people like that? Persons who gave up everything for someone else?"

"Yes, but it was basically individuals sacrificing for their kin or someone they cared about. Now the effort is organized. People are working as a group to make things better."

Dagril said, "But these very groups have done some terrible things."

Arrista said, "Yes, these groups have done some atrocious things, but that mission had only a few Earth years and had to make strictly an ideological change; they could not physically change a million beings."

Slowly, the dining area emptied, until only Alerton and Arrista remained.

Alerton said, "You lied. I've never known you to lie in all the Earth years I've known you. Why lie about this?"

Arrista pushed her long hair back, and Alerton saw it still had full color. "You know I've been on many of these voyages; I am more than seven hundred Earth years old. This will be my last trip, but you know my family have a long record of being historians."

"Yes, you and your family are well known for your public service and totally honest histories."

"Well, I never said this, but I had a relative on that mission—the mission that doesn't exist in any history. When he came home to Hamen, he was a changed man. All he ever said was that the leader of the mission, who used the name Joshua, had sacrificed himself for the good of the planet, when the ship had the means to save him. Alerton, we have been friends for a long time; please do not abuse our friendship by repeating these words."

"Arrista, my friend of many years, I understand the sacrifice you made to tell me this, and I would never abuse our friendship."

In another part of the ship, Dagril was among the escape pods. The pods could carry three occupants, and they were outfitted for the blending in and survival of the crew, but they also were self-destructive, in compliance with the rules about not interfering.

Dagril put something heavy into pod three and rearranged some other heavy objects in the pod. Dagril looked around to make sure no one was watching. There were no surveillance devices on the pod deck, for the pods hadn't been used in more than six hundred Earth years, and there was no crime on the ship.

On the deck right above the pod deck was the science deck. Alerton joined Everin and Metrool there, and on different screens, they scanned some information the ship had picked for them to review. The ship knew the type of information each one preferred.

Suddenly, the room turned red and orange, and the computer said in a loud, clear voice, "The energy pod is about to consume itself. Thirty

Earth seconds. Twenty-nine Earth seconds. All who remain on the ship will cease to exist. Twenty-six seconds."

Alerton popped out of his shock, shoved Everin and Metrool down the escape tube, and then jumped into the tube. Alerton found Everin and Metrool climbing into pod number five, and he joined them and pushed the large launch button. The hatch slammed automatically just as the hatch in front of them was blown away so they could escape. They were painfully pushed back in their seats as the computer tried to get them away from the exploding ship.

2

EXPLOSION

THE ACCELERATION DID NOT EASE UP UNTIL AFTER THE COMPUTER FELT the shock wave of the doomed ship. In a clear voice, the pod's computer said, "The ship no longer exists. Only four beings escaped."

"Four?" Everin said. "Who is the fourth?"

The computer answered, "Dagril is the fourth, in pod three."

Metrool was at the controls, and Alerton said, "See if you can find him on the screen."

Metrool said, "Yes, I have him on the screen. He's stable, with good life signs, and he has dialed in coordinates and told the computer to descend."

"Dial in those same coordinates, and follow him down."

"Here we go. This is a one-way trip."

"Yes, I know, but I feel we will be better off if we are together."

Soon the atmosphere began to batter the pod, making tearing sounds. The pod shook and lurched, and their body holders squeezed them tighter to keep them in their seats. The computer was calling out hull temperatures: 312, 417, and then 544.

Metrool said, "Something's wrong."

Everin said, "Metrool, what's wrong?"

"Not us. Dagril's pod is going too fast. It's getting too hot. It might break up."

Alerton said, "But, Metrool, other than the coordinates' override, these pods are totally automatic."

Metrool said, "True, but Dagril may have altered the controls."

Everin asked, "Why would he do that?"

Suddenly, their minds were pierced by waves of pain and anguish from Dagril. His pod was overheating, and they could literally feel his pain. The temperature in Dagril's pod was going up and up, but there was nothing they could do.

Dagril, sharing through the pain, said, "I'm sorry; I meant to do good and help these beings we caused so much pain and sorrow to."

Everin said, "I have to help him." Her body went rigid, and she began to moan. She was absorbing some of Dagril's pain. Their pain eased as they felt Dagril's life force going.

Everin said, "That bastard. He just vaporized twenty-six Hamens. Why did I feel I had to do that?"

Metrool answered, "It was the right thing to do."

"I have never heard of twenty-six Hamens dying at the same time. So many. Wonderful Arrista." She put her hands to her face.

Metrool said, "We all loved and respected them. Dassrilla! May Dagril sleep with the Lucians."

Alerton asked, "Has his pod broken up?"

Metrool said, "No, the computer has it back in control. It's going to make a fairly normal landing."

"Punch the exact coordinates of where he lands. We have to make sure these pods do what they're supposed to do."

Metrool said, "Yes, we'll be right beside him in about two Earth minutes after he lands. I have my hands on the emergency thrusters. One Earth minute till landing." He counted down with ten seconds to go. They landed.

Alerton took a deep breath. "Good work." He then told the computer, "Open the hatch."

The hatch opened with a hiss, and the three Hamens climbed out, looked around, and took test breaths of the Earth air.

Everin said, "It's very close to Hamen's air. That is why they picked it for the prime colony. This combination of water and air is rare."

Their attention went to Dagril's smoking pod. Reluctantly, they walked the short distance to it.

Alerton inspected it and then said, "Computer, open the hatch."

There was a short delay as the computer analyzed his voice to see if it was authorized, and then the hatch opened. All three stepped back. The way Dagril looked and the smell from the pod were terrible, and the three walked away.

After Alerton pulled himself together, he went back to the open hatch and asked, "Computer, why did the pod overheat?"

The computer said, "The pod was overloaded with unauthorized equipment."

Alerton said, "List this equipment."

The computer said, "One hundred Earth pounds of medicine, ten pounds of special seeds, fourteen pounds of printed paper, twenty pounds of medical equipment, twenty pounds of antique medical equipment, thirty pounds of synthetic jewels, one hundred pounds of silver coins, twenty pounds of imitation florins, and two hundred standard gold bars. The total weight is nine hundred six Earth pounds over a pod's limit."

Bewildered, Metrool said, "I'm surprised it did not burn up. That is way over the capacity of a pod."

Everin said, "The medicine was destroyed by the heat."

Alerton said, "It is just as well that it was. I feel we would have been tempted to use it."

Everin said, "What do you mean *tempted*? That medicine could have cured a lot of diseases down here."

Alerton said, "Now, listen to me. What we have been through does not change the rules. We cannot change things. We must blend in and make a comfortable and safe life for ourselves, but we cannot subvert the Controller's rules. They will come for us, and I don't want us to be criminals when they arrive."

Metrool said, "We must empty the pods before they are vaporized."

Alerton said, "Yes, thank you, Metrool. Let's work quickly. You and Everin empty ours, and when you finish, you can help me. Metrool, you have a geographic survey of this locale on your personal computer, don't you?"

"Yes, and the pod was updating it as we came down. Yes, I have a detailed map of this area."

"Ask it if there is an unused building or cave we can use to store our goods."

Metrool said after a short wait, "The computer's best choice is a cave about half an Earth mile away."

Alerton said, "It will be a lot of work, but we need to get everything and ourselves into that cave before daylight. The locals are going to be scared but curious about the lights they saw tonight."

Everin said, "A cave? I've never been inside a cave."

Metrool laughed. "Neither have I, except in a simulator. But I feel we will have a lot of new experiences."

Working quickly, they loaded the floaters to their capacity, and each picked up a heavy bag. It took three trips, and it was nearly daylight when they were through.

Alerton walked up to pod five and said to the computer, "We have removed everything we need. You can proceed with your programming." He walked back to where Everin and Metrool were, and they watched the pod begin to glow. They turned their backs. They knew a major flash was coming.

After they felt the flash, they turned to look, and the pod was gone. Metrool walked over to pod three and followed the same process.

They entered the cave, which was S-shaped and barely high enough to stand.

Alerton asked, "Do those emergency cases have mentats in them?"

Metrool said, "Yes, they both do."

"Take one to the mouth of the cave, and set it for severe fear. I don't want anyone to come into the cave. And set a comfort device to light and warm our area of the cave."

Everin said, "I think it's time we did the rememotory ceremony."

The three survivors formed a small circle, and each placed his or her right hand on the left shoulder of the next. They leaned forward, putting their heads close, and all three recalled their memories of the lost crew members one by one. Finally, they were to the last, and they could all see wise Arrista. Strangely, Arrista looked at them directly, and mentally, they heard her words: "You have a wonderful opportunity."

Mentally exhausted, the three survivors collapsed to the cave floor and slept where they fell.

Five hours later, they awoke. They activated the food producer, and it began to create edible wafers in the flavors they requested. After eating, they opened the bags containing clothes fitting for the period and locale.

Metrool, looking at Alerton, laughed and said, "If the crew could only see you now."

Alerton said, "Well, you don't exactly look like a handsome spaceman in your outfit."

Everin said, "Yes, we are all wearing too many and too fancy clothes, but at this time and place, your social position is defined by the opulence of your clothes, and we want to be perceived as rich people, so we must dress the part."

Metrool had his computer in his hands. "I took Dagril's memchip out of his pod. Look at this." He displayed a 3D projection of the local terrain. They could see traveling merchants and the city they would be going to.

Everin said, "Dagril was planning this for a while."

Alerton said, "Yes, but this will help us. Metrool, you did us a service when you saved this chip."

The three did a quick scan. They would study the information in detail later. Their lives depended on it.

Everin said, "We have to be extremely careful in what we say and do. These people believe in witches and magic, and any of our magic could get us burned at the stake."

Alerton replied, "Yes, that's why this time, the only magic we'll take is the defense built into our headdresses. And three small vaporizers."

Metrool said, "Yes, the brain-wave intensifier. Do you really think it could kill an earthling?"

Everin said, "Of course. You just go into their mind and stop their heart from beating."

Alerton said, "I repeat: you have to be very careful with your mind. Yes, we have the power to scan their minds and read their thoughts, but Hamen experts believe the earthlings would think we were the devil. So do not probe. You can let your mind be sensitive and just pick up what they're thinking at the time. Of course, you can sense their feelings, such as fear, hate, greed, and even like or dislike, I suppose."

Everin asked, "What about love?"

Metrool said, "You mean real Hamen love or what these crude people call love?"

Everin said, "I sometimes feel we Hamens have refined and controlled our emotions too well."

Metrool said, "Oh, Alerton, look out—Everin is already romanticizing these people."

They studied the information and made plans for what they would do. Finally satisfied, they relaxed, ate some wafers, and drank some synthesized nectin, a drink that relaxed and stimulated the drinker. Metrool asked, "What do you think of the mystery voyage to Earth? Do you think it really happened?"

Alerton said, "I've been thinking about it, and there are a couple of things I do know. It was in that time period that we had the great government change."

Everin asked, "What happened during the change?"

"Well, before that event, the Controller wasn't called the Controller; he was called the Faathir of Hamen. According to one story, because of some disgrace, the Faathir resigned right in the middle of his service years. Well, the citizens were very disturbed, and they changed a lot of things, so now we have the Controller." Alerton added, "Today will be a very unusual day."

It was midmorning before they went out of the cave. They couldn't help but talk about the night before.

Metrool spoke up. "We looked at Dagril's memory chip last night. I think you will find it helpful."

Alerton activated the Tok and began to scan it. "Yes, he had the merchants' travel routes laid out. He landed us close to a route leading to a city named Florence. He even has folders on some of the local businesses and traders."

"Wow," Everin said, "Dagril was deep into this."

"Yes," Metrool said, "he must have been planning this for a long time. And he must have spent years figuring out how to bypass all the safety systems on the ship."

They had buried 90 percent of their equipment; they would come back for it soon.

Alerton said, "The only devices we will take with us at this time are the brain-wave enhancers and the vaporizers. Both are small and easy to conceal, and both can self-destruct if necessary."

They checked what else they would take: ten gold bars; three bags of florins, each weighing about five pounds; and ten pounds of silver coins. Everin took a pound of selected jewels. The coins were all counterfeit; they hoped they passed. They had buried all the other riches and devices except for two: a mentat at the entrance to the cave to cause deep fear and a second mentat located close to their hoard that could do physical damage to anyone who came too close.

3

GOING TO FLORENCE

THEY WENT THE SHORT DISTANCE TO THE TRADE ROUTE BUT WAITED behind some trees so they could observe the travelers first. The first two traders who went by gave off bad vibes, but the third one, with two horse-drawn wagons and six pack mules, seemed to be what they needed. They approached him, and with a little thought-wave persuasion and two gold coins, he was their ally.

It was afternoon when they entered Florence. Taking the trader's advice, they went to the inn named the Arno and acquired two rooms on the second floor. Then they walked around the city, keeping their minds open to receiving people's thoughts. They were pleasantly surprised to find most of the people pleasant and honest. They saw the city had a choice of banks and had an artistic community, which was a major interest to Metrool, for he was an artist.

While they were eating at the inn, Alerton caught some vibes from some businessmen drinking and talking over in one corner. He leaned close to his companions and said, "This may be a break for us. One of the major banks is in trouble. The banker has a good reputation, but he financed a major trading venture, and there was a bad storm that sank three of the five ships. Now the bank is about to sink. I feel we have found our bank."

"A good bank that we can save," Everin said. "The banker will owe us, and we need friends who have obligations to us."

"Yes," Metrool said, "I caught some of the conversation, and it sounds good." He added, "Alerton, do you want to be our bank man?"

"Yes," Alerton said, "if you two approve, I think I would like that job."

Everin and Metrool both said they thought he was the right one for the task.

———————•❦•———————

The next morning, after eating breakfast with Everin and Metrool, Alerton got with the inn owner to help him. He had the owner hire a scribe and two guards to go to the bank with him.

At the bank, Alerton asked the banker's assistant for a private meeting with the banker. The assistant was suitably impressed, and soon Alerton was in the banker's private office. There was some small talk and wine. Alerton lightly probed him and saw he was an honest man in deep trouble who was hoping for a miracle. Alerton got to the point and hit hard, saying, "I heard rumors, and I searched, and I know your bank is in trouble."

The banker turned pale; he had hoped this man had not heard about his plight.

Alerton said, "My brother and sister and I have gold—a lot of gold. We can save your bank." Hamen had four ethnicities, and because of the DNA project, everyone of each ethnicity looked very much alike. Alerton, Everin, and Metrool were the same ethnicity, so they'd decided to present themselves as siblings.

The banker waited for the other shoe to drop. What did this strange, tall man want?

"Of course, we want a good return on our gold, but we want more."

"If I give you too much, my bank will fail anyway."

"We do not want extra money," Alerton said. "We want and need a friend in the business community who knows everything and everybody."

"I've lived here all my life," the banker said, "and I can be that friend."

Alerton scanned him lightly and saw he was telling the full truth. Soon they had the scribes writing up papers, and the gold man took the three bags of gold from the guards and emptied them out onto the counting table. He began weighing the Hamen gold.

Alerton asked the banker for a private talk, and once they were in the banker's office, he said, "My brother and sister and I have a lot more gold and silver. We will put some of it in your bank and some in other banks. How much we put in your bank will depend on how much you do for us."

Alerton saw that the banker had a major conflict inside him. He said, "Tell me. What is bothering you?"

The banker, obviously terribly embarrassed, sweating, said, "If I tell you, you may pull your gold back out."

"Tell me," Alerton said.

The banker said, "Your gold covers everything now, but in two months, I will need twenty more pounds."

Alerton scanned him and saw it was an honest answer. "You be our friend and help us meet people and buy houses and maybe a business, and you will have your twenty pounds of gold."

"To show you I am really that friend, and because you are new to Florence, I will tell you. The last twenty or so years have been colder than usual, and our grapes and olives have not done as well as usual. Our farmers have learned to cope, but some lost out. Then last year, the year of our Lord 1346, was very bad for business here in Florence. Three important banks failed. And now in 1347, we have had six months of rainy weather. Farmers either can't get in their fields to plant or can't get in their fields to harvest. Some of the farmers make a few grossi by catching rabbits, cats, or squirrels for the cloak makers over by the Duomo."

Before he left, Alerton had two signed and sealed copies of their wealth and an invitation for all three to a celebration the banker was giving that night. The banker told Alerton to call him Abram. His last name was Termini.

Soon Alerton was back at the inn, talking to his so-called brother and sister. He told them everything that had happened.

"Great," Metrool said.

"Yes," Everin said, "you did great."

Alerton turned to Everin and said, "You need to go shopping and buy some expensive clothes that flaunt your charms."

At first, Everin was aghast, but then she smiled. "Yes," she said, "I must remember that here, my intellect does not count; my cleavage does."

Metrool laughed. "That is putting it a little rough but is true."

Alerton said, "Remember, do not be too smart. Don't be put off by the humans' lack of knowledge. Our own people went through a period like this."

4

FLORENCE

ALERTON GAVE EVERIN AND METROOL PURSES OF REAL LOCAL MONEY that he had traded florins for at the bank. Metrool headed for the artist community, and Everin went to a clothing place. The clothing shop had several nice things about 75 percent made, but she had to stay there while they tried the clothes on her and cut and sewed. Across the street was a doctor's office. Sometimes the doctor would walk out when a patient was leaving. The first time Everin saw him, she caught her breath. He was beautiful. Earth men were not supposed to look like that. She found it hard to breathe; there was a tenseness in her chest. The doctor went back inside with a bent-over man.

Everin walked up to the window. The shutters were open, and there was no pane. She went over to where the clothing shop's owner was telling a skinny young woman what she wanted her to do. Everin said, "There is no glass in your window."

Frieda, the owner, said, "Glass is very expensive. We have shutters."

"Doesn't it get cold in here?"

"We have cloaks."

A few minutes later, Everin couldn't hold back; she scanned the doctor. *Oh my, what kind of earthling is this?* She could basically feel him feeling his patient's pain. But oh no, he was telling him to do the wrong thing for his pain. Why was he doing that? Was he a quack? She broke the rules: she scanned deeper. She found that was what he had been trained to do. She was hooked. As gently as she could, she made him aware that he had not helped his patient and made him aware of what he should do.

She saw him leave with his bag. A short time later, she saw him return, and with light scanning, she found him on his knees, thanking his god for his enlightenment.

Suddenly, she felt someone scanning her. It was Metrool.

"Well," Metrool said to her, "you have been in this place for one day, and you have fallen in love with an Earth man."

"I'm not in love with him," Everin said. "I have never met him."

⟶⟶➤●◄⟵⟵

That afternoon, Alerton and the banker went and looked at two homes owned by the bank. Tomorrow they would look at two more. They were riding horses provided by the banker.

Alerton said to him, "From time to time, I will need horses. Can you help me?"

"Of course," said Abram. "Just a short walk from our bank is a public stable that is very good and has a lot of customers."

Alerton said, "That sounds like what I need."

Abram leaned close and spoke quietly. "It is owned by Tim Petrosson, and he is old and sick. I think you could buy it for a good price." He twisted his head around, making sure no one had heard them.

Alerton asked, "Does he owe anyone?"

Abram replied, "He owes our bank one hundred florins."

"Why does he owe that?"

"It has been a terrible year for the farmers—so much rain. Some hay has been brought from the Po, and that doubles the price."

Alerton said, "I will go see him."

Then they had to separate, for the banker had to go supervise the preparations for the large celebration.

Back at the inn, Alerton found it amusing that Everin had a major interest in a well-respected doctor, and Metrool had spent several coins to gain favor with the artist set by getting six of their main players very drunk.

5

THE BANKER'S PARTY

THE THREE WENT DOWN TO THE INN AND HAD A MEAL OF BREAD AND cheese; they did not know what the banker would be serving, and some Earth meals were unnerving. At nine o'clock, they found themselves arriving with another guest. They were welcomed warmly by the banker and his wife. They were given glasses of wine, and they mingled with the other guests, picking up random thoughts. Alerton was a little surprised to see a priest there.

The banker whispered to Alerton, "He is here for my food and wine."

Alerton studied the guests, thinking, *What is each one's work?* Sipping the wine, he thought, *This is very good wine. I will have to ask the banker where he gets it.*

Suddenly, Alerton saw Metrool practically run out of the banker's home into the courtyard. He went out to see what was wrong and asked him, "What is it?"

"I almost threw up," Metrool said.

Alerton asked, "Did you get a bad drink?"

"No," Metrool said, "there is an earthling in there with a body inside her."

"That is a new earthling," Alerton said. "That is the way they reproduce here. They do not have femtechs here."

"Yes, I had forgotten that," Metrool said. "It is sickening."

Alerton said, "A long time ago, it was done that way on Hamen, but as you know, Hamen females can't reproduce anymore."

"Wonderful," Metrool said. "Earthlings are so primitive."

"Yes," Alerton said, "but that is why we came to study them. They are about to seat the guests. Can you go back in?"

Metrool said, "Yes, just do not sit me close to that female."

Everin was studying the guests' clothes and found them all to be in opulent dress. There was a lot of fabric in the wealthy women's clothes, much more than necessary, and some of that cloth was patterned and very expensive. Suddenly, her heart skipped a beat—the doctor was arriving. She quickly went to another part of the banker's home.

Later, as they gathered around the large, oval-shaped dinner table, she was formally introduced to the doctor. When he kissed her hand, it sent forbidden electricity through her. She lightly scanned him and found he was amazed by her but did not let it show. All through the extravagant dinner, he seemed to be ignoring her. But each time she scanned him, his mind was in a state of confusion. She picked up his thoughts: *No woman has ever affected me like this. What is it about this strange woman? Where are these three from? Why is my mind so impressed by her?*

When dinner was over, standing in front of her, the doctor stumbled through an invitation for a glass of dessert wine and a walk in the banker's garden.

Everin laughed charmingly and nodded. "Doctor, I did not think you even knew I was there tonight."

"Oh yes," he said, "you were all I could think of. I could not tell you what we ate tonight."

"Doctor," Everin said, "I am sure all the young maidens are after you."

The doctor blushed and said, "No one has ever filled my head with dreams before."

They arranged to meet again—with a chaperone, of course. Everin was relieved that her feelings for him were not one-sided.

But then a jibing, joking thought came from Metrool: *What would he think if he knew you were one hundred forty-two years old?*

For a moment, Everin was chagrined. But she shot a thought back to him: *If he knew the whole story, it would not matter.*

Then a sobering thought came from Alerton: *Everin, the doctor can never know the truth. You must face that from the start. The doctor can never know the truth.*

⸺⸱⸱⸱⸺

The next morning, the three Hamens met with the banker to look at houses. The bank owned several houses in Florence. By noon, they had looked at all of them, and they and the banker went back to his home, where his cooks had prepared a meal for them. They discussed three of the houses. Cost was not an object. Finally, they brought a fourth house into the discussion. It was smaller, but it was two stories like the others and was built like a fortress.

Alerton said, "This one is only two houses away from the one Everin likes. Metrool and I will buy it for our home."

"Fine," Everin said. "Yes, you know which one I like. It has upstairs balconies on two sides to catch the breezes, and I can watch the sunsets."

The banker said, "Fine choices. I will have my scribes finish the papers. Even if they must stay late, we can finish tomorrow." He winked. "You are my partners." He handed them the large keys to their new homes.

Alerton and Metrool walked with Everin to her new home. They were surprised the banker already had maids cleaning the place. As they watched the maids work, they saw the banker and three wagonloads of furniture, bedding, and cookware coming down the narrow cobblestone street. The banker came up to Everin—he obviously liked her—and said, "This is just to get you moved in. We have furniture makers who can make whatever you wish. As for the maids, look them over, and hire the ones you like. The large one cleaning the fireplace is a good cook and honest, except she likes to eat."

"Yes," Everin said, "I will hire some of them after I look them over." She thought, *I will look them over a lot better than you would believe.*

As the afternoon went by, Alerton and Metrool went to their own place. Everin scanned the women and found the cook to be honest, and she could live with Everin. The cook had a friend who could take care of Everin's garden, and when Everin scanned the others, she found two who were pleasant and honest. Once the house was set up, Everin paid off those she was letting go. Then she gave the cook coins and told her to take the maids and buy everything they needed for the kitchen, saying, "I want my brothers to eat here tonight with me."

Soon Metrool showed up with her things from the inn. He looked her new place over and said, "It isn't Hamen, but it is nice."

"It is very nice," she said. "I will make changes as time goes by, but we have a lot of time."

"We may not have a lot of time," Metrool said.

6

THE DARK CLOUD

SURPRISED, EVERIN SAID, "WHAT DO YOU MEAN?"

Metrool said, "Alerton and I were studying Dagril's Tok."

"Yes?"

"There is a terrible disease migrating across this world. It is killing half the people, and it is getting close."

"No!" she said. "The doctor will be in the middle of it, and he may die."

"We will be immune, of course," Metrool said, "but yes, your doctor could die."

"He is a good man, a special man. That wouldn't be fair."

"Life is not fair, but this disease is what drove Dagril crazy. He wanted to defy the rules to try to stop this disease. He took enough gold and jewels to build hospitals and medicine factories."

"He thought he could stop it?" Everin asked.

Metrool said, "With our medicines, yes, but they were all ruined by the heat."

Just then, the cook and maids came back with their supplies.

Everin said, "We are eating here tonight."

"Sure," Metrool said, "and I will go purchase some wine. These backward people do know how to make good wine."

An hour later, Metrool returned with a cask of wine. That night, they ate an excellent dinner. Everin had made a few changes to the local recipes to fit Hamen taste, and the cook had been cooperative. They couldn't talk about what they wanted in private until after dinner, until they were upstairs on a balcony. They scanned to ensure no one was around.

Metrool said, "Yes, it is coming and less than a few months away."

"Zabel," Everin said, cursing. "You mean a thousand people could die?"

Alerton said, "Ten thousand people could die. In some cities, they can't bury them fast enough; they are just throwing them into the river."

"That's awful," Everin said. "Can't we do anything?"

"Nothing," Alerton said. "They do not have microscopes, and they do not know about bacteria. We would wind up being burned as witches."

After Alerton and Metrool were gone, Everin stood on her north balcony. She had chosen this house because it was just down and across from the doctor's place. There was light in his window—a candle or two. There on Earth, they only had candles, torches, or fire; she missed having light.

She concentrated on the doctor and listened. He was thinking about his patients and what he did for them. His medicine was crude. Gently, she put an idea in his mind about tree bark. Next, he thought about her, and she blushed. Earthlings did physical sex. There hadn't been physical sex on Hamen for a long time.

Alerton and Metrool were back at their new home, and Metrool said, "I know you like this place, but isn't it like what they call here a prison?"

"No," Alerton said, "it is more like a fortress, and tomorrow workmen will make it even more so. Bad times are coming. We will have to bring Everin here when the trouble starts."

"The trouble?" Metrool asked.

"Yes. When people start dying by the hundreds, the ones left alive will go crazy. Laws will break down, and people will start doing things they would not dream of in normal times." Alerton led Metrool down into the cellar. "Look at this." He moved three bricks and showed Metrool a secret hiding place.

"Very nice," Metrool said, "but how do you know twenty people don't know about it?"

"Because there were eleven gold coins and ten silver coins in it. The owner must have died without telling anyone."

"Well, we need to go to the cave to retrieve some of our gold and devices."

"Yes, I have already talked to the banker about horses and guards."

"We can't take the guards all the way to the cave."

"No, we will stop a mile or so away and give them a mental suggestion that they need to rest."

"Good idea, and when we get back, we can put a little confusion into their minds."

"What if they suspect?"

"They won't, because when we get back, I will buy them a whole cask of wine."

⟶⟶⟶●⟨⟨⟵

In the doctor's rooms, the doctor lay awake in the darkness. *Why can't I get her off my mind? Why am I fascinated by her? Even when taking care of my patients, I keep thinking about her. Is she a witch? Has she cast a spell over me?* He laughed to himself. *My grandmother, before she passed away, used to say all women were witches, and I never knew what she meant until now. Everin is no witch, but I am under her spell.*

Doc did not know that Everin was hearing every thought and, strangely, rubbing her nude body and thinking of him. She said to herself, *No one in Hamen does this.* But Doc radiated such passion.

The next morning, after breakfast and after she had supervised the maids into cleaning things her way, Everin dressed in a new dress and walked to the seamstress shop, making sure she walked right in front of the doctor's office.

Doc could not help himself; when he saw her, he left his patient and went out to talk to her. She was bold and said, "My brothers will be dining with me tonight. Would you like to join us?"

Without hesitation, Doc said, "Yes, I would love to."

They parted without touching, but both were floating on air.

At the dress shop, Everin picked out fabrics and patterns. A frail young woman helped her pick out the right fabrics. Everin looked around. It seemed the owner, Frieda, got the cheapest help she could and treated them like slaves. They were underfed and not dressed well enough for an expensive dressmaker. The girl tried to help her the best she could, and when Everin had selected the fabrics she wanted, she slipped the girl a silver coin and said, "Buy some food." Tears ran down the girl's cheeks, and Everin quickly wiped them away and put a finger to her lips to let her know to be silent.

Another girl helped her pick out patterns. All were awful in Everin's eyes, but these people wore them. Finally, she picked out three, gave the bitchy owner a deposit, and was about to leave, when the owner said, "I have a dress that is nearly finished. Would you like to look at it?"

"Yes, I would," Everin said.

Upon seeing it, she decided to try the dress on. In the tiny fitting room, Everin was helped by another girl. Everin, seeing how it looked in the large brass mirror, decided to buy it. The owner told Everin the price of the dress. Everin shot back a much lower price and soon paid a price in the middle. The owner was a greedy, bitchy woman. Everin lightly scanned her and saw a lot of hate and anger inside her for no apparent reason. Her mind showed no signs of mistreatment.

Everin left the dress shop, and her cook and escort was sitting in the chaperone seat outside. She stood up quickly when Everin came out, and they began the short walk to Everin's home.

Everin said, "What do you know about Frieda?"

Donna, the cook, said, "She is evil. No one likes her. She would get a lot more business if she were nice. Some whisper that she is a witch."

Everin asked, "Where does she get those girls?"

Donna said, "They are poor orphans with no relatives and no money. She treats them like slaves, but they have nowhere else to go."

Metrool was at the barn-like building where the master sculptors worked and the apprentices practiced. Metrool had worked his way in with wine; coins, as artists were always broke; and a little scanning. He was now with Leon, looking at his latest painting. It was of an angel, and Metrool had to admit the angel truly looked angelic. Metrool asked Leon, "Who is the model?"

Leon answered, "She really isn't a model; she works at the inn down the street, the Parrot."

Metrool shook his money pouch. "I have money for wine—take me, and introduce me."

Tore and Sandro spoke up and asked, "Do you have money for us too?"

"Of course," Metrool said, thankful for the camaraderie to ease what he was feeling from Everin. The four walked the short distance to the inn. The sculptors sometimes trailed marble dust.

As they entered, the innkeeper spoke loudly. "Do you have money? No money, no wine."

Leon said, "My rich friend here always has money."

But Metrool stood transfixed. Hamen had plenty of genetically perfect, beautiful women, but he had never seen one look so innocent.

When Leon introduced him, he said, "This is Simonetta, the most beautiful woman in Florence,"

The innkeeper came to them, and Metrool woodenly gave him several coins. The innkeeper looked his fancy clothes over and said, "Maybe you are rich, not like these bums. I don't like for them to even look at my daughter."

"But you let Leon paint her," Metrool said.

The innkeeper took a deep breath. "One time. That is for the church. The padre came to me and said I would be sinning if I didn't let my angel pose for his angel."

Metrool and his friends found a table, and another girl brought their wine. Soon Metrool got up, seeking Simonetta, and his friends made catcalls at him.

Leon said, "Be careful; the innkeeper is a demon. He used to be a banker and does not really like being the owner of an inn."

Metrool found Simonetta, called Netta, by the oven and, with a soothing scan, showed her he liked her and meant her no harm. After some small talk, Metrool asked, "Will you have food with me over at that table by the window?"

She blushed. "If my father approves."

Soon they were by the window, but Metrool did not really touch the food. He asked her questions about herself, her family, and the city, and with light scans, he saw that each answer was true. Time went by quickly. Metrool kept doling out coins. The innkeeper was satisfied, and his friends were getting loud and drunk.

A thought came from Everin: *Where are you? Dinner is ready.* A laughing thought from her followed: *Oh, I see why you are late.*

Metrool said goodbye to Netta and walked to Everin's home. It wasn't far, and soon he arrived. Doc and Alerton were already there.

To impress Doc, Everin had done her best on the meal and herself. Metrool's comment about her 142-year-old age still stung. Everin was happy Doc was still gaga over her. Alerton found it amusing.

They had a good time. The table was laden with food. The four sat down at the table. Because the cook and a maid were hovering around them, even small talk was difficult, because they had to filter the discussion, but the wine Metrool had acquired was good.

Alerton asked the cook to say a prayer for them, and the cook was delighted. They had to blend in, and they knew maids and workmen talked, and gossip spread. They knew they had to act like the locals.

As they ate, Everin told them about her troubles with the dressmaker.

When she had finished, Doc said, "There are rumors that she is deep in debt to your bank and behind in paying it back."

"I will find out tomorrow," Alerton said.

Metrool talked about his new friends at the academy, saying they were a good group, and he had been surprised at how good some of them were.

"Tell us about Netta," Everin said.

Metrool grinned. "Now, there is a special girl. She posed for Leon once to be an angel. Now her father will not let her pose again. He does not like artists."

Doc said, "They are a loud group."

"Her father says they drink too much, they never have money, and they don't respect women," Metrool said.

They all enjoyed the dinner, and then Everin and Doc took wine out onto her east balcony to watch the rising moon and breathe each other's air. It was not wine they were intoxicated with; it was each other.

At the table, which was now cleared of food and dishes, Alerton and Metrool talked business.

"We need to be in business to make ourselves more respectable," Alerton said. "If that rumor about the dress shop is true, we will buy it."

Metrool asked, "What if she does not want to sell?"

"She will not have a choice," Alerton said. "Keep your eyes open for another deal."

Doc and Everin came back to the table. They had not touched each other, yet they smiled as if they were drunk.

"Charming," Metrool said. "The moon must have been bright tonight."

Doc said his goodbyes and went home.

Alerton said to Everin, "I was against this, but what can I say?"

Everin said, "Thank you, Alerton."

After Alerton and Metrool went to their own home, Everin went upstairs to her bedroom, got into her bed, and mentally turned herself off. She did not want a mental overload; these emotions were new to her.

7

BUYING THE DRESS SHOP

THE NEXT MORNING, ALERTON WAS AT HIS BANK AND IN ABRAM'S OFFICE. At once, he asked, "Does Frieda the dressmaker owe the bank?" Alerton saw Abram was not happy with the question. Impatient, he said, "Well?"

Abram said, "She owes a lot."

"Is she up to date?"

"No, she is way behind."

"Why haven't you foreclosed?"

"Some large depositors do not want me to. Some have large deposits to buy clothes from other countries, and they are afraid of losing them."

"How much does she owe?"

"One hundred twenty-five florins."

"And how much is the shop worth?"

"About a hundred."

Alerton said, "Hire some guards, get the officials, and foreclose today."

Abram asked, "What if she will not cooperate?"

"Tell her if she goes quietly, we will forgive the twenty-five florins she cannot pay, and we will give her twenty-five florins if she leaves Florence."

"And if she doesn't?"

"She goes to debtors' prison."

"That is a little harsh," Abram said.

Alerton said, "Life is harsh. We will have a buyer tomorrow."

"Who is it?"

"Everin."

Abram did what Alerton had asked, and Frieda yelled, screamed, cussed, and even threatened Abram with bodily harm. But the fight went out of her when the official read the signed and waxed official paper: "Frieda Maroni is to be held in prison until the remaining twenty-five florins are paid."

Abram told her, "Sign these papers, which will totally release your shop to me. I will give you twenty-five gold florins. If you do not leave Florence, I will have the officials arrest you."

She used some more vile language, but she was beaten.

That afternoon, Alerton met with Abram and said, "Keep guards there until I tell you to stop. Now have one of your assistants tell the girls they will be retained by the new owner. Have the assistant take them to the inn to eat twice a day." Alerton saw the look on Abram's face. "Do not worry, money counter; I will pay for it."

Late that afternoon, Alerton sent Metrool a message, and they met at Everin's home.

Of course, Everin could sense something was about to happen and asked, "What is it?"

Metrool said, "We just bought the dress shop."

"We did? How?"

Metrool said, "She had borrowed more than it was worth, and she was not paying it back."

"What are you going to do with it?"

Alerton said, "Metrool and I thought we would put a sign out front: Space Women's Dress Shop."

Everin laughed. "You want me to run it?"

"No," Metrool said, "we want you to own it. It is in your name."

She was surprised because it had happened so fast but pleased because of her concern for the girls. She said, "I do not know what to say."

"Say yes," Metrool said.

Everin said, "Yes! Yes, I love it. Now I can help those poor girls."

The next day, they just let the dress shop sit. The shop was being guarded, and the girls were being taken care of. Everin spent the day planning what she would do with the dress shop.

———⟫●⟪———

Alerton and Metrool had used the stable lately and met a young man named Dino. Abram had told Alerton the stable owner, Tim, who was in his eighties, was old and in bad health. Alerton walked up to Dino and said, "I would like to meet your master."

"I will go see," Dino said, and he ran off.

Dino soon came back and said, "He welcomes you."

Alerton felt he was welcomed because he was a partner in the bank. Dino led him to the owner's place, and Tim's adopted daughter, who was about sixty, let Alerton in and guided him to where a thin old man lay in a bed. Alerton saw that Tim was close to dying, and he was courteous and made small talk before he started talking business.

Tim told Alerton about his life before he'd come to Florence and about the forty years over which he had run the stable in Florence. He told a wonderful story of his life. But as Alerton looked at the frail dying man, he knew it was a lie.

Alerton looked him in the eye and said, "You can read thoughts."

A look of fear flashed across Tim's face, and then he relaxed and said, "You can too. Hamen!"

It was a shock. For a moment, Alerton did not know what to say. Then he asked, "Were you on the last mission?"

Tim said, "My father was. His name was Petros." Obviously reading Alerton's thoughts, he added, "You want to buy the stable, and I want my daughter taken care of. I don't have much time."

Alerton saw Tim was fading fast and said, "I will be right back with a scribe and notary."

Alerton practically ran to the bank, briefly told Abram, and grabbed the bank's scribes and notary, and on the way to Tim's, he told them the offer and told them to write quickly.

Tim was barely breathing. Alerton took hold of his hand and willed some of his strength to go into Tim temporarily.

Tim opened his eyes and mentally said, *Thank you.*

The scribe read the offer, and Tim said, "It is a generous offer. Let me and my sister and the notary sign it."

Abram entered about that time and watched the signing. Tim looked at his daughter and said, "You can trust this man. He will take care of you."

Mentally, Alerton said, *Yes, I will. Can you tell me about the last visit? Yes.*

However, after one or two confused thoughts, Tim was gone. His daughter, a frail, old-looking woman, began to weep deeply. Alerton saw that her grief was real and saw she was not Hamen. Alerton was sad, but he did not let it show. It was such a loss. If only he had known Tim was Hamen, there was much he could have asked him. Alerton went to the daughter and asked her if she would like Abram or him to arrange the burial.

Still crying, she stammered, "Yes, if you can."

Alerton was puzzled, and Abram said, "He wasn't much into church."

Alerton had met the neighborhood priest when the priest made his obligatory check-in after they came to Florence, and it had been obvious he did not care for Alerton, even after Alerton gave him a donation. Now Alerton walked to Mary's Angels Church and soon was talking to the priest.

The priest said, "I will say words over him, but it won't be a mass, and I will bury him but not in hallowed ground. I do not believe he was a Christian."

Alerton did not like the priest's arrogant ways.

Then the priest said, "I am not even sure you are a Christian. Let me see you get on your knees and start praying."

Infuriated, Alerton said, "Why don't you get on your knees and start praying for forgiveness?"

The black-robed man said, "I am the priest."

"Yes," Alerton said, "but even priests must confess mortal sins."

The priest said, "I have no mortal sins."

Alerton said, "You have a huge mortal sin that you have never confessed, so it is on your soul, and when you die, you will go to hell."

The arrogant priest said, "I have no sins on my soul."

"No?" Alerton said. "How many times did you force your younger sister to let you use her body?"

The priest was in shock.

"And when she found out she had your child inside her, she jumped into the river and killed them both."

The priest screamed, pushing him out.

Alerton walked to the inn and sat, having a glass of wine. He was about to finish his wine, when a man came in and said, "The priest has closed and barred all the doors of the church."

The innkeeper asked, "Why?"

The man said, "No one knows."

Alerton asked for another wine. Soon two more customers came in, and one said, "The priest jumped from the bell tower with a rope around his neck."

Alerton laid some coins down and decided to go to the bank, thinking, *I guess I lost my donation.* Alerton went to see Abram, and he told Abram about the priest. The news upset Abram.

Abram said, "These are dangerous times, my friend, and for a priest to commit suicide, some would say there was a witch around and start a witch hunt."

Alerton thought to himself, *My friend, you do not know how close you are.* Then he mentally told Metrool, *Meet me at Everin's home.*

Soon, out on one of Everin's second-floor balconies, Alerton told them the events of the day.

Dismayed and impressed, Metrool said, "You met a Hamen."

"Only for a few moments," Alerton said.

"But he really was a Hamen?" Everin asked.

"Only half," Alerton said. "His father was Hamen."

Everin said, "If only we had known, I would have asked him so many questions."

Metrool asked, "What about his funeral now?"

"Well," Alerton said, "I went to a different church and a different priest, and with a proper donation to the church, Tim will have a proper burial. Abram had a casket delivered, and from now until the funeral tomorrow, friends and neighbors are helping his daughter with the wake."

Alerton and Metrool left Everin's home, and Alerton waited until they were at their own door before he said, "We must go to the stable."

8

TROUBLE AT THE STABLE

"ALL RIGHT," METROOL SAID, "BUT WHY?"

Alerton said, "As Tim was going, he gave me a flash."

"What was it?" Metrool asked.

Alerton said, "It was the words *north stall*. Why would a dying man flash *north stall*?"

"It would have to be important," Metrool said.

"I believe it is," Alerton said.

When they arrived at the stable, they found Dino asleep in his crude wooden bunk. Alerton thought to himself, *I must hire him a helper.* Dino awoke and joined them. He did not have to dress, as he'd slept in his clothes. Alerton said, "We are looking for something."

"I will help you," said Dino.

Alerton asked, "What is the north stall?"

Dino pointed to a stall and said, "That one."

Metrool asked, "Will you take the horse out of it?"

They watched Dino take the dark horse out of the stall and move it to an empty one. Alerton and Metrool entered the stall and looked at every bit of it. It was an ordinary horse stall; they found nothing noteworthy or unusual.

Metrool said, "Dino, will you rake the hay out?"

Dino got a wooden rake and cleaned the stall down to the dirt. Alerton and Metrool went back into the stall and looked it over again but still saw nothing.

Metrool said, "Tim may have buried something."

Alerton got a shovel and began to dig testing holes. When he was on the fifth small hole, he heard the *thunk* of the shovel hitting wood. Metrool came in and began to dig too. Soon they had exposed a wooden box. After some more digging, they pulled the wooden box out of the dirt. All three stared at the wooden box.

Alerton removed the locking pin, took a deep breath, and opened the box. They all looked inside the box and found papyrus, parchment, and vellum with Greek and Aramaic letters.

In the bottom, they found a spearpoint. What was a spearpoint doing in the box? Alerton picked it up. It looked as if it had bloodstains on it. Why hadn't Tim cleaned it? Was it his father's blood? Reluctantly, Alerton ran his tongue along the blade. It was Hamen blood.

Handing the spearpoint to Metrool, Alerton said, "That may be Tim's father's blood; it's Hamen."

"Pure Hamen?" Metrool asked.

"Yes," Alerton said. "Then it had to be someone on that last mission."

Just then, the monsignor from Mary's Angels Church burst in with six church guards. The monsignor screamed, "Witches doing the devil's work! Grab them, and bind them. Tie them with seven knots, or they will escape."

One guard asked, "The boy too?"

The monsignor said, "Yes, him too. They killed my priest, and now they will all burn for it."

Soon the three were in separate cells in the basement of Mary's Angels Church.

It was late at night, and Alerton mentally scanned the basement prison. He could only feel one guard on duty. Alerton mentally messaged Metrool: *Can you work on the guard on duty? Tell him we were arrested by mistake, and the monsignor has apologized and wants the guard to release us.*

I will work on him, Metrool said. *Are you going to work on the monsignor?*

Yes, Alerton said, *I must get us out of this.*

Alerton opened his mind and saw that there were fourteen minds in the Mary's Angels building besides them. The first mind he came across was a prisoner, the only one besides them. He had been tortured to the point where his mind was gone. He was scheduled to be burned. All Alerton could do for him was give him a painless death.

Then Alerton found the monsignor and another mind close to his. It was female. She was a nun, and she was his lover. Alerton went into her mind first. What had he told her? He had told her he was going to arrest some witches, and when he'd come back, he had told her he'd gotten them.

Alerton saw the nun did not care one way or the other and slept with the monsignor, who was an inept lover, just for the benefits. Alerton smiled to himself; her pet name for him was Moni, and she lied to him and told him he satisfied her.

Alerton erased only what pertained to them and then went deep into the mind of the peacefully sleeping monsignor. *Zzaagran!* he thought, using a Hamen word of surprise. He was not a believer. He only had said they were witches so he could arrest them and torture them to see if they had anything to do with his priest's suicide. Alerton adjusted Moni's attitude so that he did not care why his weak priest had committed suicide.

The Vatican would send a new priest. The three in the basement were of no importance to him, and he forgot them. Alerton asked Metrool, *Will the guard release us?*

Yes, Metrool said mentally, *he is on the way. I am giving him three florins, and he thinks he is releasing us for money, so he will not talk about it.*

Soon they were outside and free, walking back to the stable. As they get close, they encountered awful smoke, and all three ran the rest of the way.

When they got there, Raphael, a neighbor's son, met them in the street with horses. He was crying. "I got them all out but two. They would not run through the fire, so they died. They fell over before the fire got to them."

Metrool went to him, put his arms around him, and said, "Thank you, Raphael. You did a great job. Thank you."

Alerton said, "Raphael, would you like a job working with Dino?"

Raphael said, "I would love it, but you have no stable."

Metrool said, "We will build a new one."

Alerton turned to Dino. "Is there a pasture you can take the horses to?"

"Yes, I can," Dino said.

Alerton said, "Raphael, go with him, and help him; you have a job now."

Metrool gave Dino ten florins and said, "Buy whatever bridles and saddles you need." Alerton and Metrool watched the boys lead the horses away.

"What a terrible loss," Alerton said. "We did not get to talk to Tim, and now we've lost his papers."

They went into the burned-out stable. The remains of the wooden box lay there. The writings had been dumped out onto the floor, and they were ashes. It was terrible to see the two dead horses.

Metrool said, "I put the spearpoint in the loose dirt." He recovered it, and it still had some blood on it. "I wish we knew if this is Tim's father's blood or not. I think you need to put it in your wall."

9

EVERIN AND THE DRESS SHOP

UNAWARE OF ALL THAT HAD GONE ON DURING THE NIGHT, AS METROOL and Alerton had kept her sealed out, Everin went on with normal business. She went to the still-guarded dress shop. She had sent word asking Abram to send carpenters and window makers to the dress shop.

The girls greeted her warmly. Everin looked the place over: the large front room, where the girls worked and displayed dresses and fabrics; the little fitting room; and the storage room at the back. It was a mess, with pieces of fabric, trimmings, scraps, and dirt. At the back of the storeroom was the facility, and it was awful. Before she went up into the attic, she went to Sarah, the healthiest-looking sewing girl.

She gave her a coin and said, "Go to my home, and tell all of the maids I want them to come here and help you girls clean this place. Tell them there will be extra coins."

Everin then sent a mental message to Alerton: *Are you still at the bank?* He answered, *Yes.*

She told him, *Have Abram send a stonemason too. Also, you or Metrool should bring a cart with a horse or mule to take a lot of stuff to the orphanage.* She would donate old cloth and cloth she did not think her wealthy clients would buy.

She climbed the stairs into the large attic. It was really like a second floor but dark. The whole place was dark. *How can the girls do good work if they can't see?* At the back of the large attic was a door. Everin opened it, and there was a small balcony. The only view was of other buildings, and it looked as if it had never been used.

Everin went downstairs, and the carpenters were there. She began telling them what she wanted.

The lead carpenter said, "That will take a lot of time."

"No," Everin said, "I want it done soon. Hire more carpenters, but get it done." She saw that the window makers were there, and she pointed to the window and said, "I want to make that window larger, add another window and shutters to the front, and add two to the attic."

The carpenters looked flustered, and Everin said, "If you do not want the job, say so."

They wanted the job; they were just overwhelmed by Everin.

Then she addressed the window makers, and the shorter one asked, "What church are we making a window for?"

Everin said, "It isn't for a church; it is for this shop."

The taller one said, "We only make church windows."

Everin, annoyed, said, "But for extra gold, you could make me windows."

They looked at each other and nodded. The shorter asked, "What image would you want?"

"I do not want an image; I want clear glass."

"We do not have clear glass; we have only small pieces of colored glass. It is all we use in our work."

Everin thought quickly, reached into her money pouch, pulled out two florins, held them up, gave them to the glaziers, and said, "When I get clear glass, you will make me four windows."

Both glaziers said, "Yes, we will."

⟶⟫◉⟪⟵

That morning, after two hours of sleep, Alerton bathed, shaved, and dressed. He was going to see the monsignor. He had to make sure their mental tricks last night had worked. In his clothes were two items: a pouch of florins and a BWI, a brain-wave intensifier. He wished he had an SFD, a strong force disrupter, but they were in the cave. Metrool and Dino were still asleep upstairs. After they had finished at the burned stable, Metrool had gone to the academy, woken up some of his artist pals, and tied one on. Because he was Hamen, Metrool would be all right when he roused. But Alerton smiled when he thought about Metrool's friends; they would be cussing him today.

Alerton arrived at Mary's Angels Church, the same place he had been in a cell last night. He went inside, found a young clergyman, and asked to see the monsignor.

"Is it for confession?" he asked.

"No, business."

The young man disappeared for a few minutes and then returned and took Alerton to the monsignor's office. Alerton took a quick look around the room. It was opulent; the monsignor liked nice things. The young clergy introduced Alerton to the monsignor, and Alerton was happy to see it had worked: Moni did not recognize him from last night. Moni asked Alerton what his business with the church was.

Alerton said, "We understand your church money is in the Patroce bank."

"Yes," Moni said.

"Well, my bank knows you can't do usury. We understand Patroce's donations to your church are small." Alerton saw Moni was interested.

Moni asked, "Your donations would be larger?"

"Yes," Alerton said. "Our donations would be more than one half of what usury would be."

"That is very interesting," said the monsignor.

When the visit was over, with another light scan, Alerton confirmed he did not remember last night.

Alerton walked to the burned stable. Looking at the charred wood, he thought, *What a loss. Not the stable but the answers in those documents and the lost knowledge of Tim.*

A man from the carpenter guild showed up, and Alerton told him what he wanted to do.

"I can arrange it all," Cosemo said, "and get it done quickly."

Alerton scanned him and saw that he could and usually did but not always. Alerton took him to Abram's bank, wrote a contract, gave him one hundred florins to start, and put an unknown fear in the back of his mind if he did not get it done.

Metrool joined him, and they began their walk out to the farm where the horses were. Metrool said, "Dino is already on the way."

Alerton already knew about the cooler climate and terribly wet year Florence was having, but upon seeing the farms, he saw why the farmers were having a bad year. Dino was waiting at the farm gate. Together they walked on to the farmhouse. Dino informed them that the owner was a widow; her husband had been killed in one of Florence's many conflicts.

When they reached the farmhouse, the owner and her two children came out to meet them. Alerton was shocked; all three were pale and underweight. He scanned the farm again and sensed only chickens. They'd sold off everything else to survive.

After Dino had done the introductions, Alerton said, "We want to thank you for letting us keep our horses here."

The widow said, "You and your horses are welcome, but we have practically no feed for them."

Alerton said, "Thank you, and we are going to buy hay now; may we use your wagon?"

"Of course," the widow said.

Alerton, Metrool, and the boys hitched two of their horses to the widow's wagon, and all four rode it back to Florence. Once there, Alerton stopped the wagon, and he and Metrool climbed down.

Alerton asked Dino, "Do you know where to buy food?"

Dino said, "Of course. The hay barn."

"No, no," Alerton said, "food for the widow and her children."

Raphael spoke up. "Yes, we do."

Alerton gave Dino some florins and said, "Go buy them a lot of food. Buy fruit if they have it. Be sure to buy honey and bread, and do you know where we can buy a milk cow?"

"I think so," Dino said.

"Well," Alerton said, "we will worry about that later. Just buy the food, and take it to her. We are going to buy hay."

Alerton and Metrool walked to the hay barn and talked to the owner.

The owner said, "Bad luck, your stable burning."

"Yes," Alerton said, "we lost two horses, the hay, and the barn."

The owner said, "I heard you lost a lot of hay."

"We did," Alerton said. "That is why I am here to buy hay for my horses."

"It is expensive," the owner said. "It has been a bad year—way too much rain. A lot of good hay molded."

Alerton and the owner haggled over the price, but Alerton could scan him and know the minimum he would sell for. In the end, Alerton bought six wagonloads: two to be delivered to the widow's farm now and four to be delivered to the new stable later.

As they were about to leave the hay barn, an old man came up to them and asked, "Did you buy Tim's stable?"

"Yes," they said.

The old man said, "I hear they are going to bury him in holy ground."

"Yes," Metrool said, "he was a good man."

"Yes," the old man said, "but he was not a Christian. I worked for him for nineteen years and saw him do many things that only a witch could do. I did not turn him in to the church, but he should not be buried in holy ground."

Metrool investigated the old man's thoughts and saw that he had thought of Tim as a father and had loved him. He was angry at the world because for the last ten years, he had cut himself off from Tim, and now Tim was gone.

Alerton and Metrool saw he was contrite over Tim, and they sat down on a bench with him and let him talk. Soon he loosened up and began telling tales about Tim. He said, "Tim could tell some whoppers. One night, when we were drinking, Tim said, 'I and my brother are as old as Methuselah.' Can you imagine someone telling one that big?"

Metrool and Alerton walked to Everin's home. The three went out onto Everin's north balcony and, for the next hour, rehashed everything that had happened.

Everin said, "You must stay for dinner. Doc is coming."

⟫●⟪

Four weeks later

The stable burning had made Alerton aware of the famine. The widow's farm, where they had put their horses, had been a shock. The widow and her two children had been deathly thin. Alerton had given Raphael money and sent him to buy a wagonload of food. Later, when he had gone to the hay barn to buy hay and grain for the new stable, he had seen that the price was nearly twice what it had been a year ago.

But food for people was getting scarce and expensive. The three were lucky they had Dagril's gold. They were rich, but most people were not. It was fall, and the situation was getting worse.

Alerton went to see his bank partner, Abram, and asked, "Are those three ships we seized in Pisa still there?"

"Yes," Abram said, "no one wants to buy ships."

"Do they have crews?"

"No, but it would be no trouble to get crews."

"I want to send them to Sicily to buy wheat and whatever kinds of food they can find. If they can only fill one ship, they can send the other two to France or Spain. I want those ships full when they come back."

"What about hogs, sheep, and goats?"

"Yes, anything that can get here healthy."

"Do you think we can make a profit?"

Alerton said, "I am not doing this for profit. People around us are going hungry. Christmas is coming, and food is a large part of Christmas. I have heard that between Pisa and Livorno, there are fishponds where they collect fish and seafood."

"Yes," Abram said, "and fish are still plentiful. They do not need good weather."

"I want contracts with them for fish, clams, crabs, and octopus for November and December."

"It will cost a lot of florins."

"I do not care. Next year, the weather will be better, and the people will not be starving. Can you go arrange all that?"

"I can go in two days," Abram said. "It will take ten to fourteen days. I can let my assistant, with your oversight, do my job. Alerton, will you be at the bank every day?"

Alerton answered, "Yes, I will until you get back. Why don't you take Metrool with you?"

Abram grinned. "That is a good idea, and you can give him a bag of florins to pay for all this."

Alerton said, "If they get the food, it will be worth it. There are so many hungry people out there on account of the bad weather, the failed crops, and the animals that starved or were slaughtered because people knew they would starve."

Abram said, "You are aware of how much this will cost? And the bank will supply the ships but not the crews."

Alerton took a deep breath. "Yes, banker, I understand, and Everin, Metrool, and I will pay for it."

Alerton left the bank and messaged Metrool: *We need to go clean out the cave.*

When? Metrool asked.

Alerton answered, *Before daylight tomorrow.*

Metrool said, *You know the law; we will have to have lanterns till we get outside the walls.*

I will buy them today, Alerton said. *Everin needs to go, plus an extra horse and two guards. Make sure we have plenty of bags.*

Metrool said, *Yes, we need to get everything.*

Everin messaged them: *Meet at my home. The cook will have breakfast at four.*

Alerton added, *Everybody keep a low profile. These are bad times, and we do not want to alert any bad people.*

⟫◆⟪

At four thirty the next morning, even though they did not need them, they lit their lanterns and walked to the nearly finished stable. Dino and Raphael already had two horses saddled and a packhorse ready for them. They were soon on their way.

The two guards had been waiting at the Arno Inn. They went through the narrow, winding cobblestone streets to the northeast, and it was still dark when they went through the new wall and started up the trade road. Soon it was daylight. They traveled the main trade road for nearly two hours before they left it, and shortly after that, they left their guards in a stand of trees to wait for them.

When they reached the cave, they scanned the area and found it clear. They went into the cave and found it had not been disturbed. They turned off the mentats and went deeper into the S-shaped cave. Soon they had dug up their treasure. They were able to load everything onto their horses, except the two floaters and their digging tools.

Metrool said, "I do not want to vaporize the floaters."

"I know," Alerton said, "but we must. They cannot be disguised."

Metrool set the vaporizer at 80 percent and pointed it at the objects, and they disappeared in a flash. They all felt a wave of heat go by them, and the objects were gone. Afterward, they went out to their horses and mounted up.

The trail was muddy, and the horses left deep tracks, but it did not matter; the cave held no trace of them. When they rejoined the two guards, they got all kinds of strange feelings: confusion, fear, anger, and aggression. The five of them traveled the trade road, and the guards were still putting out strange scans.

Alerton figured it out: the two guards had been drawn into a robbery scheme. They did not want to be involved, but they were afraid of the robbers.

Alerton messaged Metrool and Everin: *Each of you take control of one of these guards. We are going to be attacked. Metrool, give me the vaporizer.*

Metrool did, and Alerton set it for severe pain. Soon they saw the men riding toward them. When the riders got close, they drew their swords.

Alerton messaged Metrool and Everin: *Quick—make the two guards ride away.*

The two guards started riding away, and the robbers were surprised but kept coming. Alerton then used the vaporizer on them, and they dropped their swords, clutching their chests and hollering in pain. Soon they were riding away. Alerton, Metrool, and Everin spurred their horses to walk faster, and soon they were far away from the robbers.

Everin asked, "How long will they be like that?"

"About an hour," Alerton said, "if my experiment on a hog was correct."

In a short time, they reached the city wall, and as they were paying the wall tax, Alerton said, "We need to put these things away."

They went quickly to the back door of the bank. Because they were partial owners, Abram let them clear out the back of the bank and have private access to the vault. Afterward, they left and went to Everin's place. They took some things to her basement hiding place. The cook was the only one there, and Everin had sent her to the garden.

Metrool and Alerton went to their fortress home and took the rest of the things to their iron-doored basement, which had three locks. They took the three horses to the stable and told Dino and Raphael to unsaddle them, feed them, and rub them down. Metrool and Alerton then went to the Arno Inn to wind down.

They had been there for two hours, drinking and talking to the owner and other customers, when they were shocked to see fifteen people rush into the Arno: a monsignor, though not Moni; two priests; nine church guards; and the lead bandit and his two cohorts.

The monsignor screamed, "Witches and witchcraft!" He and the priest were waving large crosses and saying prayers in Latin.

The monsignor came up to face Alerton, holding his cross high. He said, "You are accused of being witches and using magic on these three innocent souls."

Metrool said, "They tried to rob us."

The largest of the robbers said, "Yes, and you used magic to stop us."

The monsignor said, "That proves you are witches. Guards, grab them, and chain them."

Metrool started to react, but Alerton calmed him. Alerton sensed something.

The guards put them in chains while the priest chanted in Latin. The monsignor said, "You are witches. You are arrested, and we will get confessions from you before we burn you."

Then the door opened again. In came the two guards they had sent away. "They are not witches," said one. "These three wanted to rob them and recruited us to help them. But when they saw we were doing what we were paid to do, they decided not to attack and rode away."

The monsignor mumbled something and then produced a Bible and had each guard swear on it. Alerton scanned the monsignor and saw he was not really a believer and loved luxuries. Alerton made him believe he would be better off with Alerton alive rather than dead.

The monsignor said, "Unchain them, and chain these three robbers. Then take them to the Bargello."

The church guards switched the chains and took the protesting robbers out. The monsignor gave Alerton a look that Alerton knew meant, *I will be expecting a visit from you.* Alerton gave him an affirming nod. Then the priest, guards, and robbers were gone.

The two guards who'd saved them stood in front of Metrool and Alerton.

The taller one said, "We did not want to rob you, but those men are very violent, and we were afraid of them. We do not know what you did to them, but we do not think you are witches. You have been good to us and other people in the past."

Alerton reached into his money pouch and gave each one three florins. He said, "In the end, you did the right thing." It was a lot of money, but saving them from the stake was worth a lot. The guards were happy and left.

The Arno owner, whom they had been drinking with, was relieved. He said, "Alerton, that could have gone very badly."

"I know," Alerton said. "Do you have strong wine?"

"For you, yes, we do," said the owner.

Alerton and Metrool left the Arno, and Metrool said, "I am going to the Parrot."

Alerton replied, "All right, I am going to see Everin to tell her everything that happened."

Soon Alerton and Everin were sitting at her large kitchen table. The cook had poured wine for them, set out excellent white bread and cheese, and then gone to her room. Alerton had messaged Everin, letting her know what had happened.

Now Everin said, "So awful. You could have been killed."

"Yes," Alerton said, "and the stake is not a good way to go."

"So it is over?" Everin asked.

"Yes, the authorities will torture them until they get the answers they want."

"That is terrible."

"Yes, but these are very bad people; they have robbed and killed for a long time."

"What about the monsignor and the church?"

"I will have to visit him and donate."

"He is not a believer?"

"Right. He is a seventh son, expected by his family to become a priest and getting no inheritance. So he accepted it to have a good life. That helped us."

"As long as you and Metrool are safe," Everin said.

"We are," Alerton said. "The cave is empty now, and things are proceeding well."

"What about Metrool?"

"Do you know where he is right now?"

"Yes, at the Parrot."

"Yes, he is very taken with Simonetta."

"They say she is the prettiest girl in Florence."

Alerton looked at Everin and asked, "What about you and Doc?"

Everin gave a guilty smile. "We are getting on quite well. In fact, he is about to use the knocker now."

They heard the *thump, thump, thump* of the iron knocker on the heavy door. Alerton went and raised the bar he had recently installed on Everin's doors. Alerton was wary of the future and the disease that was getting ever closer.

Doc entered, smiling, and soon the three were sitting at the kitchen table, and it was obvious Everin and Doc were totally involved with each other. Alerton would have preferred to leave, but protocol prevented it, so he stayed for an hour to give them some time. Then Alerton and Doc left together to walk the short distance to their separate homes.

Sometimes Alerton and Metrool would be at the table with a glass of wine, and Everin and Doc would be out in the garden, talking. They loved to talk and investigate each other's eyes and just feel good about being with each other.

Alerton got a message from Everin: *I hope you were not too bored.*

Alerton replied, *Never bored with you, Sis.*

10

THE NEW STABLE

THE NEW STABLE WAS FINISHED, AND DINO AND RAPHAEL HAD MOVED into their attic room. They were happy to have a stable again, although they had learned to love the widow and her children. She had spent a lot of time trying to improve their reading and writing. The hay barn people were bringing hay, feed, and salt. It was Dino and Raphael's job to put nearly all of it in the loft. They pulled it up with the rope and pulley at the south end of the stable.

While at the widow's place, they had lost another horse. They believed it had breathed too much smoke in the fire. Now they were down to seven horses. Alerton had told Dino they would probably go to Lucca to buy horses.

Everin was impatient. Where were the window makers? The carpenters had finished their work a long time ago. Finally, yesterday, the glass from Blunden's Wood had arrived. She had not been happy with some of it. She had taken several pieces to the basement of her home and used her creator device to take out flaws.

Now a messenger arrived and told her the window makers would be there tomorrow. She was not happy but at least knew they were coming. She looked at the glass; the pieces were not large and had many flaws. She could not resist; she picked ten pieces with the worst flaws and put them in her large bag. She was in her basement with the door latched. She got the creator out of its hiding place. She pulled out one of the panes, put it in the device, and told the device to make it clearer and larger. The device asked, "Perfect it?"

"No, just the worst ones. And thirty percent larger."

It was done quickly.

Everin held the pane up, looking at it, when Metrool messaged: *That is cheating.*

Everin was embarrassed, but Metrool was only teasing her. She proceeded to do the rest and then took them back to the shipment.

The cook was preparing lunch for Everin and Doc, who had become very close. No one had ever made her this emotional. Usually, they had lunch together twice a week, and he ate dinner with her and her brothers two or three times a week.

Because of scanning, she knew Doc wanted more. She knew he wanted to marry her. She blushed; she knew he wanted her body, and strange for a Hamen female, she wanted his body. She wanted him to do everything to her that he would have done to an Earth woman. The lunch was not ready.

11

DOC

DOC WOULD BE ARRIVING SOON. EVERIN WENT OVER AND LOOKED AT THE cooking food, and the cook reminded her that she had cooked for Doc before. Doc arrived happy, as usual. He was always happy when he was with her. The food was not quite ready, so they decided to take a glass of wine up to her balcony.

They poured the wine, and they talked and laughed as they climbed the stairs, but just as they stepped out onto the balcony, she heard Doc's wineglass shatter on the floor. Everin turned and saw Doc with his eyes closed, clutching his chest. With a five-second scan, she knew Doc was having a massive heart attack.

No! This can't happen. He's mine. Using Hamen strength, she carried him in to her bed. With her mind in a state of confusion, she ran down to the basement. She pulled out the creator and said aloud, "Antique medical syringe."

The creator said, "What capacity?"

Everin practically screamed, "Six cc! Hurry!" Quickly, there were two syringes of different sizes.

Everin ran back up to her room and slammed and latched the door. She picked a good vein and filled a syringe. She injected all of it into Doc's jugular.

Nothing happened. She grabbed the syringe, filled it with her blood again, and plunged it into Doc's chest. Doc moaned, but nothing seemed to be happening.

Doc's eyes opened, and he said, "What?" Then he was out again.

The cook was hammering on the door. Everin was not supposed to be alone in a bedroom with a man. Everin put the syringes under the mattress and opened the door.

The cook said, "You can't do that, ma'am." Then she saw how sick Doc was, and she also saw blood on his neck. The cook apologized. "I was just protecting your reputation. I did not know Master Doc was sick."

With tears running down her face, Everin wailed, "He isn't sick! He is dying!" She looked at his beautiful face, which was totally pale. She would never feel for another the way she felt for him. She began to openly cry great, heaving sobs.

The cook silently left the room. She had never seen someone so upset over someone dying; people died all the time.

When Everin had calmed down a little, she felt Metrool and Alerton mentally with her.

Alerton said, *You tried to save him.*

She said, *Yes.*

Alerton said, *You used Hamen blood.*

Everin said, *Yes, Alerton, I did, and I know it was against the rules. And right now, I do not care about the rules. If they want to come rescue us and call me a criminal, I do not care. I found something beautiful I had never found before, and now I have lost it. So do not quote me Hamen rules. You could have understood.*

Alerton interrupted. *That was not what I was going to say.*

Still irritated, Everin said, *What were you going to say?*

Doc is still alive.

Everin nearly fell apart. She grabbed Doc by the shoulders and hugged him and kissed his face, begging him to live and telling him she needed him. She collapsed onto him.

Alerton told Everin, *I believe Doc is going to live.*

<hr />

Two hours later

Everin felt Doc's weak pulse get a little stronger. It was not normal but better than it had been. Alerton and Metrool were downstairs. They came up from time to time to check on her. The servants had all been sent away because they did not know what was going to happen. It had never been done before.

Doc's body began to react; his temperature shot up. Everin called down to Alerton for water and rags. Even with the water and rags, his fever went up. Alerton knew the situation was critical.

Alerton took hold of both Doc's hands and began to draw heat out of Doc. But now Alerton's temperature was going up. Alerton stayed as long as he could and then pulled away.

Metrool pulled Alerton away and took his place. The heat continued but then slowed. With Metrool still holding Doc's hands, Doc began to act like a wild man. It was all Metrool could do to hold him. Slowly, his ravings quieted. His eyes were open most of the time, but he saw nothing.

Everin was a wreck. More than anything in the world, she wanted Doc to live, but she hated to see him suffer like this.

Suddenly, Doc's eyes became aware again. Metrool was still holding him. In a raspy voice, Doc said, "What did you do to me?"

Everin said, "We saved your life."

Doc said, "I do not believe you. What did you three do to me?"

Everin said, "If you remember, as you and I came out onto the balcony, you had a heart attack—a fatal one. We saved your life."

Doc recoiled. "Then you are witches. I want no part of you."

It took hours of talking and explaining, with Everin practically begging, to convince Doc they were not witches or evil. They would make progress, and then they would say something that Doc considered magic, and he would think them witches.

They had to get Doc settled before they could bring the servants back, and it wasn't working. Doc had lived his whole life in this environment of supposed evil, magic, and witches.

Finally, Alerton did something he did not want to do: he went into Doc's mind and showed him things no earthling had ever seen. He also put into his mind that they did not mean him or anyone else any harm.

Alerton released him, and Doc was awed. He didn't know what to say or where to start. Everin brought him back to earth, saying, "First a kiss on the cheek and then a bath, a shave, and clean clothes."

Metrool escorted Doc to Doc's home and stayed there while they both got some much-needed rest.

Alerton helped Everin clean up her room and put fresh linens on her bed. When he took the soiled rags and linens to the washroom, Alerton was impressed at what Everin had done under the limits of life in Florence. He saw rainwater going into a cistern, two masonry tubs that could be drained into the Florence sewer, and a hand pump to fill them. The pump looked ordinary, but Alerton knew some of the internal parts had been made by Everin's creator device.

When the servants returned, Alerton told them there had been some family disagreements, but they had been worked out, and everyone was happy now. Servants did not argue with their employers, so they accepted it. Then Alerton went to his home and put himself into a deep sleep for a few hours.

Four hours after Metrool lay down in Doc's home, he felt Doc rousing. He went to Doc's room just in time to see Doc practically jump out of bed. Doc went to the fireplace, picked up a large stick, and broke it in half.

Doc asked, "Can you and Alerton do this?"

"Yes," Metrool said.

"You do not show it."

"No, and you can't either. You would get in trouble."

"Metrool, you really are from another world, and it is not magic?"

Metrool said, "Yes, although a lot of things to you will seem to be magic, they are not. They are real. Do you love Everin?"

"Yes, I do," Doc said.

"Why don't you tell her?"

"I will."

"Tell her now."

"How?"

Metrool said, "You picture the person in your mind and think in your mind, *I want to send the person a message.* Then think the words."

Everin could not breathe; she was being messaged by Doc. He was awake, healthy, and back to normal. *And oh, he says he loves me!*

Doc was quiet for a few minutes, and he blushed.

Metrool gave Doc a look, and Doc said, "She says she loves me too."

12

THE DRESS SHOP WINDOWS

IT WAS MORNING, AND EVERIN HAD TO GO TO THE DRESS SHOP TO MEET the window makers. They were already there.

At the shop, she again told them she wanted four windows made: two for the first floor and two for the second. Now she uncovered the shipment of glass from Blunden's Wood, and they were amazed.

One of the glaziers said, "We have never seen glass this good. People will want to buy it."

Everin said, "You make my windows first. Then we will talk about selling the rest."

Next, she checked on the girls. They liked the second window and the extra light it let in.

Metrool had let Doc go to his office after warning him to act normal. Now Metrool went on to the artist academy, where his friends were. Leon had started a new painting of a beautiful person, but the person had wings.

Metrool said, "I have seen other paintings of these angels. What are they?"

A little taken aback, Leon said, "They are usually messengers from God."

"Does everybody see them?"

"No, usually just saints, very special people."

Metrool was curious because the angels looked just like a special type of Hamen. Besides having wings that they could either show or not show, they had special powers, and although there were only a few of them, the council had planned to convert them to normal Hamens. Somehow, they'd gotten word of it and had stolen a starship. They were never seen again.

"Well, you paint them beautifully," Metrool said.

Leon said, "I need Simonetta to pose for my angel of mercy. It is for the monsignor of Mary's Angels."

"Alerton knows him," Metrool said. "Maybe he can help."

The next morning, Metrool and Alerton ate breakfast at the inn and then went to the stable. Dino was saddling their horses; they were going to a farm a few miles west of Florence. They were only leaving five horses for customers, and that was why they were going to the farm—to buy more. A customer at the stable had told them the farmer had three riding horses he had to sell. With the weather, he couldn't raise enough hay to feed five horses.

They had to go to the Lucca horse sale soon, but they thought this might be a good buy and help them now. They mounted up and started toward the southwest gate of the new great wall. It had been finished fourteen years ago, and the people of Florence were proud of it, even if they were not proud of the taxes they had to pay to go through it.

They continued to the southwest, on the north side of the Arno, keeping a close lookout for trouble. This was a trade route. They met several traders, but scanning them lightly, they saw they meant no harm.

At a curve in the Arno, they left it and began looking for the farm. They had left the old Roman road and were now on a muddy dirt road, but they were following the customer's directions. Alerton and Metrool started picking up some bad thoughts, but they did not see anyone. They kept riding and soon saw a well-kept farm. It fit the description, and they rode up to it.

Two men came out to meet them, and then a woman, two teenage girls, and a young boy stood out in front of the house. The two men were obviously the farmer and his father. Because Alerton and Metrool were well dressed, the woman offered them wine. They were polite, accepted it, and complimented it.

With the ice broken, the farmer asked, "Are you travelers? Are you lost?"

"No," Alerton said, "a man named Montero told us you had horses for sale."

The farmer said, "He is a cousin. Will you alight?"

Alerton and Metrool dismounted and went to the farmer and his father and formally met them. There was small talk, and they complimented the farmer on his family.

The family went inside, including the father, and Alerton, Metrool, and the farmer walked down to the horses. Alerton could tell the farmer was unhappy, and it was obvious that all five of his horses were underweight.

The frustrated farmer said, "My daughters and I love to ride our horses."

Alerton said, "I do not think I would be riding them now."

"No, no," the farmer said angrily. "I meant we loved to ride them in the good times before this weather. This year, I have grown practically nothing."

Alerton knew that was a common problem in and around Florence.

Metrool messaged Alerton: *The girls in the house are crying; they think their father is going to sell their horses.*

You have a soft spot for women, Alerton messaged. *If I don't buy them, they are going to die.*

The farmer continued. "We bought them when they were very young. The girls and the horses grew up together."

One of the girls ran out of the house and down the slope to where the men were. She ran up to Alerton and, crying, said, "Please don't buy my horse." She turned to the farmer and said, "You don't have to sell him; we will get by."

"If I don't, they will probably die," the farmer said.

The girl ran bawling back into the house. Although sometimes people thought Alerton had a heart of stone, he did not. He was trying to think of a compromise.

Alerton said to the farmer, "If I buy them, it would be two or three months before I could rent them out."

The farmer said, "Yes, I know."

Alerton, being Hamen, hated to see animals mistreated. For a moment, he thought of all the trouble Hamen had gone to in order to convert their carnivores to herbivores.

Alerton said, "I am going to make you an offer, and I advise you to take it."

The farmer did not like the sound of that but said, "Tell me your offer."

Alerton said, "I will take your three riding horses to my stable and feed them right and make them healthy, and I will send two loads of hay out so your workhorses will survive; you need them. I will only give you three florins."

The farmer seemed shocked.

Alerton continued. "Then, when I have had them for eighteen months, I will give them back to you."

"You will?" the farmer said.

"Yes. You might say I am renting your horses."

"Yes, yes," the farmer said. "Let me tell the girls."

Proper farm etiquette was to offer guests a meal. Alerton read the farmer's wife, and she was terribly upset; they had nothing to offer these wealthy gentlemen.

To handle the protocol, Alerton told the farmer when he and the girls came out, "We are out of time; we must take the horses and go."

The girl who had run to the barn came to Alerton and said, "You will bring him back in eighteen months?"

"Yes, I will," Alerton said.

"And you will treat him right? No sharp spurs?"

Frustrated, Alerton said, "Yes."

The girl smiled and said, "His name is Arrow."

Soon Metrool and Alerton were leading the three horses, who were wearing only bridles, down the muddy road back to the Arno.

13

RIDING BACK TO FLORENCE

ALERTON AND METROOL FELT GOOD; THEY WERE HELPING THE FARMER
and themselves.

Alerton told Metrool, "As soon as we get to Florence, go to the hay
barn, and have them take hay and food out to the Monteros today."

Just then, the dark and threatening waves they'd felt earlier came
back all at once. Alerton, looking behind him, saw three men on horses
galloping toward them. Alerton knew the underfed horses with them
could not run, so he looked at the lead horse approaching, scanned it, and
investigated its memory for bad things—there were many. Alerton saw it
had been bitten on the leg by a snake. He made the black horse relive that
incident and see snakes all around it. It began to buck violently, and the
rider fell off. The horse would not calm down.

Metrool and Alerton reached the Roman road, and the bad men were
not trying to catch them. Metrool and Alerton kept pushing their horses,
and soon they reached the safety of the new wall. Inside the wall, they
went as straight as possible on the crooked cobblestone streets to the stable.

They gave the three horses to Dino, and Alerton said, "Feed them well.
They are our horses for a while."

It was late afternoon when they reached the hay barn, where Alerton
had bought a lot of hay and feed, as all of theirs had burned in the fire.
Alerton told the owner what he wanted, and the owner sent a man to buy
food and ordered two men to put feed and hay on the wagon.

The driver was adamant he was not going that day. Alerton was tired and angry. He took the driver to one side and, with mental persuasion, said, "You will deliver this wagon, and you will sleep in the wagon." Then Alerton told Metrool paid and left.

Alerton went to the bank. He was going to tell Abram about the horses, but Abram had something on his mind. Abram took Alerton to his private office.

Reluctantly, Abram said, "The other two partners want the bank to either buy you out or take you out of decision-making."

Although seething, Alerton calmly asked, "Why?"

Tense, Abram said, "They do not like the advice you gave me about shipping."

Alerton said, "You do not have enough gold to buy me out, and I will not be taken out of the decision-making process, so I will buy them out. How much do they have invested in the bank?"

"Each has about twelve standard gold bars invested in the bank, but they have already told me they will not be bought out."

"How many bars do I have?"

"Ninety-three."

"And how many bars are in the vault?"

"Forty-four."

Alerton said, "Demand they meet us at one and at two."

The banker quickly said, "Yes." He had not seen this side of Alerton before, and it scared him.

When their banking was over, Alerton left the bank and went to the stable. He checked on the horses, and Dino told him three bad types had been there looking for them.

Alerton asked, "What did you tell them?"

Dino said, "I told them I did not know where you were."

Alerton walked to their fortress home, and he and Metrool decided to go to the Parrot Inn.

At the Parrot, Simonetta, the innkeeper's daughter, waited on them, and Alerton did a light scan and was pleased to see the erase had worked.

They were about to finish their wine, when three rough-looking men burst into the inn. The door banged into a table.

The one in front, seeing Alerton, said, "I am going to kill you." He drew his sword.

Alerton was not wearing a sword, even though it was common. Another patron handed Alerton his. Alerton started to do a scan, but the man's brain was fueled by anger, and he was coming at Alerton. The man swung his sword, and Alerton blocked it.

Alerton moved into a defensive stance, and because he could read the man's moves before he made them, Alerton blocked stroke after stroke and lunge after lunge. As a result, the frustrated attacker got wilder and wilder. Alerton knew a bystander likely would get hurt, so after waiting for the right moment, Alerton hit him hard across the side of his head with the flat of his sword and knocked him out.

The man's partners decided not to continue the fight and dragged their partner out.

Alerton and Metrool left but stopped by Everin's to fill her in on the busy day. They were trying to use more verbal interactions to act more like earthlings.

———————

When they started to leave, Everin surprised Alerton by asking Metrool if he could stay for a moment. Alerton went on, and Everin poured wine and took her brother out into her garden for privacy.

After some hesitation, she said, "Metrool, these Earth people are totally physical people; they have not advanced enough to live in the mental state."

"No, they have not," Metrool said.

After more hesitation, Everin said, "You go to the inns a lot."

Metrool said, "Yes, I do.

"And you party with the artists."

"Yes, I do."

"I have heard several amorous tales about these artists."

Metrool thought for a minute and then said, "Probably true."

Everin had to ask what she really wanted to ask. "Have you been physical with an Earth female?"

Metrool was taken aback that such a question came from her. "Yes, I have," Metrool said.

Everin asked, "What was it like?"

Metrool responded, "At first, the physical contact was repulsive, but I proceeded to fit in with my artist friends. Surprisingly, I found it quite enjoyable."

"Are you serious?" Everin asked.

"Yes, one of the girls and I get along quite well."

"Does Alerton know?"

"Yes. He does not approve; he is too rigid. But I think he has too. Now, what is this about?"

Everin turned red.

Metrool added, "Is this about Doc?"

"Yes," she said, "I have very deep emotions for him. I never joined with anyone on Hamen, but he is an earthling; he will expect me to be physical with him."

"Yes, he will," Metrool said. "Even their religion endorses it."

"Do you think I could do it?"

"If Doc is skillful, you might be surprised."

"Surprised?"

"You see, I had an advantage: I read her thoughts, so I could tell what she liked and did not like and what she expected of me. Doc will not have that advantage, but you will. You must talk to him. Where is Doc?"

Everin said, "He says he can only doctor people for a short while, and then he must go to his home. Since the night of the heart attack."

"You know this must be radical to him. He has a thousand things to absorb and collate."

"Do you think I am wrong? I know Alerton does."

"No," Metrool said. "It looks like we will be here a long time, and I saw how you gave him mental thoughts about that medicine without his knowing it."

"Yes," Everin said.

"Well, you can do the same thing with your physical relationship."

Metrool left, and Everin went out onto her balcony. She looked down the street to Doc's home.

Quickly, she felt his thoughts. She felt chills. *He wants me both ways. He wants to share his life with me, but oh, he wants to be physical with me.*

Everin blushed. He was trying to imagine what her mammaries looked like. He was wrong, and almost unconsciously, she guided his image to what she really looked like. He was delighted with the way she looked. She read him thinking, *Oh, I hope you look like that.*

She used a sleep suggestion to put him to bed and help him adjust to what he had been through over the last few days.

14

THE DRESS SHOP GIRLS

THE NEXT MORNING AT THE DRESS SHOP, EVERIN HAD TO PRACTICALLY force one of the girls to talk to her. "Why can't you talk to me?"

The girl answered, "Every time we talked to the other owner, she was mean to us."

Everin said, "Well, I am not Frieda. You are indentured apprentices; you are not slaves. I will treat you right. Do you get enough to eat?"

Three spoke up almost in unison to say, "Oh yes, thank you."

Everin went to the new window; the window makers had not made the other three yet. She was pleased with it. It was not perfect, but it contained some of the panes she had altered. She smiled; she had a clear view of Doc's place, and he was back to doctoring people.

Suddenly, she received a message from him: *Thank you for saving my life. My mind is a little mixed up. I need to see you.*

She sent back *Come to my home for the noontime meal.*

Doc sent back *Yes.*

Everin rushed home and told the cook and maids what to do.

Alerton, as usual, went to the bank when it opened. He went to Abram's office and asked, "Did you see the partners?"

"Yes," Abram said, "one will be here at one, and the other will arrive at two."

"Good," Alerton said, "I will handle this." He could tell Abram was disturbed. "Believe me, it will be all right." Alerton then left the bank and went to the stable.

Dino and Raphael met him. They had heard about the swordfight, and being young men, they wanted to know all about it.

Raphael said, "One man who rented a horse said you were the best swordsman he had ever seen. He said you just played with Scalo before you knocked him out."

Alerton had to protest and say he was not that good. He said, "Scalo was so angry it hurt his skill." He did not want to become known as a swordsman.

Alerton went back to the bank, got Abram and the scribes and notary together, and said, "Write up contracts for both partners."

Abram said, "They do not know the price."

"You told me they had twelve standard bars invested."

"Yes, that is true."

Alerton said, "Write up the papers that they are selling their share back to the bank for eleven standard gold bars."

Abram said, "You would have to pay them a premium; they do not want to sell."

Alerton gave everyone a look. "Write it up my way—eleven bars. Everything but the signatures."

Abram nodded. "Do it his way."

At one o'clock, Alerton was in his office when the partner arrived, but he kept the partner waiting for twenty-five minutes. While he was waiting, Alerton lightly scanned the man; he opened the man's mind to receive what he thought, what he feared, things he had done, and things he had done and not confessed, sins on his soul.

Then Abram's servant let the partner, named Ander, into his office.

Ander was flustered and angry. "I am not used to being treated like this."

Alerton ignored the remark and began talking to him, and Ander began to relax.

Then Alerton said, "Does the priest know your real father was a Jew? That your married mother had an affair with a Jewish painter?"

The partner stood up and tried to draw his sword, but Alerton was like lightning and had his sword at the partner's throat. Alerton said, "Sit down, or I will kill you and tell everyone all your secrets."

The partner sat and gasped. "How did you find out?"

Alerton replied, "If you are willing to spend gold, you can find out anything."

Soon Ander had accepted the eleven gold bars and signed all the papers, and Alerton assured him his secrets were safe.

A short time later, the other angry partner, Dante, was there. The servant brought him into Alerton's office, and their talk was casual for a while.

Then Dante told him flatly, "You do not have enough gold to buy me out. I am a man with principles."

Alerton was quiet for a few minutes and then spoke. "A man of principles? Yes, well, your wife was very sick for a while."

"Yes," Dante said, "and the doctor came to see her many times. And I hired people to take care of her."

Alerton said, "Yes, you did, and one of the people you hired was the innkeeper's daughter, Simonetta."

All the color left Dante's face, and he looked sick.

Alerton continued. "What would the innkeeper say if he knew you forcibly took his daughter's chastity?"

Dante, nearly choking, said, "He would kill me."

"Yes, he would," Alerton said, "and everyone would say he had a perfect right to. And then, with a sin like that on your soul, where do you think you would go?"

Dante was crying now.

Alerton said, "Accept the eleven bars, and sign the papers, and maybe no one will find out."

Alerton would not tell Dante that two days ago, he had erased all memory of the attack from the poor girl's mind. Dante signed and then stumbled out of the bank.

Alerton went to Abram and said, "Now we are the only two owners of the bank. Are you all right with that?"

Abram replied, "Of course."

Alerton read that Abram was afraid of him. Alerton assured him that he only had done what he had to do, and if the partners had been happy, they would still have been partners.

As Alerton walked to the inn, he messaged Metrool and Everin to meet him there, and they agreed. Soon Alerton was sipping a glass of wine. He was thankful the inn had good glasses to drink their wine from. When Metrool and Everin arrived, Alerton told them the news that they and Abram owned the bank.

The door opened, and to their surprise, Dante walked in. Alerton saw he was carrying a guard's compact crossbow.

He pointed it at Alerton and said, "You will tell no one."

Alerton saw that it was drawn and latched, with Dante's finger on the trigger. Alerton pushed his mental power to the limit; he first froze the arm holding the weapon and then went into Dante's mind. He saw that other than the incident with Simonetta, Dante had led an exemplary life. With no good solution at hand, Alerton erased the attack. Now neither Dante nor the girl remembered it. Alerton turned Dante toward the open door and then released his arm.

Dante stood there not knowing why he was there. The innkeeper took the weapon and told Dante to sit down, pointing to a table away from them. The innkeeper gave him a glass of wine, and Alerton gave him memories that made him believe selling his part of the bank had been what he wanted to do.

Soon Doc arrived, and after one glass of wine, Doc, Everin, and her maid chaperone left.

Metrool turned to Alerton and said, "She is going to marry him."

Alerton replied, "You are sure?"

"Oh yes, she has verbally asked me many questions about these earthlings and their man-woman relationships. She knows the crowd I hang out with are very earthy."

"And you told her you've been physical with earthlings?"

"Yes, I told her that I had several times, and it is an amazing thing."

"I know," Alerton said.

Metrool said, "Why, you faker!"

"Well," Alerton said, "it was strictly for science. Hamens gave it up long ago, but you were making such a big deal over it, and Everin is getting involved with Doc, so I thought I should know."

"Yes, sure," Metrool said. "I totally understand; you did it just for science."

Simonetta brought Metrool and Alerton another glass of wine, and Alerton scanned her and was pleased to see that all memory of the attack was gone, and in her memory, she had never been with a man.

Metrool felt Alerton's mental activity and asked, "What are you doing?"

Alerton said, "I removed a bad memory, and I just wanted to know if it was still gone."

Metrool felt there was a little more to it than that, but he let it go. Metrool was drawn to Simonetta and had come to see her several times. He thought, *If something bad happened to her in the past and Alerton erased it, I do not want to know what it was.* Now, watching her serve food and drinks to other people, Metrool picked up that she liked him. But he knew she was not like the girls who played with his artist friends.

Doc and Everin were in her garden, and the maid and cook were inside. Doc looked at Everin and said, "I think I deserve some answers."

Everin said, "Yes, Doc, you do. First, there must be some rules. You cannot tell anyone ever the things I am going to tell you."

"I agree," Doc said.

Everin asked, "Will you swear on your Bible?"

"If you will swear that it is not witchcraft or magic," Doc said.

"Yes," Everin said, "I will. These things are science, not magic."

"What are you?" Doc asked.

Everin said, "I am human just like you but from a different place and a different time."

"How can we be the same if we are from different worlds and different places?"

"Oh, Doc, that goes so far back in time that even Hamen does not have a clear picture of it. Sit down on that bench."

He did, and Everin said, "I am going to shock you." She began projecting images into his mind: the journey to Florence with the traders, the escape pods sitting on the ground, the view from inside the pod as it fell to Earth, the exploding ship, the ship's dining area, and a view from space of her sparkling planet.

Everin stopped, and Doc's first comment surprised her. "You have all this wealth and all this power. Why did you choose me? Why did you save me?"

She leaned over and, for the first time, kissed him on the lips the way earthlings did. "Because I love you and plan to marry you."

Doc grinned. "You really are a witch."

15

LUCCA

METROOL AND ALERTON HAD AN EARLY BREAKFAST AT THE INN AND THEN walked to the stable.

Dino assured them he could run it while they were gone.

Alerton said, "You have Everin and Abram if you need them, and if there is trouble, there is the captain of the people."

"I know, I know," Dino said.

Alerton, Metrool, and Raphael were going to Lucca to buy horses. Alerton pulled out two money pouches, handed one to Metrool, and said, "We are each carrying half for safety." He handed three florins to Dino and said, "This is for an emergency. When we get back, I want them back."

Dino grinned broadly; he couldn't believe he was holding three gold florins.

The route they were taking to Lucca was an old Roman road. In some places, the thousand-year-old road was still good, but in some places, it had disappeared, and there was just a muddy path. They reached Prato by noon and were thankful the Roman bridge over the Bisenzio, a tributary to the Arno, was still in good shape. They only stopped long enough to buy some bread, cheese, and wine to take with them. They waited for a grazing place for their horses before they stopped to eat. Then they started out again. They wanted to be in Pistoia by nightfall. Even though Hamens had excellent night vision, they knew it was not safe to travel at night.

There was still some daylight left when they got to Pistoia, but it was not worth the risk to use it.

They found a stable first and took care of their horses. They saw a farrier and his apprentice making horseshoes. The apprentice was working a bellows to make the fire hot.

Alerton and Metrool took Raphael with them as they looked for an inn. They did not like the first one they came to, but the next was all right. Only one room was available, but that was all they needed.

The next morning, they were up at dawn. Bread, butter, and honey were all the inn offered for breakfast, but that was enough. As they saddled up, Raphael talked to the apprentice. Then they were on their way, still following the old Roman road.

Alerton found it ironic that he and Metrool knew more about the road than the locals. The fall of the Roman Empire had had a profound effect on that part of the planet.

Alerton and Metrool stayed wary. There were times when they knew they were being watched. Close to nightfall, they were approaching Lucca. The first thing they spotted was the top of the Torre Guinigi. Then they came to the outer wall and entered the eastern gate and soon heard the noise of a crowd.

Soon they could see the San Frediano Basilica, along with a huge crowd. Sitting on their horses, they could see over the crowd. Near the basilica, outside the old Roman colosseum, they saw two priests, three officials, and some guards. Between them and the crowd were two women. One was tied to a large wooden stake about six feet tall. The other was prancing around her, haranguing her about how she was a witch. She could move things without touching them, and her garden was always green, when everyone else's garden had dried up. She went on and on, and people began to bring wood and place it around the woman tied to the stake.

The woman pleaded when she got a chance, saying she was no witch, and she had harmed no one. One of the priests sent a guard to gag her. The accuser grinned at that.

Alerton scanned the woman on the post and saw that she was not a witch; was a good person; and, shockingly, had an amount of Engel—a type of Hamen—blood. Alerton knew he had to do something to save the woman, but what?

He put a hand inside his loose local clothing to grab a device he carried nearly all the time. Mentally, he reconfigured it for what he wanted to do.

But first, he went into the accusing woman's mind and made her want to confess that she had falsely accused the woman because she was jealous of her. But that was not enough for the crowd.

Someone brought a burning torch, and others in the crowd lit their torches from it. Metrool sent him a message: *Alerton, we must save her.*

Alerton again put his hand on the device. Suddenly, most of the crowd went silent, mesmerized. The accuser was floating six inches off the ground. She screamed, "I am not doing this! There is a witch in the crowd!" Her legs would not cooperate; she was floating and moving.

Alerton picked one of the priests, and after a little mental message, to the other priests' surprise, the chosen priest told two of the guards to go release the woman, and they did. Quickly, she left the scene. Alerton sent her a message: *I need to talk to you.*

What about? she replied.

Your cousin, whom you say is cursed.

There is no cousin.

Alerton cranked up his mental power. *Do not try to deceive me. I have more of the gift than you do.*

All right, she said, *but no one knows about him. They would kill the whole family.*

Tell me where and when to meet you.

She did, and in two different ways, they left the scene.

As they went on to the horse sale, Metrool pressed Alerton, asking, "What did you see in her mind?"

"First," said Alerton, "the Hamen blood in her system is not normal."

"Then what is it?" Metrool asked.

"It is Engel."

"Then there was another visit, an Engel visit. Tell me about the cousin."

"The mix did not go well. His tall body is like a skeleton, and he has large, sickly wings. He looks more like a bat than an Engel."

They asked directions and were told the horse sale was inside the old Roman structure. They rode through an entrance that obviously had been made recently. Inside was a large, flat surface. There was a fence across the middle of it, and fifty or more horses were on the other side. Alerton and Metrool left Raphael to take care of the horses and went to meet the people running the sale. The sellers told them the sale had been going for nine days and would go on for nine or ten more days because people brought horses to sell to them nearly every day.

Alerton decided they would not wait for more horses to come in; they would just buy the best of the ones there. Metrool, Alerton, and the sellers entered the horse area. They eliminated the seven workhorses first. They wanted riding horses. Alerton saw a black horse with a white blaze that was acting up. Because he was acting badly, Alerton got him for a low price. Then they looked at the others' hooves and teeth and checked to see if they had spur marks, and they bought four other males and three mares. The sellers separated them and put them in a holding pen to keep them till morning. It was now dark, and the sellers directed them to a stable and inn built into the old Roman structure.

After they had eaten and Metrool and Raphael had gone to the room, Alerton went back to the stable, got his horse, and rode east out into the country to meet the woman he'd saved from being burned at the stake.

The small farm was about two miles east of Lucca. As he neared the farm, Alerton messaged the woman: *I am near.*

Are you alone? she asked.

Yes, he said. *I can be your friend. If I intended to be your enemy, I could kill you without getting near your home.*

Alerton showed her his power for a minute as a message.

Yes, she said, *you can come in.*

Alerton smiled to himself. *A wise decision.* He entered the farmhouse.

"How did you find it?" she asked.

"I followed your thoughts."

"You can do that?"

"Yes, I can."

"You look like an earthling."

"I am Hamen."

"You do not look like the Hamens I have seen."

"The ones you have seen are a very small subset. Hamens who stole a starship and escaped."

"Escaped?" she asked.

"Yes, they were going to be changed into normal Hamens."

"Your government can do that?"

"They do what they think is best for the most people."

With thoughts, Alerton invited the cousin, Uriel, to come into the room.

A thought came back: *I am not pretty.*

Alerton said, *You do not have to be.*

Slowly, a gray shape entered the room. He was right: he was not pretty. He was tall and underweight; Alerton could see the shapes of all his bones under his gray skin. His large wings had practically no feathers.

Alerton said, "I want to help you; you are not safe here. I will get you a place much closer to Florence, probably around Prato." He stood up, went to Uriel, and put his hands on his shoulders. "I want you and Andromeda to accept my offer. The three Hamens will try to help you." He turned to Andromeda and said, "I will send you a mental message when I have your new home." Before leaving, he gave Andromeda five florins.

As Alerton started back to the inn, he sensed danger ahead of him and turned the power of the BWI up to max. When two men on horses with swords drawn rode at him, Alerton caused them both to fall off their horses.

Back at the inn, Alerton found the room. It only had one small bed, and Metrool was asleep in it. Raphael was rolled up in a blanket on the floor. On the floor were another blanket and pillow. It did not take a Hamen scientist to figure out they were for him. Alerton lay down on the blanket, and soon he was rolled up in it and asleep.

The next morning, they rose at dawn, and the inn surprised them. The inn staff had gathered fresh eggs and boiled them, so they had yesterday's bread, butter, and jam and fresh boiled eggs with a little salt. They were tasty. Then they went to the stable to get their horses and then to the horse sale.

The sellers led the horses out in single file. As they started out, three horses did not want to cooperate, but with a few messages from Alerton that it would be in their best interest to be like the other horses, the string of horses smoothed out, and they were able to proceed through the narrow streets.

Two hours later, they came to a shallow clear stream and let the horses drink their fill. On the other side was an unfenced meadow, and they let them graze. Metrool got with Alerton off to one side and asked, "What did you find?"

"A lot," Alerton said. "Some by what they told me and some that I pulled out of their memories. Do you remember the story of the Engels' escape?"

"Of course," Metrool said. "Twenty-seven Engels, with the help of certain Hamens, stole the newest, largest starship and disappeared."

"Yes," Alerton said, "twenty males and seven females. Well, female Engels cannot reproduce."

"They do not need to; they have a femtech," Metrool said.

"No, they do not. They thought their Hamen conspirators had supplied them with one, but it was fake."

"Can't their creator make one?"

"No, the tightest-controlled things in the world are femtechs and population."

"Everyone knows that," Metrool said.

"That ship is huge and could support them forever, but they can't reproduce. So they came to Earth. They put their ship in orbit. There are no telescopes or cameras; no one sees their ship. They can orbit for years. They breed and take the new Hamens back to the ship," Alerton said.

Metrool asked, "What about Andromeda and Uriel?"

"They do not take rejects back. They were lucky they were not terminated," Alerton said.

"Their ship was not in orbit when our ship arrived," Metrool said.

"No. My estimate is they are in orbit around a star a little over four light-years away. Their ship can shield them from the bad rays."

"Yes, it was investigated and written off a long time ago. And the Engels would know that."

"Yes, and we would be unlikely to come back. There was one other thing, and they did not tell me this. It was just like a shadow in Andromeda's mind. The Engels took three females back to the ship."

"Why not more?" Metrool asked.

"The Engel females do not like it."

They resumed their journey on the horses. Alerton thought about the best place to find safety for Uriel and Andromeda. After two more water and grazing stops, they came to a place well known for its warm springs.

Alerton went to Metrool and asked, "Could you and Raphael safely take the horses to Florence?"

"Of course," Metrool said. "You want to do something else?"

"Yes, I want to go southeast through this farmland and find a good place to buy a farm."

"All right, we will take care of the horses."

16

ALERTON LOOKS FOR A FARM

ALERTON RODE THROUGH THE ROLLING FARMLAND. HE SAW MOSTLY small and medium-sized farms with olive trees and vineyards everywhere. It was nearly dark when he rode into Altopascio. He found a good inn just as he rode in. It had a stall and feed for his horse. He went inside and saw it was a good-sized inn. It had six tables with benches on each side. There were about twenty people eating and drinking. Talking to the owner, Alerton found there were six rooms upstairs, and two were empty. Alerton paid him for one and went over to a half-empty table. By the way the patrons were dressed, Alerton assumed they were traveling merchants, and a light scan proved him right.

A waiter came to the table, and Alerton chose the beef stew and good white bread and ordered local wine. Soon he was talking to the travelers about the surrounding farmland. Of course, they had to tell him about the great battle that had been fought there twenty-two years ago.

Afterward, Alerton went up to his room, barred his door, and put himself to sleep.

The next morning, Alerton awoke early, dressed, and went down. The inn had a good breakfast. After he ate, he checked his horse, and yes, it had been watered and fed. Alerton gave the stableman two grossi and started on his way.

He continued to the southeast, and after riding through a lot of farmland, he came to a small town named Vinci. Looking around, Alerton thought it would be a good place. After a few inquiries, he was told the bank had two farms for sale. Alerton was soon talking to the banker, and it did not take long to see the farm to the north of Vinci was just what he wanted. Alerton signed the papers, gave him a deposit, and told him his banker would be there within five days.

Alerton continued south at a faster pace. When he reached the Arno, he turned east. He would follow the small dirt road along it back to Florence. But as darkness approached, he saw smokestacks with smoke. It was the town of Montelupo Fiorentino, which was famous for its pottery. He would have to spend one more night.

———⟫◉⟪———

Metrool and Raphael made Pistoia by dark. They helped the stable hand, the farrier, and the apprentice secure the horses and then got a room at the inn. Since it was not a holiday, the porridge was plain, with no spices, but the inn offered good bread, cheese, a slice of ham, and a glass of local wine. Afterward, they went to the room.

The next morning, after the standard inn breakfast of bread, butter, and honey, they went to their horses. The stable people were already there. Metrool had paid them well, and Raphael had talked a lot to the apprentice and found out he was out of indenture.

Raphael came to Metrool and said, "We do not have a farrier, and Marko would come work for you."

Metrool said, "Bring him to me."

Raphael did, and Metrool asked him several questions about his work. By light scanning, Metrool saw he told the truth and was qualified. Metrool offered him a job and pay, and he accepted. Thus, when they left Pistoia, there were three of them. Marko rode one of the horses they had bought, with only a blanket for a saddle.

That day, they pushed; they were anxious to get back to Florence. They arrived at Prato before noon, and Metrool only paused to buy bread and cheese. Metrool and the boys would let the horses drink each time they crossed a stream, but they stopped for only two grazings. At sunset, Metrool and the young men could see the new Florence walls and the towers soaring above it, and it was a joyous sight. Metrool messaged Alerton and found Alerton was not coming to Florence that night. Metrool counted out the coins for the gate tax for them and the horses. Once inside, they hurried along the cobblestone streets to the stable. The three of them had had their hands full in driving the horses that last mile. Everin had messaged Metrool earlier in the day and found out Alerton was not with him.

They arrived at the stable, and Dino was glad to see them. He told them business had been good, and they really needed those horses. Metrool introduced Dino to Marko and told Dino what his job was. No, he was not taking Dino's job; Dino was the boss of the stable. Raphael and Marko would work for him. But Marko was a trained farrier, and he knew how to shoe and doctor horses. He and Dino together would buy his tools and supplies.

Metrool left the young men to take care of the stable. He went to the Parrot, the inn owned by Simonetta's father. He hoped she was there.

One day later, when Alerton got back to Florence, he looked the stable over and talked to Dino and Marko. Everything was going well, so Alerton went to see Abram.

Abram welcomed him back, and after the normal pleasantries, Alerton told him, "I have bought a farm in Vinci."

Abram was surprised, but he had learned not to question Alerton's motives. Even so, he asked, "Who will farm it for you?"

Alerton told him, "I met two people in Lucca. I promised the banker I would send a scribe and notary with the florins inside of five days. Is that a problem?"

"Not at all," Abram said.

Alerton asked, "Do you know Cerano, who owns the Parrot?"

"Yes," Abram replied cautiously.

"Is he a good man?"

"Yes."

Getting impatient, Alerton asked, "Was he a good banker?"

"Yes, he was. He was a partner in one of those banks that failed last year," said Abram.

"Was it his fault?"

"I do not think it was."

"I have heard that the Gondolfo bank is about to fold."

"That is the rumor."

"Why?"

"A very common thing. Bad things happen, and they do not have enough gold to cover everything."

Alerton went to his office, and he sent a message to Everin: *If I gave you many large jewels, could your creator make them into small ones by morning?*

Everin replied sarcastically, *Well, hello. I am glad to be home.*

I am sorry, Alerton said. *I did not mean to be rude.*

Everin said, *Tu-arta*, which was Hamen for *You are forgiven.*

Thank you, Alerton said. *The gems Dagril made are too large for the market. Can your creator make smaller ones out of them?*

Yes, she said, *how many?*

About two pounds.

Oh, it will take several hours, but I will do it.

It is important. We are buying a bank.

⟶➤●⟵

When Metrool got back from the horse-buying trip, he first went to the Parrot. Then he went to the art colony. Some of his artist friends were there. When they saw he was carrying a cask, they came to meet him.

"Metrool," Piero said, "you always know how to cheer us up."

Metrool asked, "Why would you be down, Piero?"

"Well, you know we are supported by the rich like you."

"I am not rich," Metrool said.

"Oh, but you are, my friend. But some of the rich have setbacks, and when they do, we do. But you have been most generous with us."

"I love art, and I wish I were better."

"For a young man, you do wonderful work. Someday you will be famous."

"No, Piero, you will be." Metrool could not tell him he was 133 years old.

Filippo, Celli, and Carlo came to join them. When the cask was empty, Metrool gave Carlo coins to find more wine. Metrool never asked for his change. Alerton was making them a lot of money, so why not share it with their friends?

The next morning, Metrool woke in an earthling woman's bed. He had to reach into his mind to remember last night. He recalled he had

80

given Carlo coins three times to go find more wine. *Whoa, can't drink like that.* But everyone had been happy and had a good time. Some women had joined them, and wine had flowed like water.

With his Hamen body, thirty minutes after he awoke, Metrool was back to his normal state, but he found Piero and Filippo were in bad shape. Piero said, "Oh, Metrool, next time, do not be so good to us."

Metrool knew as soon as his head quit hurting, he would change his mind.

"You are the devil," Filippi said. "No one can drink that much and feel as good as you do the next morning." Metrool was taken aback, and Filippi, seeing Metrool's face, said, "No, I did not mean it that way. It is just a saying."

"Thank you," Metrool said. "I do not want you thinking badly of me."

"Never," Piero said. "You are the most decent man I know."

17

MOVING URIEL

ALERTON AND DOC WERE GOING TO LUCCA TO MOVE ANDROMEDA AND Uriel to Vinci. They were taking a new cargo wagon with a false bottom. It was pulled by two strong draft horses. Alerton and Metrool took turns driving the wagon, and Doc was riding his favorite horse from the stable.

They could not use a regular wagon because they would have to keep Uriel hidden. Uriel would have to stay in the hidden compartment all the way to Vinci. They would put a load of regular household items on top of it. Alerton had messaged Andromeda to say they were coming to move them to their new farm.

As they rumbled along, they were glad most of the Roman road was still in good shape. They stopped in Porta just long enough to buy some food and then pressed on. With the wagon, they could not travel as fast as on horseback, and it was dark when they reached Pistoia.

They found the same stable and inn they had used on the horse-buying trip. Gerano, who owned the inn, greeted them warmly this time. They got the same room with one small bed, but this time, there were two narrow feather mattresses with blankets on the floor.

They rose early, and the cook had risen even earlier. He must have remembered the grosso Alerton had given him. There were fresh boiled eggs, fresh white-flour bread with butter and marmalade, and a plate of hard cheese.

When they walked into the stable, they were shocked. The stableman was lying on the straw-covered ground, killed by a sword. With the relaxed moment gone, Alerton and Metrool drew their swords as they became aware of the three killers. Anger fueled Metrool, who lunged forward at Hamen speed, and soon a killer's arm was lying on the floor. A moment later, its owner joined it.

Metrool and Alerton were fighting experienced swordsmen. Again, getting into their minds gave Metrool and Alerton the advantage. After a dozen thrusts, slashes, and parries, Alerton saw an opening and thrust his sword into the killer's chest. Alerton read his thoughts as his mind faded; the man was in disbelief.

Metrool finished off his second killer with a fast slash across his throat. Suddenly, there was Gerano, saying, "Bravo! I have never seen such swordplay. Those men were known by everyone; they were bad."

Alerton said, "Gerano, you need to summon the podesta or the captain of the people."

"Of course," Gerano said. "Are you all right?"

"Yes, yes," Alerton said, "just get the officials."

Gerano sent two of his servants for the podesta and soon brought out special wine, which they were thankful for.

Alerton went to Doc, who was in a state of shock. Alerton used his power to calm Doc down to normal.

Doc said, "I must talk to you later."

Alerton said, "Yes, you will." The poor stableman was now covered by a cloak. They could not move him until the officials came.

Gerano said to Metrool, "You did not tell me you were expert swordsmen."

"It was best we did not," Metrool said.

"I know, I know," Gerano said, "but that fight was amazing."

Soon the podesta arrived with his people, and he was surprised Metrool and Allerton had killed the three bad men without getting a cut. Gerano bragged to the podesta about the fight.

Gerano said, "Oh, it was beautiful. Those three locals were totally outclassed by these experts."

The podesta said, "Well, it is obvious by Geno the stableman's death that these men were killers, and you were justified in fighting them, so you can go."

Alerton recognized that some coins needed to change hands, but it had to look normal. He said, "Do you think three florins would bury these people?"

Alerton saw the podesta was secretly delighted, and the podesta replied, "I am sure four would."

Alerton handed him four florins from his money pouch.

The podesta said, "Yes, I will see that they are properly buried."

Alerton and Doc saddled the horses, Metrool hitched up the wagon, and they left the terrible scene. As they rode away, Alerton read the podesta, who was thinking, *Who are these rich swordsmen?*

The rest of the day was uneventful until they arrived at Andromeda's farm. Doc and Metrool wanted to meet Uriel. Alerton talked to Andromeda, and they talked to Uriel and assured him Doc and Metrool would not be shocked by him, nor would they hurt him in any way.

Into a dimly lit room, Andromeda brought Doc and Metrool to meet Uriel. They were shocked but masked it. The tall being was light gray, even his long, thin hair. The shape of his bones was obvious under his skin, and of course, he had large angelic wings. They should have been beautiful, but they were not. They were gray and had practically no feathers.

Alerton told them about the farm he had bought for them just outside Vinci. "It will give you a new start, and you will be much closer to us."

Andromeda asked, "Why are you doing this?"

"Well," Alerton said, "your being tied to that stake got me into this, but I guess it is because I like you two, and we are relatives."

Uriel was tense; he had something on his mind.

Alerton asked Uriel, "What is it?"

Uriel looked at Doc and said, "You are an earthling."

"Yes," Doc said.

Uriel said, "But you are part Hamen."

"Yes," Metrool said, "we used Hamen blood to save his life."

There was silence around the table for a few minutes, and then Uriel said, "Will you use Hamen blood to save my life?"

"You are not dying," Metrool said.

Uriel smacked a hand down on the table and then held the long, thin, nearly translucent hand up to the four-candle fixture hanging over the table. "I do not have a life. I am a walking corpse. I cannot go out into the sunshine; if a child saw me, it would scare them to death. Will you help me?"

Alerton spoke up. "There is no protocol. This was never necessary on Hamen and never done. Doc nearly died when his body reacted to it."

"But he did not die," Uriel said.

Metrool turned to Andromeda and asked, "What do you say?"

"I love him," she said. "I want whatever he wants."

Alerton said, "If both of you are willing to accept whatever happens, we will give you Hamen blood treatments after we get you moved to another farm."

Metrool said, "There is only one condition."

Uriel tensed up. "What is it?"

Alerton answered, "You and Andromeda must tell us all you know about the Engels."

Uriel quickly said, "Agreed."

Andromeda spoke up. "Don't you know about them?"

Alerton replied, "Two hundred Earth years ago, we knew all about them. Then they stole a starship, and we know nothing after that."

The ice had been broken, and large glasses of wine were poured. Andromeda served the food she had prepared for them and said, "You may call me Meda. Uriel does."

Doc had mixed feelings but kept them hidden. Uriel looked exactly like some artists' paintings of the devil. But Doc knew he was an Engel.

They had wine with their meal, and then, sitting together with their glasses, Uriel and Meda asked many questions.

Uriel asked, "How will we travel in daylight?"

Metrool answered, "Our wagon has a false floor. You will have to lie on your back, but you will not be seen. There will be no sunlight to harm you."

They asked many questions, and Alerton asked about the Engels.

Meda went to a chest and got some drawings she had made of them: one standing in front of the farmhouse; a wing; two Engels flying, one light and one dark; and other drawings.

Finally, Alerton said, "We must get ready and go."

Meda was surprised and asked, "In the middle of the night?"

"Yes," Alerton said, "the wagon is slow, and I want to get there in one day."

They put all their bedding in the bottom of the wagon. Uriel lay down on it, and Alerton and Metrool installed the false bottom. Then they loaded Meda's meager possessions on top of it. Meda rode on the wagon seat beside Doc.

Even though Alerton and Metrool had excellent night vision and Doc's was better than it had been, they were careful. In less than an hour, they reached the Roman road. They would be able to use it for a while.

Two hours later, Alerton switched places with Doc and began to tell Meda about the small BWI he gave her. Alerton had had Everin make it. It was not powerful, but it could be useful. Alerton even went into her mind and planted three different engrams. She could never show it to anyone or tell anyone about it.

As they moved along the Roman road, Alerton and Metrool were constantly light scanning, looking for people who might give them trouble. With Uriel trapped inside the wagon, they felt vulnerable. Alerton was amused; three different times, he saw someone's dreams.

Alerton messaged Uriel: *Are you all right?*

Uriel messaged back: *Yes, I am.*

It was dawn when they went through Alto Pascio. A few people looked them over but judged them to be regular travelers. As they pushed their horses, they let them drink often but did not stop to graze; they had brought grain and feed bags for the horses so as not to lose time.

It was midday when they went through the edge of Monte Catini, leaving the Roman road to travel dirt roads through farm country. They were traveling southeast, and in that area, the farmers grew a lot of wheat. The first six months of the year had been very wet, which had hurt that year's wheat crop.

Alerton thought to himself, *We are fortunate that the latter part of the year has been dryer, or this road would have been bad.* In places, there were deep ruts left from earlier travel.

Meda had prepared food and wine for the trip. They ate as they traveled. They only stopped at the streams to let the horses have plenty of water. The farther southeast they went, the fewer wheat fields they saw and the more olive trees they saw.

Alerton had already told Uriel and Meda that their new farm was basically olive trees and vineyard. It had a garden for family use. It was about a mile north of Vinci, at the start of the foothills. Allerton thought it should be great for olives.

They traveled on, and it was getting dark. Alerton did not want to go through Vinci at night, so they went around it. Finally, they were at the farm. Metrool and Alerton could see it well. Abram had asked the banker to prepare it, and he had. It was clean, and there was a box of candles on the table and wood beside the fireplace.

Metrool checked the two other rooms and said, "They are bare and clean."

They had made sure it was safe, and now they unloaded the wagon to get Uriel out. They took the bedclothes out of the wagon, and after they had taken care of the horses and put them in the corral, they went into the farmhouse and, using Meda's bedding, found a place on the farmhouse floor and went to sleep.

The next morning, Alerton left Metrool and Doc to put the farmhouse together and inspect the farm while he took his cousin to the bank to make sure the papers were all in order. They were, and Alerton opened Andromeda an account with two hundred florins, a large amount of money.

They were in the wagon, the false floor was back in the farm's barn, and Alerton took Meda to buy food and whatever else she needed for the farm. Alerton had seen the farmhouse had two rope beds with no rope, so he took Meda to a place where they could buy rope.

After they arrived back at the farm, Metrool, Alerton, and Doc got ready to go home. The grapes had been harvested in September, and the olives had been harvested in late October, so the farm could just sit until the next spring. Uriel and Meda were effusive in their thank-yous and goodbyes.

The trio left the farm, heading southeast. When they reached the Arno, they turned east and traveled in sight of the river. When they came to Montelupo, a city well known for its pottery, they decided to stop for the night. Alerton had had a good experience with a large inn there, and they decided to use it again.

They arose early the next morning. They wanted to get back to Florence.

They arrived in the afternoon, and after giving their wagon and horses to Dino and Raphael, Alerton went to see Everin.

She was happy to see him but even happier to see Doc. Sometimes the way they reacted to each other amazed Alerton. There was a mental and physical reaction when they came into each other's presence.

18

THE BANK

ALERTON LEFT EVERIN'S, AS HE HAD OTHER THINGS TO DO. SOON HE WAS at their bank, going over everything with Abram. Everything was in good shape, and they were to buy the Gondolfo bank tomorrow. Abram and his people had examined the bank they were going to buy and found it to be in good shape. It was just overextended.

The next morning, Alerton was getting dressed for the big day. The Gondolfo bank was a large bank, with a large amount of good loans. It had run short on florins and because it had been cutthroat with the other banks, so no one wanted to help the owners.

Alerton was not helping them bank-wise. He was getting the bank, worth one hundred thousand florins, for fifteen thousand florins. The owners had no other way out. With Florence law, if the bank failed, they would be criminals. That would mean being in prison, tortured on the rack or wheel, or thrown out to the crazed crowd to be torn apart. It had happened before. After today, they would be free—a lot poorer but free.

It was hard to believe Alerton and Abram were getting that large of a bank for that price. Alerton hoped the Gondolfos were not going to be enemies.

Alerton pulled on the stocking garment his tailor had made at his request. It was one piece, like Hamen trousers, not separate stockings like the locals wore. Then he put on his linen shirt, his knee-length trousers, his gold-studded belt with the gold-studded sheath that held his new gold-trimmed sword, and his formal jacket with lots of real gold thread woven into it. Of course, there were the clunky shoes. Alerton missed Hamen shoes.

Alerton came out of his room, and there was Metrool in sartorial splendor. "Are you ready?" Alerton asked.

"Yes," Metrool said, "and Simonetta's father will be there to officially take over the bank."

"Yes," Alerton said, "we will own eighty percent, but it will appear that Cerano does. We are just there as loyal friends."

"Does Simonetta know what is going on?"

"I don't think so. She is thrilled that her father is back in the banking business."

"Do we have a buyer for the Parrot yet?"

"Not yet, but he signed it over to us for his share of the bank."

They left their fortress-like home and walked the short distance to Everin's home. Everin invited them in warmly and informed them that breakfast was nearly ready.

It was strange in a way, but the months of pretending to be brothers and sister had begun to feel real. The cook served fresh boiled eggs, fresh white-flour bread, marmalade, honey, butter, and roasted sausages. The three ate at the large table, with the cook hovering around them.

Everin asked, "Are you going to ride?"

"Yes," Metrool said, "it isn't far, but for propriety's sake, we need to ride."

Alerton added, "Dino will have horses ready for us and ride with us and then take our horses back to the stable."

They finished their breakfast and walked to the stable. Dino had everything ready, and at ten o'clock, they arrived at the Gondolfo bank.

Cerano was there, and all three of the Gondolfos were there. Abram and his scribes, accountants, notaries, and two large guards, standing beside a chest, had evidently been there awhile.

Abram and his people were still checking the accounts. They had been doing it for days and had only found two medium-sized accounts that were bad. The lawyers, accountants and notaries all went over the contracts, for this was a large and important bank that was changing hands.

Wine was flowing, and they opened the chest and counted the gold. That went smoothly, and then it was done. Cerano pledged to keep as many employees as he could, and Alerton insisted on talking to each one alone. Alerton found only two who were unacceptable. One had a burning grudge against the new owners, and the other was an embezzler who had gotten away with it.

Alerton thought for a few minutes and then went into the man's mind and caused him to faint. While the man was out, he put an engram into his mind that anytime he touched gold, it would be red hot and burn him. Those were the only employees Cerano did not keep. Alerton read mixed emotions in the Gondolfos: relief, pain at the loss of their bank, and some anger with no real target. So now it was over. Everyone had said the proper things. The Gondolfos left, and the bank was Cerano's.

Cerano invited all his friends and partners to the Parrot to celebrate. The trio owned the Parrot now, but they had no problem with Cerano using it to celebrate.

Metrool messaged Everin to say they now owned the large Gondolfo bank and to tell her about the party. Everin messaged back: *Great, and I know Simonetta will be there.* Metrool nearly choked.

Later that night, they had a well-done party with two barrels of beer, four casks of wine, large amounts of boiled or roasted vegetables, four ducks, eight chickens, a roasted half-grown hog, and a long table of sugary sweets. After about thirty minutes, when three short speeches were made, they threw open the doors to the hungry public, and they loved it.

Of course, they were made aware that this was a gift from the new Gondolfo bank. The highlight of the night for Metrool was when Simonetta came to him with tears that made her eyes shine even more and told him, "My father makes me stay out of business for my safety, so I do not know what happened. But I know in my heart that you, Alerton, and Everin put my father in that bank. Thank you." She gave him a quick kiss and disappeared into the crowd. It was his first kiss from her, and later, when he walked home, he felt as if his feet were not touching the ground. He could have floated literally, but this was not Hamen; this was just a feeling for a beautiful girl.

19

THE FOOD

It was late November, and they got word that the ships had just docked in Pisa. Alerton got with Dino and told him they would take all their horses and both wagons to Pisa the next morning. They had three shiploads of food, but according to what he'd been told, Pisa had claimed one whole ship. They had found food in places like Sicily, which had a better growing season than Florence.

It took two days to get there and two days to unload the ships. It cost Alerton money, as he had to hire five wagon teams and drivers. It took two long days to get the wagons, carts, and packhorses all back to Florence.

They were met by a large crowd of people who had heard about the food. The crowd were adamant and shouting, "We have money! Sell us food!"

Alerton picked a large amount of food and told Dino and Raphael, "Unload this food here, and sell it to the people just slightly below the going price. I do not want to start a riot."

Alerton, Metrool, and their hired help took the rest of it to the stable and put the grain and dry food on the large second floor. The hogs and sheep were to be taken out to the widow's farm; she would be paid for keeping them.

Dino said the crowd were pushing hard for a hog. They said they would be happy with one hog. They had a butcher, and he would divide it up.

"All right but just one large hog." Alerton watched the fat hog being led off to slaughter. They did not do that on Hamen. They had not for thousands of years. He did not like it, but it was part of life there on a planet that was probably fifty thousand years behind Hamen.

They put everything else in the dress shop's storeroom. The seafood would not come until late December; it was for the Christmas fish meals. Alerton and Metrool were on horses, while Dino and Raphael were on foot, as they herded the sheep and hogs along the cobbled streets through the city walls and down the dirt road to the widow's farm. The widow and her children came out to meet them. Alerton looked at them and could tell all three were healthier than the last time he had seen them. Alerton had sent Dino out to them with food twice. Alerton and Metrool dismounted and walked over to them.

The widow, clearly nervous, said, "Thank you so much for the food, but I can't pay you for it."

"You do not owe us," Metrool said. "It was a gift."

Alerton said, "If you will keep these hogs and sheep for us until we need them, we will gladly pay you."

Her face lit up. "That would be wonderful. My children can shepherd them."

Raphael went to draw water from her well and quickly came back to Alerton and said, "Part of her well is caved in. What are you doing for water?"

The widow, clearly embarrassed, pointed and said, "There is a spring down there. My son takes buckets down there and brings us water."

Metrool asked Raphael, "Can you and Dino fill the troughs that way? If you can, Alerton and I will send well diggers out to fix the well."

"Yes," Raphael said, "we can, but it will take a while."

"All right," Alerton said, "you two stay till you get the troughs full; we will go find a digger." Alerton reached into his money pouch, pulled out a handful of grossi, and handed them to the widow. He told her, "I will pay you the rest for keeping our animals later."

They left the farm as tears ran down the widow's cheeks.

Alerton and Metrool rode back to Florence. They had put twenty-six sheep in her fields and nineteen hogs in her sty. Back in Florence, Metrool went to look for well diggers, and Alerton tried to get things back to normal. Three days went by, and things worked out.

———— ✦ ————

Everin had hired another cook and maid for the season, because food was a large part of it. Cerano loved his new bank, and he and his wife and two children, Simonetta and Silvano, had become part of their group.

There were going to be four nights of celebration. The main one was Christmas Eve, the seven-fish night. They would bring the hogs to the butcher two at a time about every other day. Their butcher was not on the Ponte Vecchio anymore. Too many people had complained about the butchers dumping into the Arno. There were butchers to slaughter and then butchers who took part of the meat and processed it, such as into sausage or smoked ham. There were a lot of hungry people, and some religions preferred sheep, so they would be bringing sheep in also.

———— ✦ ————

Alerton was with Abram at the bank; they were going over the bills from the voyage. It had been expensive but no more than he had expected. In Sicily, they had sold two of the ships to grain people. That made Abram happy. The grain people had sent skeleton crews back with the ships, and now they were gone. The gold from the sale was in Abram's bank.

Alerton said, "We still have money coming in; those hogs, sheep, and ducks are making a profit."

"Yes," Abram said, "more than I expected."

"Yes, and we are charging last year's prices."

"There are some people who do not like that."

"I know, because we are taking some of their sales. When Christmas is over, we will be out of the food business." Soberly, Alerton added, "Abram, you know there is a bad disease coming, getting closer every day, and it will change many things. A lot of people will die."

"I believe you," Abram said. "But how do you know this? Sometimes you make me feel you are a witch, and I do not like that."

Alerton said, "Have I ever cheated you or done wrong by you?"

"No," Abram said. "That is the conflict: you seem to be an exemplary man, and then you do something—like the way you handled our ex-partners—that makes me think you are different."

Alerton looked Abram in the eye and asked, "Even though you have doubts about me, can I trust you with my life?"

"Yes," Abram said, and a light scan told Alerton it was true.

20

SETTING A DATE

THAT NIGHT, THEY ALL CAME TO DINNER AT EVERIN'S HOME: ABRAM AND his wife; Cerano and his wife; Simonetta; Doc; Metrool and Alerton; Dario, the owner of the Arno; and Dino and Raphael. They had hired Farno to run the Parrot until they sold it, but he wasn't in their circle. There were two other people there: the monsignor who loved good food and good wine and his special nun. With a quick scan, Alerton saw that Sister Nancy was thirty; was, like her boss, a nonbeliever; and liked the same things the monsignor liked.

The dinner went well. A month ago, Everin had hired masons to come in and build her a second kitchen fireplace, even adding an oven with an iron door. The two cooks had done wonders with it.

Everin looked at Doc, and he grinned. She stood up and said, "Doc and I have set a date. We are going to be married." Everyone applauded.

The monsignor stood up and said, "They have been talking to me, and I have posted the bands. Now I will say a blessing, and then we will have a toast." The monsignor spoke in Latin, blessing them, and most of them understood it. Then, in Florentine, he proposed a toast, and they all took a good drink; everyone was happy for them.

Doc and Everin were still gaga over each other and had decided to marry on December 18, a Tuesday, with a full moon to celebrate by. Everin had her girls working on a special dress, and Alerton had his tailor making new clothes for Doc, Metrool, and himself.

The dinner ended. The desserts had been sugary and rich, and the dessert wine had been good. Everyone wished Everin and Doc the best as they left. Everyone left except Alerton and Doc.

After some long silent looks between Doc and Everin, Alerton pulled Doc away, saying, "All right, Doc, soon you can stay all night," and they walked down the street together.

It was hard for Doc to believe this angel he loved was not from Earth. Doc was part Hamen now, because Hamen DNA was aggressive, and it had slowly made some changes in him. Doc had grown a beard to help hide the changes.

Doc, Alerton, Metrool, and Everin had talked about the plague coming toward them, and just two days ago, Doc had told Alerton there had been some suspicious deaths in Pisa. Now they were able to tell Doc how they knew about the plague. Doc and Everin had had many deep discussions about Hamen. Sometimes Everin had to say, "No Hamen tonight, just Earth and us."

Doc would always grin, apologize, and say, "I am sorry. There's just so much I want to learn."

Everin had taught him a few minor things he could work into his medical practice, but he had to be careful, as the citizens were still burning witches. Just last week, while riding their horses, they had come upon a witch burning. The poor woman already had been badly burned. All they could do was put her out of her misery.

Doc asked her about medicine and many questions about their home, Hamen—about why they did not have rock, about their planet being attacked, about the Engels, about the temporary warriors, about their four continents and the four ethnicities, about their ethnic-change device that let any Hamen be any of the four ethnicities, and about the way they altered some plants to have the same properties as meat to satisfy their previous carnivores. Sometimes Everin said, "No Hamen tonight."

Two nights later, Everin and Doc were having one of their special nights. Everin's cook and maids had prepared a special meal for them, as well as Alerton and Metrool. The food had been good, the conversation had been pleasant, and the wine had been excellent. Now, as prearranged, Alerton and Metrool stayed in the dining room, and Everin and Doc went to her balcony.

Sometimes it was difficult to stay upper-class proper. They had each brought another glass of the excellent wine. They kissed politely before they settled into their chairs and made the small talk that lovers did.

Doc turned serious. "Everin, I must ask you about Hamen."

Everin asked, "What would you like to know?"

"Well, except for being male and female, you, Alerton, and Metrool look very much alike. That is why everyone accepts that you are brothers and sister. Does everyone favor as much as you three?"

Everin answered, "It is a little complicated and the reason for one of our wars. Our planet has four continents, and when the DNA project was started, there was resistance."

"Resistance?"

"After about a hundred years of trouble, there was a war."

"What happened?"

"The DNA project went forward."

"And the results?"

"Well, ninety-nine percent of our DNA is the same. On the four continents, each has an appearance subset, and within each ethnicity, the DNA is 99.7 percent the same. You can change your ethnicity at any time."

"You mean you could look quite different tomorrow?"

"No, not here, but on Hamen or on a starship, I could."

"Does this apply to everyone?"

"To all regular people."

"Regular people?"

"Well, there are two others. One is Engel. You met Uriel, who is part Engel. They are tall and strong, they can fly, and they have no age protocol. They say Michael may be six thousand Earth years old."

Doc said, "But there are no Engels on Hamen now."

"Yes," Everin said, "and the others are warriors who are temporary beings for Hamen's defense. There are no real warriors at this time."

"What are they?"

"They are duplicates of Hamen's citizens who fight our wars. They were invented when it became a crime for Hamens to fight in a war. A citizen volunteers to be duplicated, and he can volunteer seven times. Normally, citizens only have one duplicate at a time, because they feel a lot of what the warrior feels."

"What if a warrior gets killed?"

"It causes great pain and anguish to the citizen."

"Do you use them often?"

"At times, but they have not been used in the last two thousand Earth years."

21

URIEL

ALERTON AND EVERIN RODE HORSES TO THE COUNTRY TOWN OF VINCI.
Alerton had bought Andromeda and Uriel a farm there for them to be safe.
It was a working farm with a lot of olive trees and a large vineyard that
Andromeda could hire people to work. And it was a long way from Lucca,
where Andromeda had been accused of being a witch.

As they rode up, they saw smoke coming from the chimney. They were
greeted warmly by Andromeda, who took them into the farmhouse. Uriel
came out of his room, and they began to talk.

Uriel asked, "Are you here to help me?"

Everin took his bony hand in hers. "We will do what we can, but the
only thing we have to help you with is our blood."

Uriel looked confused.

Everin pulled out a syringe. "We would pull some of our blood out
with this device and then inject it into you."

Uriel asked, "Is that what you did to Doc?"

"Yes," Everin said.

Uriel asked, "Will it help me?"

Alerton said, "Probably, but there is no guarantee. We would do a
small dose at a time every six hours."

Uriel asked, "What will it do?"

Alerton said, "That is unpredictable. It may have a lot of effect, or it
may have none. You are a combination of earthling and Engel. At worst,
you could die. At best, you could become a perfect Engel. Or you could

become more Hamen. We do not know what it will do, but it will change you. We can do it or not—it is up to you."

Uriel did not have to think long. "Yes, I want to do it. I want to do it even if I die. If I die, it is not your fault. I want the chance."

"When?" Alerton asked.

"Right now," he said.

Alerton turned to Meda and said, "We have only done this once. Sometimes the patient gets violent. Are you all right with that?"

Meda replied, "I want him to have what he wants."

Alerton gave Uriel three ccs of his blood. Uriel was lying down and soon began to moan.

Uriel said, "I feel so strange."

They had arrived in the afternoon, and the first injection was at sunset. They took turns watching him, and they all knew he used his strong will to control his body at times.

At midnight, Uriel said, "I want another."

Everin asked, "Are you sure?"

Uriel answered, "Yes."

Everin gave him three ccs of her blood. Immediately, his body reacted violently, and Alerton went to the barn and got rope. Soon they were tying him down, and Alerton started to explain.

Uriel interrupted and said, "Yes, I feel it is necessary."

Within minutes, they saw his body viciously fighting the ropes. He screamed at them. Some words they did not even know. This went on for nearly four hours; there were bruises and raw spots all over his body from the ropes. Finally, he was calm, and they saw his vital signs were normal. An hour later, they were confused; his vital signs were going down. Thirty minutes later, they were still dropping.

Everin took his hand. "Can you hear me?"

After a minute, Uriel said, "Yes."

Everin said, "Your body is shutting down. If you want to live, you have to use your mind to control your body."

Uriel asked, "Can I do that?"

"Yes. I am going to scan you and put a few things in your mind if I have your permission."

"Yes," Uriel said faintly. He was sinking fast.

Everin probed his mind and encountered vast reactions of grief that she had to turn off or bypass to get to what she needed. Finally, she was there and began doing what she needed to do. At first, there was no result; he was still dropping.

Everin rallied all the strength she had and said, "I am not going to let you die." She put her hands on his temples and, using all her mental power, began controlling his vital organs. His heart, his lungs, and whatever he needed, she kept going.

Thirty minutes later, Uriel said, "I am back."

Everin fell to the floor, unconscious. Alerton scooped her up and carried her to Andromeda's bed. He took both her hands in his and willed some of his strength into her. When he saw she was safe, he left her and went back to Uriel.

Uriel was conscious and able to talk now. He said, "You can untie me now; it has done all it is going to do."

Alerton looked him over. There were obvious changes. He untied him. Because Uriel was part Hamen, the bruises and raw flesh were already starting to heal. When Uriel sat up, Alerton could see that his wings were visibly smaller.

Alerton said, "That will be all for this session. Everin is a wreck."

"I know," Uriel said. "I was dying. If she had not helped me, I would have died."

"Yes, and she really sacrificed her body, but because she is Hamen, it will repair itself."

"I can never repay you."

"You do not need to. Doc and Metrool will come here in seven or eight days."

Uriel asked, "Will it be like tonight?"

"I do not know," Alerton said. "You can stop if you want to."

"No, I want to be as normal as I can. But right now, I am hungry."

Meda laughed out loud. "I have never heard him say that." She went to prepare food.

Alerton said, "Your body must be wanting to replace what it used up last night."

"Yes," Uriel said, "it went through a lot."

Alerton again said, "You can stop anytime."

"No, no, I must finish," Uriel said.

They went to where Andromeda was cooking. Uriel asked, "Do we have eggs, milk, and bread?"

"Yes," she said, "I read your mind." She laughed again.

Alerton let Everin sleep and repair until nearly noon. He had already saddled their horses, and after Everin nibbled at some food, they said their goodbyes and started for Florence. Alerton saw Everin was still weak, but her Hamen body was busy repairing itself.

It was fully dark as they approached Florence's new walls, and they got their lanterns out and lit them. They rode along the cobbled streets to Everin's home, where Doc, the cook, and the maids were waiting for her.

Alerton took their two horses to the stable, where Dino and Raphael were waiting for him.

Metrool messaged him: *Where are you?*

Alerton replied, *I am at the stable, but in a few minutes, I will be at the Arno Inn.*

Metrool replied, *I will meet you there.*

Alerton walked the short distance to the inn, went in, and told Drago, "A large glass of your best wine." Soon he was sipping it. It had been a hectic time; he was thankful it had turned out as well as it had.

Soon Metrool came in and wanted to know everything.

After Alerton had told him, Metrool asked, "What will happen now?"

Alerton said, "I believe the worst part is over. Uriel still wants to look normal and to be able to go out into the sunshine. He wants to be able to help Andromeda with the farm and maybe herd some sheep. He has simple desires, which is good for our types."

"Yes," Metrool said, "it is so easy for us to get into trouble."

Alerton asked about the new farrier, and Metrool said, "He is doing well. Dino and Raphael have helped him get an anvil, a forge, and tools and supplies to do his job."

Alerton asked, "Do they get along well?"

"They seem to. All three have beds and pegs for their clothes in that large third-floor attic." Now they were walking to their fortress home.

Alerton said, "That illness is getting very close."

"Yes," Metrool said, "and those images Dagril had of it were terrible."

Once in their home, Alerton went to his room and was quickly asleep.

22

THE DRESS

On his horse-buying trip to Lucca, Everin had asked Alerton to visit a silk merchant there for her. She had told Alerton what she wanted, and he had flashed her four images. She had loved one of them and messaged, *Buy it. Buy a lot.*

Alerton had bought all they had. The heavy white silk with a pattern of real gold thread woven into it was to make Everin's wedding dress.

A month ago, she had searched for a goldsmith who could make fancy tiny gold roses for the dress. There would be fifty of them. The girls in the dress shop all seemed to be happy to work on it. Some were working on other things for that day and night. The girls loved the new windows with clear panes that let in light but not the cold.

Now only when they had a rush job they had to finish at night did they have to burn candles. Now that the weather was cool, a man with a horse-drawn cart came by once a week to deliver wood for the fireplaces.

Everin had learned quickly that Frieda had been terribly stingy; the girls had had only three thimbles they had to share, two pairs of scissors, not enough needles, and no special needles. Now each girl had her own basket with everything she needed.

They were happier, and Everin got more work done. The floor-length dress with a train in back would be a snug fit in the waist and torso and flare from the hips down. It would lace up the back with braided silk and gold strings.

Dona and Sala took the project and were happy to do it. Everin had increased business, and the reputation of the shop had improved. Now she was getting some of the large-money crowd, who set up appointments for Everin and two of her girls with fabric samples to come to their mansions. They did not go to shops, and some wanted the most extravagant dresses.

Everin had gotten the payment situation in hand early. She continued to make improvements on the shop. Now both the shop and the large attic had two fireplaces. Two glass windows were on each floor, on the side that faced the street.

23

JEWELS

EVERYTHING THEY HAD DONE IN THE LAST FEW WEEKS HAD INVOLVED gold, so Alerton was doing something he thought prudent. Alerton, Metrool, and four guards rode to the Jewish part of Florence. Through a goldsmith name Joshua, they had been working on a project for a month. Alerton carried a little more than two pounds of finished gems ready to mount. In that area, there would be Florence buyers and buyers from other places.

They pulled up in front of a large, plain brick building. Two young Jews in traditional clothes met them. They welcome them, and then one led them through the door into a hallway and through two locked doors into a large, well-decorated room. Part of the room was raised, and there was a large, heavy dark wood table with four large dark chairs behind it. In the lower part of the room was a plain table with eight chairs around it.

Metrool and Alerton, with their two fancy leather bags, were guided to the lesser table and seated facing the large dark table. Two young Jewish men covered both tables with fancy green velvet. One of the young men brought them each a small glass of dark red wine and indicated they should drink it now. Two different young men entered the room, carrying scrolls. Then eight older men came in. Four sat at the dark table, and four sat at their table. A man at the dark table said two prayers that Metrool and Alerton did not understand.

Now Alerton and Metrool would show some of their gems to the men at their table, and they would show the ones they liked to the men at the dark table for further approval. It took hours. Even with their Hamen bodies, Metrool and Alerton were tired.

The men purchased nearly all the gems, and Metrool and Alerton left with a pouch full of florins and papers guarantying large deposits to both their banks.

The sun was going down as they rode back to the stable. They paid the guards, gave their horses to Dino, and headed to the Arno for a drink.

Two days later, Metrool and Doc left for Vinci. They left at first light, and it was sundown when they arrived at the farm. Andromeda and Uriel greeted them warmly. After a glass of wine, Uriel had a long talk with Doc, because he knew Doc had been injected.

Then Uriel lay on his bed as Metrool injected four ccs into his arm. For the next six hours, Metrool and Doc took turns watching him, but nothing extreme happened. Metrool filled the syringe again and stopped at three ccs.

Uriel said, "No, use six."

Metrool said, "Are you sure?"

"Yes, I want to get on with this."

Metrool asked Andromeda, and she said, "It is his life."

So Metrool finished filling the syringe and injected it into Uriel. There was an almost immediate reaction. Uriel jumped up and started to run out of the farmhouse. Metrool and Doc had to tackle him and pull him to the floor. Uriel's wings were visibly shrinking, and his body was filling out.

Soon he calmed down and said, "I am hungry." Uriel's looks were changing.

Metrool and Doc stood beside him as he ate the food Meda had prepared.

At the end of six hours, Uriel asked for another six ccs, saying, "I want to be normal now." His wings were just stumps now, and he was calm, so they gave him what he wanted.

At the end of six hours, they examined him every way they could. He looked Hamen, and he tested Hamen. His long, thin gray hair was dark and thick now. Uriel looked at Doc and Metrool and studied them.

Uriel asked Andromeda, "Will you get something to cut my hair like theirs? I want them to take me to Vinci. I want to go to an inn." He turned to Metrool and asked, "Will you take me to an inn and eat and drink with me?"

It was a simple request, but Metrool felt such deep emotion in it that it shook him. He had never felt such emotion over such a simple thing.

As Andromeda was cutting Uriel's hair, Metrool said, "Of course I will, and Doc will too."

"I would be glad to go with you," Doc said. He had felt Uriel's emotion too.

Andromeda said, "Yes, take him. He has heard people's thoughts so many times and dreamed of going among them."

The three men rode horses into Vinci and found an inn. The innkeeper greeted them, pointed to an empty table, and asked if they wanted wine.

"Yes," Metrool answered, "three glasses of local wine."

Soon a young woman brought the wine and asked if they wanted something to eat.

Uriel quickly said, "Yes."

Metrool, amused, asked the woman what they had. Metrool smiled; Uriel would have ordered all of it. Metrool ordered three bowls of lamb stew with bread.

Uriel watched the young woman take the order and walk away and then said, "Thank you, Metrool. I am new at this."

Doc had been studying Uriel, and he said, "I am very happy for you and Andromeda."

Uriel said, "Oh, Doc, I owe Meda so much. I would have been—"

Metrool read what he was going to say and stopped him. He messaged him: *You must be careful what you say in public. They can still do those things to you.*

"Thank you," Uriel said, "but I owe Meda so much."

Their food came, and the young woman obviously looked Uriel over. Metrool read her thoughts: *He is good looking. Are these men travelers?* Her thoughts made Metrool look at Uriel again. For an earthling, he looked thirty to thirty-five years old, and looking at him, Metrool felt there were traces of earthling and traces of Engel. Metrool knew Uriel had heard the young woman's thoughts too.

Later, back at the farm, Metrool warned Uriel it would be complicated and dangerous to mate with an earthling.

Uriel said, "I understand, but your Everin is marrying Doc."

Metrool took a breath. "Yes, but Doc has some Hamen blood now, and Everin has Alerton and me to support her."

Uriel changed the subject and asked, "Are Andromeda and I invited to the wedding?"

Doc spoke up. "Yes, and it is only a week away."

The four went out and walked around the farm, talking about the olive trees, the grape vines, and what they would have to hire people to do in the spring and the other seasons. Andromeda was pleased there was a large, well-prepared garden plot. Metrool gave Andromeda a small bag of mixed coins and reminded her that she had a bank account to finance the farm operations.

Andromeda said, "I can't believe our fortunes have changed so much. Why have you done it?"

Metrool smiled. "First, it was that they were going to burn you. Then we found out you were kin to us."

It was obvious Meda and Uriel were both grateful, and they waved to Metrool and Doc as they left for Florence.

They rode south to the Arno and then rode east along the Arno. They hoped to reach Montelupo before dark. The city was famous for making pottery and had a good inn.

24

WEDDING DAY

EVERIN COULD NOT BELIEVE HER WEDDING DAY HAD FINALLY ARRIVED after many days of preparation and all the gold they had spent.

The value of gold there on Earth had shocked her at first, and it still amazed her. Hamen was made from gold. It was a golden planet with an iron-and-nickel core and a gold shell a thousand miles thick. Gold was a useful and common thing there. Pipes, wires, roofs, machinery, and even sidewalks were made of it, and it lasted forever. But on Earth, it was scarce. To look proper in their proper setting, they had to show gold and flaunt it. Her wedding dress had real gold thread in the fabric and small gold roses around the neckline and scattered around the dress.

The special coach Alerton had built mainly for the wedding had gold-plated trim. Even though Doc hated wearing a sword, he wore one for ceremonies, and just like Alerton's and Metrool's, Doc's had gold on it.

Uriel and Andromeda had ridden horses to Florence two days ago. They were staying with Metrool and Alerton. Uriel was enthralled with Florence.

Doc had told Everin that Uriel was handsome now, and he was. It was hard to believe he was the same person. His good looks and naive personality got him a lot of attention there in Florence.

The wedding breakfast had been at the Parrot, which had been closed to anyone else. Cerano and his wife and children had done it all. It had been wonderful. Now her home was full of people, including four girls from her shop, Meda, two cooks, and two maids. Her home was spotless and decorated for a combination of wedding and Christmas.

The girls and Meda were fussing over her fancy silk underclothes, getting her hair just right, and making sure her elevated shoes fit right and were laced right. She was reluctant about wearing them, because she was already taller than Doc, but Doc was wonderful. He said, "That is the style. Wear them."

Her beautiful wedding dress laced up the back with golden strings, so it was snug around her slim torso and then flared and went all the way to the floor with a long train—lots and lots of cloth. She was ready. She was also anxious; she had never been married. On Hamen, she had never joined with anyone—a mental marriage—and she had never been physical with anyone. Her tension rose.

Alerton and the coach arrived, and Alerton acted as her father.

Nearly everyone in Florence proper did the wedding walk to the church, which was close, but that was not good enough for Alerton. He properly knocked with the knocker, and Everin was led out to meet him.

Alerton and the two drivers had splendid clothes, which Alerton had paid for, and Alerton and one of the drivers helped her and her long dress into the coach. Then Alerton joined her, and as the coach rolled over the cobblestone, Alerton told her that she was beautiful, which he had never told her before, and that he was happy for her.

Everin replied, "Oh, thank you, Alerton. I am so glad you changed your mind."

"How could I look at you and Doc together and not change my mind?"

They arrived at the church. Many people had their weddings in front of the church, but Alerton and the monsignor had insisted it be inside. Metrool and Doc were in wonderful clothes. Everin was proud of Doc. As he looked at her, his eyes got shiny with tears. Doc had shaved his beard, and now Everin saw no wrinkles and no gray. Everyone but Everin, Alerton, and a young priest went inside. A few minutes later, the music started, and the young priest guided them as they entered. As Everin walked down the long aisle, she saw Metrool and Doc standing there, facing the monsignor.

Now, as she rode in the wedding coach with her husband, it all seemed like a dream. The coach was taking them to the Arno Inn. It was afternoon, and the Arno was closed for a special wedding feast.

The coachmen helped them down and escorted them into the Arno. Everin saw a table, set with a fancy tablecloth, large enough for twenty-four people. There were other tables set up, and at both ends of the inn were all kinds of food.

Everin whispered to Doc, "I don't understand."

Doc said, "The first hour is private. Then everyone will celebrate our marriage."

It was a wonderful afternoon with many happy people—some happy for them and some happy to have food in their stomachs. Everin again rode in the coach, this time to their home. The maids had made sure there was plenty of their favorite wine, and the cooks had prepared anything they might want. Doc let the staff know it was time for them to go.

After they were gone, Everin and Doc knew that the shivaree would start soon. Drums sounded, people sang songs, some made speeches, and then there was more music. Doc and Everin stayed there on the first floor, listening to their friends, sipping wine from two beautiful glasses, and enjoying the moment for a long time. Then it was time, and they both knew it. Doc took Everin over to the fireplace, and each took one last sip from his or her beautiful glass and threw it into the fireplace. It was a traditional gesture that had deep meaning.

Doc helped her up the stairs in her long train. In the hallway, Doc picked up her train and placed it in her arms. He then picked Everin up and carried her and the dress into the bedroom. She stood facing him, and he took her into his arms.

For Doc, at that moment, the world was perfect. It was a once-in-a-lifetime moment. Everin turned her back to him, and he saw the golden laces. Doc untied the laces and pulled the sides wide, Everin did a couple of wiggles, and the dress fell to the floor. Everin stepped out of it, and Doc picked it up and carried it to the other bedroom.

Once back with Everin, he took her in his arms, and soon they were kissing. Doc found these kisses much more intense than before. Then she stepped back and turned her back to him. At first, Doc did not understand, but then he saw her undergarments laced up the back. With nervous fingers, he untied them, and they fell to the floor. Everin turned to him. With only the moonlight from the window, Doc saw her in all her noble beauty.

The Parrot went back to regular business. Metrool, in his splendid attire, had gone to the academy and recruited several of his friends, and they were tying one on. It was strange; he was happy for her and thought Doc was great. He guessed it was like a real Earth sister getting married.

Metrool was shocked when his buddy Alerton joined them and gave the waiter a whole florin for wine.

25

CHRISTMAS

CHRISTMAS WAS NEAR, AND THE SHIPMENTS OF SEAFOOD ALERTON HAD ordered were arriving. They were so plentiful that they could sell some at low prices and still have enough for the Christmas fish meals. The different families were taking turns with the special days. The Christmas sweet treats were being created by the tableful.

They were celebrating Calendale and the tradition of the thirteen desserts, a symbol of Jesus and the twelve apostles. December 24 came, and it should have been the happiest, most boisterous night of the year, with the seven-fish meals, gambling, and the midnight mass.

However, there was a dark cloud hanging over it. Travelers were now telling everyone terrible tales of the plague. At first, people did not want to believe them. The tales were too terrible. But they kept hearing similar tales from every traveler who passed through Florence.

They went ahead and had their New Year's Eve celebration at the Parrot. They invited their friends and people they did business with. Most of them came, and there was music, dancing, gambling, and drinking, but the mood was grim.

Late on New Year's, Metrool and Alerton sat at the large table in their kitchen. There was a fire in the fireplace, and they had sent the maid home.

Metrool asked, "Do you think we should leave?"

Alerton hesitated and then said, "There is no place to go. It has traveled two-thirds of the known world, and it will travel the rest. We have no way of getting to the other continents, so we are here."

"We should be immune."

"Yes, and I messaged Andromeda to say they should stock up now and stay on the farm."

Metrool asked, "Do you think Doc will be immune?"

Alerton took a deep breath and said, "No. And he will not quit doctoring. He may die."

The next morning, at the home of the newlyweds, Everin rose early. Even though she had told the cooks what to prepare for breakfast, she still wanted to supervise. On the table, she placed a vase of silk roses. She had taught the girls how to make them. She could have had her creator make a vase full of real roses but did not want to get burned as a witch, and with the tales of the plague, people were looking for things to blame.

Doc came down the stairs. She loved his smile, and he nearly always had one for her. She remembered Alerton's early words to her: "You may only have him for forty years and have five hundred years without him." Well, whatever years she had with him, she would treasure them for a lifetime.

Even Metrool had warned her that marrying an earthling was like getting a pet, saying, "You have to be prepared to watch it age and die."

Well, in her eyes, Doc would never age; he would always look the way he had on their wedding day.

Doc looked at this lovely woman. He found it hard to believe she, probably the smartest woman in the world, had married him.

26

THE PLAGUE

IN FEBRUARY, DOC GOT HIS FIRST PATIENT WITH THE DISEASE. EVEN though Doc by then had heard the disease described at least fifty times, it was still a shock. He had seen and talked to this man three days ago, and he had been healthy. Now Doc knew he was close to death.

Doc pulled back his bedcovers and was suddenly nauseated. He had been told about the odor, but it was bad. Doc overcame it and continued. Yes, the man had the buboes—small ones in his neck, egg-sized ones in his groin, and large ones under his arms that were stretched and ready to burst.

Doc's colleagues had advised him that buboes this bad should be lanced because they were terribly painful and probably would bust on their own. Doc reached into his bag and got out his small, razor-sharp knife. He touched it to the worst buboes and cut. Greenish-black blood shot out, nearly hitting Doc, and this time, at the smell, Doc had to rush outside to empty his stomach.

In a few minutes, Doc went back inside and finished, even though he knew the patient was dying. When Doc went home, he was shaken. Being told about the disease was not the same as seeing it.

Seeing Doc's condition, Everin pried everything out of him. She decided to help. She and her cook—she only had the original now—walked to a cobbler's shop. She asked if he had ever made a surgeon's apron. He said yes, he had made three of them, and he described them.

Everin said, "Yes, make one for my husband, only more wraparound, not just the front."

"It will cost you more."

"That is all right," she said. Then she asked him about a mask. "I do not want one of those terrible bird masks that some doctors are wearing."

Finally, he agreed to make a leather half-face mask.

Everin went back to her home. Doc was sitting at the table. Everin said, "Doc, you cannot help them."

Doc said, "I cannot just abandon them."

"Doc, it is pointless."

"Everin, I must live with myself, and some survive."

"Do you not think those would have survived anyway?"

The next day, the man was dead, and he was one of the fortunate ones who had a proper burial. A week later, six or so were dying every day.

Doc would not stay home. He kept going to the sick, giving them medicine that did not cure them but eased their pain a little. Everin had broken the rules and had her creator device make a pain reliever, which Doc mixed with his local medicines.

She had the same device put a filter inside the leather mask the cobbler had made. She used logic, fear, and love to get Doc to wear the mask and apron.

Nearly every day, when Doc came home, the apron had traces of patients' fluids on it. In her basement, with the door locked, Everin cleaned it every night. Sometimes she had to clean the mask. The maids had to wash Doc's clothes every day.

The smell of the disease was terrible and permeated everything. As time passed, people were dying faster. Men, women, children—it did not matter to the disease. So many were dying that they had given up on proper burials.

Many of the clergy, who had been doing burials, were now buried themselves. Now the townspeople dug long, deep pits to bury the dead. The death carts would come by in the morning to pick up the dead who had been laid out for them. They would take them to the pits and throw them in. When a pit had a layer of bodies, a layer of dirt would be added to be ready for the next bodies.

The city had to pay higher and higher wages to the death-cart men, for they were dying too. Doc would not stay home, even though he admitted that nearly everyone who got the disease died, whether he lanced the buboes or they burst on their own.

Even though Everin had closed the dress shop, had food and the things they needed delivered to them, and just let the girls live in their upstairs room, two of them caught the disease and died.

Two people at Abram's bank were dying.

27

THE PLAGUE STRIKES HOME

METROOL BURST INTO DOC'S OFFICE. "DOC, I NEED YOUR HELP. SIMONETTA is sick. I think it is the death, and Cerano is letting one of those quacks in a hood and bird mask doctor her."

Doc rose quickly and then almost fell over. Metrool looked at him. Doc was sick. A quick scan told Metrool that Doc had the death. Doc had been trying to treat sick people, even though he knew it was useless. Doc could not just sit in his office or in his and Everin's home.

Metrool messaged Everin: *Doc has the death.*

Everin messaged back: *Where is he?*

Metrool replied, *In his office.*

Everin said, *I am out the door.*

Quickly, because their home was close, Everin and Nan, the cook, were there. Hamens did not cry, but Everin was crying and angry. Everin and the cook took hold of Doc and guided him to their home.

Metrool listened to Everin's thoughts and heard Hamen curse words: *Zarin! I told you not to doctor those people.*

Doc replied, *I took an oath to try to help people.*

Everin said, *Well, that oath may have killed you.*

Metrool messaged Alerton: *Where are you?*

I am at Abram's bank, Alerton said.

I will be there soon.

When Metrool was in Alerton's office, he said, "Simonetta has it."

Alerton asked, "How do you know?"

"One of the quacks with a bird mask is treating her, and I asked Cerano her symptoms. She has large buboes in her armpits and groin, dark spots on her arms and legs, and that awful odor."

"What is the bird mask doing for her?"

"He gave her something to drink, which she threw up, and then burned some sort of incense. Cerano will not let me see her. He says it is the doctor's orders."

Alerton could see Metrool was very upset over Simonetta.

Metrool said, "We have to help her."

"How?" Alerton said. "Even we do not have medicine that will cure it. And the bird mask and Cerano will not even let us see her."

"We could give her my blood and lance those buboes."

"It might work, and it might not. She is so advanced, I just do not know. How would we do it?"

"We could use mental pressure to send Bird Face away, but Cerano's wife has already died from the death. It would be hard to drive him from Netta's side."

"And how would you, a man, be able to lance those buboes, when you cannot even be alone with her?"

"Everin could do it. She is a woman and medically trained."

"Metrool, she has just found out that Doc has the death. Do you think she would leave Doc?" Alerton messaged Everin: *Can you have your device make a dozen syringes?*

Everin replied, *I did that a week ago. Why?*

Simonetta has the death.

No! Everin, who was with Doc and the cook, turned to the cook. "Do you trust me?"

Nan said, "Yes."

"Do you like me?"

"Yes."

"Do you sometimes think I am a witch?"

The cook turned red.

Everin said, "Nan, I am not a witch." But at the same time, she put Nan into a trance and put three engrams into her mind. She would not tell anyone the strange things she was about to see.

120

They put Doc in a downstairs bedroom. Everin sent the cook to the kitchen to boil water, and she undressed her husband and examined him. Yes, he had it bad; he had buboes under his arms and dark spots forming on his skin.

Everin latched the door and got out one of the syringes. From her own thigh, she drew four ccs of her blood, and she injected it into an artery in Doc's thigh. After putting the syringe away, she unlatched the door and let Nan in.

She asked Nan to get a shallow bowl from the kitchen. Nan did, and Everin placed it under the buboes in Doc's right armpit. Doc had the awful odor that was common with the death. Everin pulled out a small surgical knife she had made with her device. She asked the cook to hold the bowl, took a deep breath, and lanced the buboes. Green, black, and red liquid came out of them, and Doc's bad odor got worse. Nan had to run to a garbage pot to heave. When Nan was back, they did the left armpit. Everin had checked his groin and seen that the ones there were quite small, so she would do them later.

She put a strip of cloth deep into each bubo, with part of it hanging out so it would continue to drain. Everin did not know how Doc would react to the blood this time. But now, for a moment, she could think about Metrool's problem.

Simonetta had the death and was being treated by one of the many charlatans taking advantage of the death. Simonetta was about to die if they did not help her. How could she help?

Well, Everin was a female; she could examine her and open the buboes. She had to have help. Could she trust Nan that far, even after she put protective engrams in her mind? Whose blood, Metrool's or Alerton's, should she use, and how much? The first time, months ago, Doc had reacted violently. Would it cure her? It seemed Simonetta was deep into the disease and might die no matter what they did.

But yes, Metrool is deeply involved with Simonetta, and we must try. But what if she did survive? Would she be different?

Everin was torn apart. She messaged Metrool and told him to come to her. They got together and decided Alerton would stay with Doc, and Metrool, Everin, and Nan would go to Simonetta.

Cerano was adamant that only the hooded doctor in the mask could see Simonetta. Metrool tried to enter anyway, and the hooded doctor stood in his way and made an insulting remark. That was over the limit for a distraught Metrool.

Metrool hit him with a brain message much harder than he intended, and the masked doctor grabbed his heart and fell over. Metrool stepped over him and went in to see Simonetta. She looked terrible, and she smelled terrible, but Metrool did not care.

He knelt beside her and took her hand, and she tried to smile at him. Everin and Nan came into the room, and Everin messaged Metrool: *She does not have much time.*

I know, Metrool said.

Everin said, "Find the kitchen, boil some water, and find some strong wine if you can." Metrool touched Netta's face and left.

Immediately, Everin and Nan took Simonetta's gown off. She was in terrible shape, with large black buboes in her armpits and groin, smaller ones in her neck, and dark spots on her skin. Her odor was terrible. Everin went to the kitchen, where Metrool was, with a syringe and pulled six ccs of blood from him. She hid the syringe in her clothes and went back into Simonetta's room. She had Nan leave and quickly injected the blood into a major thigh artery. Quickly, she put the syringe away and called Nan back in.

Metrool knocked and handed Nan a bottle of strong wine. Everin set it to one side and pulled out a bottle of disinfectant her creator had made. Everin pulled out her surgical knife and rubbed the buboes with disinfectant. Then, one by one, she opened the dreadful buboes, draining the foul mostly black liquid, and inserted cloth strips so they would continue to drain.

Metrool brought the boiled water, and Everin and Nan lifted Simonetta out of the soiled bed onto a clean sheet on the floor. There they used the boiled water and soap to bathe her. They pulled everything off the bed, even the down mattress.

Everin went to another room and got a new mattress and sheets. They put a clean gown on Netta and lifted her into the bed. Barely awake, Simonetta managed to say, "Metrool."

They had cleaned Simonetta and the bed, and Nan had carried all the foul stuff away, but the room still smelled bad. However, Everin knew how love was, so she went and got Metrool. She and Nan left Simonetta's room, and they saw that the masked doctor had been taken away.

Metrool went into the room, and after a few minutes, he messaged Everin: *Did you inject her?*

Yes, Everin answered, *but I do not know if it will save her. She is fading fast.*

Metrool asked, *Will you inject her with your blood?*

Everin thought for a moment. *You know it could get very complicated if we made a Hamen out of a young person.*

Metrool was quiet and then said, *If she becomes Hamen-like and goes rogue, I will terminate her.*

Hamen oath? Everin asked.

Yes, Metrool said, *Hamen oath. Inject her.*

Everin left Nan outside Simonetta's room and went in. Metrool gave her the syringe and watched her pull four ccs into it but said, "More." Reluctantly, she filled it to six.

With the full syringe in her hand, she looked at Metrool and said, "Are you sure?"

Metrool said, "Yes, inject it."

She injected it into the poor girl's thigh artery. Everin then said, "The buboes are drained, and we have given her two large injections close together. That is all we can do right now. I have to go help Doc."

"I know," Met said.

"I will leave Nan here with you; you are not supposed to be in this room without a chaperone."

Outside, Cerano was acting wild, praying, cussing, and asking, "Why me? What have I done so bad that I should lose my wife and daughter?"

Everin called Nan into Netta's room and told her, "You stay in this room so Metrool can be with Simonetta. I must go help Doc."

When she went outside, Cerano asked wildly, "How is she? Is she going to live?"

Everin used her powers to calm him down and convince him they would have to wait and see. She took him into Simonetta's room for a few minutes and then asked him to escort her the two blocks to her dress shop.

Things were dangerous now that the death was killing as many as six hundred a day. There were no individual graves. Now there were large open trenches filled with layers of bodies barely covered with dirt.

Cerano quickly walked Everin to the dress shop, and after checking the dress shop and making sure the remaining four girls were all right, she had two of them walk her the short distance home.

Everin ran to Doc. Alerton was with him. She asked, "How is he?"

"Stable," Alerton said. "That's all. The injections we gave him when he had the heart attack helped him, but they are not enough to make him immune."

Everin retrieved a new syringe and said, "I wish we had a real medicine to fight the death. Using our blood is very primitive medicine."

"I know," Alerton said, taking the syringe. "Your device told you it did not have the formula for this disease." Alerton injected four ccs of his blood into Doc's carotid artery.

Doc began moaning, and then he began clutching at the buboes. "Oh, they itch." His body began to jerk and have violent movements. Alerton and Everin had to hold him down. The buboes were getting smaller and smaller.

They had quit draining, so Everin pulled the linen strips out of them and washed them with alcohol her creator had made.

Two hours later, Doc sat up and asked them, "What happened?"

Everin said, "You had the death, but I think you are nearly well now."

Suddenly, Everin got a message from Metrool: *I need you here as soon as you can.*

After scanning Doc, Everin kissed him and said, "I will be right back. Metrool needs me."

Quickly, Everin and a servant went to Cerano's home. He was crying wildly outside his home. She went inside and was surprised to see Simonetta in the main room of the home in just her gown. She had returned to look like her beautiful self, but she was raving. "You are witches! I always knew you were different, you rich newcomers able to do anything you wanted. But now you have bewitched me, and I know you are witches. I see things I should not, and I hear things I should not. I hear what people are thinking."

Everin messaged Metrool: *Have you tried to explain to her?*

Netta screamed, "I heard that! You can talk to each other without talking out loud. Total witchery. I have sent the servants for the priests. I am going to tell the church about you. I will see all of you burn."

Metrool tried to make mental contact and did but did not get what he expected.

She was strong and mentally yelled, *Get out of my head!* and turned his mental waves away.

Metrool saw they had a major problem and sent a message to Alerton: *I need you and a BWI.*

Simonetta said, "Yes, yes, tell Alerton to come. I want all three of you here. You are all three witches. I hear insects in the dirt. I hear the winds blowing. I can hear what my own father is thinking. He thinks I am a witch—and I am a witch, but you did it. I do not know how. Something about blood. But that does not matter. I am a witch, but now I know that you three are witches, and that is why you were so nice to me. Metrool, you wanted to make me into a witch. Well, you did, but now we will all burn together."

Metrool was crying. He tried to talk to her, but she sent a mental shock wave to stop him. Simonetta said, "I am not going to let you put any more spells on me. I saw how you killed the doctor. You did not want him to help me. You wanted to use your magic on me when I was sick, so you could get me when I was weak. Well, you did it; you made me a witch, but I do not have to stay one. I am going to get us all burned. I will go to heaven for it, and you three will go straight to hell for making a witch out of one of God's children."

Metrool tried again to speak verbally to Simonetta, and again, she sent a strong brain wave, knocking him to the floor. Alerton came in and was unprepared to see Metrool on the floor, trying to stand up.

Simonetta said, "You witches picked the wrong person to make a witch," and she hit Alerton with a strong wave. It was all he could do to stand, and mainly on reflex, he hit her with the BWI. It was set for deep sleep, and Alerton should have used it for only one second, but her wave dazed him, and he used it for six seconds. Simonetta fell backward onto a couch.

Metrool ran to her and scanned her, but there was no brain activity. She was dead. Metrool began to cry.

Alerton was trying to get back to normal. He had never been hit by a brain wave like that. Suddenly, he received a message from Everin: *Alerton, you have priests and witnesses coming, and they are nearly there. Get a story together and a plan. Get Metrool back in control of this, or we will burn.*

Yes, I will, Alerton said. He used all his abilities to get back to normal. Then he went to Metrool, put his hands on him, and tried to help him. Slowly, Metrool came back to normal, and Alerton informed him of what they must do.

"Every servant must be cleansed, and the priest's memory must be changed, or we will be in major trouble."

First, they quickly brought Cerano into Netta's room and redid his memory of how his daughter had died. The bird-faced doctor had been doctoring his plague-stricken daughter, and they both had died from it. But his daughter was so beautiful and pure that a miracle had happened: her body had been returned to its normal beautiful self.

It was easy to convince Cerano of this. All the witch things were erased from his mind. His daughter had died an angel.

Just then, servants, three priests, and six guards arrived.

Alerton, Metrool, and the BWI put them all to sleep. They all collapsed onto the floor, and one by one, either Alerton or Metrool re-created their memories of what had just happened. When they were finished, they woke them all at the same time.

Cerano could not wait to take the priests into Simonetta's room to show them the miracle. At first, they doubted she had been sick. But then the servants confirmed she had had it and had looked and smelled terrible.

The priests prayed, put on their purple vestments, and gave Simonetta extreme unction. The priests knelt beside the beautiful girl in the pristine bed and prayed for a long time. They asked God for confirmation that this really was a miracle.

The lead priest told Cerano, "She will not be thrown into the pit like the others. She will be entombed in the church."

Cerano was thrilled by the news; it was a great honor. Alerton donated to the priests, and then he gave the captain of the guards three florins in front of his men and said, "See that she gets safely to the church, and then buy your men good wine."

An hour later, Alerton, Metrool, and Everin were sitting at Everin's large kitchen table. Alerton was shaken by the events of the night. Metrool still had tears in his eyes.

Alerton said, "We must leave Florence."

"What?" Everin said.

"We must leave Florence," Alerton repeated.

"Why? When?" Metrool asked.

Alerton said, "Not tomorrow but soon. There have been too many events. Too many times we have had to erase memories or create new ones. Someday one of those creations is going to wear off. A hit on the head, a brain disease—many things can alter the mind. We must decide where and when. We must disguise and ship some things ahead of time. Metrool or I will have to take a trip there. Maybe even go ahead to receive the shipped things. But we must leave soon."

Everin was hesitant. "What about—"

"Your husband is alive and going with you," Alerton said. "All the incidents we have had here in Florence in this year make it certain that someone will remember. To earthlings, we do not age, so no place can be permanent. In nearly perfect conditions, we will be in a place for twenty-five to thirty-five years. We will always have to be aware of our situation and be ready to move on. I have been inquiring about Paris, and it seems perfect for our needs."

Everin asked, "What are your requirements for a place to move?"

"First and foremost, it must be a major distance from our present location, so a neighbor will not show up. Second, it must have a good-sized population, and it's better if it is a cosmopolitan population. Paris fits all these, and because of the plague, its population is in turmoil. Our normal moves will be twenty to thirty years, but it could happen anytime."

Metrool asked, "What other places are on your list?"

Alerton answered, "Barcelona, Amsterdam, Lisbon, Bordeaux, and Madrid."

Metrool asked, "When?"

"In three months."

28

1477

130 years later

PORTUGAL WAS THEIR FOURTH EARTH LOCATION. IN LISBON, ALERTON and Metrool were successful businessmen, and Doc was a doctor. They had capital and were always on the lookout for a good buy, and when they could make a profit, they sold it. They liked Lisbon; it was a bustling cosmopolitan city. It had a lot of ships coming and going. Alerton and Metrool had found that spending some time in the seaside taverns was a good way to find deals. Alerton had found something else: he had met a young man, Colombo, who had dreams of sailing west to China.

Alerton was talking to Metrool about the possibility. Metrool said, "His numbers are all wrong. This round ball is a lot larger than he thinks it is."

Alerton said, "Yes, but if he sails west, he is bound to find the continents that Europe does not know exist. It could make him famous and give us a lot of opportunities. If they knew about the other continents, there would be a lot of new ships built. Thousands of sailors would be recruited. I am going to encourage him."

Metrool told Alerton that in that context, it was the right thing to do.

As time went by, they found that the young man, though from a modest background, was in some of the upper circles. The young man had an eye for the ladies, and they seemed to have an eye for him. He worked as a mapmaker and a sailor and had been on long voyages.

Doc had quickly become one of the favorite doctors in Lisbon, and of course, Everin was proud of him. Everin told Alerton, "Every place we move to, Doc becomes one of their favorite doctors."

Alerton smiled and said, "That is because Doc is very dedicated, not doing it for money."

Everin said, "We do not need it. You and Metrool have made us rich."

"We are trying to make us even richer," Alerton said. "There is a young man named Colombo who has a scheme to sail west to China."

Everin said, "Alerton, you know he can't do that."

"I know, but he would discover the other continents."

"Oh, I see. You do not expect him to reach China."

"No, we expect him to discover a new world."

"I know of this young man. He is going to marry Filipa Moniz."

"I am sure we will be invited to the wedding."

Indeed, they went to the wedding, and time went by. Colombo's father's tavern burned, and Metrool helped him acquire another one. Two different times, Colombo got encouragement from King John II of Portugal, but both times, the plan fell through.

More time went by, and Alerton heard a rumor that Queen Isabella of Spain had money and might be receptive to the deal. He passed that information on to Colombo. It was not long before Alerton received a written message. It read, "My great friend Alerton, on the seventeenth day of April in the year of our Lord 1492, I received from the queen of Spain the funds for my journey. I plan to sail in August."

Everin, Metrool, Alerton, and Marie, an earthling Alerton had fallen in love with, continued as a foursome. Tragically, they had lost Doc, and because of their long lives and unchanging appearances, they had to move periodically. England was their nineteenth move. They moved to England in 1895, a time of rapid progress in inventing things and manufacturing things. They traveled to different sites where things were invented or manufactured and invested in the ones that showed promise. Metrool loved automobiles, and there was huge action in that field. He invested in four different automobile manufacturers.

29

DAGRIL'S LEGACY

Early July 1914

METROOL WAS DRIVING HIS STUTZ THROUGH THE ENGLISH COUNTRYSIDE to Alerton's home. The English countryside was green and smelled of moisture. The house came into view. Arrista was a large but not huge home. Alerton had bought it a year ago and renamed it. Once the major repairs had been completed, Alerton had turned Arrista over to Marie. Marie would have to handle the rebuilding of Arrista. Alerton had plenty to do with his new job in the aeroplane industry.

Metrool enjoyed driving the Stutz, shifting the gears and mashing the pedals. Being from Hamen, Metrool could see how terribly crude the machine was. But it was amazing how suddenly the earthlings were making progress. As Metrool pulled into the circular driveway, Alerton, Marie, and a servant came to greet him. The servant took the Stutz to the car park in the back. Alerton and Marie both hugged him and held him for a moment. They had been through much together. Alerton and Marie had been together for nearly two hundred years. Things were getting more advanced, with steamships, trains, and automobiles.

They went inside, and Metrool set his valise down; a servant would take it up to his room. Marie asked if he was hungry, and he said no. Alerton told him he had some good Tuscan wine.

Metrool replied, "Now you're talking. That should bring back memories."

Alerton told Marie, "Metrool was an artist in Florence during part of its glory period."

"Oh," Marie said, "that must have been wonderful. Did you get to meet some of the famous artists?"

"Yes," Metrool said, "I met some who later became quite famous, and some of the people you see in famous portraits I knew personally."

Marie said, "Oh, that is wonderful. You are going to have to tell me about some of them."

"Of course," Metrool said. "I will enjoy it. I am limited in talking about the past."

"Yes," Alerton said, "they do not burn witches anymore, but there are a lot of ways to get in trouble."

They spent a good while talking about personal things. Then, sitting with Marie and Alerton in the library after dinner, Metrool said, "War is coming."

"I know," Alerton said.

"No," Metrool said, "I do not mean in general. Within one month, a major war will start."

"Well, what do we do?" Alerton asked.

"That is why I am here—to find out what you want to do. I communicated with Everin, and she is going to take the English American side."

"As wealthy manufacturers in both America and England, we cannot stay neutral."

"I have factories in Germany and Austria also."

"You need to sell them quickly."

"One is a pharmaceutical company, and I have put a lot into it."

"I know; you lived in Germany for nineteen years."

"I think it would be a disaster for someone else to take over the pharmaceutical company right now."

Alerton said, "You would have to put it in someone else's name and be very careful. I think we must appear to give our full support to England, even though Hamen rules say we cannot take part in a planet's wars."

Metrool said, "According to the noninterference rules, we cannot invent weapons of war for them to use. We cannot give them new technology. We can help them with things that already exist. We can facilitate manufacturing."

"All right, that sounds appropriate."

"You are aware that these earthlings are inventing things at a rapid pace without our help."

"I know. Do you know how many companies are trying to build aeroplanes and rapid-firing rifles they call machine guns?"

"Do you think we should get into those companies so we can keep an eye on them?"

"That is a good idea. We do not want one side to get a huge advantage over the other."

Late at night, they went to their rooms.

The next day, the planning continued. It continued for two more days because the trio of Everin, Metrool, and Alerton owned a lot of companies large and small.

The next two weeks were a business nightmare, including selling out of some companies and buying into others—diverse companies, such as lumber in Alaska; engine companies in France, Spain, and America; and shipbuilding in Scotland.

Alerton and Metrool put the operations into the hands of zombies, people who had total loyalty to them. They had volunteered for the job and were paid well. Alerton and Metrool put engrams into their minds so they could not betray them.

Centuries ago, they had been betrayed twice and learned their lesson. Alerton started a new company that managed resources, whatever they were. Metrool started an engineering resource company to help companies solve problems. Alerton's first problems were engines that had not enough power, had too much weight, and were unreliable. Those were common technology problems he could help with.

Alerton's first business trip in his new job was to Barcelona to acquire aircraft engines and get them shipped to England. In dealing with the company, Alerton found Germans were negotiating too, and because he could scan them, he outbid them.

Later, only being Hamen saved him when he was attacked in his hotel hallway. He put his attackers in the hospital, because he did not want to involve the police. The incident was educational: war business could be deadly.

Two weeks later, he was trying to get to Alaska to secure a contract on their Sitka spruce. Whether it was aircraft cloth, aircraft glue, or dope, he and his associates were always chasing something. Marie was a good sport; she always supported him. Sometimes she told him he had not made the best choice, but she always supported him.

Just a few years after they'd met, Marie had been about to die. As Everin had done with Doc, Alerton had injected her with his Hamen blood. He had saved her life, but she had been in shock. She had not known who or what he was. He'd had a lot of talking to do. But Marie already had loved him and had been willing to give him time to explain everything.

Those injections were why, 192 years later, she still looked forty.

Alerton missed seeing Everin, his earthly sister. They had lived close to each other for many years and been through many things.

30

JULY 28, 1914

THE WAR HAD STARTED. WITHIN A FORTNIGHT, ALERTON WAS CALLED TO 10 Downing Street to have it pressed upon him how important his companies were to the war effort.

Alerton messaged Everin: *We are now at war, and I am overly concerned about these earthlings and their ability to create weapons. In the last fifty years, they have develop trains, automobiles, aeroplanes, and fast-firing weapons. There is no telling what they will develop next. It appears that many nations are about to enter the conflict, committing millions of men. The more they commit, the more will die. Their mechanical development is way out of its natural timeline. Our colonies did that forty thousand years ago.*

Metrool worked with Hawk, making their planes more reliable. He believed that was a suitable thing to do. Because of his work there and Alerton's success with parts, Metrool was offered a high technical position at an English air base in France.

The ocean was rough as Metrool's ship made the eleven-hour crossing. It got smoother as the ship got close to the port of Le Havre.

Metrool took a taxi from the port to the train station. At the train station, he asked for a private compartment, but one was not available, so he settled for a semi. Cost was not an object; he had been building his fortune for a long time.

When the other person entered the compartment, Metrool was surprised; it was a pilot going to the same aerodrome. His name was Jack Simons, and he had been in Le Havre to visit a wounded pilot. Metrool asked him about the local air battles.

Jack said, "The Jerrys in this area are good. They have good planes, and they have good discipline. If you make a mistake, you can die."

They went to the dining car, and soon they were dining with wine and finished with absinthe. Metrool found out Jack was from a wealthy English family. He did not have to be there; he had chosen to be there. He told Metrool about his hotel in town; he did not stay in the crude barracks.

At the train station in Troyon, they caught a taxi to Jack's hotel, and Metrool secured a room there. It was nighttime, and Metrool unpacked his valise and hung his suits on racks. Maybe they would not need to be pressed, he thought.

The next morning, he ate breakfast at the hotel, checked his suit, and went to the base.

He checked into the general's office. The general said, "Welcome, Mr. Metrool. We have been expecting you."

After a short conversation, Metrool was turned over to Colonel Dubeau. Dubeau escorted Metrool around the base, especially the maintenance and supply areas.

Nearly all the planes sat out in the open. They only had three of the French Bessonneau canvas hangars, and they were reserved for repair work. Metrool went back to the main maintenance hangar and gathered all the different repair people. He explained to them why he was there: to help them keep the planes flying. Metrool then went to the office he had been assign to and tried to make some telephone calls. The telephone service was terrible, and he could not complete a call.

So he did what he needed to do. He locked his office door and messaged Alerton. Metrool asked, *Do you have time?*

Alerton answered, *Yes, give me one hour.*

Metrool had a staff car take him to his hotel. He went to his room, sat back and relaxed, and then messaged Alerton. He told Alerton of some of the problems he had seen in the repair hangars. He asked Alerton if he was familiar with those problems. Alerton knew about some but not all. He told Metrool he would investigate all of them.

<hr>

Three days later, Metrool began looking for a secretary. He advertised, and each day, two to four applicants would see him to apply. None of them had all the talents he required. Typing was a new skill, and these women were not good at it. Metrool was about to give up and hire one of them anyway, when she walked in.

She said her name was Margaux Dubois, but he could call her Marg. Metrool looked at her application. She was a widow and was well educated and a certified typist. It was not her application that grabbed Metrool, however; it was her. She was thirty-nine and had a radiant personality.

Metrool did a light scan and saw her credentials were real, and he hired her on the spot. He had her sit down at her desk with the large Olivetti typewriter and dictated a letter to one of the manufacturers he was having trouble with. She had no trouble in typing it. He read it and then asked her some questions. She lived with her sister because her husband had been killed in the war. She had an eighteen-year-old son who lived with her. Metrool told her the job's hours and told her to start the next day.

After she left, Metrool sat there thinking about her. What was it about this woman? Why did he keep thinking about her? Did she remind him of someone else? In his 567 years on Earth, he had gotten emotionally involved with only three earthlings, and all had ended badly.

The next day, Marg arrived on time, and Metrool spent most of the day dictating letters to different manufacturers. Marg typed them all up and mailed them.

Metrool spent most of the next day in the main maintenance hangar, getting his hands dirty with the problems. He gained points with the mechanics, who saw that he was not just a paper helper. Piere, Max, and Charles, all maintenance officers, went to the officers' mess with him and continued to discuss the problems. It was late when they left the mess, and Piere, who had an auto, drove Metrool to his hotel.

Metrool found out that Piere had a home with a wife and child in the town. Metrool had scanned Marg before he hired her; she'd had to flee her previous job when Germany took over a large part of France. Her husband had been killed in the First Battle of the Marne.

Watching Marg type on the upright Olivetti typewriter, Metrool was constantly amazed at the earthlings' progress. When they had arrived on Earth, the metal type-printing press had not been invented yet. Marg's job was to answer his phone, type up his papers, and receive any notes his maintenance people sent to him. She ran the office every day, even when Metrool was out of town.

A week after he arrived, tales about one of their newest planes started circulating. Tales of wings breaking. Tales that were hard to believe. One morning, Metrool and Jack took off in two of the planes and, over the aerodrome, put them through aerobatics. At first, they did basic aerobatics, and then they moved on to maneuvers that put high stress on the aircraft. Because he was Hamen and had much more sensitive senses, Metrool was able to realize when the upper wing spar started breaking, back off, and gingerly bring it down and land it.

He immediately messaged Alerton because he worked with the manufacturers. He told him the plane's upper spar was not nearly strong enough. He had Marg type up the results and telegraph them directly to the manufacturer. The manufacturer replied that they would fix it but that he should not have sent that information over the telegraph. Metrool said, "My men are dying."

It was amazing to Metrool the inventions the earthlings had made in the last hundred years. He looked at Margaux typing on her Olivetti typewriter, which had been invented only a few years before. Nearly a hundred years after they'd arrived, the printing press with movable metal type had been invented. Metrool remembered when Gutenberg had printed his Bible. Alerton had known Johannes.

The aeroplane Metrool was dealing with had been around for only a few years. Metrool went out to the maintenance hangar. Lieutenant Charles Eker and his team had been assigned to uncover the upper wing. When the plane was sitting there in the hangar, the cracks were barely visible, but with just a little more stress, the wing would have come apart.

Lieutenant Eker said, "Mr. Metrool, you were right."

Metrool said, "Take pictures of it, and twist that wing so the cracks open."

Lieutenant Eker said, "We will have to get the base photographer."

"Do that," Metrool said, "and do not let anyone mess with this airplane, no matter who wants to move it or repair it, not even the commandant."

Metrool found out Lieutenant Eker was about to go to town, and Metrool asked if he could take Marg to town. He said, "But of course." Metrool had to have dinner with the commandant that night to keep him informed.

The next day, Metrool had a staff car take him to town and then taxied to three different auto dealers, and he wound up buying a Daimler. Behind the engine compartment, there was a windscreen and then an open front seat, with a closed-in rear seat. The salesman explained the controls, and Metrool drove it back to the base.

Metrool was aware that the trio had been lucky to start with wealth and increase it several times. He also knew they had benefitted individuals and companies with their investments. *You cannot build a factory unless you have money or credit. You can have a great invention, but you must be able to make it and sell it*, he thought. Dagril's gold had been their start.

Late that afternoon, two men from the maker of the faulty spar arrived at the aerodrome. Metrool took them to the main hangar. They did not want to believe what they were being told. When Metrool and Eker showed them the spar with the cracks in it, one said, "That pilot must have pulled nine g's, and we are not asked to build for that."

Metrool said, "The pilot of that plane only pulled four to five g's."

The taller of the two factory reps said, "Let us talk to the pilot."

Eker spoke up. "The pilot was Mr. Metrool."

Metrool said, "Unless you want the whole contract canceled, you will fix that damned spar so it will take eight g's. I want those wings to be bulletproof. I want my pilots to be able to do anything necessary to win a fight."

Chastened, they said they would redesign both spars. Metrool said, "Do not ship any planes until you have fixed those wings." They gave Metrool a look, and he said, "Yes, I have the authority to cancel the whole contract."

Metrool, in his new Daimler, drove them to the train station, and they caught the next train out. Metrool then went to the club. Several pilots and maintenance officers were there, and they insisted on buying him drinks.

The club served food at night, so he had a meal with them. He then went to his hotel and faded out.

He awoke to another day of getting twenty aircraft into the air on a mission. Twenty and thirty-five minutes later, fighters returned with troubles. That was average. They would go to the maintenance hangars to see if the problems could be found and fixed.

Ninety minutes later, they started returning from the mission. Metrool counted fourteen. *Where are the others?* A few minutes later, another appeared with its motor sounding awful and landed. Three were dead or captured. It hurt. Metrool did not like dealing with this. He sometimes thought of going someplace else, such as Africa or a remote island, and staying there until this catastrophe was over.

———◦———

For Alerton, dealing with the manufacturers was at times frustrating. They always had excuses for why they made bad parts: they were rushed, or they did not have enough machinery or people. But Alerton always told them they either had to find ways or would lose their contract. The maker of one type of bad part had the audacity to say, "You cannot pull our contract; we are the only company that can make these parts."

Within thirty days, Alerton put together a company and had it making those parts. Now the old company was searching for a new contract. Alerton hoped word got around. The pilots fighting this war depended on these planes to survive.

———◦———

One morning, Margaux was not at work, so Metrool did a light scan, and he saw that her son was extremely sick. Metrool also saw she had no way to get him to a doctor. He drove to town, to her sister's home. Margaux was surprised to see him. She asked how he had known her son was sick.

"You are a particularly good worker. I deduced that only you or your son being sick would keep you home."

Metrool drove Marg and her son to the doctor and waited to drive them home. He left them there and drove back to the base. Just as he got back to the aerodrome, a fighter plane, in flames, was trying to land. The tires must have been flat, for when the wheels touched the ground, the plane tumbled and became a ball of fire. The pilot was dead before the fire truck got to the wreck.

Damn, Metrool hated this war. He did not know yet who the pilot was, but it did not matter. It was such a waste. The maintenance people had learned he cared and were always letting him know about their problems. He tried to help them, but sometimes he could not.

Alerton was dealing directly with the manufacturers, one of which manufactured the Peregrine. He had been having an awful time with them. It was a sound company with lucrative contracts, but they would not agree to fix their problems. Alerton had even gone to their board of directors. That day, he was going to the banking center of London.

He went into a bank and adjusted two accounts. Then he went to a building two streets over. The timing was crucial. At two thirty, Alerton launched a large sell order of Peregrine stock to a fake buyer, who was really himself, at a low price.

The next day, he contacted the top board members, and they were much more receptive about fixing the problems. Alerton messaged Everin in America and informed her. She was happy for him. She was working with some of the suppliers in America, and she was familiar with his problems. Alerton quizzed her about her private life.

Oh, I have friends, she told him, *male and female.*

But no one special? Alerton asked.

No, Alerton, it has not been that long since I lost Doc.

Alerton did not say anything, but it had been more than a hundred years since she'd lost Doc.

They messaged some more, and then Alerton said goodbye. Everin was smart, and she was tough. Of course, she was a Hamen.

As Alerton's chauffeur drove him to Arrista, he was glad he had Marie. They had been together for two hundred years, and it had been close to perfect from the start. She'd had major roles in the past, but right now, finishing the resurrection of Arrista was her occupation. The chauffeur drove up in front, and Alerton got out. The driver took the Rolls on to the garage in back. The driver was also Alerton's butler. Alerton did not want to have too many servants. Hamen did not have servants.

Marie greeted him with her beautiful smile. They hugged and kissed and then sat down with a cup of tea. She told him of the things the workmen had done that day. She was pushing them because next month, there was to be a major dinner with the prime minister in attendance.

Everin had just returned to her apartment. She looked out the large window, which looked out onto Central Park. Alerton's asking about her personal life had resurfaced many memories of Doc—the fabulous times, the terrible times, and 450 years of loving and being loved. It still hurt. Four different times, she had come close to losing Doc but had not. She activated the engrams in her mind that brought better moods, and there were memories of Doc and all the love and good times they had shared. Now she could sit down at her large mahogany desk with her Royal typewriter and think of the current problems.

There was a company whose quality control was terrible. Fifty percent of their products that got to the field had to be sent back. Because of all the rejects, the company was not making any money. Why did they not fix their quality control? Tomorrow she would take the train to Ohio. These companies did not like working with a woman, but that was tough. She had not had to use mind control in this war, but if she had to, she would.

Mavis, her cook, came in and told her dinner was ready. She went into the dining room and said, "Mavis, dine with me tonight." About half the time, she did. She had been with Everin for eight years. That was about as long as she could employ someone. If they were around longer than that, they learned too much. Sometimes they were dismissed quicker than that.

After dinner, Mavis cleaned up and put things away and went to her own room. Everin packed her small suitcase. She did not overpack. After a few hundred years, she'd learned how to travel. She sat at her desk with her briefcase, making sure she had all the facts and figures she needed. Then she turned in and turned herself off.

The next morning, she took a taxi to Grand Central and boarded a train. America was not at war yet, but it seemed like it was. Because of time lost to being sidetracked for other trains and delays, the trip took more than eight hours. She was irritated that she could do no business that day. She just checked into her hotel. The hotel restaurant was adequate, and after checking her papers one more time, she programmed herself to go to sleep.

The next morning, she rose early and was at the factory at eight thirty. She was not impressed when some of the people she needed to see did not get there till nine o'clock and still had sleep in their eyes. After three hours of searching, it became obvious to Everin what the trouble was. The inspection and certification department were overseen by the major owner's son. It was obvious he was not up to the job. It was evident that people under him were aware of his faults and only did what they had to do. She requested a meeting with the major owner. She was stonewalled.

Everin messaged Alerton and told him what she needed. Alerton sent two telegrams. Everin knew it was too late to use them that day, so she went back to her hotel. Because of the time difference, the telegrams arrived in the middle of the night, and she did not pick them up until morning. They were both from the British government, and they stated exactly how much authority she had. One said if the company wanted to keep its doors open, they would do exactly as Everin said.

At 10:00 a.m., she had a private meeting with the major owner. Immediately, Everin told him, "You must get your son out of the plant."

He replied, "I don't want to do that."

She said, "Do you want to lose your contracts? I am about to cancel them all."

The major owner was still resisting.

Everin said, "You are going to fire your son and Jacob Danes and Charles Jobbs. Then you will put John Todd over the inspection department. If you do not and I walk out of here, this plant will close."

The owner was red-faced and sputtering. "What makes you think you can walk in here and make these demands?"

Everin replied, "Young men dying and my authority. If you do not comply, this plant will close." Sensing his thoughts, Everin saw that he wanted to physically attack her, but he did not. She said, "Read the telegrams again."

He did, and he collapsed like a wet rag. "All right," he said, "when do I have to do it?"

"Now," she said. "Bring them to the office now."

With tears of anger in his eyes and his face red, he sent for the people she'd mentioned. The next hour was chaos. If Everin had not been Hamen, she would have feared for her safety. She had a BWI in her pocket but did not have to use it.

Everin met with John Todd. She told him, "You have a major opportunity here; our warplanes need these parts, but they need to be good parts. This company can make a lot of money, but these parts must be good, or I will pull the contracts." She could tell Todd was excited at having the opportunity to advance.

Everin left the plant, checked out of her hotel, and caught a train to New York.

<hr />

Three days later, Metrool rose early, ate at his hotel, and drove his Daimler to Margaux's sister's house to see if her son was well enough for her to return to work. Her son, Henri, was a lot better. Metrool talked to him while she dressed.

Metrool drove her to the office. She was behind on her typing, and there were problems in the maintenance hangars that he had to investigate. Every time he thought he had things smoothed out, something else showed up. He was slated to go to another fighter base, but he had to finish here first. Now there was a problem with the dope. It was not holding the fabric tight. When the fabric wrinkled and flapped, it came loose and separated. The doping paint was made in America by a major paint company. Metrool investigated the problem to be sure and to be able to give Everin facts. He chased the problem for two days, and all the gripes were true.

The next day, Metrool and a pilot named Riker went up in two of the planes with problems and took them up to full speed. Metrool could see the wrinkles undulating on the lower wing. It was probably doing the same on the top wing. Then, looking at Riker's plane, he saw the fabric come loose at the rear of the lower wing. The fabric was flapping and tearing loose. Metrool wagged his wings to get Riker's attention and made motions that pilots recognized as "Land now." Only because Riker was a damned good pilot did he get the plane down safely, with half the fabric gone off the lower wing.

Metrool went to his office and had Margaux type up an order that no plane with wrinkles would go on a mission. He had Marg type up a long telegram for Everin and send it. Then he messaged her: *Hi, Sis.*

He could feel Everin's smile as she said, *Hi, Brother.*

Then he went on to describe the problem. She listened to it all and then told Metrool that the dope was being made by a subcontractor and that she would investigate them. The original dope had been good. She would have to find out what had happened. She would have to go to Pittsburgh.

The next afternoon, Everin was in Pittsburgh. She got a copy of the original formula, and they had samples of recently produced dope by the subcontractor. Everin took some of them to a testing company.

The next day, they gave her a certified analysis showing the samples were different. The Pittsburgh company investigated and found they had substituted a chemical for trichloroethane. They canceled the subcontractor's contract. Everin told the Pittsburgh company that the next ten batches had to be certified by an outside lab. They gave her the names of all the manufacturers they had sent the bad stuff to and the batch numbers; it was complicated.

Metrool was a troubleshooter with authority. Every day, he saw men fly out on missions and not come back. It caused terrible conflict inside him. Metrool ate, drank, and partied with the squadron pilots, and when they did not come back, it hit him hard.

The Germans had timed machine guns and had an advantage. Metrool and his people had to help their side catch up. Metrool got command of maintenance and tried to work the problems out of the planes.

One day he was watching a plane take off and saw the elevator on one side come apart. The plane nosed into the ground, killing the pilot—a pilot Metrool had talked to an hour before. He brought the wreckage to a maintenance hangar and went through it piece by piece. He found several pieces that were about to come apart.

He gathered the mechanics together and asked them why they had not found the faulty parts. They said they had not been trained to look for glue problems. Angry, Metrool told them they were responsible for the whole airplane, nose to tail. "Do not tell me something was not your job."

They were reluctant, and Metrool told them, "If you do not want to take proper care of our planes, I am sure the commandant can find a place for you in the infantry." That got their attention. "Check every part of every plane for bad glue. These planes should not be out in the weather, but we do not have hangars for them. From now on, after every four hours of flight, pull and clean every spark plug." That brought a string of protests.

One said, "We do not have enough hangars to do all the maintenance inside, and the weather is getting colder day by day."

Metrool said he knew that and would try to get them proper clothing. He told them, "These spark plugs are terrible; they barely do their job, and our pilots' lives depend on them."

Metrool messaged Alerton about the glue. Alerton traced it down, and at first, the manufacturer said they'd changed the glue because of shortage. Using scanning, Alerton saw that cost was the real reason, and he forced them to fire the person responsible. The man was terrible, and Alerton saw he planned to do harm to people in revenge, so Alerton put it into his mind to join the army. Alerton worked hard to find the best supplies. He could not improve their designs, but he could improve their supplies, including glue, dope from America, and wood from Canada and Alaska.

Metrool tried to stay aloof from his pilots, but they were so young, raw, and naive. They kept going day after day. Occasionally, he would see one in tears or getting drunk over a lost friend. It was amazing they kept flying day after day. The pilots were young; they were not worldly, and most were not political, but they were patriotic.

Aircraft were only eleven years old, and they were changing week to week. Many parts were weak: spark plugs, valves, lubrication, cooling systems, and hoses. The engines were changing, usually for the better but not always. Alerton traveled to the different suppliers, sometimes by train and sometimes by ship. He traveled to help Hispano make a deal with other manufacturers to build their engines. Hispano's factory could not build enough engines.

Metrool had been sent to aerodrome number seven because it was having more than the normal amount of problems. Slowly, it was improving. The large town of Troyon was just over two miles from the base. It had several bars but only two large ones. Those two were the ones patronized by the aerodrome people.

Because of his job and looking out for them, Metrool got close to a dozen pilots. When one went down, it hurt, and he always tried to find out why. Was it a pilot mistake, the design of the plane, or bad maintenance? He found all kinds of reasons, from bad spark plugs to plain bad luck.

Some men were as cold as ice about being fighter pilots, and some got the shakes before every mission. Stevens was the ice-cold type. He acted the same if he came back with bullet holes in his fighter or if he had shot down a German. He would go to the club after every mission, drink two drinks, talk to any fliers there, and then go back to the aerodrome. Jenkens was the other extreme. Metrool had seen him throw up before he climbed into his plane. But his buddies said once he got into the air, he was good.

The air service was quick to replace the men they lost. They did not want empty spots to remind people.

Because he was Hamen and because he, Everin, and Alerton stayed abreast of earthling progress, Metrool had been flying since 1906, and he was an expert pilot. Except for the last year at an airplane manufacturer's airport, nearly all Metrool's flying had been done surreptitiously.

Before he left England, Metrool used all his Hamen abilities to learn everything he could about every available plane. One morning, a flight of eight Hawks took off to go on a mission. Soon another Hawk joined them. They recognized the Hawk but not the pilot; they assumed it was a replacement. The mission turned into a major fighter melee. At one point, Stevens had a Fokker on his tail, and the new guy shot the Fokker down. When the flight got back to the aerodrome, they found out the extra Hawk was Metrool. After that, the whole crew had more respect for him.

Metrool messaged Everin: *I need your help.*

Everin messaged back: *Anything I can do to help you, I will.*

Metrool said, *We have parts coming from America with terrible quality control. I need for you to go to those factories and make changes.*

Everin said, *You want me, a woman, to do that?*

You are not just a woman; you are Hamen, and you have bags of money.

I will need papers and letters of introduction.

I will get them.

Then Metrool messaged Alerton: *I need Everin's help with parts coming from America, but she needs papers.*

That is not a problem, Alerton said. *I will get her everything she needs. It will take two or three weeks for them to get to her. That will give her time to pick her targets and arrange transportation. What are your mechanics having trouble with?*

Everything from bracing wire to spark plugs.

Metrool listened to his mechanics and tried to get them what they needed. Several times, he bought special tools with his own money. As time went by, because they found out he was real, the pilots and mechanics opened up to Metrool. Metrool got close to several of them. He saw many ways he could improve the planes, but Earth technology was jumping ahead on its own. He could not justify breaking the noninterference rules.

Three weeks later, Everin went to a manufacturer in Indianapolis. At first, they did not want to talk to her, but after reading her letter of introduction, they knew they had to. After they realized she had authority over their contract, they let her talk to their engineers. Two of them tried to fluff her, but she cut them down. She answered every question they asked, and they could not answer some of her questions. Their quality was awful because they were using unskilled machinists. She told them the issue and impressed on them that men's lives depended on their parts.

She said, "The bottom line is, if you do not get your quality under control, I have the authority to cancel your contract."

They did not like it. The changes would cut into their profits. She convinced them that if they did not fix the issue, there would be no profits.

Metrool was amused when Everin told him about the visit, and he thanked her and told her she had done great.

Metrool talked to Riker as he got ready for his flight. Riker was one of his favorite pilots. Metrool watched a mechanic spin the prop, and the engine started with a cloud of castor-oil smoke. Then Riker taxied out to the runway with Metrool still watching him. He revved the engine, and the fighter accelerated down the runway. It lifted off—and then the engine sputtered and died. The fighter fell to the runway.

Metrool and a mechanic jumped into a car and raced to the crash. They pulled Riker out and found he had a broken arm. They took him to the sick bay, and the doctor set his broken bones and put his arm in a plaster cast. The arm was wrapped in fluffy cotton and then cotton cloth, and then a plaster-of-paris mixture was applied to that. The doctor made them wait till it dried before they could take Riker away, and the doctor forbid him to fly.

Metrool got his Daimler automobile, and he, Riker, and the mechanic, Brown, used it to go to the club in town. Riker had a female friend there. She was both happy and sad. She was happy to see him, but his injury reminded her of how many pilots died.

Other pilots came in who had been on Riker's mission, and they were down, as two of their flight had not come back. Metrool bought several rounds of drinks and then helped them cram into his Daimler and drove them back to the base.

Three days later, Metrool saw Riker dressed for flight. Metrool reminded him that the doctor had said no flying. Riker said, "The cast is on my left arm, and I fly with my right."

Metrool said, "You should not fly, but that is between you and the commandant. The commandant wants planes in the air."

Riker said, "See that new eagle over there with number four on it? It is mine."

Metrool did not know what to say except "Good luck."

They always wanted more planes in the air. They never had enough flyable airplanes. If the planes were shot up or broken, they were fixed. If they were too bad, the mechanics salvaged the good parts and had them taken to a dump. The commandant did not want bad reminders sitting around.

Three different planes had been flown back by wounded pilots who later died. They had been repaired, repainted, and renumbered, but people knew their stories, and no one wanted to fly them.

Some of the manufacturers complained, and Metrool was called to Paris. He was not scared, as he did not have to have this job; he was rich. But he did resent the manufacturers continuing to push faulty products. With his connections, he got a room at the Ritz. *Let them chew on that.*

The next day, at one o'clock, they met at the Grand Palais. The manufacturers tried to trap him fourteen different ways, but his Hamen mind had the facts and figures. He also had them on paper, including the percentages of bad parts, how bad they were, and the new parts they'd had to scrap. Metrool even had a suitcase full of bad parts.

One manufacturer rep got so violent that Metrool went into his mind and made it so he could not speak. Then the man got apoplectic and ran away.

A week later, the rep came to see Metrool at the base and, writing on paper, told Metrool he knew Metrool had done this to him, and he begged him to undue it. Metrool told him he did not know what he was talking about but thought that by the time the man arrived home, he would be well.

The meeting at the Grand Palais lasted until six o'clock, and he was exonerated. Two of the manufacturers had wised up, and they went with Metrool back to the Ritz and bought him and some of the general staff an excellent dinner.

Quality improved, but Metrool realized that sometimes they did not know how to make the part right, and when possible, he went to the factory and showed them. When they asked about his knowledge, he quoted them his degrees and colleges. He had to compress the time some, but the degrees were real.

A new type of fighter arrived with a whole new set of problems. It was faster, but pilots had to be careful with the speed. If one maneuvered too violently, the plane would come apart. Metrool messaged Alerton: *Can you go to the factory making the X-7 and show them that the motor mount needs to be stronger and that the fuselage needs more longerons? Pilots cannot use the top speed and maneuver too.*

Within a month, they were getting the X-7b, and it was a much better airplane.

Then, one black day, two pilots Metrool was friends with did not come home. One they saw go down in flames in a high-speed crash, and the other made a crash landing behind enemy lines, and they did not know what happened to him. Two carloads of pilots went to the club in town and soaked up a lot of alcohol.

Metrool saw and sensed that Riker and Lola were now involved, although they kept it well concealed. The group drank till late and were lucky they made it back to base. The next day, there were men who flew with headaches, but the cool air up there was refreshing.

When Metrool heard of all the men in the trenches being shot or blown apart, he thought, *Why are all these people dying? What can they gain? Building and destroying so many things. So much production wasted. So many young men wasted.*

Some of the pilots flew with parachutes, and some did not. The English air service did not supply them, and they did not always work. Nearly all the pilots had seen someone bail out and fall to his death.

The group had had losses lately, and several pilots had wounds, so they were noticeably short on pilots. Metrool volunteered. He had made several friends in the group. He suited up, talked to maintenance, got a plane, and fired up with the group. The castor-oil smoke and smell were awful, but the spinning prop blew the smoke away. The fighter was nimble as it raced down the runway and climbed into the air. It was hard to believe earthlings had been flying for only eleven years. Now they had at least a hundred different flying machines.

The flight of Hawks climbed up to their cruising altitude and headed for their target. The nine planes were cruising along, when one of the group's motors started smoking. Soon the pilot was wagging his wings and turning back. The remaining eight continued. They were nearly to the target, when they were jumped by a whole flight of Jerrys.

The Hawks were zooming, twisting, and turning, trying to get the enemy in their sights. They heard the sounds of machine guns and sometimes the sounds of bullets zipping by. At one point, Metrool saw bullets go through his wing. By pushing his plane to the limit of the stress it would take, he got behind an enemy and fired his guns. He must have hit the fuel tank, for the plane immediately burst into flames.

Metrool did not know if the German had a parachute, but the man went down with the plane.

Metrool was not happy on the flight back to base. He had caused a man to die. It was what he was supposed to do, but he felt wrong about it.

The base was just ahead of him, and he cut back on power. As he got lower, he keyed the mag button. The main wheels touched, and after a short roll, the tail skid touched. Metrool taxied to the tie-down area and stopped the engine.

Soon he and the other pilots went to the club, but he felt down. Being Hamen, he realized Riker and Lola had gone elsewhere.

Metrool spent five more weeks at the aerodrome, and in that time, Margaux became a lot more than an employee. Metrool was in love with her. They worked together, and they ate many meals together. They took long walks together and talked about life after the war.

They were in love, but they were not intimate. Metrool was now about to move to another aerodrome. It was forty miles away, and he made no secret that he was moving. Metrool was a little surprised that Margaux asked if she could work for him there.

Metrool said, "You could not live with your sister and work there."

Margaux replied, "You pay me well, and I could find a boardinghouse. It would probably only be for five months, like here, and my son could stay with my sister for five months."

She was a good worker and an excellent typist. Metrool was in love with her. He had no reason to turn her down.

Two days later, he watched her say goodbye to Henri and load her three cases into the Daimler. Metrool informed her there had been a change of plans.

"Oh, what is the change?" she asked.

Metrool said, "I am taking you to Paris first."

Marg replied, "Oh, that is wonderful!" and she kissed him three times.

It was cold weather, so Metrool asked Margaux if she wanted to ride in the glassed-in back.

"No," she said, "I am wearing a coat. I will ride up front with you."

As they drove to Paris, they saw war damage and planes overhead. Metrool navigated through the war trucks and damaged roads, and after three hours, they saw the top of the Eiffel Tower. In a short time, they were in Paris, working their way through the fortifications and the war damage. In thirty minutes, they were at the Ritz. A porter took their bags, a valet took the Daimler, and Metrool's sign-in was quick because they knew him. They were escorted up to their two rooms.

After the porter showed Margaux her room and left, Metrool held her and kissed her and said, "Warm up, and take a nap. We will dine out later."

Metrool went to his room and unpacked his suitcase. He was happy to be in this fabulous city with this fabulous woman. In the months he had known her, he had found nothing bad about her, and when he scanned her, he found her professed feelings for him were real.

Room service brought wine to both rooms, and Metrool poured himself a glass and relaxed. Later, he knocked on Margaux's door and found she was ready. He was taking her to Les Deux Magots for dinner. Metrool knew the new owner, Auguste Boulay, and he hoped they might see someone famous.

The wine was good, the food was good, and Metrool recognized two well-known people. The owner came by their table, saying, "Welcome back, Mr. Metrool."

Afterward, driving back to the Ritz, Metrool was glad he had Hamen night vision, for there were war fortifications and war damage to drive around. Back at the Ritz, Metrool went into Margaux's room, and they hugged and kissed. Then he poured wine, and appropriately, they sat on the love seat and talked.

Metrool knew she wanted more; she wanted their relationship to proceed. He had been emotionally involved with three Earth women, and all three had ended badly. Metrool was in love with Margaux, but at his age, which she did not know, he was in no hurry; he felt there was plenty of time. He knew if they married, it would last a long time.

He hugged and kissed her good night. In his room, lightly scanning her, he picked up a thought from her: *Does he find me physically attractive?* He did—very.

The next morning, up and dressed, they ate breakfast at the hotel and then went up to their rooms to put on their coats, for it was quite cool weather.

The valet brought the Daimler, and Metrool drove through Paris's wartime streets to the Notre Dame cathedral. They toured all of it, with a priest showing them some artifacts. Margaux loved all of it but especially the rose window. Later, they drove the short distance to the Eiffel Tower.

They rode the two elevators all the way to the top, where the panorama of Paris was wonderful. Metrool pointed out certain sights, such as Les

Invalides, the Trocadéro, and the Grand Palais, which was now being used as a war hospital. Each would point out something, and they would talk about it.

They dined at the tower restaurant, and it was a wonderful treat. Then they took an elevator ride back to the top for one last moment of this experience. Then they took the two elevators down, and Metrool drove them back to the Ritz.

At eight that night, Metrool knocked on her door and found her dressed elegantly, and he told her she was beautiful. He was taking her to the Moulin Rouge for a dinner and show. At the windmill, she loved the entertainers and the colorful costumes.

The next morning, after breakfast at the hotel, Metrool drove them down the Champs-Élysées to the Arc de Triomphe. After circling it and reading many of the inscriptions on it, they entered and soon were climbing the 180 steps to the top. They were breathing deeply when they got there. The view was wonderful. They looked one way toward Sacré-Coeur and then the opposite way toward the Eiffel Tower. Looking another way, they saw downtown Paris. It was a wonderful experience.

Soon they were driving on the Champs-Élysées again. They were almost to the Place de la Concorde, when they heard the roar of the Gotha bombers' engines. They heard an explosion behind them, and then a hundred meters in front of them, another bomb exploded. The Daimler's windscreen blew out, and Margaux screamed and collapsed. Metrool looked at her and was shocked. The woman he loved had a jagged piece of metal sticking all the way through the right side of her chest.

Metrool's mind raced about medical things. There was a clinic at Rue 10, about four blocks away. Metrool made the Daimler go as fast as it would and pulled up in front of the place. It was a limestone building with a black door. He carried Margaux into the clinic and pushed past the nurse into the exam room. The doctor was angry at the intrusion at first, but when he saw the situation, he was involved.

After a moment, the doctor turned to Metrool and said, "She is dying; we cannot save her."

"No," Metrool said. "She is not going to die."

The doctor said, "If we pull that metal out, she will die immediately."

Metrool asked, "Do you have sucking chest-wound seals?"

The doctor said, "No, I do not."

Metrool put a plan together. He put the doctor and the two nurses into trances. He grabbed a syringe, pulled eight ccs of his blood, and injected it into Margaux. He cut the tops off his patent-leather boots, used scissors to make seals out of them, and made sure he had plenty of tape. Using all his mental power, he put Margaux as far out as he could. Then he cut the clothes off the top half of her body. He took hold of the metal and pulled it out of her. Blood gushed, and working as fast as he could, he sealed the wounds front and back. Using the syringe again, he drew another eight ccs of his blood and injected it into her.

It was her only chance. It was a massive amount of Hamen blood, and it was aggressive. Some people injected with it became violent. Marg moaned, but that was all. Metrool found a bag and put her bloody clothes in it, along with some medical supplies. He laid out a large sum of money and put a doctor's robe on Margaux. He carried Margaux and the bag out to the Daimler. He put her in the back and drove away. As he drove, he took the doctor and nurses out of their trances.

Metrool drove up to the Ritz valet and said, "My wife was injured by a bomb blast. Get the auto cleaned up." He gave him a large tip.

Metrool carried the strangely dressed Margaux into the fancy hotel and got some looks. But the onlookers had heard the bombs and understood she had been injured.

As Metrool got her to her room, she was starting to react. She was fighting him, so he went deep into her mind and put her into a trance. He took the rest of her bloody clothes off and bathed her as well as possible. Using his senses to see, he saw the wounds were healing. He got a syringe out of the bag and gave her four more ccs just for insurance.

At nine o'clock that night, Metrool could tell the chest wounds were healed, so he took the leather and tape seals off. He finished bathing her and put her in a clean nightdress. At midnight, he could tell she was completely healed. He woke her, and she was in shock because she remembered the injury and being carried into the clinic.

She opened her gown and said, "How is this possible?"

Metrool said, "Marg, I am going to tell you something you will not believe."

"Tell me," she said.

"I am from another planet."

Margaux laughed.

Metrool continued. "You had a piece of metal stuck through you. Do you have any scars?"

Marg looked down her gown and said, "No."

Metrool showed her the bloody clothes and bandages, and Marg got terribly upset and began crying. She wailed, "I do not remember any of this! I remember the explosion, being hurt terribly, and the doctor saying I was going to die. But I did not die. I am well."

Metrool said, "I have powers, and I saved you."

Margaux was about to cave in. She had too much to absorb. Metrool went into her mind and calmed her. Margaux was an intelligent, educated woman with college degrees.

She said, "Metrool, what you are telling me is right out of books by H. G. Wells and Edger Rice Burroughs."

Metrool was perplexed. *How do you convince an intelligent woman that you are a man from Mars?* He looked around the fancy hotel room. Besides central heat, it had a wood-burning fireplace. He went to the fireplace and got the wrought-iron poker. He handed it to Margaux and said, "Bend it."

Marg said, "I cannot bend that."

Metrool said, "Humor me. Try to bend it."

Marg took it in both hands and bent it in two as if it were nothing. She was shocked and said, "I cannot do that."

Metrool said, "I injected you with my blood to save you, but it also made changes in you." It was the middle of the night, and Metrool said, "Go to the window, and look out."

She did and said, "I can see as if it were daylight."

"Yes, you will see and hear better, and you will heal much faster."

"Metrool, this is rough."

"I know. That is enough for now. Can I put you to sleep?"

Margaux asked, "Can you do that?"

"Yes," Metrool said, "I can."

Margaux said, "Well, then put me to sleep. I am stressed out." He put her to bed and to sleep.

Metrool poured a large glass of wine and sat in a large chair, watching the woman he loved sleep. He was stressed out too. Normally, Hamens were not, but this was not a normal situation. He had seen the woman he loved get a spear through her chest. He'd had to pull the jagged piece of metal out of her and save her with crude doctoring.

He did not know of any case in which a person had been injected with twenty ccs of Hamen blood. But she had been so gravely wounded that he'd felt he had to. What would he do when she woke up? She still did not know who he was. She now believed he was an alien but had no details.

What should he fill in, and what should he show her? Visions of the exploding spaceship and the ride down in the pod had worked before. Metrool had many fond memories of Doc, the wonderful earthling who had fallen in love with Everin and married her.

When Doc had had a massive heart attack and been dying, Everin had injected him with twelve ccs to save him. His recovery had been rough, but he'd recovered, and Doc had been with Everin for about 450 years. From a recent conversation, he could tell she still missed him.

———⟫●⟪———

Metrool woke himself at seven o'clock the next morning and went down to the valet desk. He found the valet manager and asked, "Did they clean my auto?"

The manager said, "Yes, they totally cleaned it."

Metrool asked, "Can you have the windscreen replaced today?"

The manager said, "Yes, we can. The Daimler dealer is only a few blocks away."

Metrool said, "I will need an auto for today."

The valet said, "No problem, sir."

Metrool went back up to his room and ordered breakfast to be brought to Margaux's room for both; he knew what Margaux liked. Now she was awake, and they began to talk. About two hours later, they were at a Lagrangian point. Metrool said, "Let me take you to the Louvre."

Margaux agreed. They put on their proper warm clothes and went down the elevator. Metrool said, "I have reserved a hotel auto." Margaux thanked him.

Metrool drove the hotel auto the short distance to the Louvre. They started on the lower level and saw the foundations of the original fort. Then they went to an upper level to see the works of art.

They saw statues and great paintings. It was late afternoon when they left the Louvre. Metrool felt they had been dancing around real talk all day. They went back to the Ritz to relax and refresh. Metrool went to his room, and he messaged Everin, telling her he had brought Margaux over and why.

Everin said, *Oh, Metrool, that sounds terrible.* She was sympathetic for what Metrool had had to do but was cautious about the aftereffects.

She says she still loves me, he said.

Everin asked, *Do you still love her?*

Yes, I do.

After some more talk, they ended the messaging. At about eight o'clock, Metrool knocked on Margaux's door. She opened the door and looked great, even better than she usually did. They were going to the Le Grand Véfour, a high-dollar restaurant.

The best Paris restaurants were expensive, but Metrool did not mind. He wanted to impress Margaux and get her mind off what she had been through. The meal and the service were great.

They left the restaurant and went to the Paradis Latin show. She had not seen it before and seemed to enjoy it.

While driving back to the hotel, they heard the roaring engines of zeppelins, and Margaux shrieked. Metrool forcefully went into her mind and calmed her.

Soon they were in the hotel, and in her room, Metrool carefully put her to sleep so she would not hear the sounds of aircraft or munitions. He decided they would leave Paris in the morning. Metrool went to the garage, and the Daimler looked as good as new. He went up to his room and programmed himself to sleep.

The next morning, Metrool told Margaux of the change in plans, and after they had breakfast in her room, she packed. Checkout was quick, and the repaired Daimler was sitting there with the motor warming up. For obvious reasons, he asked Margaux if she wanted to ride in the back. Again, she told him, "No, I will ride up front with you."

As they drove out of Paris, they saw several bomb craters, but they saw no aircraft over Paris that day. Once out into the countryside, they saw many fighter planes, but they were not their targets.

Metrool had already investigated aerodrome number nine and the town of Bayous. He had seen that it had only one good hotel, so that was where he drove first. At the desk, he told the clerks that he had a three-month job at the aerodrome and that Margaux was his employee. They looked at her and how attractive she was, and they did not believe him. But this was France, so they pretended to believe it. A porter helped with their luggage and picked out the best of the available rooms, and Metrool tipped him well.

Metrool left Margaux to settle in, and he drove to the aerodrome. It was remarkably like the other one, and Metrool assumed it had many of the same problems. The commandant did not welcome him.

The commandant said, "I know the air service sent you, but I do not need someone looking over my shoulder."

Metrool said, "I am not here for that. I am here to make aircraft fly better."

The commandant let one of his junior officers show Metrool his run-down office and then the maintenance hangars. They were worse than those at the other aerodrome. They had three Bessonneau hangars, but Metrool saw no heaters. For lighting, he saw only some kerosene lamps that a helper had to hold for the repairman. Metrool asked for the head mechanic. When he came to Metrool, he asked the head mechanic to summon his best two or three men.

The mechanic summoned three, and when they arrived, Metrool began asking them questions. They told him things, and he checked them out. They had little dope or glue and had to use them only on the worst jobs. One said, "We have very few spark plugs. All we can do is take them out, clean them, reset the gap, and put them back in. We are very short on castor oil, which the rotary engines must have. We give each rotary only the amount it must have—no extra."

They told him several other problems they could not get help with. Metrool was disgusted; he believed pilots were dying because of this mess. He drove back to his hotel and first saw Margaux.

She could tell he was upset and asked what was wrong. He told her that maintenance was a mess, and he had to talk to Alerton. In his room, with the door locked, he messaged Alerton: *I need to talk to you.*

Alerton replied, *I will lock my door, and we can talk.*

Metrool told him everything that had transpired at the aerodrome. Metrool said, *I scanned the commandant. He is skimming, putting money in his own pocket. I cannot prove it, but I know it is true.*

Alerton said, *We have a lot of friends in government. Why don't you come to London, and we can present your case?*

Metrool said, *If it does not work, I will resign this job. I cannot work with this commandant.*

I understand, Alerton said.

Metrool said, *I have an idea. Margaux is having a hard time accepting what I am. Can I bring her to meet you and Marie?*

Alerton said, *That would be a great idea. We would love to meet her.*

Metrool said, *We should arrive in London late tomorrow afternoon.*

Metrool went to Margaux's room and knocked. She answered, and he asked if she would like to go down to dinner. She said yes, and they went down to the hotel dining room. She ordered something Metrool knew she liked, but she barely picked at it. He knew she was having trouble adjusting. Metrool told her, "I must go to London tomorrow."

She said, "All right," with no emotion.

Metrool said, "I would like for you to go with me."

She smiled at that and said, "Yes, I will."

Metrool said, "Just pack a small suitcase; we will just be there one or two nights."

The next morning, they rose early, ate at the hotel, and then took a taxi to the train station. Metrool got a compartment for the five-hour ride to Le Havre. Then they took another taxi ride to the ship. After Metrool bought their tickets, they had a two-hour wait for the ship.

They went to a nearby club to have a glass of wine. While they were sipping their wine, Metrool said, "We will get there too late to do business today, but I have two friends who are going to meet us."

"All right," Margaux said, again noncommittal.

The ocean was rough, but Margaux did not get sick, for she was a large part Hamen.

Metrool thought, *How do I tell her that now she is going to live a long time?*

The ship docked on the Thames riverbank, about twenty-six miles from London proper. Out among the taxis was a black Rolls that Metrool recognized. He guided Margaux to it, and a good-looking couple were standing beside it.

Metrool introduced them. "These are my longtime friends Marie and Alerton."

The introductions went well, and the small talk as they drove went well. Finally, Arrista appeared in front of them. Marie said, "This is our home."

Margaux said, "Oh, it is beautiful."

The Rolls came to a stop, the four passengers got out, and the chauffeur drove to the car park in the rear. Marie took Margaux on a partial tour of the house, and Metrool and Alerton talked about Marg's problem. Then the four went to the library for a glass of wine before dinner.

Dinner went well, and afterward, they gathered in the huge, wonderful drawing room at the front of the house. They made small talk for a while, and then Marie said, "So your man is from another planet."

Margaux nearly came unglued. She thought, *Am I going crazy?*

Marie said, "No, honey, you are not going crazy; it is real. Yes, your man is from another planet, but I have known him a long time, and he is a wonderful man."

Margaux was dumbstruck. "How?" was all she could get out.

Marie said, "How do I know? Because I married his buddy. Alerton crash-landed with him."

Margaux managed to ask, "How many were there?"

"Three. These two and a female who lives in America."

"You are married to one?"

"Yes, honey, I am. Now ask how long I have been married to him."

"How long?"

"Two hundred years."

"That is not possible. You are not over forty."

Marie said, "He has not told you yet? Lady, you are going to live a long time. I am two hundred thirty years old."

Margaux said, "You cannot be."

Marie said, "When he saved your life and injected that Hamen blood into you, he changed you. Surely you have noticed you are stronger, you see better, and you hear better. You will probably live at least seven hundred years."

Alerton said, "Metrool, I think it is time to show her the crash."

Margaux said, "How can he show me?"

Metrool came to her, kissed her, and said, "Please just lean back and relax in that large chair."

She did, and then Metrool used his mind to relax her even more. Then he showed her the exploding spaceship, the rough pod ride, and the three standing together.

When Metrool woke her, she said, "Was that real?"

Alerton said, "Very real. Only four of us got off the ship."

"Four?" Margaux asked.

"There was one other, but his escape pod overheated, and he died on the way down."

"How can you show me things in my mind?"

"It is something we developed many thousands of years ago, but you can do it too."

"Yes," Metrool said, "you are a large part Hamen now. I injected twenty ccs of Hamen blood into you—that is a huge amount. You can try it by thinking of Henri and thinking, *I would like for Marie and Alerton to see him.*"

She did, and Marie said, "A handsome young man in a blue shirt."

Margaux said, "You really saw him then?"

"Yes," Marie said. "There will be changes in you. Hamen DNA will make changes. I calculate that it will take your body back to a twenty-four- or twenty-five-year-old level. The Hamen blood will make one serious change in you, but if Metrool had not given it to you, you would be dead."

"Yes, I know," Margaux said. "Tell me the change."

Marie said, "Hamen women do not bear children. You will not have another child."

Margaux teared up, but Metrool took her hand and said, "That does not matter to me. We already have a child."

They talked until late and then went upstairs to their separate rooms. As Metrool kissed her good night at her door, she asked, "Will you sleep beside me tonight?"

Metrool said, "Yes," and they entered her room.

There was a wine cart in the room, with several kinds of wine, and Metrool poured two glasses. They sipped the wine and talked. Metrool could feel her emotions and her need for him to love her and protect her. He kissed her and reassured her that he would always be with her. He said,

"In all my years on Hamen and on Earth, I have never felt this love I have for you." He took her in his arms and held her, and she clung to him."

"Oh, Metrool, I love you, and I need you. I do not know what I would do without you."

Metrool answered, "As long as I live, you will never be alone."

Metrool got up, poured two more glasses of wine, handed one to Margaux, and said a toast and made a promise they'd always be together. "Always and always," Margaux said.

The next morning, the four dined together with light conversation. Margaux would spend the day with Marie while Alerton and Metrool went to London to pursue help with the commandant.

Metrool and Alerton rode in the back of the Rolls as the chauffeur drove through the wartime traffic. Alerton told Metrool about the strikes at the different wartime plants. Metrool said, "You're telling me one reason I am not getting parts is because the workers are on strike?"

"Yes," Alerton said, "we have had some plants totally shut down."

"How can they do that?"

"They have unions."

"It has not been in the papers."

"No, because the government does not want the Germans to know. The Germans are trying to panic the masses with their bombings."

"Can the government force people to work?""

"When you force people to work, you get shoddy work."

"I would have thought patriotism would have kept the people working."

"Patriotism does not put food on the table."

The chauffeur pulled up in front of the Royal Air Service building, Alerton and Metrool went into the building, and the chauffeur drove on to the auto park. Alerton was taking Metrool to see a general who was a good friend. The general's secretary ushered them into the general's office.

The general was courteous but cautious as they told him the situation. The general said, "Going over someone's head is not the way we do things."

Metrool said, "General, young men are dying because of this commandant, and if I had gone through him, the papers would have been trashed."

"Yes," the general said, "I understand that. And if, as you say, men are dying because of him, he will be replaced."

They were about to leave, when Metrool brashly asked, "General, can you give me a letter of authorization to the aircraft parts warehouse?"

The general laughed. "I have heard you two are rich. Do you want to buy parts?"

"Yes, I do. I have airplanes falling out of the sky."

"Well, if you are serious, my secretary will type your letter."

Metrool said, "I am serious, and thank you."

They thanked the general for seeing them and then waited in the outer office while his secretary typed up the letter on her new Royal typewriter. Afterward, they went to the front of the building, and the chauffeur was there. He told them he would have the auto there in a few minutes and hurried away.

Metrool asked Alerton, "Do you know where the warehouse is?"

"Yes, I do," Alerton said. "I go there often."

The chauffeur brought the Rolls, and soon they were back in the heavy traffic. Alerton told the chauffeur where to go, and Metrool and Alerton continued their talk about the strikes.

At the warehouse, Metrool, from memory, picked out a list of parts and shocked the warehouse man by writing a personal check for many thousands of dollars. Metrool gave them information about the aerodrome and how to ship the parts.

Back in the Rolls, Alerton took Metrool to the mahogany-walled club he belonged to. Alerton introduced him to two friends who happened to be there. They talked over drinks, mainly about Metrool and Margaux, and then they got back in the Rolls, heading for Arrista.

The night was a dress-up night. Marie and Margaux had become fast friends, and Marie loaned Marg an elegant dress. They went to the Royal Coach restaurant and then to a play. Later, at Arrista, Metrool again slept beside Margaux.

The next morning, they ate together, and then Metrool took Margaux to the garage and showed her his Stutz. Alerton and his chauffeur took them to Portsmouth, where they would take the ship back to Le Havre. They said their goodbyes, and Alerton and his chauffeur left.

Soon they were boarding the ship and were escorted to their first-class compartment. Margaux took Metrool in her arms and said, "I believe in you, and I trust you."

"Thank you," Metrool said, "but do you love me?"

"With all my heart," Margaux said.

Metrool knew now that taking her to meet Marie and Alerton had been the right thing to do.

The sea was smoother than on the trip over, and in ten hours, they were at Le Havre.

The train from Le Havre was running late, so they ate dinner in the dining car. It was nearly midnight when they took a taxi to their hotel.

The next morning, they went back to work. Metrool talked to Maurice, the head of maintenance, and was downhearted to learn that two planes had gone down behind enemy lines because of engine failure.

Back at the office, Metrool gave Margaux a long handwritten page to type up and watched her type it. He was amused and wary. He went to her and told her she was Hamen now and had to be aware of herself. No earthling could type as fast as she just had.

She said, "I was not aware. I thought I was just typing normally."

"You will find all your abilities will be heightened."

"Metrool, thank you for saving my life."

Metrool said, "I could not lose the love of my life. Because of my past life, I tried to resist loving you."

Margaux said, "I knew you were holding back."

"Well, when the doctor said you were going to die, I quit fighting it. I let my love loose."

"You have loved someone before."

"After loving you, I would say no, but I was emotionally involved before."

"That was here on Earth?"

"Yes. Emotions are much more restrained on Hamen."

"Do people marry there?"

"Not in the Earth sense. Two people bond, but it is strictly mental."

Margaux blushed. "What about making love?"

Metrool answered, "There has not been sex on Hamen for many thousands of years."

"Then how do you reproduce?"

"Well, as Marie told you, Hamen females have been altered so they do not reproduce. This was done thousands of years ago, when our DNA was perfected, and we began to live for a thousand years, so population control became mandatory. Hamen has a device called a femtech that, given two sets of DNA, can create a person or, given one set of DNA, can create a clone."

"It all seems rather cold."

"Compared to Earth, it is very cold. Hamen is a very peaceful place, with practically no crime. If people commit a crime, they do not go to prison; they go to the Purgon, a device that removes the defective part of their mind. Prisons are very wasteful of resources; Hamen does not have them."

"If people commit a crime, how are they judged?"

"They are not judged; their mentect sends everything they do to Central Memory, and if they commit a crime, they are sent a signal to come to the Purgon. They cannot resist."

"What is a mentect?"

"It is a mental implant."

"Do you have one?"

"All Hamens have one."

"Do they know what you are doing?"

Metrool smiled. "I am twenty light-years away; I am out of range."

No one was in the office, so Metrool gave Margaux a real kiss before he went to the maintenance hangar. He talked to Maurice, the chief mechanic, and told him that parts were coming and that he was trying to get more castor oil. Maurice thanked him and told him he knew Metrool was trying to help. Metrool just stayed out of the commandant's way.

Two days later, the parts arrived, and the mechanics were happy. The next day, a group of air service people came to the aerodrome, and the commandant was escorted off the base.

Two days later, Metrool got a telegram from the general that said, "Mr. Metrool, this is not the way things are normally done, but he was doing wrong."

Things were beginning to improve at the aerodrome, and Metrool got a message from Alerton. Alerton said, *Everything has a price. The general wants you to do something for him.*

Metrool said, *What does he want?*

They have a new prototype of the Peregrine, which has killed two test pilots. The general wants you to take over the test program. He will send someone to the aerodrome to fill in while you are gone.

Metrool said, *Tell him all right.*

Alerton said, *He wants you there tomorrow.*

Metrool said, *All right.*

Metrool took Margaux out to the Daimler, and being Hamen, she quickly learned how to drive it and drove it to the hotel and then to the train station. They hugged and kissed goodbye, and Metrool said, "Lady, I really love you."

Metrool took the familiar train ride to Le Havre and then an all-night ship to London. He landed in Portsmouth and took a train on to London. Metrool arrived at the Peregrine factory airport, which was a large, flat open pasture with hangars at one end. The pilots liked it that way, so they could always take off into the wind. A new Peregrine was sitting there, and Metrool looked it over thoroughly. He saw nothing obviously wrong.

Soon two maintenance men and two test pilots arrived. They all introduced themselves and asked Metrool what he wanted to do. Metrool said to the pilots, "You have not found anything wrong with its flying characteristics?"

They told him it flew great.

"Well then," Metrool said, "the five of us will take this Peregrine apart and check every nut, bolt, wire, piece of wood, and piece of skin."

At the end of the second day, the sharp-looking fighter plane was a large pile of parts. They had found no bad parts, and Metrool asked the two test pilots, "Will one of you fly one tomorrow?"

The two pilots hesitated, and then one said, "We will cut the cards to see who flies tomorrow."

Thompson got the low card, so he would fly tomorrow, and Simmons would fly the next time.

Metrool let all of them go, went to the pile of parts, and tried to picture what could be wrong. He messaged Alerton, telling him what they had done, and Alerton approved.

The next morning, Metrool, the two mechanics, and Thompson were there at seven o'clock for Thompson to make his first flight. There was another brand-new Peregrine sitting there for Thompson to fly. The first flight would be a mild checkout flight. There would be at least two more flights as the pilot went into aerobatics.

Thompson got into the deep cockpit of the Peregrine and said, "Switch off," and the mechanic spun the prop. Then Thompson said, "Switch on," and the mechanic was careful as he spun the prop. Being new, it fired right up. The smoke blew away, and it sat there rumbling, warming up. Metrool went to Thompson and made sure this was just a routine flight. Once warmed up, Thompson headed into the wind across the field and quickly was aloft.

Metrool sent a message to management that he needed a plane to fly chase. An hour later, about the same time Thompson landed, the factory towed an older Peregrine down to them tail first. It was guaranteed to be in good shape, but Metrool and a mechanic checked it out. About an hour after he landed, Thompson took off again with Metrool right behind him.

Not many people knew that Metrool was an expert pilot, but he was. On this flight, Metrool would just watch the Peregrine as Thompson put it through mild aerobatics. Thompson took it up to top speed and from top speed to a vertical climb. He stayed in the climb until he stalled, then did a tailslide, and then rotated into a dive. Thompson zoomed up out of the dive, leveled off, and did a four-point roll. Thompson was a particularly good pilot. Metrool watched him do a few more maneuvers, and then they returned to the field. They landed and took a break for tea as the mechanics added fuel and oil to their Peregrines.

Soon they were about to make the flight during which the trouble always occurred, and no one knew why. Once they were in the sky again, Metrool stayed close. If something started breaking or flapping, he wanted to see it. Soon Thompson was putting his plane through extreme aerobatics, as if he were trying to get away from someone's machine guns. Thompson did a lot of maneuvers, getting more vicious all the time. Metrool looked at the belly of the Peregrine as it went into a dive. At first, Metrool thought it was on purpose.

But no, the Peregrine stayed in the dive until it slammed full speed into the ground.

Metrool headed back to the factory airport. He did not have good news for them. Metrool walked up to the office and told them that Thompson had crashed and that they would need another plane tomorrow. Metrool told what had happened. One man in the office was upset because he had been a friend of Thompson's. Metrool said, "Have another new Peregrine there tomorrow, and we will keep testing."

Metrool messaged Alerton, telling him to come pick him up, as he had had a bad day. About an hour later, Alerton's Rolls and chauffeur showed up. They went to Alerton's club, and Metrool made himself unwind as they talked and sipped whiskey. They went over the whole thing with the Peregrine. Then, of course, they talked about the terrible war and how many young men were being lost.

Alerton also told him that he and Marie really liked Margaux.

Alerton and his chauffeur took Metrool to his hotel, where he programmed himself to go to sleep.

Metrool slept until five o'clock the next morning. He arrived at the test site at six forty-five. Simmons arrived at the same time, and after Metrool told him about Thompson's crash, Simmons quit. He said he was not going to fly the Peregrine anymore and left.

Metrool looked at the brand-new plane sitting there. They had taken one apart and not found anything wrong. Metrool went to the two mechanics and told them to get it ready. They asked who was going to fly it. Metrool told them, "I am. Get it ready." Metrool knew it was not the intelligent thing to do, but he felt compelled to do it.

Soon he was climbing into the deep cockpit and checking it out. He said, "The switch is off," and watched them spin the wooden prop. He said, "The switch is on." They spun the wooden prop again, and the new engine started quickly. Metrool let the engine warm up and then signaled the mechanics to stand clear. He taxied a short way and then went to full power.

The plane seemed to leap into the air. He eased back on power and circled the airfield twice, checking all the control surfaces. He went to full power and top speed with no problem. Metrool started doing aerobatics—mild at first and then more drastic. He started to do the same series of aerobatics Thompson had done right before he crashed, and in the middle of it, he saw something. He repeated the same series again, and there it was: an invisible killer. Holding his breath, he did the series of maneuvers three more times. On four of the five tests, the killer was there. He turned and flew back to the field. It was terrible that it had killed three pilots.

Metrool landed, taxied up to the hangar, and sat there for a few minutes. It was depressing that the flaw had killed three men before they found it. Metrool slowly climbed out of the plane, walked to the mechanics, and simply said, "I found it." He kept walking, and soon he was at the airport office. He pulled out the phone number of the general who had sent him and asked the operator to connect him.

Ten minutes later, the general was on the phone, and Metrool told him what he had found. Metrool said, "The Peregrine has a low pilot's seat, and it has holes in the firewall for engine controls. The cockpit is not ventilated, and fumes build up. Under certain maneuvers, exhaust actually blows through the cockpit. The pipes on the exhaust are too short. It needs an air scoop to ventilate the cockpit. I would raise the pilot's seat three or four inches."

The general said, "I will get people on it right now."

Metrool said, "I will be checking Peregrines as they get to France."

Metrool walked out, walked away, caught a taxi to the train station, and caught the next train to Portsmouth. When he got to Portsmouth, he found the next ship was three hours away, so he went into a sailors' bar and had a couple of pints. He had a cabin on the ship and slept most of the eleven-hour crossing.

Another train ride followed, but he was happy to be getting close to Margaux. He had taught Margaux to message, and they had messaged each other when he was in England, so she knew when to meet his train. Soon there was a flurry of hugs and kisses. He was happy to see her, and she seemed to reciprocate. They went to the hotel and first dined at the hotel restaurant and then took a bottle of wine to her room and talked into the night.

They went to the aerodrome the next morning, and Metrool met his temporary replacement. He seemed like a good man and appeared to have been doing a good job. Metrool, walking through the repair hangars, saw a lot more supplies now.

Metrool received a message from Alerton: *Get somewhere where you can talk to me. We have trouble. The commandant must have some very influential friends. They checked you with a fine-toothed comb. They found you really own that huge pharmaceutical company in Germany and that you lived there for nineteen years. They know you, through dummies, own things in Austria. They are going to arrest you and charge you with being a spy.*

Metrool asked, *What about all my work with the aerodromes?*

They say you were spying, and you found out every weakness of the Royal Air Service.

Metrool asked, *What are they going to do?*

Alerton said, *They are going to arrest you and charge you with being a spy in the next few days.*

What should I do?

I would say run. As a spy, you could be shot. You need to get out of Europe and disappear.

I must talk to Margaux.

Yes, talk to her, but get out of Europe quickly.

Metrool went to Margaux and told her, "I have a serious problem."

Margaux asked him what it was.

Metrool said, "I am going to be charged as a German spy."

"Are you a spy?" she asked.

"No," Metrool said, "I have been working extremely hard for the Royal Air Service."

"What are you going to do?"

"I must leave Europe quickly."

Metrool saw Margaux thinking deeply, and then she said, "I will go with you."

Metrool said, "Wonderful."

Margaux said, "I must take my son with me."

"Of course."

"I have not seen him much lately."

"All right, pack here, and then we will go to your sister's. You and your son pack up there, and then we'll go catch a train to Le Havre."

Margaux asked about the Daimler, and Metrool said, "Alerton will handle it."

An hour later, they were packed at the hotel and loaded the luggage into the Daimler. Then they drove to Margaux's sister's house. Margaux spent a good while talking to her son and sister.

Margaux came to Metrool and told him, "My son wants to come."

Metrool said, "Good. Help him pack."

Metrool waited, and an hour went by before Margaux kissed her sister goodbye. The Daimler was loaded, they drove to the train station, and when the train came, an elder porter was helpful in getting their luggage stowed on board. As Metrool was about to board the train, he looked at the Daimler, and then he looked at the porter, handed him the key, and said, "It is yours."

They had a compartment for the six-hour train ride. After they arrived at Le Havre, Metrool hired a train station truck to take their luggage and boxes to the hotel, the Paulista, and their taxi followed the truck. At the hotel, Metrool got them a suite and a room for their baggage and boxes. He then went to the row of offices that handled freight and people traveling on the ships. The first two offices had nothing to offer him. The manager at the next office was helpful but kept telling him, "The only ships that go to Brazil are Brazilian ships, because German submarines have sunk some ships going to Brazil."

Metrool said, "Whatever the case, I must get to Brazil."

The manager looked at all his ships going to Brazil. He said, "The only one that is close to your needs is a multistop freighter, and it will take between thirty-five and forty-five days to get there."

Metrool asked, "Where is it docked?"

The manager replied, "Dock four. The *Brazilian Star.*"

Metrool left quickly and caught a taxi to dock four. He boarded the ship and went to see the captain. After he told the captain what he needed, the captain sent the first mate with him to show him the ship. The available quarters, the dining room, and the kitchen were all satisfactory. The freighter had twelve passenger cabins, and Metrool claimed cabin numbers nine through twelve and got a written note from the captain. The crew's language was Portuguese, but the captain and first mate were both fluent in English. Metrool went back to the shipping office and booked those four cabins.

The manager said, "It leaves in two days."

Metrool went to the hotel, and since it was already dusk, they would stay in the hotel that night. The three went down and walked around the hotel's neighborhood. They found an elegant restaurant and decided to dine there. Later, when they got back to the Paulista, even Metrool was ready to get some sleep.

The next morning, after breakfast, Metrool saw the Paulista's manager and acquired the hotel van. He got the porters to go up to their baggage room and bring all the luggage down to the van. Metrool tipped them well, settled with the hotel, and told the van driver to follow their taxi. At the ship, Metrool again had to acquire people to get their things up to their cabins, this time the ship's crewmen.

Metrool had not used their real names when he booked their passage, and because he had paid in gold, the manager did not care what his name was. Because it was a long trip, after he got Margaux and Henri settled, Metrool left to buy supplies. Five hours later, he returned with a truckload of supplies, everything from cases of wine to tinned delicacies to one of the new devices that played music. There were some boxes marked with words and some boxes marked with numbers.

Before they had left the base close to Paris, Metrool had gone to major banks in Paris and drawn out a huge amount of gold, and he had gotten five huge vouchers, for he did not know how much trouble the commandant's people would cause him.

The next morning, Metrool took Henri into Le Havre and basically let him buy whatever he wanted. Then they returned to the ship; it was going to leave with the tide. Later, they stood on a railed-in deck at the top of the ship and watched the port of Le Havre slowly slide past them. Metrool messaged Alerton: *We are on a ship leaving France now. I have bought supplies, and I have a lot of gold and five exceptionally large vouchers.* My plan is to go to São Paulo, buy a large ranch, and live there a long time.

Alerton messaged back: *That sounds excellent. When this damn war is over, Marie and I will visit you.*

Soon the conversation was over, and Alerton wished them good luck.

Slowly, the ship left Le Havre. It was not fast; this was going to be a long trip and not a direct one. São Paulo was the ship's sixth and last stop. They found there were five other passengers: an older couple and three businessmen, all Portuguese. The ship had twelve passenger cabins, and on the voyage, four of them were unused. The crew's language was Portuguese, but some spoke English, and Metrool was fluent in Spanish, so he could get by. Metrool arranged for the first mate to give Portuguese lessons to Margaux and Henri. Things settled down, and on the fifth night of the voyage, Margaux and Metrool were on the foredeck. It was dark, but the stars were bright, and the breeze was pleasant. They had their favorite wine with an excellent evening meal. Metrool pulled out a small jewelry box and gave it to Margaux.

"What is it?" she asked.

Metrool said, "Why don't you open it and find out?"

She opened it and caught her breath. "What does it mean?"

Metrool replied, "It means I want to marry you."

Margaux did not hesitate. "Yes, but how? When?"

Metrool took her to a cabin they used for storage and handed her a large box. She opened it and found it contained a white lace wedding dress. Tears filled her eyes, and she embraced Metrool and held him tightly. With shining eyes, she asked him again, "How? When?"

Metrool told her, "Right here on the ship. The captain can marry us."

Margaux embraced him and said, "Oh, I love you."

Metrool then said, "We must go talk to Henri; he must approve."

They talked to Henri, and he quickly approved. Henri and Metrool got along well.

The next day, Metrool was busy. He went to the storage cabin; got a camera and its accessories; and took them to the main cook, Mateo, whom he had talked to earlier, and discussed its operation.

Metrool then went to the baker to see how the cake was going and to the captain to make sure the proper forms were filled out. Metrool then went back to the storage cabin and retrieved two new suits he had bought for Henri and himself. He set the gramophone up on the foredeck with a copy of the "Wedding March" on the turntable. The first mate was going to manage the gramophone.

Just before sundown, nearly the whole crew was there. The other passengers were all there. Henri and Metrool, in their new suits, were there, and the first mate started the "Wedding March." Everyone turned to see Margaux appear in her white lace dress. The ship's officers were in their best uniforms. The captain, with a Bible in his hand, spoke the words he seemed to know by heart and asked them the proper questions. In a short time, he said, "Metrool, you may kiss the bride."

The crew had decorated the large dining room with paper and ribbons Metrool had provided. There was an excellent meal with champagne, wine, and beer. It was a wonderful, happy occasion, and Margaux glowed. The first mate brought the gramophone into the dining room and played a record for them to dance to, and the cook took more pictures. It was a wonderful wedding, and Margaux loved having Metrool's ring on her finger. At ten o'clock that night, she and Metrool retired to her room.

The routine settled down. The ship was a good ship but slow, and it plowed through the Atlantic west to the Americas. The first mate spent two hours every day teaching Margaux and Henri Portuguese. Metrool, because he was Hamen and was fluent in Spanish, had already learned the difference. Margaux, because she was Hamen now, was learning the Portuguese language quickly, and that was going to cause a problem.

One night, in his cabin, Metrool messaged Everin to catch her up. Everin told him she was sorry that his work in France had not been appreciated. Metrool thanked her. They messaged for a while; she congratulated him on his marriage; and at the end, he brought Margaux into the message.

The voyage went on seemingly the same day after day. Nearly every day, Metrool and Henri went out exploring the ship. One day Henri asked Metrool, "Why do they always have two lookouts up there?"

Metrool did not want to answer, but he did. "The Germans' submarines have sunk some ships."

The Atlantic-crossing part of their voyage ended when they docked in Caracas. There was cargo to unload there, and that would take two days. The first night, the three went into Caracas to dine, and the next day, Metrool hired an auto and driver to see the countryside around Caracas. After one more night there, the ship was on its way again. Henri had enjoyed seeing the Caracas countryside, but Margaux had noticed him acting different lately. Maybe it was because she had married, she thought.

More days went by as they went south to Colombia. Henri was still acting strange, so Margaux finally sat him down and asked, "What is wrong?"

Henri surprised her by asking, "Are you my mother?"

She said, "Of course I am your mother."

Henri replied, "I have watched you, and you can do things my mother cannot do. You lift things, remember things, and add stacks of numbers in an instant, and you're already passable in Portuguese, while I am just beginning. How can my mother do all this?"

Margaux was shocked. She said, "I will explain, but first, I must talk to Metrool."

She went to Metrool and asked, "What in the world do I do? To tell him about me, I must tell him about you. How do I tell him his stepfather is a seven-hundred-year-old being from another planet?"

They discussed what to do. It was obvious Henri had to be told; he knew too much. First, with an iron-clad engram, he was told that Metrool was not an earthling. Then he was given another fact: Metrool had been on Earth for five hundred years and was quite wealthy. As they proceeded, more and more information was added.

Eventually, they came to a tough point: telling Henri how his mother had become Hamen. It was painful to all three. They were up all night long. Henri had some conflicts. He told them, "My mother would not have been hurt if you had not taken her to Paris. But if you had not saved her, she would be dead. Because I love my mother and don't want her to be hurt, I would not have told anyone about this anyway, but I do not blame you for implanting the engrams."

It was dawn, and all three crashed; it had been a stressful night.

They slept for most of the next day, but it did not matter. They were going eight knots per hour on their way to Georgetown, Guyana. It was a three-day voyage. They smoothed out some rough spots with Henri, and then the ship was at Georgetown for two days. Then they were in Paramaribo the next day, though for only a few hours, and then they were steaming again. Their next port was Belém, and it was several days away. In those days, Henri asked his mother a hundred questions about what she was.

Belém was only an eighteen-hour stop, but they were able to get off the ship and go to a wonderful restaurant with a crowd, because Metrool invited everyone on the ship to come, and it turned into a real party. As they steamed out the next morning, several of those on board had headaches. They would be in Recife in two days.

Henri tested his mother on her strength and her mental capacity, and she tried to downplay it. The ship steamed into Recife and, six hours later, steamed out. Their next port was Salvador. The next morning, they entered All Saints' Bay. Salvador was the capital of the state of Bahia. The captain was from there, and he had told them about the neighborhood of Pelourinho.

It had cobblestone streets, large squares, colorful buildings, and baroque churches. That afternoon, they hired an auto and driver to take them there and walked around and looked. They especially liked the São Francisco Church. That night, they dined out with the captain and first mate. The next day, they were on their way to their real destination: São Paulo, Brazil. They still had several days of steaming ahead of them, and Henri was pushing for more and more information.

Margaux knew where he was heading with his questioning and dreaded it. On the third day, he asked her if Metrool could make him like her. Margaux got the three of them together to explain the good and bad points of the process. Metrool explained to him that it was not a scientific process; it had always been used in desperation. The results varied, and the procedure could even result in death. If they did it and it was successful, Henri might appear as eighteen years old for sixty or seventy years.

Margaux controlled the situation by not saying no and by saying there was no rush. She said they should watch her for a while for side effects or problems.

It was the middle of the day, and Metrool and Henri were on the foredeck. The captain had told Metrool they would arrive in São Paulo the next morning. Looking at the smokestack, Metrool saw twice as much smoke as usual. He went to the captain to see what was wrong. The captain told him the ship was all right, except one of the lookouts thought he'd seen a periscope, so they were burning more coal to go a little faster. After about two hours of the dark smoke, it went back to normal.

The next morning, the ship entered the Port of Santos. After they were docked, Metrool went ashore and acquired a truck and a taxi for the twenty-two-mile trip to the Intercontinental Hotel in São Paulo. After they were all packed, they went to the crew and thanked them for their hospitality and hired three of them to take all their stuff down to the truck. The three travelers went down the gangway to the waiting taxi.

On the car ride, the scenery was varied, and in some places, the road was steep. São Paulo was more than two thousand feet above sea level.

Soon they were checking into their wonderful hotel, which had just been built in 1910. It was one of the first hotels in São Paulo to have electric lights.

The first few days were relaxing; they spent time sightseeing and making connections. One of the connections Metrool made invited the three out to his mansion on Paulistas Avenue for dinner, and it was wonderful. Metrool also met a real estate agent who dealt in ranches and country properties, and through him, he hired a truck and driver.

The first two days they went out were not very satisfying; the places the agent showed him were either too small or too swampy, or the vegetation was wrong. On the third day, by noon, they had looked at two properties that were close to what he wanted. Metrool watched the agent rearrange his papers, and something caught his eye. He asked the agent to show him the picture. The agent asked, "What picture?"

Metrool told him, "The picture of the large, fancy gate."

The agent quickly told him, "That ranch is not for sale. The owner is very secretive."

Metrool looked at the picture. It could not have been chance. What should he do? The name of the ranch was Hamen II. It could not have been a coincidence.

Metrool sent an open message: *Are you Hamen?*

There was no answer as the truck moved along. Finally, a message came back: *Yes. Are you?*

Metrool said, *Yes. Can I meet you?*

Yes, but only you. Come to my gate. My man will come for you.

Metrool told the agent to take him to the gate. The agent told Metrool the owner would not see him, but Metrool insisted they go. Nearly an hour later, they pulled up to the large, ornate gate.

Besides the guard, there was a driver and a shiny black Model T Ford pickup. The agent did not know what to say when Metrool walked through the gate to the pickup, and the driver helped him climb in.

The driver was well dressed and well groomed. He told Metrool his name was Carlos. It was nearly a mile to the large hacienda. Carlos walked him to the door and told him, "Lopez will take you to Senor."

The door opened, and Lopez ushered him in and led him to a large room with several pieces of large, overstuffed leather-covered furniture.

Sitting in a wheelchair was an incredibly old man. His skin was nearly transparent, what little hair he had was white, and his muscles obviously had withered.

"Hamen?" Metrool asked.

The man replied, "Yes. My name is Talaron."

At that time, Lopez pushed a cart of refreshments into the room and offered many things. Metrool only accepted lemon water. Metrool told Talaron that he was Hamen, told him what his name was, and asked if Talaron was Engel. That drew a scowl, and Talaron told him, "No, but that is why I am here. But first, tell me how you are here."

Metrool saw no reason to refuse, so he started their story. "We were on an observation mission on a starship, and something went wrong so fast that only two pods escaped. Three were in my pod. Something went wrong on the other pod, and its occupant did not survive."

The old Hamen said, "You were able to salvage both pods?"

Metrool told him yes.

Talaron replied that the Engels had given them only a few pounds of gold and pushed them out.

"Why were they so crude?" Metrool asked.

Talaron said, "Even though the three of us helped them steal the starship and escape, they were angry at us."

"May I ask why?"

"The femtech on the ship was a fake, and they thought we knew."

Metrool looked at Talaron; he had never seen a Hamen look so old, not even in a recorded image. He did not probe, but it was obvious Talaron did not have much time left.

Talaron asked about the other two Hamens, and Metrool told him, "Alerton, the other male, is in England with his wife."

"Do they have children?"

With Hamen senses, Metrool saw he was about to get into some deep questions. "My agent and driver are waiting at your gate, and it is getting late. We must reach São Paulo before dark. May I and my wife return tomorrow?"

"Of course. Forgive me for being a bad host."

"No," Metrool said, "you have been most gracious."

Lopez led him out, and Carlos drove him to the gate in the polished Model T. The agent was upset and dismayed, and Metrool had no logical explanation, so he had to use some Hamen mental persuasion. It took two hours to reach the Intercontinental, and on the way, he silently messaged Everin and Alerton.

In the hotel, Metrool quickly got Margaux alone and asked if she would go with him to the ranch tomorrow. She told him of course and asked many questions about the old Hamen.

"How old is he?"

"He appears to be fifteen hundred years old."

"How is that possible? You have told me Hamens live a thousand years."

"Yes, I told you that, but that was only part of the equation. Because Hamen has ultimate population control, a femtech cannot create a new Hamen unless a Hamen has chosen to depart, and the extremely old custom on Hamen is to depart at one thousand."

"On Earth, that is called suicide."

"That is our custom," Metrool said.

"How old are you now?" Margaux asked.

"Seven hundred."

"Are you going to commit suicide and leave me when you reach a thousand?"

Metrool laughed and said, "I will never leave you," and they kissed several times.

They invited Henri out to dinner, but he had other plans. Metrool and Margaux dined in the hotel's fancy dining room.

Metrool looked at Margaux and said, "Other plans?"

She laughed and told him, "He has met a girl who works at the hotel."

Metrool laughed too. "That is a familiar story."

The next morning, after breakfast, Margaux and Metrool walked out to their waiting driver and truck. It was red and black, with red wood-spoke wheels, and it had one bench and a canvas top. It was the best Metrool could hire. Margaux sat between the driver and Metrool for the two-hour drive. When they pulled up to the large gate, Carlos was already waiting.

Soon they were at the hacienda, and Lopez pushed Talaron outside. Margaux did her best to cover her feelings at how ill Talaron looked. The three exchanged warm greetings, and they were real. Lopez pushed Talaron inside, and Margaux and Metrool followed. Lopez pushed Talaron into the large drawing room with the stuffed leather furniture. Talaron bid them to sit, and Lopez went out of the room and then pushed a refreshment cart in.

Lopez left the room, and Talaron told them they could speak freely; his servants did not eavesdrop. Talaron, practically staring at Margaux, said, "You are his wife?" When Margaux replied that she was, Talaron said, "You are an earthling, but you are also Hamen; you are a hybrid. How is that possible?"

Margaux replied, "In Paris, I received an injury that was certain death, and Metrool saved my life."

Talaron looked at Metrool and said, "How did you do that?"

Metrool said, "I treated her wound and injected Hamen blood into her."

Talaron was stunned. "Is that possible?"

Metrool answered, "It is not scientific. It has only been done six times, and one resulted in death. It has only been done to save the dying."

Margaux changed the subject and asked, "Have you married?"

Talaron looked startled but answered, "Yes, three times."

Margaux pushed again. "Did you have children?"

Talaron, upset and exasperated, took a deep breath and said, "I would have to tell you a story."

Margaux said, "Please do."

Talaron looked at Metrool and then at Margaux. "I married three times to good women. Each marriage produced one beautiful child, and each one of those beautiful children was so bad that after each one had killed several people, I terminated them." Tears streamed down his withered cheeks. "They had remarkable powers; I could not leave them loose in the world."

Margaux was crying, and Metrool said, "I know it was terribly hard, but you did the right thing." Margaux, wiping her eyes, went and embraced Talaron.

The old man looked at Metrool and asked, "Can you inject me with young blood?"

Metrool replied, "It has only been done to people who were dying."

"Am I not dying?"

"It might kill you."

Talaron smiled. "Then it would not cheat me out of much."

They went to lighter subjects and found he had claimed the ranch two hundred years ago.

Metrool asked, "How have you managed to live in one place this long?"

Talaron said, "I live a very secret life. I deal with very few people, and I have had five funerals." Talaron asked Lopez to push him out to the garden.

Margaux and Metrool followed them into the unusual garden, which had roses, gardenias, hedges, azaleas, chrysanthemums, and many tombstones. It was well kept. There were five fake markers for him, with different names on them. There also were three large, beautiful markers for his three wives and three medium-sized plain black stones for his three sons. Lopez pushed Talaron back into the drawing room. Talaron asked up front, "Will you inject young blood into me?"

Metrool saw no real reason to refuse him and said, "Yes, we will."

Talaron said, "There are some things I must do; can you start on the third day from now?"

Again, Metrool saw no reason to say no, and he said, "Yes, we can."

Lopez escorted them out to the polished Model T. Carlos helped Margaux climb aboard, and then he and Metrool climbed in. As soon as they were gone, Talaron got on the phone with his doctor and his lawyer, getting things done.

Margaux and Metrool rode in the red-and-black truck back to São Paulo. They felt Talaron's actions were not all logical, but he was not in a normal situation. They messaged Alerton and let him know everything that had happened. Later, after relaxing, bathing, and putting on fresh clothes, they invited Henri out to dinner. At first, he hesitated, but then he asked, "May I take Alinda?"

Margaux quickly said yes, she wanted to know the young woman.

They dined at an excellent restaurant only a block from the Intercontinental. Metrool had called and changed their reservation from two to four persons. Metrool and Margaux had been seated for only a short time, when Henri and the lovely girl arrived. Margaux, as any mother would have, with Hamen senses, checked her out, and she was pleased. She found Alinda was a nice girl who was from a poor background but extremely high in basic intelligence.

Margaux was impressed by her and saw her affection for Henri was real. Margaux quietly observed her throughout the formal meal with multiple utensils and saw she waited on Henri and followed what he did. With mind reading, Margaux saw it was not just to please her; it was because Alinda wanted to know.

When the dinner was over, they went their separate ways, and back in their suite, Metrool said, "Why don't you take her and buy her an outfit tomorrow?" He smiled. "That will give you more time to read her mind."

Margaux blushed and said, "You saw?"

Metrool said, "Yes, and I understand; you are a mother."

The next morning, Metrool went out looking at ranches again. It took about two hours to get to the area Hamen II was in, which was where the best land was. One ranch's name translated as Black Bull Ranch, and it was a desirable ranch. Metrool asked the elderly man why he wanted to sell it.

He replied, "It has made me a lot of money, and I was able to send my two sons to the best colleges. One became a lawyer, and one became a doctor; neither wants to operate a ranch."

They talked about a price. It was reasonable, but it was not cheap. Metrool told the man he would consider it, and they went on to another ranch. This ranch's name translated roughly as Beauty Ranch, and it was beautiful, but it was only two-thirds the size of the Black Bull.

Soon they were back in the truck, and the driver was taking them back to São Paulo. Metrool told the agent he was considering the Black Bull but was not ready to buy yet.

Back in his suite, Metrool took a hot shower. It felt wonderful. He dressed, and sipping a drink, he talked to Margaux.

Margaux said, "I did what you suggested, and the girl loved the clothes."

Suddenly, Henri rushed in, screaming, "What did you do?"

Margaux said, "I took her and bought her some clothes."

Henri shouted, "Well, her father thinks she did something wicked to earn them and has beaten her!"

Metrool asked, "Do you know where they are?"

Henri said, "Yes, their small house."

"Take me to it. We will get a taxi."

"Wait. This man is dangerous."

Metrool said again, "Take me to them."

Quickly, they were riding in a taxi, and in twenty minutes, they were there. As Metrool and Henri walked up to the house, a large man burst out of it and ran at Henri.

Metrool knocked him to the ground. He got up and lunged at Metrool. Metrool reached deep into the man's mind and stopped his heart. The large man grabbed his chest and then coughed, gasped, and fell over. After two minutes, Metrool started his heart back up. After a fit of coughing and gasping, the large man got up and came at Metrool again, and again, Metrool went into his mind and stopped his heart. He told the man's mind, *I can stop your heart anywhere anytime.* Now the coughing dying man shook with fear.

Metrool said, "Get the girl."

Henri went into the house, and Metrool started the father's heart again. The father stood up, and Metrool put him in a frozen state. Metrool looked at Alinda; she had a black eye, one side of her face was purple, and Henri said she had bruises on her body. Metrool went into the paralyzed man's mind and told him, *I am going to release you, and we will fight.*

He released him, and the man grinned, for he was much more heavily built than Metrool. Metrool, with Hamen speed and strength, began hitting the man in his face, stomach, and ribs. The man was turning black and blue all over.

Metrool went into his mind and told him, *If I ever find out you have hurt anyone, I will have my men come cut you into little pieces while you are still alive.*

Alinda's father did not know if Metrool was a witch or what, but he was crying now, deathly afraid of him. Out loud, Metrool said, "We are taking your daughter with us until she is well. Do not ever hurt her again."

As they got into the taxi, the driver said, "From what I saw tonight, he will not even look at her."

When they got to the hotel, Margaux immediately took Alinda under her wing.

When Metrool and Henri were alone, Henri asked, "Was what I saw tonight Hamen?"

Metrool simply answered, "Yes."

"Well," Henri said, "I want it more than ever, but I am willing to wait for a while."

Metrool said, "A wise decision. Thank you."

Margaux came to them and said, "I have doctored her, and, Henri, I gave her your bedroom. You will have to sleep on the divan in the drawing room."

The next morning, Metrool had breakfast for the kids served in the room, while he and Margaux went down for breakfast in the main dining room. Then Metrool went to the manager and covered for Alinda's absence from work for several days.

The shiny red-and-black truck with the red wood-spoke wheels was waiting for them outside. Metrool was taking Margaux to see the two ranches he liked. There was no agent; it was just Margaux, him, and the driver.

The hotel had packed a large wicker lunch basket for them. It was a warm day, and the driver, at lunchtime, parked under a large tree. Margaux opened the lunch basket and gave the driver lunch and a glass of wine, and he went over to another tree to give them privacy. Margaux had liked the Black Bull, but at this time, they were not buying. It was cool under the large tree, so they took a slow lunch. At one point, Metrool took the driver another glass of wine.

Margaux put the remains of their lunch back in the basket, and the driver carried it to the truck. He started the truck, and they were on their way to the other ranch, Beauty Ranch. After about five miles, the driver pulled into an unguarded gate, and Margaux read the name and asked, "Does it live up to its name?"

"That is for you to decide," Metrool said as they drove the mile-long road to the hacienda.

An hour later, as they left, Margaux said, "Yes, it does live up to its name." It was only half ranch; the other half was coffee.

The next morning was similar, except no lunch had been packed, and Metrool carried a medical bag. When they were out of São Paulo on the west side, the roads were either dirt or gravel. After the two-hour drive, they were at Hamen II. Carlos and the polished Model T were waiting for them. As they arrived at the hacienda, Lopez was pushing Talaron out to meet them, and they embraced with real affection.

Soon they were following Lopez and Talaron into the drawing room. Talaron spoke up immediately and said, "I want to get started."

Metrool said, "Are you sure about this?"

Talaron said, "Totally. Your lovely wife is proof of what your Hamen blood can do."

Metrool used alcohol to sterilize Margaux's and Talaron's arms and then drew three ccs from Margaux and injected it into Talaron. Now it was a matter of observing him for a few hours.

Lopez wheeled in a cart with iced lemon water, hot coffee, several sweets, and local specialties. The main thing they took was coffee; it was a tense situation. Talaron's vital signs seemed to improve slightly. When four hours had passed and his vitals were still strong, Talaron said, "I want another injection." Metrool did not want a confrontation, so Talaron got his second three-cc injection.

It was time for Carlos to take Margaux to the gate. She had to go back to the Intercontinental to take care of Henri and Alinda. Before she left, she and Metrool embraced and kissed several times, and then she was in Carlos's Model T, going down the long driveway.

Metrool went back to his job of observing Talaron. All night, his vital signs were stable, and when Margaux returned at ten o'clock the next morning, Talaron was pushing for another injection. Within thirty minutes, they gave him another three-cc injection.

At two thirty that afternoon, his vital signs dropped slightly, and Metrool said, "We should not give you an injection at this time."

Talaron was adamant. He insisted, and he wanted Metrool's blood this time. He got what he wanted, but his vitals continued to drop—not quickly but steadily. Metrool messaged both Everin and Alerton, asking for their advice. At first, they had no advice. After Margaux had left for the hotel, Alerton messaged him back.

You will have to get his help on this. Alerton explained to him what to do.

Metrool thought to himself that Alerton was exceptionally good at pulling up ancient Hamen programs. Metrool went to Talaron and, sitting close to him, told him, "This is not going well. To save your life and maybe give you what you wanted, you must cooperate with me."

Talaron said yes, he would, and Metrool began telling him what to do. "You must go deep into your Hamen memory banks, where so much is stored, and find ancient Hamen physical stasis, and you must apply it to yourself now." Metrool scanned him lightly as he searched the memory banks of his mind, and he saw that Talaron had found it. Then Metrool scanned as he applied it. However, when it seemed he had finished it, he started dropping fast, and in a few minutes, Talaron's vital signs were zero.

Metrool sat there for thirty minutes, scanning Talaron, but there were no vital signs. Metrool messaged Alerton and told him everything that had happened.

Alerton said, *You need a technostasis device to keep him alive.*

Metrool replied, *I have never heard of one, and I darn sure do not have one.*

You could make one if you had a creator.

You know Everin has the only creator on Earth.

I know. Can she bring it to you?

I do not know, but I will find out.

Metrool ended that messaging and opened a message to Everin. After normal greetings, Metrool said, *Everin, I need your help.*

Everin replied, *I will do anything I can.*

Metrool said, *I need you to bring your creator to São Paulo as soon as possible.*

Wow, she said, *you do not ask for a small one.*

Metrool told her everything that had happened in the last few days, and Everin told him she would bring it as soon as she could.

Metrool called Lopez into Talaron's bedroom and told him that Talaron had passed away. Lopez surprised him by leaving the room crying. Metrool gave him some time to settle down and then went to him and asked, "Can you call Sanchez?"

Lopez said, "I will call him now." He went to the phone, and in a few minutes, he returned and told Metrool, "He will be here in one hour."

The phone was strange to Metrool; they had to crank it, and they had a phone but no electric lights.

Metrool went to the drawing room, sat in one of the large stuffed leather chairs, and programmed himself for thirty minutes of deep sleep. It had been a trying night.

Metrool woke a few minutes before Sanchez arrived. Sanchez's eyes were red, and when he arrived, he wanted a few minutes alone with Talaron.

Metrool said, "Of course," and while Sanchez was there, Lopez told Metrool that Talaron had been like a particularly good father to Sanchez.

Metrool told Sanchez, "Have a glass case made for him. I am having one built in São Paulo, and whichever is best is the one we will use. He does not need to be embalmed; his body will not decompose."

Sanchez was a little tiffed; he did not see the need for a glass case, because he did not believe Talaron's body would not deteriorate. Sanchez said, "Those two days you were not here, Talaron had his lawyers and clerks here to rewrite all his papers; he wanted them read soon."

Metrool said, "Whenever you want to."

Sanchez left, and Metrool went to Lopez and told him that Talaron would be put in a glass casket, but until then, no one was to touch him. Margaux arrived, and Metrool filled her in on everything.

She was down about Talaron, and with tears in her eyes, she said, "He was so old and frail, but I thought we could help him."

Metrool phoned the contractor in São Paulo about the glass casket. "I want it here tomorrow, even if they must work all night."

The contractor said, "That will cost you extra."

"That was not our deal," Metrool said, "but I will tell you what: you have it here by noon tomorrow, and I will pay you double. And if you do not, you can keep it."

As soon as Everin ended the message with Metrool, she thought, *Airplanes.* What was best, and what was available? She soon found out two of her choices were not available. She had friends in the army, and she had friends at airfields. She began calling people. After several dead ends, bingo. She grabbed her purse and her checkbook and headed for the elevator.

The doorman hailed a taxi for her, and soon she was heading for an airfield. It was not much of an airfield; it was just a large pasture with maintenance and manufacturing hangars all the way down one side. Out there on the pasture were lots of planes. Her friend John walked with her among them. They carried kerosene lanterns.

She looked at John and asked, "What can you let me have?" John gave her a look, and Everin said, "John, I have money, and this is important. I will pay you well."

John said, "Do you want one plane or more than one?"

Everin told him she wanted four.

"Wow," John said, "the only type I could take that many serial numbers off the books would be JN-6s."

Everin said, "They only have a range of one hundred fifty miles, and I have a long way to go."

"We have extra fuel tanks that we put in some of them."

"Can you have four of them totally checked out, with the largest tanks you have, by morning?"

"Damn, girl, you are asking for a miracle."

Everin waved her checkbook at him. "As baggage, two quarts of motor oil and four new spark plugs in each plane. Find me three good pilots who are willing to take a flying vacation for damn good money."

John said, "All right, but who is the fourth pilot?"

Everin said, "Me. I am a well-qualified pilot." She held out her checkbook and asked, "How much?"

He told her, and it was a high price, but she was in a bind.

She wrote it for 10 percent more than he asked and said, "Have it done by daylight and the planes in great shape. Do you have army supplies?"

"Yes, I do."

"I want a sleeping bag, a canteen full of water, ten army chocolate bars, and an army flying suit in each airplane."

"That is no problem," John said as he walked her back to her waiting taxi.

She left the airport and went back to her apartment, where she packed a small bag. She went to her safe and opened it. She put six pounds of eagles and double eagles and twenty one-thousand-dollar bills into another bag. She got the creator out of her closet. It was in a case she had made for it. It weighed twenty-two pounds; that made all her baggage amount to thirty-six pounds. She put coffee on to percolate, and she got Mavis out of a sound sleep. Mavis was much more than a maid. She had her own room and did not wear a uniform; she dressed like Everin.

As they sipped coffee at the dining table, Everin told her she was taking a long trip and might be gone for a month. Mavis always carried a card in her purse with eight different phone numbers that were important to Everin.

Everin said, "Buy food and supplies just like you always do."

Then Everin went to her bedroom and programmed herself to sleep for three hours.

Three hours later, she was dressed, and she carried her flying jacket and her flying overpants just in case John did not deliver. Mavis helped her get all her stuff down to the waiting taxi.

Everin and Mavis embraced, and Mavis said, "I will miss you."

Everin said, "And I you."

When she got to the airport, the three pilots were already there and drinking coffee.

Everin laughed and said, "Do not drink too much." She asked them if they had warm suits, and they did. She said, "John has supplied us with army flying suits. You can have your choice but not both; we cannot afford the weight."

She found out the pilot named Mike was a fully qualified mechanic and was pleased with that. Dawn was breaking, and the planes had been finished only about thirty minutes.

All four put their flight suits on and climbed into their planes. Mechanics spun the props, and the engines fired up. Everin set her fuel-selector valve to the new extra tank. She had told the three pilots to do the same. Everin wanted to make sure the system worked.

They all worked, the engines were warmed up, and soon all four were in the air, climbing and flying south.

After many hours of roaring engines, numbing cold, and the odor of castor oil, they landed in Savannah. It was about to get dark. While the planes were being refueled and checked, Everin went into the airport office and called the Jacksonville airport. The airport operator said they closed at dark.

"No," said Everin. "I have four planes you can sell a lot of fuel to, and I will pay you tie-down fees. Just put out two rows of lanterns, torches, or whatever so we can see where to land."

The airport personnel said yes, and she told them the estimated arrival time and ended the call.

Everin went out, and per her instructions, the engines were already running. Soon the four JN-6s were climbing into the air. It was getting dark, and they followed the coastline. It got very dark, and they kept following the moon-illuminated coastline. When the time was right, they began looking for a town, and they saw one. They descended and flew over it, and soon there was a lit-up pasture. One by one, they landed, and they were guided to the fuel service and parked their planes there.

The airport manager said, "We will settle in the morning."

They were pleased when a woman handed them sandwiches and cold drinks, and then everything went dark. It had been a tiring day, and when they finished their sandwiches, they pulled their sleeping bags out of their planes, got into them, and went to sleep.

The next morning, Everin awoke at first light and woke the others. The service people were not there yet, so they checked their own planes. Charlie's plane was using more oil than normal, but it was running well, so they just added oil. The fuel pumps were not locked, so they refueled their own planes. As they finished, the airport manager and his wife arrived.

They found out his wife was the one who had given them the sandwiches. This morning, she had coffee for them and gave each one two egg sandwiches. Everin ate one and then wrapped the other and put it in her airplane. She then went into the office with the manager. She paid him and thanked him for his hospitality.

Their engines were warmed up, and soon they were climbing into the air. They were headed for Miami. After Miami, they would go on to Cuba and then sleep under their planes in the Dominican Republic.

<hr />

Metrool was staying at the ranch all the time, while Margaux was going back and forth because of Henri and Alinda. Margaux felt that Henri was too young to be so involved with a girl, but he was. Metrool had consulted Alerton by message, and they had agreed he should give Talaron one cc per day until they got the technostasis device. The São Paulo glass casket had arrived, and Lopez, Carlos, and Sanchez had put Talaron in it. The glass case had removable legs, and it was in the large drawing room.

One late afternoon, Sanchez had the lawyers, the accountants, Carlos, Lopez, and six other workers gather in the drawing room. The lawyers got everyone's attention and began to read the will. To Carlos, Lopez, and the six other workers, he gave large cash awards. He gave a separate large cash award to Sanchez. Hamen II was to go to Metrool immediately with no restrictions but with one provision: every January, 50 percent of the previous year's profits would be distributed to the two hundred employees named in the will.

Sanchez seemed surprised, and Metrool sensed some anger in him. The accountants gave Metrool the ledgers and explained them to him. Soon after, everyone was gone except Carlos, Lopez, and Metrool. Making sure he was unobserved, Metrool gave Talaron one cc with a long needle in the area of his heart. He then poured himself a large glass of wine and sat down in one of the large chairs in the drawing room, thinking. He did not need the ranch or the bank accounts. He had his own plans and wants. But he would take care of it, and maybe they could bring Talaron back.

Everin was flying through Caribbean sky. They had just refueled in Puerto Rico, and Charlie's plane's Hispano-Suiza engine was still using a lot of oil. When they took off and climbed to altitude, Charlie's plane started smoking badly. After watching Charlie try to stay up with the other three in his smoking plane for ten minutes, Everin signaled for him to go back to Puerto Rico. Each pilot had an info pack that Everin had typed, telling them what to do in different situations.

Everin was wearing earplugs and a leather flying helmet, but the exhaust roar was still punishing hour after hour. They were flying at 90 percent power. As they flew over towns, Everin looked for flags to see which way the wind was blowing. With a strong tailwind, their range might be four hundred miles, but with a strong headwind, their range might be three hundred miles. She had to keep going over the numbers. Their next fueling stop was Dominica, and it went well; quickly, they were back in the air.

It was almost dark when they reached Trinidad and Tobago, and because of her Hamen night vision, she had told the other two pilots that if it was dark, she would lead them in and would land last. That was what they did, and after the airport staff showed them where to park, they shut the airport down. One of the airport workers came to them and said, "If you give me money, I will go get you good food."

They did not believe him, but Everin thought, *You've got to trust somebody,* and she gave him forty dollars. Nearly an hour later, when they were about to give up and eat a chocolate bar, the man came back with a lot of good food.

The next morning, the routine started again at daylight with fueling the planes. They checked them out, grabbed a bite, and soon were back in the air. They headed southeast to Georgetown, Guyana. The Georgetown fueling went well, they each grabbed something from a food vendor, and then they were back in the air, going to Paramaribo, Suriname. Unfortunately, when they got there, things did not go well. After they refueled, Mike's plane would not start, and the airport staff spun the prop many times. Mike came to Everin and said, "You may need a mechanic. If you want me to, I will fly Randol's plane."

Everin said, "Thank you, Mike. Let us do that."

Soon two JN-6s were climbing into the air. They had a long flight to Macapá.

Metrool was staying at the ranch all the time basically, guarding Talaron—not that anyone would have wanted to do anything bad to Talaron, but he could not tell them the situation. So Metrool guarded him, and each day, he gave him an injection. He thought he was keeping it secret, until Lopez came to him and asked, "Why do you still give Talaron injections?"

Metrool told Lopez, "Believe me, I do not do anything to hurt or disparage him." Metrool used a mental suggestion to help Lopez believe him.

Margaux had not been to the ranch for the last two days; she was trying to defuse the Henri and Alinda situation. Henri wanted Margaux to either adopt Alinda or let him marry her. Margaux did not want to do either one. Henri would not let the matter drop, saying her father would permit either one.

Everin rose before daylight and began fueling her plane. That woke Mike, who began checking both, and then he fueled his. There was a small restaurant about a block from the hangar, and they went to it and wolfed down eggs and toast. Everin paid for their fuel, and airport employees spun their props. Both planes started right up, and after a warm-up run, they were climbing into the sky, going to Belém. They arrived in Belém at midmorning. The airport staff fueled the planes, and Everin said, "Mike, I need to talk to you." They walked away to a quieter spot.

Everin said, "We have been following the coastline because that is where the settlements are. Now, to save time, I would like to fly cross-country, but it will be dangerous, with jungles, swamps, and vicious animals, including snakes and crocodiles. If you say no, I will respect your decision, and we will continue to follow the coast."

Mike said, "Let me think about it while they are fueling and checking the planes."

Everin was anxious; she wanted to go cross-country, but she could not do it alone.

When the crew had finished and Everin and Mike were drinking coffee, Mike said, "I will go with you."

Everin smiled and said, "Oh, thank you, Mike."

Soon they were climbing into their planes and going through the routine: switch off, the prop was spun, switch on, the prop was spun, and the still-warm engine started. They took off into a mild headwind and began climbing to their cruising altitude. Everin had been hot and sweating in Belém, but soon she would be cold. They were flying south over dangerous country to a small place called Parauapebas.

When they got there and wanted to be fueled, the staff wanted to see their money first, and they would not accept American paper money; Everin had to pay them with gold. She did, and quickly, they were on their way. They flew nearly due south to Ilha do Bananal, and again, she had to pay with gold. It was a remote place, and Everin was going to push for Brasilia.

She told Mike, "I have very good night vision. Just stay on my wing, and I will lead you into the airport."

It was about 240 miles to Brasilia, and it was fully dark when they arrived, but with her Hamen vision, she led Mike in to land, and she made a circle and landed. The fuel pumps were already locked up, but the airport had a small restaurant hotel. They went to it, Everin got two rooms, and they had a good meal and good wine. *Oh, what a night.*

Everin was up at daybreak, knocking on Mike's door. They ate a quick breakfast at the restaurant and then went out to their planes. Again, they were in the air, still flying nearly due south.

Their next stop was Uberlândia, and it went well; they were quickly back in the air. About two hours after they left Uberlândia, Everin's Hispano-Suiza engine began to steam. It had developed a water leak, and soon it would be seizing if she did not get it on the ground. Mike saw she was in trouble and looked for a place for her to land. He pointed to a pasture-like area and motioned for her to try to land there. Everin was lucky the Jenny had a low stall speed. She touched down, and after a short roll, she came to a stop. Then, to her surprise, Mike was landing.

With his motor still running, Mike said, "I have half my fuel left. The original tank is full. Take off your heavy outer flight suit, get your device and money, and climb on board."

She did as he said, but she knew his plane was still heavy because of the extra tank and the plumbing for it. Mike's engine roared, and he let the tail rise, but he kept the main wheels on the ground as they built up speed. Then they were flying. Everin messaged Metrool, telling him her situation.

Metrool told her, *There is a pasture beside the hacienda. Lock on to my message, and use it to guide you here. Using that, estimate your distance and if you have enough fuel.*

She said, *We have just enough. Mike thinks I am crazy, telling him the headings. I must get this device to you.*

Metrool said, *Thank you, Everin. You are wonderful to do this for me.*

After an hour, Everin knew they were running on fumes, when Metrool messaged her: *I see you; we are at the large hacienda.*

Everin replied, *Yes, I see it.*

Soon Mike landed the Jenny in the pasture and taxied close to the hacienda before he stopped the engine.

Everin ran to Metrool with the creator, and together they ran into the hacienda. Mike climbed out of the Jenny slowly; he was worn out. Mike walked slowly to the hacienda, and inside, he ran into Lopez, who recognized his condition and took him straight to a room. Later, Lopez came back with food and drink and found Mike sprawled asleep on top of the covers in his clothes.

As soon as Metrool got the creator to the drawing room, he set it up on the large, heavy dining table. Metrool began to make parts for the technostasis device and assemble them. Although the creator was fast, it still took more than an hour for Metrool to ask for all the pieces and assemble them. Soon the assembled technostasis device was in the glass case with Talaron. The device had about fifty small lights on one side, and at that time, nearly all of them were red. Everin, Metrool, and Margaux stood there watching.

Margaux poured wine, and they found chairs and watched the device. Every so often, one of the red lights would turn green, but progress was slow. It would take several minutes for another green to appear. They began to relax a little, but they were still afraid it would not work. Talaron had been technically dead for four and a half days. Metrool said, "It is hard to tell whether he is dead or in stasis; the appearance is the same." Metrool sent Margaux to the hotel to take care of Henri and Alinda. Metrool and Everin took turns watching Talaron.

Lopez was still devoted to Talaron, and he approached Metrool in the drawing room and said, "I heard what the lawyers said, but I really did not understand it. What did it mean?"

Metrool replied, "It boils down to this: Margaux and I own half, and you, Sanchez, and two hundred named employees own the other half."

"What if we wanted to sell our half?"

"We would not stop you."

"Is that true?"

"Margaux and I have a lot of money."

"I can tell your friends have money. To acquire four airplanes overnight is impressive. Where did she get the device she brought in the Jenny?"

Metrool brushed off his question by saying, "She has had it a long time."

Metrool went back into the viewing room. He sat with Everin, and they talked about several things. She liked Margaux and said Metrool was fortunate; she could have been different after the Hamen blood injection.

Metrool said, "Yes, I know. I am truly fortunate. Talaron did all right with women but had terrible luck with children."

The fifty lights on the device slowly continued to change from red to green.

Metrool messaged Alerton and asked, *If nearly all change to green, would it mean he is all right?*

Alerton replied, *I do not know; it has been thousands of years since one of these has been used, and I do not think one has ever been used this way.*

Everin asked, *What about the blood? Metrool and I are debating about continuing or not.*

Alerton said, *I would advise doing it for five more days.*

The message ended, and Metrool became aware of Everin's exhaustion, which she had been trying to hide. He went to Lopez and asked, "Do you have a room for Everin?"

Lopez said, "Of course. We have several rooms."

Everin thanked Metrool and let Lopez lead her to a room. He lit the coal-oil lamp for her and left. She stripped off her clothes; got in the shower for a few minutes; used a plush towel to dry; climbed between the crisp, clean sheets; and was out.

Five hours later, as she had programmed it, Everin awoke refreshed. It was early morning, and she dressed in the only clothes she had. She messaged Margaux and asked, *Are you in São Paulo?*

Yes.

Will you buy me some clothes? I could not bring a suitcase.

I would be happy to; you have put yourself in so much danger for us.

They had some girl talk about clothes and shoes before they ended the message.

Many hours after Mike had fallen across the bed, he was eating breakfast in the kitchen. He asked the cook if the ranch had gasoline. The cook said yes, there were tanks of gasoline, white gas, kerosene, and diesel. Mike said, "I want to put fuel in my plane. Everin gave it to me for helping her. If someone wants to go to São Paulo, I can get them there quick."

The cook told him, "Carlos would be the one to help you with that."

Later, Mike saw Carlos, and with two five-gallon cans and the Model T, they made three trips and fueled the Jenny. Carlos took Mike to the equipment repair barn, where Mike borrowed some tools, and then took Mike back to the plane and watched him take the large extra fuel tank out of the Jenny. Then Carlos and Mike took the borrowed tools and the fuel tank to the repair barn.

With a clear, refreshed mind, Everin went to the room where Metrool was watching Talaron. She told Metrool, "I have revised what I think we should do."

"All right," Metrool said, "what do you think we should do?"

"Talaron was too old and frail and has been through too much for us to play it safe."

"I agree, but what should we do?"

"I say give him six ccs every three hours."

"That is drastic."

"I believe we must be. I feel he is dying the way we are treating him now."

"All right, when do we start?"

"Now," Everin said, rolling up her sleeve.

Metrool put Lopez in a trance so they could open the glass case. They injected six ccs into a neck artery, closed the case, and took Lopez out of his trance. Three hours later, they went through the same procedure, only they injected into a trunk artery, using Metrool's blood. Three hours later, they drew six ccs from Margaux and, using a long needle, injected it into an artery close to his heart. When Lopez was brought out of his trance, Metrool asked him if he would cover the glass case. He said he would, and soon it was covered.

Margaux asked, "What was that for?"

Metrool said, "Talaron is changing. I do not know if it is for good or bad, but his body is changing."

Three hours later, they sent Lopez on an errand and uncovered the glass case. It was obvious Talaron was changing, seemingly for the better. They opened the case, drew six ccs from Margaux because she would be leaving soon, and again used the long needle and went for a chest artery. They closed the case and recovered it.

Lopez and Carlos returned from the gate with two large boxes, and for the next hour, Everin and Margaux had girl fun with clothes. Soon Metrool was saying goodbye to Margaux with hugs and kisses. He was working on a plan, but it was not complete.

At the next injection time, Lopez was helping the cook, and they used Metrool's blood and a neck artery. They did not know if he would live or not, but there were major changes in his body, and he had vitals.

Metrool was planning how they would handle the situation if Talaron survived. They would have to bury an empty casket, and they would have to get Talaron out of the ranch and then bring him back.

As Metrool was talking to Mike, Mike told him what he had done to the plane. Metrool asked, "Can you fly someone to São Paulo?"

Mike said, "I would be glad to."

Metrool hesitated and then said, "No questions asked?"

Mike replied, "No questions asked."

Three hours later, when they used Everin's blood, Talaron looked normal, only much younger, and all his vitals were nearly normal. Three hours later, they were normal, and Talaron looked different. Metrool went ahead and gave him the injection and then reached into the glass case and turned the technostasis device off.

Metrool went through a tense three minutes, and then Talaron opened his eyes.

Talaron coughed a few times, tried to sit up, and said, "Water." They got him water and helped him sit up, and he looked around and said, "What am I doing in this thing?"

Everin said, "That is a long story."

Talaron, looking at Everin, said, "Who are you, pretty lady?"

Everin said, "That is another long story."

They got him out of the glass casket, and Metrool told Everin, "Hide him in your room for the moment." He then told Talaron, "Do not leave her room."

Talaron said, "Why should I hide? I own this place."

Everin pulled him to a large wall mirror.

Talaron grinned broadly and said, "Oh my God, it worked."

"Yes," Metrool said, "but you are not Talaron anymore; he died. We must get you off the ranch and bring you back as someone else. Since you look a lot like us, I will say you are my brother, but right now, stay out of sight."

Talaron could not stop grinning—he looked like a forty-five- to fifty-year-old earthling. They got him out of sight, and Metrool told Lopez to have workers dig a new grave in the garden, as they had decided to bury Talaron.

Lopez said, "That is a wise decision."

Soon Metrool saw six workers in the cemetery garden, busily digging the grave. Metrool asked Lopez and Carlos for a few things, and he used them to seal and wrap the glass casket. Lopez told Metrool that the grave was nearly ready, and Metrool asked him to call Sanchez, the priest, and the workers. An hour later, they were all there, and six of the workers carried the wrapped glass casket out to the garden cemetery.

The priest did a burial mass with the Eucharist. Then the workers lowered the casket into the grave. Everyone who was there passed by the lowered casket and tossed a symbolic handful of dirt into the grave. Some of the workers showed a lot of emotion. When the funeral was over and everyone had left, the six workers who had dug the grave filled it in and packed the ground. Metrool made sure he knew where everyone was and went to Everin's room.

There was Talaron, looking at himself in the mirror, saying, "I feel I have a couple hundred years left."

Metrool answered, "I believe you do."

Talaron said, "Oh, Metrool, how can a man thank you for giving him years and years of life?"

"It was not just me," Metrool said. "Four of us worked on it, and Everin was the key. She flew a Jenny from New York to this ranch to bring us the only creator on Earth. She started with four airplanes, and three of them fell out."

Talaron said, "It is amazing, and I will find a way to reward her."

Metrool said, "What we need to do right now is, in the middle of the night, when everyone is asleep, get you off the ranch. I will come for you. I will take you out to the plane, and you will get into the front cockpit and slump down. I will bring you a blanket. We do not want anyone to see you. At dawn, Mike and a mechanic will come to the plane. Mike will get into the rear cockpit, and the mechanic will spin the prop for him to start the engine. Mike will fly you to São Paulo, and Margaux will meet you at the airport. She will then take you to buy clothes and then to the Intercontinental Hotel, where I have already reserved a suite for you. After a week or so, you will come out to the ranch, and I will introduce you as my brother. Then we will work on turning the ranch over to my so-called brother."

Talaron asked, "You do not mind giving it back to me?"

Metrool said, "No, I am very wealthy. I do not need your ranch that you have lived on and worked on for two hundred years."

Talaron was looking at himself in the mirror again. "We Hamens do favor a lot."

"Yes, we do."

"All right, I will do exactly as you say."

Metrool now made one change. "At ten o'clock, everyone on the ranch is asleep. I will come get you and take you to my room to stay until four o'clock in the morning."

Talaron said, "All right, I understand. Your sister is an attractive female."

Metrool just shook his head and said, "I will see you at ten."

They carried a kerosene lamp as they went to Metrool's room at ten, seeing no one. They played cards and talked until four o'clock. They had never undressed, so Metrool just took a blanket off the bed, and they walked out of the hacienda and into the pasture.

Metrool helped Talaron climb into the front cockpit and said, "Slide down or hunker down; no one is to see you."

Talaron said, "Yes, I understand."

Seeing that Talaron was doing what he'd asked, Metrool walked back to the hacienda, waited until four forty-five, and then knocked on Mike's door.

Mike opened the door, still sleepy, and Metrool told him, "Go out now, start your engine and warm it up, and take off as soon as you can see. I do not want our passenger getting jumpy."

Mike said, "I understand. I will dress and go out now."

Metrool went outside the hacienda on the side where the plane was and, with his Hamen night vision, saw Mike and his helper walk out to the plane. After a few minutes, he heard the engine start up. It idled for about twenty minutes, and then Metrool saw Mike taxiing around to find the wind.

The engine roared, and after a short roll, the Jenny was in the air. Mike circled the ranch to check his plane, and then he was off to São

Paulo. Thirty minutes later, Mike was taxiing up to Margaux and her taxi. Margaux had not seen the new Talaron, and she was amazed at the difference. She took him to three different places to buy clothes and shoes. They kept the taxi waiting at each place, and then, with the car full of bags and boxes, they arrived at the hotel and arranged for staff to bring the purchases up to Talaron's suite.

At that time, Metrool and Carlos arrived in the Model T, and Metrool let Carlos go on. Margaux helped Talaron unwrap and unbox his new clothes and hang them up in his closets, and then she went to her own suite.

She told Metrool, "It is amazing he went from looking like he was one hundred fifty years old to forty or fifty years old."

"Yes," Metrool said, "it is amazing what this aggressive Hamen blood can do."

Thirty minutes later, there was a knock on their door. It was Talaron in a suit of his new clothes. He said, "Metrool, come walk around São Paulo with me. I want to be seen."

Metrool was not thrilled by the request but thought, *What harm would it do?* So for one and a half hours, Talaron and Metrool walked the streets of downtown São Paulo.

Back in Talaron's suite, Talaron poured wine and said, "I need a new name."

Metrool said, "For what you want to do, you have to have a new name and papers to match."

"How do I get those?"

"I can get you those, but you must come up with a suitable name."

They came up with twenty different ones, but none of them really clicked. They thought maybe Tom Laron. They brought Margaux into the discussion and told her the name Tom Cabral, and she suggested Álvares Cabral.

She said, "You know Pedro Álvares Cabral discovered Brazil; you would have a famous name."

Talaron said, "I think I would like that name."

Metrool said, "You'd better like it; you might be stuck with it for two hundred years." They all laughed.

Talaron said, "Yes, I like the name. Can you get official papers with that name?"

Metrool assured him that he could. He did not tell him that those papers and a history would be expensive.

Talaron said, "I want to go out at night to go places and be seen. Can you arrange it?"

Margaux said, "I will arrange that."

Metrool and Margaux went back to their own suite, and Metrool poured wine. Sipping it, Margaux said, "We have a problem."

Metrool asked her what it was.

"Alinda's father says she is well and should return home, and Henri does not want her to."

"Yes," Metrool said, "that is a problem. Have you talked to Henri?"

"I have talked and talked, but he is being stubborn."

"I will talk to him tomorrow. Maybe I can change his mind."

Later, they dined with Álvares and then went out on the town with him. Álvares loved it as if he were a teenager. He was good looking, obviously rich, and a flirt, and women seemed to love him.

When Metrool and Margaux came back to their suite, Alinda was there, crying.

Margaux asked her what was wrong, and crying and gasping, Alinda said, "My father jumped into the river and did not come out."

Metrool was shocked and felt there had to be more to it than that. Metrool went to Henri and asked him about it, and Henri told the same story, but Metrool, being Hamen, saw it was a lie. He secretly scanned Henri to get the truth, and he did and was shocked. He had to get away.

Metrool went down to the hotel bar and ordered a double whiskey on ice. How could Henri have done such a thing?

At that moment, someone said, "Order me one too." It was Álvares. He said, "I felt your vibrations; you are upset."

"Yes," Metrool said, "by something my stepson did."

"Tell me," Álvares said.

Metrool told him about the fight they'd had over the father beating the girl.

"You were justified," Álvares said.

"Yes," Metrool said, "but Henri kept threatening him with me and drove him to suicide."

"What will you do?"

"I will tell Margaux."

"No, you will not. It would destroy their relationship and serve no purpose. There is no evidence here that could be used in a court. You go to Henri, and tell him you are Hamen and you know what he did. If he never does anything like that again, you will not tell his mother. But if he does something else, you will have his Hamen mother scan him, and you cannot lie to a scan."

Metrool said, "You are right," and he ordered another round.

They talked about Hamen and sipped their drinks and then called it a night.

The next day, Metrool got Henri alone and said, "I know you were driven by trying to protect Alinda, but what you did was wrong. It was murder. You made him commit suicide."

Henri started to protest, and Metrool said, "If you do nothing else, I will not tell your mother; it will only hurt her. But if you do anything else, I will have her scan you." He saw that Henri wanted to ask him something but did not. Metrool read what it was and said, "Yes, I will make Alinda's small house safe for her."

For a week after that, Álvares was out on the town, showing off his new self and flaunting the new stylish clothes the French Margaux had picked for him. He was going by the name of Álvares Cabral, and he was having fun. He spent money, and the ladies liked him. They did not know he was 1,500 years old.

Ten days passed, and he was riding in a new Daimler that Metrool had bought. Álvares, Margaux, and Metrool were going out to the ranch. When they arrived at the ranch, Metrool introduced his brother Álvares Cabral to everyone, and he was accepted. Metrool noticed that both Lopez and Carlos acted a little strangely around Álvares. Metrool, through connections, had bought Álvares papers and a history. It was not long before Álvares began to press for the transfer of the ranch back to him.

Metrool contacted Sanchez and asked him and the lawyers to come to the ranch when possible. The next afternoon, they were there. When Sanchez found out what they wanted to do, he was aghast. He was loud and vocal and said no.

Metrool, Álvares, and Sanchez went into another room, and Álvares began telling Sanchez many things that only Talaron would have known. Sanchez went into shock, and Álvares told him, "I am Talaron."

Sanchez embraced him and began to cry. When he regained control, Sanchez looked at Metrool and said, "You and Margaux did this."

Metrool said, "Yes."

Sanchez said, "It seems like the devil's work, but I do not care. Thank you for giving us Talaron back."

After Sanchez found out Álvares was Talaron, he let him do whatever he wanted. The ranch was transferred to Álvares for a large sum of fictitious money. Quickly, Carlos and Lopez were brought into the charade, and engrams were put into their minds that no one else could have known. Mike basically knew, but he was part of the team.

Mike had a job now: to keep the Jenny in top shape, clean and shiny, and fly Álvares into São Paulo two to four times a week. Álvares was spending a lot of money for a large motor-driven generator for the ranch, and he was going to turn the pasture into an airport.

Álvares said, "I want to be able to fly to São Paulo to have a good time and then fly home."

Mike and Carlos were working on the details. Carlos had hired workers to add a shed onto the repair building, and they would run wires to the hacienda and the airstrip. It would have a row of lights on both sides, and workers were erecting a forty-foot tower with a rotating light to guide Mike to the ranch. Per Mike's request, the landing strip would have a lit sock. One of the mechanics was sent to a trade school in São Paulo to learn electricity.

Metrool was negotiating with the owners of the Beauty Ranch, and they were close to agreement. Margaux really liked it, and because it had a guesthouse, Henri liked it. Half of it was devoted to raising coffee, and that was new to Metrool. Margaux was thrilled that Álvares's hacienda was going to have electric lights. She told Metrool, "If we buy this ranch, there is no reason we cannot buy a generator and have electric lights."

Metrool had no reason to deny her, because he enjoyed the many benefits of electricity. Working with electricity had Metrool's interest, and he checked out the whole electricity situation around them.

São Paulo was powered by one company. Rio was powered by one company. That was the way it was—a lot of small companies. Metrool saw they all needed more financing. Which one needed it the most? Which one showed the most potential? The ones that were burning coal were burning Brazil's brown coal; the others were burning trees. They did not have enough resources for high-calorie coal to come in by ship.

Metrool went and talked to the head man of the company that powered São Paulo, and it seemed the company wanted his money but not his advice. He began to look for a solid company that wanted to build a hydroelectric dam. He found one, but several people had invested, and he could get secure bonds but at a low return.

They bought Beauty Ranch and started the process of taking it over and changing it to suit them. They drilled a new water well and dug a new sewage system far away from the hacienda. The ceramics company in São Paulo was making progress on the bathroom fixtures and asked Margaux if they could have the rights to market them. Margaux had gone to a company that made brass fittings and gotten them to make the valves for the kitchen and bathrooms.

Like Álvares, Metrool ordered a large diesel generator because Margaux wanted it and because Beauty Ranch had coffee sheds that needed to have lights. He was thinking of buying a dryer for the coffee, but what to buy: diesel, wood, or electric? All the workers were staying, and right now, several were working on the hacienda, painting, sawing, and hammering.

Metrool found out two of them worked full-time on planting, trimming, and watering. Mike wanted Margaux to build an airstrip like the one Álvares was making, and she was trying to talk Metrool into doing it.

Margaux said, "You are a pilot. Buy us a two-seater, and you can take us places like Rio."

So Metrool, in a pasture close to the hacienda, marked off a landing strip a hundred feet wide and a thousand feet long. He had a dozen workers search it for holes or rocks. Metrool thought he would fix it up just like Mike's.

31

STEAM YACHT

EVERIN WANTED TO GO BACK TO NEW YORK, BUT EVERY SHIP THAT WENT there went totally out of the way first. One day, when she was searching for a ship with a shorter route, she was told about a steam-powered yacht in the Port of Santos. She was told it had been sitting there for two weeks, so she decided to check it out. Margaux took her in the Daimler and stayed with her until the harbormaster sent her out to the yacht. When the captain welcomed her on board, Everin got a surprise. She did not know him, but she had seen him many times around functions in New York, and she had heard talk about him.

He was from an old New York family with a good name and money. Unfortunately, the money had run out. The captain's good name was Frank Eisely, and he had parlayed that good name into marrying an extraordinarily rich woman. He and Everin introduced themselves, and he told her he had seen her at functions as well.

After a good bit of small talk, she asked why he had been in the Port of Santos for two weeks. Frank was embarrassed and said, "Since we run in the same circles, I am sure you have heard the stories about me—that I'm a man with a good name but no money, and because of that, I was able to marry an extraordinarily rich woman."

Everin blushed and said, "Yes, I had heard that."

Frank laughed and said, "It is all true. The only part they left out is that my wife and I really care a lot about each other."

Everin smiled and said, "I am happy to hear that."

Frank said, "Now that I have that out of the way, I will answer your question. I, with her money, bought this yacht for us. Then I decided to take it around the world, and she did not want to leave New York for that long, but she said I could go. Well, just before I got to the port, a pressure-relief valve on the boiler stuck and ruined the boiler. She had sent a large amount of money with me, but buying a new boiler and having it installed absorbed all my money. She is a little tiffed at me, so she is taking her time in sending the money."

Everin asked, "Is your yacht in good shape now?"

Frank told her it was in excellent shape.

"How fast will she cruise?"

"Thirteen knots on a normal ocean."

Everin asked, "How much money would it cost you to steam to New York?"

Frank thought for a moment and then told her an amount. It did not seem a huge amount to Everin, so she said, "If I gave you that amount, would you take me to New York?"

Frank quickly replied, "You are damn right I would."

Everin asked, "When can we leave?"

"When could you give me the money? If you gave it to me tonight, we could leave tomorrow afternoon."

"I will have it for you tonight."

They shook hands on it, and Everin messaged Margaux: *Can you come back to the yacht to get me?*

Margaux answered, *Of course.*

When Margaux came back for her, Everin asked, "Can you go out to Hamen II with me?" Everin then messaged Metrool: *Where are you, and can you come to Hamen II?*

Metrool replied, *Yes, I am at Beauty, and I will come to Hamen II.*

While they drove, Everin told Margaux all about it. Everin said, "If things go right, I have a fast ship that leaves tomorrow."

After a while, everyone was at Hamen II: Metrool, Margaux, Everin, Álvares, and Mike. The mood was mixed, half party and half wake. They were happy Everin had found a way home, but they had enjoyed her company, so it was sad to see her leave. Even Lopez and Carlos had grown fond of her.

Margaux helped her pack her new clothes. Margaux and Metrool would be driving her to Santos, and then they would drive to the Intercontinental to spend the night. They all exchanged their goodbyes. Everin was taking her creator home with her; however, she had made a few things for Metrool that he could not buy, such as a new BWI and a VPR, which was an immensely powerful device.

The three arrived at the yacht, and all three went on board. Two crewmen carried Everin's things on board, and Metrool carried the creator. They took everything to her room and looked the yacht over. It was a steam yacht that still had two masts and sails for emergencies. They met Frank and his crew, and Frank and Metrool looked at everything on the boat. Then Everin gave Frank the amount he had asked for in one-thousand-dollar bills, and he gave her a receipt.

Margaux and Metrool left. The Daimler's dim lights and their Hamen night vision would get them to the Intercontinental. Frank thanked Everin again for getting him back out to sea, and he brought the crew of fourteen in to meet her before she went to her cabin.

The next morning, Everin took two crewmen into Santos to buy supplies, and they brought back several boxes of goods. Most of the crew were loading brown coal onto the yacht, and they wanted the bunkers to be totally full, because brown coal did not contain the calories of hard coal. At four in the afternoon, all was ready, and Everin messaged Metrool, Margaux, and Álvares to say the yacht was leaving the Port of Santos. Within two hours, they were in real ocean, and Frank had the yacht up to cruise speed.

The first part of the voyage would be up the eastern coast of South America to Caracas to top off their bunkers. Then they would cross the large Atlantic Ocean. All of a sudden, Everin got a strong message from Metrool: *Everin, have Frank be very careful. The Germans just sank a ship, the* Lusitania.

The voyage was long because the ship was slow, but on a freighter, it would have been twice as long. Every day at noon, Metrool would send Everin an update on the war. Every day at sundown, Everin would send one of the Hamens a short message to let them know she was all right.

Two days later, Metrool watched Mike land at the Beauty Ranch airstrip, and when Mike taxied close, Metrool walked over to the Jenny and climbed on board. Soon the motor roared, and the Jenny was climbing into the air. They flew to a ranch west of Rio, where they saw an English biplane sitting just off the runway. With the war in Europe winding down, a lot of surplus warplanes were coming up for sale. They landed, and soon Mike and Metrool were having a good conversation with the owner.

Mike checked the airplane and then climbed into it, and a ranch hand helped him start it. Mike taxied around the airstrip some and then lined up on the runway to take off. Mikes turned the power on, and the plane moved down the runway, but then Mike quickly shut it down. He taxied over to where Metrool and the owner were and stopped the engine. Mike climbed down out of it, came over to Metrool, and told him the engine was in bad shape.

The ranch owner became angry, insisted the plane had a good engine, and hollered for his pilot to show them it had a good motor. The ranch owner's pilot took it up, buzzed the airstrip, and then went into a climb with the engine at full power. The engine was running at maximum rpm, and the engine seized. The large propeller wanted to keep turning and tore the engine off the plane. Now the engineless airplane was tail-heavy and fell straight to the ground.

The ranch owner instantly sent people to rescue the pilot, but it was no use. There was not anything Mike or Metrool could say, so they climbed into the Jenny and soon were in the air.

As preplanned, they flew west in a zigzag pattern to cover more territory. It was not long until they saw the crash-landed Jenny. It looked as if it might be savable, and they looked the area over. They saw a road about two miles away. They turned south and flew to Beauty. After they landed, they talked about the poor dead pilot. Mike said, "I told them the engine was about to go. That was all I could do."

"I know," Metrool said. "You are good at what you do."

About the Jenny, Mike said, "We might be able to fly it out."

Metrool replied, "If not, we could salvage it for parts."

Mike said, "We could take horses and a sled." Mike then climbed into the Jenny, waved goodbye, and flew it to Hamen II.

Mike was doing a lot of flying with Álvares now that they had lights. Mike would fly Álvares to São Paulo, usually at dusk, and now, with the landing lights, it might be midnight when they flew back to the ranch.

Álvares got Margaux and Metrool a suite and invited them to come to São Paulo, where he threw a thank-you party for them. Only the three of them knew what the party was for. It was for bringing him back from near death. At the party, all three messaged Everin to thank her. It had been a long voyage back to New York.

Metrool was busy with his half ranch and half coffee plantation, and he was still investigating the evolving electric business. Since other things had settled down, Henri was again pushing for what he wanted. He wanted to be Hamen now, and he wanted to marry Alinda. In some ways, his marrying Alinda was not that big of a deal; she was a good girl. Margaux just did not want it right now.

The other was the real problem: Henri was demanding to be made into a Hamen. Even Álvares begged him to wait. For several months, the conflicts went on. Then, speaking to Margaux, Henri practically threatened to expose them as aliens. Afterward, there was more talk, fighting, and arguing over whether they were going to do it. Alinda did not know about it. It was driving Margaux crazy; she did not want to do it. But finally, they gave in.

With Henri lying on his back, they began. The first injection caused little reaction. The second injection four hours later caused violent reactions, and he had to be heavily restrained. The Hamens had all conferred, and Metrool, Margaux, Everin, Marie, and Álvares had agreed four injections four hours apart of four ccs would make him as Hamen as possible. With the third injection, his body was still reacting violently. Then it stopped, and his vital signs took a nosedive. They wanted to hold off on the next injection, but Henri demanded it. Then the fourth injection was done, and all that was left was to watch him. Several hours later, as Margaux was watching him, Henri sat up and said, "Margaux, I am all right; you do not have to watch me."

During the next few hours, she saw him testing himself to see what his abilities were. Margaux and Metrool both talked to him, and in looks and ways, he appeared to be like a thirty-five-year-old man. Henri went out onto the ranch, and after a few hours, Alinda came to Margaux and asked, "What did you do to him? He is so different. He is a different person; he would not even kiss me. He says he wants to go to Europe, and he looks fifteen years older. He aged fifteen years overnight. What did you do to him?"

Margaux could not answer her, so she went into the poor girl's mind and changed some things.

Henri came to Margaux and Metrool and told them, "I want to go to Europe. Will you finance me?"

Metrool said, "Of course. Are you going to a university?"

"No, I am going to join the air service. The Germans killed my father, and I am going to get a few of them."

Metrool saw that Henri was very Hamen now, so there was no point in trying to talk him out of it. Metrool said, "I will find a ship for you, and I will give you five thousand dollars in gold to open a bank account in France."

Henri thanked them, but Metrool and Margaux saw his emotions were cool.

Two weeks later, they were seeing him off on a steamer, and he was not any warmer. As Metrool drove the Daimler away from the Santos dock, Margaux cried, saying, "He is not my child anymore. Oh, Metrool, what did we do?"

Metrool answered, "My love, we did what he made us do. Henri figured out what you were and what I was, and he wanted it, asked for it, and demanded it."

Margaux said, "He is so different."

"Yes," Metrool said, "but he is also much the same."

Mike got his mission to salvage the crash-landed plane, with four large trucks and twelve workers. It took them four days to get there; they slept in the trucks and cooked over campfires. When Mike got to the Jenny, he saw a large snake on it. Three workers with axes took care of the writhing critter. Then they pulled two more regular-sized ones out of it. They found it had been damaged by the elements and other things, and all they could do was salvage parts. They got the Hispano engine, wheels, radiator, fuel tank, and control surfaces. Mike was disappointed, but at least that was something.

⟿⟾⊶⟽⟾

It took Henri two months to get to France, and two weeks after that, he messaged Metrool and told him he had been accepted for flight school. Metrool knew that would take three or four months, and he was glad, because the war was ending, and he did not want Henri to get killed. Margaux was in a despondent state that he could not get her out of. Normally, Hamens did not get despondent, but then again, Hamens did not normally give birth.

32

SPECIAL MARINE AIRCRAFT

BECAUSE OF HIS WORK WITH THE DIFFERENT AIRCRAFT MANUFACTURERS, Alerton was invited to join an aircraft company named Special Marine Aircraft. It had been started in 1913 and, at that time, had been called Special Aircraft Southampton. During World War I, they had built amphibian aircraft. After the war, they entered a contest for a large contract for amphibian aircraft and won, but they were having trouble making the aircraft perform to the government's demands. They had heard of Alerton's reputation, and two executives came to Arrista to talk to him. Alerton wasn't working at the time, but he was rich, so he did not have to work. Marie was a gracious host and invited the executives to dine with them. As they dined, it was obvious they enjoyed Alerton's taste in wine and the cook's beef Wellington.

Alerton told them he would accept their offer as an adviser. They accepted, and soon Alerton was spending time at their factory. Being Hamen, he found some of their problems obvious. When they were hesitant about making the needed changes, he closed his briefcase and told them to call him when they would use his expertise.

Two weeks later, the same two executives came to Arrista again and told him there had been some changes in management because they had to make improvements on the aircraft or lose the contract. Alerton told them he would be there the next day. Marie was a gracious lady and invited them to dine again, and they accepted.

The next day, Alerton went to the factory and handed them a folder of changes they needed to make. He then walked around the plant to see anything else he could help them with. They now took his advice seriously, and he only came to the plant one or two days a week. Within thirty days, the aircraft met the government's requirements, and Alerton knew it could be even better. Thirty days later, the aircraft exceeded the requirements by 15 percent, and Alerton dropped out.

Every year or two, the company would want to make a new aircraft, and he would rejoin them. He made several friends there. In 1930, they were building an aircraft for the Schneider Trophy race. They called it the S.6B. It was streamlined and sleek, and Alerton was proud of it. Some later said it looked like a fighter that was built later on.

⎯⎯⎯⎯⎯⎯⎯⎯⎯⎯

1930

Alerton messaged Metrool and told him, *I have been having a lot of trouble with your pharmaceutical company in Germany.*

Metrool asked, *What kind of trouble?*

Trouble of all kinds, but the most trouble is in getting and keeping people. You need to go to Germany, Metrool.

Metrool told him he would and contacted Mike. He asked Mike, "Can you acquire a good plane to take me to Germany?"

Mike said, "If you are willing to spend the money, I know of a nice Vega."

"What is its range?"

"With a light load, maybe eight hundred miles."

"Tell me about it."

"It is a real sturdy plane. The pilot sits up front, and there are six passenger seats behind him."

Metrool said, "Make a deal on it. Come by the ranch to get a check. Rip out five of those passenger seats and anything we do not need, and install the largest fuel tanks you can where those seats were."

Mike said, "It will take some time."

"Then let me know when it is finished."

Metrool got with Margaux and made sure everything was all right and secure. Twenty-three days later, Mike was landing the Vega in Munich.

The next morning, rested and refreshed, Metrool went to the main part of his company. After he proved who he was, he demanded records. He scanned them, but with his Hamen memory, it was not a scan. The president of the company came to the records department and said, "Mr. Metrool, you do not have to trouble yourself with these boring records."

Metrool laid down the file in his hand and said, "All right, let us go to your office."

In ten minutes, they were in the luxurious office. Without hesitation, Metrool asked, "Why can't you keep employees?"

The company president replied, "I think our turnover is about the same as other companies'."

Metrool got in the man's face and said loudly, "I did not ask you about other companies. Why does this good-paying company have a high turnover rate?"

The president sputtered and did not really answer him.

Metrool scanned him, and there it was. Metrool said, "You hire a lot of Jews."

The president haltingly said, "A lot of the people in pharma are Jews."

"That is perfectly all right. Why can't you keep them?"

The president did not want to answer him, and Metrool scanned him again. Metrool said, "Munich has a lot of Nazis, doesn't it?"

The president turned red but did not answer.

Metrool continued. "They do not like Jews, do they?"

The president croaked out, "No."

Metrool said, "You do not do much to protect them."

The president said, "What can I do?"

"You do not ask their religion. You purge all religious questions from your records. If Nazis come to ask questions, you make sure they have authority and are not just browsing. I want you to go down there and start this now, and it will be done before I leave Germany, or you will be out of a job."

The president was angered, but he went to start the changes. Metrool looked around the fancy office and found some excellent peppermint schnapps and poured a glass. This was terrible—people were being harassed and having their lives ruined because of their religion.

The president came back and said, "It is all started."

Metrool said, "Good. I will stay in Germany until it is finished. Does your personnel manager have authority?"

"Yes, full authority."

"Then fire him right now. He should have been on top of this."

Metrool could tell the president was angry, and he got in his face again. He said, "Pick up the phone, and call him, or do I fire you both right now?"

Struggling with his emotions, the president made the call.

Metrool said, "Now call security to send two guards to take him out. If I ever hear he has been inside any of our facilities, you are gone too."

The manager and the guards arrived at the same time, and the manager looked at Metrool and said, "Who are you?"

Metrool said, "The man who just fired you." He then turned to the guards and said, "Take him straight out—no stops." The manager was talking loudly as they pulled him out the door.

The president said, "Wasn't that a little drastic?"

Metrool said, "It was an example for you and everyone who works for the company."

That night, Metrool took Mike to an expensive cabaret that put on a good show. Using Hamen scanning, Metrool was able to see who was a Nazi, even if the person was not wearing a uniform. After that, they went to their hotel and their separate rooms. Metrool sat in a large chair and messaged Alerton and told him all that had happened. Alerton told him he had handled it well. Then Metrool took a shower and lay down for a good rest.

The next morning, Metrool ate breakfast at the hotel with Mike. He then left Mike at the hotel and went to meet some local Jewish leaders alone. They were skeptical of him, fearing he just wanted to learn information. Before the day was over, they had warmed to him, and he wrote a large check for their emergency fund to help people.

That night, Metrool and Mike went to an expensive German restaurant. It had been a good while since he had been to one. The next day, he went back to the main pharma factory. He first went to the records department, where there was a flurry of activity. He next went to personnel, and they were also busy with the records. It took personnel three days to finish, and it took the factory records department nine days. Metrool had an amicable meeting with the company president on the last day. Metrool reminded him, "Our employees are more than just a number."

Metrool did a light scan and was satisfied that the president had learned his lesson. Metrool went out to his waiting taxi and told the driver to go to the airport, where Mike and the Vega were waiting for him. Within an hour, Metrool was able to message Margaux and tell her, *My darling, I am on my way back to you.*

Forty-eight hours later, Mike was putting the Vega in its hangar. Mike took his plane out of the hangar, and it was warming up. Within an hour, Margaux was in his arms.

1931

Brazil was in turmoil. The American stock market had crashed on October 29, 1929, and that had depressed the price of commodities all over the world. Now Brazil had gone through a revolution. The whole country was upset. Metrool had made deals with different electric companies and had started the venture of building a hydroelectric dam in the wilderness.

Metrool hired Mike, and they flew over vast expanses of Brazil, looking for the perfect spot. They found one, and Metrool went back to São Paulo and started negotiating, but it did not work out. So he and Mike flew again. Finally, for the fourth place they found, he got approval from all the agencies and participants.

Because it was in a remote area, they had to create a major road with four bridges to be able to get their trucks and heavy equipment to the dam sight. The project was burdened by its location, the weather, and the heat, as well as the flies, mosquitoes, snakes, and animals.

One early morning, Metrool got up off his cot and pulled on his damp clothes and boots. He opened the flap of his tent; it was beginning to get light. He walked over to the mess tent and poured coffee. Several supervisors of different crews arrived, trying to get their work started before it got hotter. One of them came to him and said, "One of our temporary bridges fell with a cement truck on it."

"Well, get whoever and whatever you need; we must have the road," Metrool said.

The road was a dirt-and-gravel road they had created through the wilderness. It was new and was large and rough. There were four temporary bridges, and one of them had just failed. They had to get it repaired; between fifty and a hundred trucks used that road every day. There were a thousand workers living in tents and working seven days a week. Everything they needed came down that road. There was no refrigeration, so food for the cooks had to come every day. Metrool went to the food line and got the same basic food everyone got. It was not gourmet, but it had protein and calories to keep the people going.

They had been on-site for a year at a wilderness place on the river. They had to clear the vegetation and burn it and find a place nearby for a quarry to supply rock. Metrool had the crew clear a large, flat place for an airstrip; he had bought a plane for the company, and occasionally, Mike would come get him and fly him to Beauty Ranch for two days.

One of the supervisors came to him and told him it would be more than a week before they could get pontoons for the failed bridge. Metrool said, "Well, tell the cook shack about it, and have them cut back, or there will be some hungry people around here."

Metrool went to his planning table in the office tent, and as he looked at the plans, he got an idea.

He messaged Margaux, and after greeting her and telling her how much he missed her, he said, *I need you to see if Mike can bring me fifty pounds of eggs, twenty-five pounds of dry beans, twenty-five pounds of rice, and a hundred pounds of meat every day for a week.*

Margaux said, *I will asked him. What is this about?*

You know the road we had so much trouble building?

Yes.

Well, one of the temporary bridges collapsed, and it will take at least a week for them to repair it, and I have a thousand people to feed.

I am sure Mike will do it. This project is important to the country.

Well, the country is kind of mixed up right now.

Then Metrool went to see Raymon and asked, "Can you rig a boat as a ferry for some stuff, using the flowing water to push it back and forth?"

Raymon said, "Yes, I think I can. Refresh me on how that works."

Metrool took a large sheet of paper and drew him a sketch of how a water-powered ferry worked.

Next, Metrool went to the quarry site. They should have had a conveyor to take the rocks to the dam, but they had to use trucks. Metrool went to Montez, who oversaw that operation, and asked him, "Can you run for a week with no supplies?"

Montez replied, "Five days, yes. After that, I do not know."

They were already over budget, and every problem pushed them more over budget. Metrool was not doing this for money; he had grown fond of the hardworking Brazilians, and they needed this dam. They were having to burn trees to make electricity.

Metrool went to the dam site, where they had built a cofferdam to divert the river while they built the real dam. The dam site was working all right, but their three cranes were being pushed to the limit. Metrool walked back to the tent city, and two people hollered, "Go to *medico*!" He walked faster and went into the large medical tent. There was a worker lying on a cot with eyes closed, shaking.

Metrool pulled the doctor off to one side and whispered, "What is it?"

The doctor calmly said, "Snakebite. He is dying. It happens about every few days."

Metrool said, "Can we not do anything about it?"

The doctor said, "We came into their territory. We kill what we find, but we are surrounded by swamp, jungle, and morass."

Metrool left the medical tent, disgusted. It was not supposed to be this way. Margaux messaged him and said, *Mike said he will be there about three o'clock in the afternoon.*

Metrool thanked her and told her he loved her. He then went to Winston, an English hydroelectric engineer who oversaw the gates and power plant. Metrool had scanned him once when he doubted him and found he had the same attitude about the dam and the people as Metrool did. After that, they had become good friends. Metrool told him about the snakebite victim. Winston said, "Yes, we have lost three men here at the dam site."

At Beauty Ranch, Juan, the foreman over the cattle part of the ranch, came to Margaux. She had an open-door policy with both foremen. Margaux saw Juan was upset, but rather than scanning him, she preferred for him to tell her what was wrong. Juan said, "The men are talking about leaving."

"Why?" Margaux asked. "Do they not like it here?"

"Yes, they like it here very much, but the hands at the Black Bull have worked a year without pay, and with your husband having to work at another job, they feel you may not be able to pay them."

Margaux said, "First, my husband does not have to work on another job. I am insulted that they think that. He took this job to build this dam for the benefit of the Brazilian people. As for your men, if they promise not to take the money and run, I will pay them six months in advance."

Juan apologized if he had offended her and told her he was sure his men would be happy with what she had offered. Of course, she had to give the coffee workers the same offer, and amazingly, in the next few months, only one took the money and ran.

Margaux was lonely without Metrool. She loved him so much that when he was gone, she felt part of her was gone. Margaux had plenty to keep her busy, and Mike and Álvares both came to see her. On one special day, they flew in a new shiny airplane that Álvares had bought. Álvares was getting serious about a woman. She appeared to like him a lot, but she did not know he was 1,500 years old.

———⟫●⟪———

Two years later

Metrool was a happy man standing there with his beautiful, loving wife, watching the water flow through the dam to make electricity. They had officially turned it on that day, and Metrool was leaving it that day and never coming back. It had been a worthy cause but a dark three years. The further the project got along, the more time Metrool could take away from it to be with Margaux, but it put a lot of wear and tear on Metrool. Margaux was still hurt that Henri seldom communicated with her, and if he did, it was usually to ask for money.

———⟫●⟪———

1935

For the last two years, Metrool's sources in Germany had been sending him troubling information, but now it was critical. Hitler had been appointed chancellor on January 30, 1933, and the lives of Jews had gotten worse. On November 15, 1935, Hitler had revoked the citizenship of all Jews in Germany. Metrool's spies were telling him to get out of Germany. Metrool consulted the other Hamens about where they should go. America came up, and Álvares said they could come to Brazil. Both were good ideas, but some of his spies suggested Israel. Metrool had people check Israel out, and based on what they found out, he started building a pharmaceutical plant in Tel Aviv.

Metrool and Mike went to Munich again. This time, when they arrived, they were put through a hassle at the airport, and there was a limit on how long they could stay. Talking to the local Jews, Metrool learned the best way to contact Jewish workers in his plants. He used the local rabbis and leaders to contact Jewish pharma workers.

Word of mouth spread the message to others. Metrool gave the rabbis maps and instructions and let them know it could mean death if the Nazis saw those papers. Metrool gave the rabbis a large sum with instructions to use it to help Jews escape Germany. Metrool waited until Mike had them totally clear of Germany before he told him their new destination: Tel Aviv.

Mike was surprised but not dismayed. Mike said, "Hold the yoke so I can look at my charts."

They flew out of Germany into France and then turned east and flew into Italy. They landed at Amerigo Vespucci Airport in one of Metrool's favorite cities, Florence. Mike got the Vega taken care of, and Metrool took him into Florence in a taxi. Metrool had the taxi driver go to all the famous sites, for Mike had never been to Florence.

Then the driver took them to a famous hotel right beside the Arno and close to the Ponte Vecchio. After securing two rooms, Metrool went into the city. They picked a good restaurant and had an excellent Italian meal. They circled the Duomo and, a little later, went back to their hotel. They had to fly the next morning.

The next morning, after a hotel breakfast and a taxi ride to the airport, they fueled and checked the Vega and soon were climbing into the air.

They refueled in Athens and flew on. Then came a fuel stop at Antalya, Turkey. It was nearly dark when they landed in Tel Aviv. Mike went through the airplane regulations, and then Metrool got them a taxi to take them to a hotel. It was a nice one right on the ocean. They ate at a kosher restaurant there in the hotel and then turned in for the night.

The next morning, they looked for and found a restaurant that had American breakfast. Metrool used the hotel phone to call his scouts, Moshe and Yigael, and they told him they would pick them up at eleven.

The scouts were on time, and Metrool and Mike got into the vehicle with Moshe and Yigael. They had been telling him about properties that were available, and now they took him to them. As they did, Metrool inquired about prices and restrictions.

Yigael said, "You know, of course, number one is Shabbat."

Metrool said, "Of course."

They spent that day and the next looking at property and talking to agents. Metrool did not learn until much later that these men were not land agents. They were members of an Israeli organization, and they were checking him out to see if he was real. When they were through on the second day, Moshe took Metrool to one side and told him, "Before you invest a lot in this venture, I want to point out that you are assuming Jewish pharma people will be coming here from Germany."

Metrool said, "Yes, I am."

"Well, you should be aware that a lot of people do not want them to come here."

"Who?"

"The English authorities do not want them here, a lot of the locals do not want them here, and the surrounding Muslim countries surely do not want them to come."

They talked for a few more minutes, and it only made Metrool more determined to build his pharma factory there in Tel Aviv.

The next day, he met with the owners of a large parcel of land. They knew he was wealthy and at first tried to offer him an unfair price. Metrool sent a dark message through their minds: *You are going to lose this sale unless you offer him a bargain.* They offered him a good price, and he bought it. Metrool knew some of his pharma management people had already fled to Israel, and he looked them up and picked three of them to work with the engineering firm he had chosen to build his factory.

After working with those three and a team of engineers for two weeks, he chose Izak Abramson of the three to be the plant manager, and the three would oversee everything, including the building of the plant and the hiring of personnel. Metrool wanted to get back to Margaux and his home.

The next morning, after Mike checked the Vega over, they took off and headed west.

They still had fuel when they flew over Benghazi, so they flew on and landed at Tripoli. Then they flew on to Casablanca. They spent the night there and went to a nightclub run by a man named Rick. He told Metrool they were talking about making a movie at that location.

The next morning, they were in the air again, flying southwest along the west coast of Africa. They refueled in Monrovia and turned west. They flew across the narrow part of the Atlantic and landed at Recife. It was getting dark, but they knew São Paulo's airport had lights, so they flew on. When they landed, Mike parked the Vega, got his plane out of the Vega's hangar, and flew Metrool to Margaux's arms at Beauty Ranch.

In the coming months, Metrool became involved with what he had started, even though he stayed in Brazil. He had agents in Germany helping people escape. He also had agents in Israel helping immigrants avoid the authorities. Metrool did not feel guilty about it, because he felt it was a good cause. This project went on year after year.

<hr />

January 1940

Metrool kept hearing of the coming war in Europe, and he was getting restless. Margaux, after twenty years of running a ranch, admitted she missed France. São Paulo had restaurants and nightlife, but it was not Paris. Metrool got word that the Royal Air Force needed fighter pilots badly— so badly they were accepting them from Poland and other countries. Metrool's old Hamen jousting complex came on. It was part of the hidden memory the Controller and his people had initiated after deciding some things should not be available to Hamens. They put the secret ability in the restricted information banks.

In Florence, Metrool and Alerton had been expert swordsmen, even though they had never touched a sword until they came to Earth. Doc, a peaceful man after he became Hamen, once had been attacked by a ruffian with a sword, and when a bystander had handed Doc his sword, those hidden memories had come out, and Doc had become a swordsman and killed the ruffian. Hamens all had fighter-type devices. Metrool knew they had them; he had pondered it a lot. From the first time he'd gotten into a fighter plane, he'd known it. Everything was natural to him. Metrool knew he was better in it than he should have been. There had been times in World War I dogfights when he would do something he had never done before, and it would seem as if he had done it many times before.

Metrool thought about wonderful Arrista, the voyage historian. The Controller had sent his personal envoy to tell her that the peace mission to Earth 1,900 years ago was a myth and had not happened. They'd warned her not to look for it anymore. If it had not happened, what could she possibly have found out?

<hr/>

February 1940

Metrool said, "I think it would be best if we went to England."

Margaux replied, "What about your trouble there?"

"Alerton and the lawyers cleared that up a long time ago. We will go in with different passports and be different people. They would expect us to be old-looking people, and we look the same as we did when we left. I want to be around Alerton and Marie. We have only had their company four times in the last twenty-two years. Because we do not appear to change, we would have to leave here in eight to ten years."

"I know," Margaux said. "I have already had women friends ask me if I dye my hair to cover the gray."

A few days later, Beauty Ranch was put on the market, and because it was deluxe and made a good profit, it sold quickly. After that, they spent two weeks packing what they wanted to ship. They had a lot of things to give away. Metrool talked to Mike about their Twin Beech. Mike had gone to Wichita, Kansas, to take training and deliver it to them in 1939. Metrool asked Mike, "Do you think Álvares would want to buy the *Beauty Bird*?"

Mike said, "Oh, I am sure he would; he has said many times he wishes he had one just like it."

"All right, if he buys it, you will fly us to New York."

"Great. I bet Álvares will go with us, and he and I will spend some time in New York."

Six days later, the Twin Beech was landing in New York City, and Mike had been right: Álvares was with them. Metrool and Margaux were going to the Waldorf Hotel, and Mike and Álvares were to meet them there that night. Mike and Álvares came to the hotel at eight o'clock, and the four went out into the New York nightlife. Later, they said their goodbyes. Metrool and Margaux would board the *Queen Mary* the next day to go to England.

Sailing on the *Queen Mary* was vastly different from sailing on the *Brazilian Star*. It was a pleasant crossing. When they got to Southampton, the ship had already arranged for a private compartment on the train to London. When they arrived in London, Marie and Alerton met them in Alerton's new Rolls. They went to Arrista and spent hours catching up. They talked about Metrool joining the RAF, and then Metrool got a surprise: Marie, with fake papers, had joined the American WASP. She would be leaving for America in a few days. Marie asked Margaux if she would live at Arrista and take care of it for her.

The next few days were a jumble of things, with Marie getting ready to go, Metrool joining the RAF, and Alerton telling Metrool all he knew about the new German planes. Then they were seeing Marie off. To Margaux, it seemed sad because Marie and Alerton were so happy together.

With Marie gone on her quest, Alerton jumped on Metrool. "Why do you want to join the RAF?"

Metrool answered, "I am a fighter pilot."

"That was World War I. A long time ago."

"I am Hamen—that was like yesterday. If something does happen to me, just take care of Margaux."

In Brazil, Margaux had tried to discourage him, but he had told her, "It is something in my Hamen blood."

Margaux had said, "Yes, I know, and if you promise to come home to me, go do it."

Alerton got him the proper papers, and the RAF thought he was a Polish ex-pilot. Metrool had lived in Poland for twenty-three years, so the language, maybe a little archaic on his part, was not a problem. In a few days, he showed up at the base named in his papers. Now they would check him out to see if he could live up to his credentials. A two-seat trainer sat there, and the tester said, "I will be talking to you over the earphones. I want you to do what I tell you and only that. Do not try to impress me."

Metrool recognized the trainer was right and only trying to stay safe. They climbed into the trainer, and for the next two boring hours, Metrool performed every standard move the tester told him to do. After they landed and climbed out of the trainer, the tester said simply, "Tomorrow I will see if you can fly a fighter."

Metrool had bought an English Ford, and as he drove it to Arrista, he felt as if he were floating. Margaux, with hugs and kisses, showed she was happy for him. When Alerton arrived at Arrista, Metrool convinced him to go out with them to celebrate. After some hesitation, Alerton said, "Yes, but only if we take my chauffeur and Rolls, not your Ford."

The next morning, Metrool arrived at the hangar thirty minutes early and carefully went over the planes outside. They were beautiful; they had twelve-cylinder Rolls-Royce Merlin engines, elliptical wings, and Perspex canopies and were wonderfully streamlined. An hour later, Metrool was climbing into one and looking at all the instruments—no more spinning the prop to start the engine. The crew chief gave him the OK to start signal, and Metrool closed the switch. The sky appeared to turn when the large prop turned. It started with smoke and a rumble; it was a beautiful sound.

The plane ran on the new aviation gas that had been developed in America, which gave them more horsepower. A hundred feet away, another plane just like his was starting up—that was his tester. The tester called him on the radio to make sure they could communicate. After the planes were checked out and warmed up, they took off. When they reached ten thousand feet, they headed east, with the tester flying along like a wingman. When they got to the test area, the evaluation started. The tester told Metrool to do several things, and he did them.

Then the tester said, "Get on my tail, and try to stay on it." The tester went through many evasive maneuvers, but Metrool was able to stay with him. Next, the tester got on his tail, but Metrool was able to lose him. The tester asked him to do it again, and Metrool lost him again.

They flew back to the base, and after they landed, the tester said, "I am not sure about your history you gave us, but you have flown a lot somewhere. By the way, you passed. And one more thing. I know you have been told this, but it is important. Your plane will have twenty-four hundred rounds, but they only last fifteen seconds. Use them wisely; you are useless if you are out of ammo."

⟶⟶⟶⟶⟶⟶

July 10, 1940

Two days later, Metrool found out which squadron he was being assigned to: Squadron 303 at Northolt. He was disappointed; it was equipped with Hurricanes. The Hurricane was a great airplane, but it was not as streamlined as the Spitfire. Both had their strong points: the Spitfire was faster, but the Hurricane could take more punishment. Metrool reported to his Polish squadron and soon found out that several of them were highly agitated in light of the childish tricycle training and the mandatory English classes. The Poles wanted to fly and kill Germans. They were not permitted to get into the fight yet.

Metrool went through the training just like the real Poles, and because he had lived there for twenty-three years, he was fluent in their language and could talk to them about places and customs, so they accepted him completely. He was one of them; he ate with them, trained with them, and talked to them. The Poles were angry: the Germans had attacked their country and, with the Russians, conquered it. Many of their pilots and soldiers had escaped; had gone first to France to fight the Germans; and, when it had fallen, had escaped to England. The Polish pilots wanted a chance to get even. Their desire to fight was not just patriotic; it was visceral. They would get angry and red-faced just in talking about the Germans.

Part of their training was to learn all about the Germans' Me-109E, including what it did well and what it did not. The instructor said, "Fight your fight, not his. He is faster than you, but you can outturn him. He is short on fuel; he cannot do an extended dogfight and get back to France, so believe me, he is constantly looking at his fuel gauges. When he goes into a tight turn, his automatic slats extend; that slows him down some. If only one extends, it makes him roll. You are lucky with the Hurricane: it will not do a high-speed stall in a turn, no matter how hard you pull back on the stick. Remember, his MB-601 engine has fuel injection; it will run upside down. Your Merlin has a carburetor and will not."

Finally, they were cleared to get into the fight, and some of the Poles amazed him. Some would dive into a bomber formation, get dangerously close to a bomber before they fired, and pump a lot of rounds into it before they broke away. They were not just shooting airplanes; they were shooting Germans. They had that drive because of what had happened to their country. They ate and slept close to their planes.

One day the alarm sounded, they ran to their planes, the Packard-built Merlin engines were started, and they watched their gauges and soon headed for the runway. England's secret radar told them where the RAF thought the Germans were. It turned out they were right, and soon they were diving into the German formation of fighters and bombers. The Me-109s had to fly at the bomber's speed, which made them sluggish in performance. Metrool picked out a bomber and dived on it, and when he got close, he fired his guns two or three seconds into the left engine. The left wing was immediately on fire, and the bomber fell out of formation. It would not get back to France.

Metrool started to line up on another bomber, and a Hurricane appeared awfully close to it and appeared to fire five or six seconds into the fuselage. The bomber came apart with fire, debris, and a possible explosion. It was gone.

As Metrool went for another target, bullets zipped past him. Bringing his Hamen senses to full alert, he could sense the 109's position. He knew it had attacked him from above. Metrool did a diving turn as tightly as he could. The 109 continued his dive, and with a gut-wrenching climbing turn, now Metrool was behind him. The German had made an error; maybe he was looking for another target. Metrool had him in his sights; he lined up on the left wing and fired his guns two or three seconds. The wing folded up, and Metrool saw the 109 start to do rolls as it fell. Metrool was glad to see the pilot was able to bail out.

Another 109 crossed in front of Metrool, probably six hundred yards away. Metrool turned hard and went after him. The pilot of the 109 must have seen him and gone to full power, because he pulled away from Metrool's slower Hurricane. To do that, he was burning a lot of fuel, so he might not make it back to his base, Metrool knew.

Air raids and dogfights happened every day. Every day there were heavy losses on both sides. Part of surviving was luck, but most of it was skill. Some of the pilots were just damn good. Flight Sergeant Urbanowicz shot down four bombers in one day.

The losses saddened and angered the Polish pilots; they were a close group and felt the losses deeply. One pilot, Josef Frantisek, shot down seventeen German planes before he was shot down. The Hurricane was a workhorse. It could land at the base out of ammo and out of fuel and be refilled with both in ten minutes. With a Spitfire, that time was twenty-five minutes. The Hurricane could take a lot of punishment and still get one back to base.

Then the Germans changed their plans and their attacks, and the Battle of Britain was over. Metrool withdrew from the RAF and relaxed at Arrista with Margaux.

One day Metrool felt Everin messaging him. She had subleased her wonderful New York apartment overlooking Central Park and moved to Washington, DC. She wanted to get into the power circle so she could really make a difference. She had admitted to Alerton that she had used her Hamen mental power a lot to make connections with generals, admirals, industry leaders, and, most of all, Eleanor and her circle of about twenty women, wives of senators and congressmen. She told Metrool, *Claire Chennault is forming a fighter group.*

That was all she needed to say. Metrool knew him from way back. Claire had had one of the first precision flying teams ever. Later, Claire and his two wingmen had toured the country, wowing the crowds. In 1932, his group had been called Three Men on a Flying Trapeze.

33

MINGALADON, BURMA

December 1941

BURMA WAS HOT AND HUMID AND HAD MANY BUGS. THEY HAD TO tolerate the general's grade school for fighter pilots. If they wanted to be in the general's AVG, they had to learn every vital part of a Zero and where it was located. They had to learn what a Zero did well and what it did not. There were mock dogfights, with two P-40s playing as if they were trying to shoot each other down. Unfortunately, one made a mistake, and it took both down. Then it was not playing anymore, and the mood in the camp was terrible. Both those men had been liked and respected by everyone. This was not a regular army, and his buddies found six or seven versions of homemade alcohol. Metrool had learned from his artist friends in Florence that sometimes alcohol was the answer.

The general stayed out of sight for two days. Then he gathered everyone together for a talk. "All right," he said, "now it is time to put the alcohol away. This has been a wake-up call; this is a deadly business. If the Japanese do not kill you, then the weather or the P-40 may try. I know most of you will survive this but not all. Fate is fickle. I have seen some damn good pilots, better than me, crash and burn. Gentlemen, in three days, we go to Kunming, China."

Metrool was lucky he had friends who were well connected. Although Metrool was an exceptionally good pilot, those friends and fake papers had gotten him into a Spitfire squadron in Britain, where he had gotten a large number of confirmed kills. A certain widow, Mrs. Dante—Everin—had made friends with Eleanor Roosevelt and had gotten him the fake papers for his quest. Ever since World War I, Metrool had looked upon aerial combat as a form of medieval jousting.

Sixteen days later, Metrool was on the alert crew, and he heard the moaning sound of the hand-cranked air-raid siren. Metrool ran to his P-40 and climbed into his parachute. Then he climbed into the cockpit and tried to hurry the chief. But the chief would not be hurried. More than once, the chief had said, "The general has strict rules about start-up, and he is right. I do not want you to get killed trying to take off in a sick bird."

The engine roared, and the twelve-exhaust was like music to his ears. Metrool saluted his crew and pulled out into the line of P-40s. After a fast takeoff roll, they were climbing up to meet the Japanese. In minutes, Metrool was in a melee of twisting, turning aircraft. Tracers flashed by Metrool's canopy. *Damn, I have one on my tail.* Metrool used every move he had ever been taught, but he could not get rid of his pursuer. He felt bullets hit his plane. Suddenly, Metrool dropped his engine to idle, lowered the flaps, and fired a long burst with his machine guns. The Zero flashed past, and Metrool had already reversed those actions and now was on the Zero's tail. He lined up a perfect shot and fired. After a few rounds, the guns were dead. He hollered, "No! Damn it, no!"

Automatically, Metrool did a full-power scan, and he found the Zero's pilot. Metrool sent hard left ailerons until the Zero crashed into a hillside. After a moment of elation, Metrool felt bad. That was not the way he was supposed to win a joust. Next time, he would have to be better.

A few days later, he got another chance. He paired off with a Zero, and the fight was on, with twists, turns, zooms, and dives. Metrool fired a few shots but could not get a good, clear shot. However, the Zero had slowed, though it was still trying to maneuver. Maybe one of his bullets had hit something vital, he thought. Metrool could not just fly away; he put the left wing in his sights and fired a short burst. He saw bullets hit the wing, but the Zero kept flying. He lined up on the right wing, thinking, *Why doesn't he bail out?* Metrool fired a short burst, and suddenly, the Zero was a fireball. With both hands on the stick, Metrool pulled hard to avoid the flaming wreckage. Once clear, Metrool looked around, and there was no other aircraft in sight, so he flew back to the base. On the way back, he kept asking himself, *Why did he not bail out?*

Back at the base, there was gloom. They had two pilots confirmed dead. Lieutenant Bond spoke up and said, "It was that bastard with the yellow spinner; he is damn good."

Over the next few days, Metrool trained himself to be better and better with the P-40. He told himself, *It is not cheating to use my Hamen abilities to save my friends.*

One day they received warning that Japanese bombers were headed for Kunming. Metrool ran to his plane and again had to go through the tedious process of getting it ready. Although he griped about it, he admired the chief and was thankful for having him. Soon he was in the air, and his engine roared as he climbed to meet the enemy. Metrool was leading the flight that day, and he took them high. They did two holding circles, and then they saw them: six bombers and six Zeros escorting them. Yellow Spinner was daring them to attack his flight.

Metrool, leading the flight, brought them as high as he could so they could make a fast-diving attack. He gave his flight the signal and nosed his P-40 over into a dive. He chose the bomber being escorted by Yellow Spinner and fired a long burst into its right engine and wing. The whole right wing erupted in flames, and the bomber fell out of the sky. As Metrool dived past Yellow Spinner, he knew he would be angry as hell and on his ass. Metrool went full power and began to maneuver.

Over the last week, he had experimented with how much of his Hamen strength he could use without damaging the controls. Now he had a better chance, but this pilot was damn good. *Hey, a clear shot.* His guns barked, but Yellow twisted away. The gut-wrenching twisting and turning went on, and then another clear shot opened up, and he fired. Metrool could see bullets hitting the Zero, but tracers were zipping past him. He saw Yellow Spinner flame big, but bullets were striking Metrool's aircraft. One hit him. He had heard many stories about Japanese strafing, so he got as low as he dared before he bailed out.

On the ground, he used his knife to make a waist bandage out of his parachute. He saw that a flaming bullet had passed through his left side. Because he was Hamen, he was able to run three miles to get away from the crash site. Then he collapsed among some bamboo. Finally, after he got his head together, he messaged Margaux and told her he was all right.

———————

A day and a half later, Metrool made it back to base. They had presumed him dead, and now they sent him back to the world to heal. While on his journey back to the world, he got a message from a seven-hundred-year-old man in England: *We need you here.*

Within two weeks, Metrool was in England, and the first thing he did was go to Arrista to surprise his lovely wife.

After many hugs and kisses, she asked, "Are you through with sky-fighting?"

Metrool said, "Yes, I am finished."

Margaux practically jumped up and down and said, "Oh, darling, let it be over! Every night, I prayed for you. I was so afraid I would lose you."

The next day, Metrool looked up the seven-hundred-year-old gentleman, who was living in a London flat because of his intelligence job. Metrool was surprised to find him uptight and asked, "What is wrong?"

Alerton said, "Marie is flying a B-24 across America, and she just lost an engine."

"Yes," Metrool said, "she joined the American WASP."

"Yes," Alerton said, "she flies military aircraft all over the country."

They continued to converse as they walked on a London sidewalk.

34

PROBLEM WITH HENRI

THERE WAS A PROBLEM WITH HENRI, METROOL'S STEPCHILD. METROOL asked, "What has he done now?"

Alerton said, "Normally, he will not let me scan him, but two weeks ago, he got drunk, and his guard was down."

"What did you find out?"

"With his scanning ability, he has become a Jew hunter and is selling them to the Germans."

"I will go stop him," Metrool said.

Just then, someone in a passing taxi fired six shots at them. Only their Hamen reflexes allowed them to be missed.

Alerton said, "Well, they know who I am now. I will have to leave soon."

The next day, Metrool left for Lisbon to make his way to France. Two days later, Metrool messaged Alerton to let him know that he had arrived and found Henri, and everything was all right.

The next day, Metrool messaged Alerton and said, *I was wrong. Henri is a demon. He can give you a false scan. I have been arrested by the Gestapo; I do not know if I can escape.*

Alerton was revolted at the thought of Henri turning his own father in. Alerton got into his secret place and got out pounds, francs, gold, and a vaporizer. In an hour, he was flying to Lisbon; he then boarded a train to occupied France. He boarded another train that would take him to Paris. Even though he had particularly good papers and was a tall,

German-looking man, he still had to use some mental persuasion. Once in Paris, he first had to neutralize Henri. Alerton scanned for more than an hour before he found him. He was in an expensive cabaret with some Gestapo buddies. Alerton waited until he left the cabaret and then followed him to his apartment.

Scanning it from outside, Alerton was surprised that someone else was there. Alerton scanned the person: it was a woman—a scared-to-death woman. She was educated and beautiful and was his slave because she was a Jew. Alerton was as angry as he had ever been. He messaged Henri to come outside.

Henri came outside with a Luger in his hand and fired four shots as he came out the door. Alerton dodged the bullets and, after hesitating for only a second, hit Henri with the vaporizer. It was set to low power, which was its most painful setting. Henri was on the ground, moaning, twisting, and sometimes screaming. Alerton scanned the apartments, and no one was looking out; they knew better.

Henri said, "I do not know what you did, but something is eating me. Finish me off."

Alerton said, "Why should I? You are turning innocent people in to be tortured and killed."

Henri said some terrible things, trying to get Alerton to finish him off. Alerton asked him, "Why were you doing this? We gave you all the funds you ever asked for."

Henri replied, "These people are right, and I want to be one of them."

Alerton went inside and found the woman, Helga, to be totally messed up. He put her in a trance with instructions and placed the vaporizer in her hand. She walked outside, and with Henri screaming dirty words at her, she pointed the vaporizer at him, and he quickly turned to gas and disappeared.

Alerton retrieved the VPR, took the woman inside, and did a lot of mind cleaning. He thought, *I should not worry about her; she may get us caught.* But then he used Henri's phone to call a contact and took her to him. He told him, "Keep her until I come back, and make her some good papers."

Alerton went to his real job. He had brought new papers for Metrool, but he gave them to Krueger and said, "Make another set for him." Krueger was an artist—an expensive one. He could make any kind of papers.

Alerton took two different taxis and got out of the second one four blocks from the Lutetia Hotel. When the Germans had taken over Paris, the Gestapo had taken over this classy hotel. Now the Gestapo were using the basement to hold people. Metrool's looks had probably saved him so far; he looked like an Aryan poster. Also, it was obvious he was English.

Alerton messaged Metrool: *Why haven't you tried to escape?*

I did not want to get Henri in trouble.

Alerton said, *Do not worry; you will not. It is three thirty in the morning; there should not be many people on duty.*

Soon, using scanning and their mental powers, Metrool was in the new clothes Alerton had brought for him and able to walk out. Again, Alerton used two different taxis to get to Krueger's. Krueger changed his location often. Four top-level Gestapo who were not Hitler believers were also his clients. They used his services to buy property and to deposit money in other countries.

Alerton went to Helga, the woman he'd saved. He had erased a lot of memories, and now he erased a lot more.

She looked at Alerton and said, "My God, who are you? What are you? What have you done to me? I cannot remember anything of the last year."

Alerton said, "I am a psychiatrist, like Herr Freud. You had an awfully bad year. A bad person found out you were a Jew and made your life hell. If you want, Metrool and I will help you get to Lisbon."

She said, "Oh, that would be wonderful, but isn't it dangerous?"

Alerton said, "Yes, it is, but did not your family disappear on one of those Jewish trains?"

Tears came to her eyes. "I want to go."

Alerton turned to Krueger and asked, "Did you make papers for her?"

Krueger replied, "We are in the process; my associate is doing research."

"Yes," Alerton said, "your work is so good it is normally accepted."

Metrool asked, "Will taking her make it worse for us?"

"No," Alerton said, "it would probably make it better." He turned to Krueger and asked, "Can you make Helga into Frau Metrool?"

"Yes," Krueger said. "*Das ist* a good idea."

"Wait," Metrool said.

Alerton cut in with a message, saying, *Metrool, it will make it better.*

They went to the train station at seven forty-five in the morning, one of its busiest times, so the authorities would have less time to look at their papers. Soon they were in a compartment on a train bound for Lisbon. Metrool leaned back with his eyes closed. Helga curled up against him and fell asleep. Scanning her, Alerton saw it was the first time she had relaxed in months; he also saw she had no memory of vaporizing Henri. Alerton did not regret vaporizing Henri. It had been the proper thing to do.

The scene looked normal; the conductor did not look twice. Someday Alerton might tell Metrool that Henri was gone but not now.

The train made a stop about halfway to Lisbon, and then it was on its way again. They could not go to the bar or dining cars, because they might be checked again. At one point, a conductor tried to add two people to their compartment, but a handful of francs sent him on his way. Alerton's job in London was with intelligence. He knew how to contact people in Lisbon. In a short time, Alerton was turning Helga over to people he trusted. He gave her a phone number of a drop phone in London.

Alerton said, "If you get into trouble, they can help you."

Helga put her arms around him, clinging to him. She asked, "Will it be you?"

"No," Alerton said, "I must go far away." Alerton knew she was in a terrible emotional state, but these people would help her become herself again. In her mind, Alerton had seen what she had been before Henri, and he knew she could be that again.

Two hours later, Alerton and Metrool were at the airport, boarding a Portuguese airplane that was really owned by the British. Twenty minutes later, the plane was climbing into the air. Neither relaxed until they landed in London. They talked about normal things, including what Metrool should do now.

Alerton said, "I can get you papers."

Metrool said, "That will not be necessary. Everin got me papers to get into the RAF."

Alerton said, "Yes, I recall."

Three thousand miles away, Everin was at a luncheon party with Eleanor and fifteen other women. Nearly all the women were wives of senators or congressmen. Seldom did Everin scan; she just kept her senses wide open. She had developed high contacts in the army and navy who needed to know what Washington was thinking and doing. Everin had learned Eleanor was a good person—not always right but a good person.

Everin messaged Alerton, and after pleasantries, she said, *It seems they are creating a huge project to build a bomb.*

A bomb? Alerton said. *They are building lots of bombs now.*

An atomic bomb.

Zarin! We had those one hundred thousand Earth years ago. There has been some talk among scientists here about the possibility, but I did not know someone was going to put that much money into it.

They are going to put a lot of money into it.

Thank you for telling me. I should be into this.

You are welcome. How is Metrool?

He and Margaux are disappointed in Henri, but they will be all right. Henri's departure was Alerton's secret.

<hr>

Alerton got off a ship in Santa Cruz, Mexico, and within three hours, he was on a Mexican bus, heading north. The bus was hot and dusty, and he had to spend a night on the way, but finally, he was at the border. Simply by saying, "California," he walked into the United States. There was no record of his crossing. He took a taxi to a used-car lot and paid cash for a 1939 Ford. He drove carefully because Americans drove on the other side of the road.

Alerton drove north to the Texas capital. He went to the college, and using scanning and fast reading, he acquired all the names of electrical engineers who'd graduated in the last ten years. He then went to the newspaper archives. He searched the obituaries and found three of the engineers had passed away. He picked one name and went to the driver's license office.

The lady behind the wooden desk gave him a little book and said, "Study this, and come back and take the written test."

Alerton walked to a nearby restaurant and sat on what he later would learn was called a barstool. The waitress was friendly and brought him a glass of water.

Alerton asked, "What do you recommend?"

Strangely, she said, "Honey, you are not from around here, are you?"

Alerton mumbled, "New York."

She said, "That explains it. Honey, I would say the hamburger steak with pinto beans and mashed potatoes."

Alerton said, "All right, I will try that," even though he had no idea what she was talking about." It took him about five minutes to learn the book, and then he looked around. Food names were different from those in England. He recognized a red Coca-Cola sign and ordered one when she brought his food. The meal was passable, and it was something he could order as he drove across America.

He finished his food, went back to the driver's license office, passed both tests, and received a temporary license. He went to the records department, and with the driver's license and some scanning, he walked out with a birth certificate.

The next day, he went to the college and got copies of all his records. Now he was set up, and he began his drive to Washington, DC.

⟫●⟪

When Metrool came back from Burma, his wound from the war had healed, but it had been a major wound and had shown him he was not invincible. Margaux was happy he was home and not sky-fighting, as she called it. When Marie had joined the WASP, she had asked Margaux to live in and take care of Arrista. Alerton was gone to America for some secret project and the chance to spend some time with Marie. Margaux and Metrool talked about Henri, and they were shocked and saddened by what he had been doing, but Alerton had assured them he would not do it anymore.

Metrool got into the secret radar project. It was one of the reasons they had won the Battle of Britain. Usually, but not always, they could see the Germans coming. Metrool's group were armed, and that was unusual. They were trying to make radar better more reliable. They were a major target of the German agents in England. They had found one of their group tortured and dead. They did not know if he had given the Germans any information. Metrool did not feel Hamen rules applied to this job and was really trying to improve the radar. So far, their main results had made it more reliable.

After their man was killed, they were issued weapons, which was unusual for Britain. Three days later, Metrool was riding in a taxi and suddenly sensed major danger. He loudly told the driver to get down, and Metrool hit the spacious floor of the London black taxi. But the driver did not heed his words, and when the taxi was sprayed with bullets, he died. Metrool's senses were at their peak, and he immediately rose, drew his weapon, and shot the gunman in the thigh. By the time Metrool got to him, he had used a cyanide capsule. Metrool had wanted to question him. There was a secret inquiry about the incident, and Metrool was cleared.

Metrool kept hearing things about a new type of airplane engine. He pulled some strings to get into the project. He got into it and found they were on the right track, but it was primitive compared to Hamen propulsion devices. They needed better materials, better designs, better oiling systems, and better oil; it was nearly hopeless. It was frustrating. Sometimes he would suggest something he knew would be an improvement and be told, "Maybe we can try that next year." The Germans already had a fighter flying with axial-flow compressors, but this group was stuck on centrifugal compressors. Metrool had to move on. He had heard the Americans were working on something called a computer.

Metrool smiled and thought, *Hamens had them more than a hundred thousand years ago.*

In a month, Metrool was on the *Queen Mary*, heading west across the Atlantic. Margaux was staying at Arrista to take care of it and repair the damage she had covered up and not told Metrool or Alerton about.

Arrista had a large separate garage behind it. A German bomber had crashed behind it, and the garage had burned to the ground. In some ways, the garage had protected Arrista, but both Alerton's Rolls and Metrool's antique Stutz had burned. Margaux was going to rebuild it, but building materials were scarce.

Metrool was going for an interview with a company known for its electrical products. They were also a supplier of turbochargers for aircraft.

It was located in a city named Lynn in New England. The *Queen Mary* docked in New York, and soon Metrool was on a Greyhound, heading for Lynn. He arrived in the afternoon, phoned the number on the letter they had sent him, and arranged an interview for the next day. Metrool spent the night in a hotel and then went to his interview the next day. When they found out he had worked on the English engine project, they hired him immediately.

Alerton drove north from the Texas capital to a place called Fort Worth. He ate lunch there and saw they were proud of their rustic western heritage. It seemed like a genuinely nice city, and when he stopped to refuel, the person who put fuel in the Ford also cleaned his windscreen and checked his engine at no extra charge. When Alerton asked for a road map, the attendant gave him one. Alerton scanned the map and saw the road he needed to take to the eastern part of America; it was called the Bankhead Highway. Using the map, Alerton found it and started east.

Alerton felt it was a road, not a highway. As he drove east, the first town he came to was a sleepy little town of seven thousand called Arlington. Alerton proceeded east, and it was getting dark as he drove through Dallas, where stopped at what the Americans called a *motel*. Alerton assumed that was short for *automobile hotel*. After he acquired a room, he went to the restaurant next door for dinner. The people who worked there were friendly, and the food was good. Alerton messaged Marie and told her where he was.

She said, *Darn, a few days ago, I picked up a P-51 from a factory just west of you.*

Alerton said, *I wish I had been here.*

Marie said, *I love you, and we will work it out. We will be together.*

Alerton said, *Marie, when this is over, I will take you back to the Cocos.*

Marie replied, *Oh, Al, that would be wonderful. It was so beautiful.*

They said good night. Alerton was in Dallas, and Marie was in Florida.

The next morning, Alerton went back to the restaurant for breakfast, and then he was back on the so-called Bankhead Highway, making his way east. It was near dark when he entered a state named Arkansas, and he pushed on to a town named Arkadelphia before he stopped for the night.

Every night, Alerton messaged Marie. She was happy he was in America. She was flying to different places and hoped that soon their paths would cross. Everin lived in DC now, and Alerton messaged her and told her where he was. She was the main reason he was there. She had told him America was going to build an atomic bomb. Using her Hamen mental abilities, Everin had developed many important contacts, and she knew much about what was going on, including what the government was telling the public and what it was not, such as the shipping losses.

Alerton went to a restaurant and took his time eating. He had noticed these people's accent was a little different. He had adjusted his accent to Texas because he was Texan according to his papers.

America was short on roads and highways, but it was a new country; they did not have a two-thousand-year-old Roman road system to start with. Europe had had a major road system at the time of Christ.

The next morning, the pattern continued; Alerton was crossing one southern state a day. He did light scans, absorbing Americana, so he could blend in. He was going to be working in an airtight society that would be looking for anything out of place.

The next morning, he went through Mississippi, Alabama, and then Georgia. When he got to Atlanta, the Bankhead turned to the north, and he followed it. The highway took him through South and North Carolina, then to Virginia, and at last to Washington, DC. Alerton messaged Everin and told her, *Finally, I am here.*

Everin said, *Wonderful*, and she recommended a hotel. She told him it had a fabulous restaurant, and if he wanted, she would dine with him at eight.

Alerton told her, *Fine. I will see you at eight.*

Alerton gassed up his Ford and asked the attendant for a city road map, and the attendant gave him one free. Alerton scanned the map, and soon he was driving into the valet area of the Mayflower Hotel. The fancy-dressed valet obviously looked down on the used Ford as he took the keys. Alerton did not care since he knew he had the funds to buy that hotel. Alerton acquired a room in the fabulous hotel and settled in. He relaxed and messaged Marie and found her on a train going back to Wichita. She assured him they would have time together soon.

At eight o'clock, he was at the restaurant. Everin looked good; she did not look a day over three hundred. Alerton saw that the maître d' knew Everin, and it was obvious he gave them one of the best tables.

When the sommelier came, Everin talked wine with him and accepted his suggestion. Soon the bottle was opened, and a small amount was poured into Everin's wineglass. She sipped it, rolled it, and then smiled and said, "Yes, I will take it." Two glasses were poured, and when they were alone at their table, Alerton tasted it, and it was a quality wine, but the wines of Tuscany had shaped his taste in wine.

While they were dining, three important people came to their table and spoke with Everin. He knew they were important because he scanned them. All through the meal, they kept their conversation light. They talked about his drive, the war, Marie, and England. Only when they were in a remote spot in the huge lobby did they talk about the project.

Alerton said, "I want to be in it. I know I can help them."

Everin said, "You do not think that is breaking the rules?"

"No, I may be saving lives."

"I will look over their project for you."

"Thank you. Try to get me somewhere I can contribute."

"Overall, this is going to be a huge project."

"Yes, mining the ore, refining it, separating the uranium out of the refined ore, and then bombarding the pure uranium with neutrons to create plutonium in reactors, and then you have to separate the newly created plutonium from the uranium with a chemical process in large plants they call canyons. Each one of these steps requires a huge facility. I am surprised at the American ability to build factories and get their massive production going. They are building huge numbers of planes, trucks, tanks, and ships. It seems nearly impossible that a sleeping country could become this productive."

Over the next two weeks, Alerton and his Ford explored north and south of DC. It had been more than one hundred years since he had lived in America, and it was different. Alerton got a message from Marie: she was flying to DC and would have three days there. Alerton told her, *Wonderful. The Mayflower is a great hotel. We will have fun.*

He met her at the airport as she delivered a B-25. He met her flying partners and invited them to the hotel too. For the next three days, Alerton,

Marie, and the Ford spent a lot of time together. Marie knew more about American food than he did and guided him to things she thought he would like. Their nights came back naturally to their wonderful married life. The three days went by fast, and soon he was driving her to the train station. Twice, Everin and Marie had spent some time together, and they got along great. Alerton helped her aboard and then watched the train leave for Wichita.

Everin messaged him, telling him she had a great opportunity for him. He asked her, *What is it?*

They are building a nuclear enrichment facility in Hanford in Washington state, near a curve in the Columbia River.

This is a major enterprise.

Yes, it is. Do you want to be part of it?

Yes, I do. Set it up.

A week later, Alerton had sold his Ford and was boarding a train for Hanford. He had said his thank-yous and goodbyes to Everin. The train was loaded, and only sit-up seats were available. Alerton was lucky he could program himself to sleep sitting up and look as if he were awake. After three and a half days, he arrived in Yakima. The government had a building there where they were receiving people and sending them on to Richland on buses. As Alerton rode the bus, he was aware of the workers—concrete workers, bricklayers, plumbers, electricians, and welders. All the building trades were there.

Richland was controlled chaos. There were four different places to process people. Alerton went to the one that processed scientists. There was a line, and processing was slow. The person processing him went through all his papers three times. She was obviously stressed out, saying, "We must be so careful, and we must process so many people." Alerton did her a favor and sent a calming wave through her troubled mind.

Upon leaving that place, Alerton had housing and a job location and had been told which mess hall to use. Currently, his job site was a major construction site. He soon found out that a scientist's job right now was to oversee construction of the reactors and other equipment. For many months, Hanford was just a huge construction site, with as many as forty-four thousand people employed. As parts of the complex were completed, people were sent on their way.

More and more of the facility was completed, and finally, in September, they were permitted to fire up reactor B and start making plutonium. The reactor worked. It did what it was designed to do, adding neutrons to uranium. Two months later, they got to start up reactor D. These were good people to work with, and they accepted some of his suggestions. Soon they would begin shipping plutonium to a place called Los Alamos in New Mexico. Alerton had done about all he could do in Hanford, but he knew he could help in Los Alamos, where they were trying to make a bomb. Alerton messaged Everin and told her what he wanted.

She exclaimed, *You do not ask for much! That is the most restricted site in America.* A minute later, she told him, *I will try.*

Alerton thanked her, and they ended the message.

He worked at his regular job with reactors B and D, and one day his boss handed him a letter—it was a transfer to Los Alamos.

December 1945

Alerton had resigned from Los Alamos. He had caught a bus to the nearest railroad and bought a ticket to New York City. His lovely wife, Marie, was already there. In this transition period, she had been able to acquire a nice apartment not far from Everin's Central Park apartment. Everin had gotten the tenants to move, and she and Mavis had moved back from Washington, DC. Marie met Alerton at Grand Central, and right there on the platform, they hugged and kissed. Marie cried joyful tears.

When Alerton had been in her calm apartment for two days, he talked to her about Los Alamos. "Overall, it was a great group of dedicated people. There were a few spies, but I could not tell how I knew. What really bothered me were the primitive tools these dedicated people had to work with. They could have gotten enough radiation to kill them easily. I am going to start a company here in New York. I am going to call it Alerton Electronics, and some of the things we make will be tools for working with dangerous technologies."

Marie told him that was wonderful and that she had been terribly worried about him while he worked on the project. Then she had a surprise for him. She said, "Alerton, because of my experience in flying B-17s and

B-24s across America, an airline has hired me to be one of their captains. On my papers and job, I am listed as Mark because they do not want to frighten people."

Alerton said, "You're joking."

"Why? You do not think I can do it?"

"Oh, I know you can do it. You are a Hamen. But, darling, we are rich, and we have already been apart for years; you do not need to do this."

"Alerton, please. This is something I want to do for myself. Please give me your blessing."

Alerton loved this woman and had loved her for more than two hundred years. How could he turn her down? In answer, he gave her a real kiss and said, "Fly the wings off the damn thing."

Marie kissed him back several times and said, "Oh, thank you, Al!"

Everin, Mavis, and two cooks hired for the night gave Marie and Alerton a wonderful dinner. Everin appeared to be happy, but leaving his senses open, Alerton could feel a large emptiness from losing Doc.

In the coming weeks, Alerton scouted property. He acquired offices in one of New York's skyscrapers. The country was in transition; the war was over, and a lot of war plants were closing. Brand-new warplanes were being flown to either desert storage in Kingman, Arizona, or the scrapyard. Brand-new P-51s were being sold to the public for $1,500.

Alerton secured a closed factory for his company and began to search the wealth of engineering talent available. Alerton hired fifteen people and basically turned them loose after telling them what he wanted to do. Alerton, Marie, and Everin developed a habit of holding a once-a-week meeting at one of New York City's fabulous restaurants for dinner. Everin's four years in DC and all the contacts she had made had followed her to New York and had put her on the boards of directors of three corporations.

Metrool messaged Everin: *We are wrapping up developing the M-47 jet engine. From here on, it will just be production, so I am going back to Margaux at Arrista.*

Everin said, *That is wonderful, Met. I am so glad you had success with it, and I am so glad you are going to be with Margaux.*

Marie said, *I need to tell you that Alerton and I talked about this: since Margaux has been so wonderful about taking care of Arrista, we want to deed it over to Margaux.*

Metrool said, *Oh, that is wonderful. Margaux loves Arrista. But that is way too generous of you. You know I have plenty of funds to buy it.*

No, this cannot be a sale. It has to be a gift.

I understand, Metrool said, *and thank you with all my being. I have been offered a job with the Falcon Aircraft Company; they want to build a jet airliner.*

Wow, Everin said, and she brought Alerton into the message. *Alerton, did you catch that?*

Alerton said, *Yes, I did. Metrool, you know building the first jet airliner will be risky.*

I know, Metrool said, *but America has a near monopoly on building airliners, and England thinks speed will sell.*

Alerton said, *I am sure it will, and good luck.*

Every so often, Alerton would get a message from his relative in Brazil telling him he was still alive and doing well.

One evening, Alerton was in his office working late and was shocked that his mentect implant became semiactive for fifteen minutes. Then there was nothing. He immediately messaged Everin: *Did you just feel something?*

Yes, she said, *my mentect tingled.*

Alerton said, *You know what that means.*

Everin said, *Yes, it means a starship was close.*

Relatively. It may not have been in this solar system.

Would it be coming here?

It might be.

Why now?

Because of the nuclear explosions.

Then they are not coming for us.

Probably not. They do not know what happened to us.

Alerton, would you want to go back?

No, Eve, I have been here for five hundred seventy-seven years, I have a wife I love here, and I do not think she would like Hamen. Hamen is a wonderful place with no crime and no problems, but compared to Earth, it has no excitement.

Everin said emotionally, *I would not want to leave. Doc is here.*

Margaux and Marie did not get the tingle, because they did not have mentect implants, but Metrool got one and messaged Álvares.

Yes, Álvares said, *I got it. I have spent nearly eight hundred years here. I am way over the customary age to expire. I would be expected to expire, which, strangely, I am not ready to do.*

In the group's communications, it came up that they had broken many Hamen rules. They knew that their creating the hybrids would be a crime in Hamen eyes. They all agreed that now they were more earthling-like than they were Hamen. They all agreed that even if their mentects became fully active, they would not make contact.

A month later, with no further contact, they put aside the mentect tingle.

Metrool contacted Alerton and said, "The Falcon Aircraft Company is terribly busy working on the new jet airliner."

Alerton told him, "That is great, but this is a large jump in speed and altitude. Check and recheck everything."

Metrool replied, "Yes, we know we are in new territory, but this is our only chance to cut into the American monopoly. You know England spent a lot of money building an exceptionally large airliner, and no one bought it. They feel that speed will sell."

"I am sure it will," Alerton said. "Just be careful."

The next day, Alerton was in his office, and his secretary buzzed him, saying, "Your wife is on the phone."

Alerton sensed immediately that something was the matter and answered the phone by saying, "What is wrong?"

Marie said, "I landed in Chicago."

"You told me your flight today was Los Angeles to New York."

"Well, I had a propeller come off."

"How much damage did it do?"

Marie messaged him a mental picture of the slice the spinning propeller had taken out of the fuselage.

Alerton said, "Marie, you could have been killed."

"But I was not," Marie said. "I landed, and everyone was safe."

"Maybe Metrool is right. Jets may be the way to go."

"You are overreacting. This does not happen very often."

"Well, I love you and do not want to lose you."

Marie kept flying for the airline. Then, in June 1948, Russia shut off access to Berlin, and America decided to supply Berlin with hundreds of flights a day. They were short on airplanes and short on pilots, so Marie volunteered. That made Alerton angry.

Alerton said, "This will be terribly dangerous, flying in all kinds of weather. With hundreds of flights into one airport, there are going to be crashes."

Marie replied, "Alerton, it is for the good of those captive people. I must do it."

The next few months were terrible on Alerton because there were crashes. Finally, in May 1949, it was over, and Alerton could relax a little. He relaxed more when Marie did not go back to her airline job.

Alerton said, "Marie, I need a new boss for the Jacobs factory. Do you want it?"

He was pleased when she said, "Yes, I do." It was his largest factory, and it was a real job.

It was not long before Metrool messaged him to tell him they had a prototype flying, and it was a beauty. Alerton told him that was wonderful.

Metrool added, *It will cruise at four hundred ninety miles per hour.*

Alerton replied, *Well, Met, if it can cruise that fast, it will sell.*

In June 1950, the Korean War started, and Alerton went to Korea to see if he could help the situation. He soon found out that Kim and Pak were under heavy influence from outside forces, and he could not affect their actions.

Metrool's airliner went into service, and it was a fast beauty. However, it was not long until problems began to show up. Without telling Metrool, Alerton put some of his best engineers on the problems. About the time Alerton's engineers were finding answers, the English airliner was grounded, which depressed Metrool.

Two years after they had the mentect tingle, they got solid contact, but no one answered. The contact was active for forty days before the ship departed. No one felt a loss when the ship departed.

Alerton went back to Korea. Young men were fighting and dying in freezing weather, and he wanted to try again to use his Hamen powers to help. It was no use; the outside influence was too strong. Alerton came home disheartened.

When Alerton messaged Álvares, Álvares became aware of Alerton's down feelings and invited him to Brazil for Carnival. He told Alerton that Carnival had become a huge event. Marie learned of the invite and persuaded Alerton to go. Everin learned of it and said she would go too. When Álvares learned they were coming, he messaged Metrool and Margaux, the people who had saved him, to come too. Metrool and Margaux had been his saviors and neighbors for more than twenty years.

Everin, Marie, and Alerton flew together on the long three-segment flight from New York to São Paulo. On the flight, Everin recounted some of the adventures she'd had on the many-segmented flight to take the creator to save Álvares. Álvares met them at the airport, and he still looked fifty, even though he was over 1,400. He and a new pilot flew them to the ranch, Hamen II. Mike had lived with Álvares until he passed away and never revealed their secrets.

Álvares said Mike had a special place in his garden. He had lost Carlos and Lopez, but he still had loyal servants.

Margaux and Metrool flew in the next day, and for them, it was like old times, being at Hamen II with Álvares.

After a week at the ranch, Álvares flew them to Rio, and soon they were in a wonderful hotel on Copacabana Beach. It was on the beach and had a rooftop pool. Soon they became part of the crazy, wonderful world of Carnival. Thousands of people were in costumes.

They rode the cog-rail train up the mountain to visit the Christ the Redeemer statue and later rode the cable car up to the top of Sugarloaf. While up there, they wondered, *How did they build it?*

The city was a party town at Carnival, and with Álvares's connections, they were invited to three major balls. Before they flew back to the ranch, they gave their costumes away, and then Álvares flew them back to Hamen II. They spent a week just enjoying one another's company, and they knew it was a magical moment that would not happen again.

35

2014

THE SALTY SPRAY STUNG WHEN IT HIT ALERTON'S FACE. IT WAS EARLY March, and the western Atlantic very cold. His Garmin said he was 120 miles east of his Manhattan headquarters. Several of the people around him got upset every time he went out on his boat like this, but they did not know who he really was.

Suddenly, his head hurt terribly, and he received a message: *I have been trying to reach you, but when everyone was alive, the others' waves interfered with mine. The engines are quiet now; we must be out of fuel. The plane is falling; we are at latitude 12.20 south and longitude 97.30 east. You will find me there, if I can stay in one piece. I love you and have had a wonderful, fulfilled, and happy life with you. Thank you for sharing so much with me. Tell Everin and Margaux I love them, and I hope to see all of you again. The plane is going very fast, and I think this will be the last. Latitude 12.25 south and longitude 98.10 east. I love—*

That was the end of it. Alerton collapsed on his sailboat. That message had been in real time. His wife had sent the Hamen message from more than ten thousand miles away. Could it be that she was really gone? They had gone through so much together, and most of it had been wonderful. Alerton let the coordinates register in his mind. The place and the memories hit him. Sixty-two years ago, he and Marie had spent a whole month with their sloop anchored at the beautiful Cocos Islands. It had been beautiful; it had been idyllic. After more than three hundred years and five different infusions of Hamen blood, Marie had been almost a

Hamen. He had difficulty putting her in the past category, even though he knew her message was real. Her airplane had crashed. Later, it would be on the news. He had to get back to land.

He sailed the small sailboat just for enjoyment, and he was far out to sea. Several people thought he was crazy to sail so far out into the rough ocean, but they did not know his strengths or his resources. He had an autonomic speedboat that could come at his calling. He thought about calling it now but decided not to. He could not save Marie, but he still had to move. He had saved her from death four times in the past, but this situation was different. If only she could have opened a door and jumped out. But if she had disintegrated, there was nothing to work with. Five infusions had made Marie 99 percent Hamen, but there were certain things even a Hamen could not survive.

In their early Earth years, they had found that Hamen blood was aggressive and tried to turn the patient into a Hamen.

Alerton called his pilot and told him, "Get the 37 ready to fly to Australia—max fuel and only one passenger."

"Will do," the pilot said. "When do we leave?"

Alerton replied, "As soon as you can, send a chopper out to get me."

The pilot asked him about his boat.

Alerton said, "Have him bring a sailor out to sail it back."

Then Alerton did something Hamens did not do and he had never done: he let his emotions run wild and wept, letting his whole body feel the loss. They had shared everything, the wonderful times and the terrible times.

Then he called an old friend in Australia and told him, "Lease me the largest and strongest seaplane you can find. I know they are expensive, but I don't care. Have it at max fuel and crewed when I get there, and have a chopper with rotors turning waiting to take me to the seaplane."

Alerton watched the news on his phone, but they reported nothing about the plane crash yet. He could have told them it had crashed and where to find it, but he had learned over the centuries to keep a low profile.

He continued to sail until he heard the chopper and then dropped sail and waited. Soon a sailor was lowered down to the boat, and he gave the harness to Alerton. Quickly, Alerton was in the chopper, flying back to land. Eighty minutes later, Alerton was sitting in his private modified

737, waiting in line to take off at Kennedy Airport in New York. A backup crew were in a compartment at the front of the plane. There would be no twelve-hour flying limit on this plane. As the engines roared and the plane started to move, Alerton thought about why he was going. Even with Hamen superregeneration power, he knew Marie was gone. But he had to try. She had saved his life before. How much of a sample did there have to be, and what kind of condition did it have to be in, to regenerate a Hamen?

He went into his private compartment, put himself into a trance, and stayed in it until they reached Perth. After leaving the Boeing, he quickly walked the one block to the waiting running helicopter, and as soon as Alerton buckled up and put his earphones on, the chopper lifted into the air.

Twenty minutes later, they landed on a windy peer beside a large rocking seaplane. Fifteen minutes later, the turboprop engines on the seaplane came to life, the crew went through their checklist, the large plane began to move, and they were flying. Alerton, in his large chair, pushed the intercom button and confirmed the coordinates.

Four hours later, on his direct order, the plane landed in a rough sea. The crew did not want to, but on his order, they opened a hatch right above the waterline. Alerton sat in the open hatch. He was getting wet but did not care. He put his hands into the water and pushed his senses to the limit, but there were no vibes or thoughts, just a blank. Had he expected there to be? He did not know. He put his hands in the cold water again and opened his mind again. Still nothing.

The pilot demanded they close the hatch because they were taking in water. Alerton demanded five more minutes with the wet hatch and then let them shut and lock it.

On the speaker, the pilot said, "Mr. Alerton, we need to take off now."

Alerton thought for a moment and then said, "OK."

The pilot said, "As soon as you are buckled in your seat, we will take off. It will be rough."

When buckled in, Alerton said, "I am ready," and immediately, the already running engines roared, and they began to move. As they picked up speed, the collisions with the waves got rougher, and the plane slowed down.

Alerton asked a crewman, "What is wrong?"

The crewman said, "The pilot is looking for a better cycle of waves. That cycle was too rough."

Alerton thought to himself, *This is a hell of a place to crash.*

The pilot kept the engines running, and they moved slowly into the wind. After about fifteen minutes, the engines roared again, and the collisions were rough but not as rough as last time. Then the plane left the rough ocean and began to climb. Because he was paying for it, Alerton was able to tell the pilot to level off at five hundred feet and circle those coordinates. The pilot did not like it but had no reason to refuse.

After thirty minutes of circling and not feeling anything, Alerton said, "Head for Perth."

Alerton's mind went to Everin. She had gone through this when she lost Doc. He had not quite understood at the time. But losing someone after three hundred good years left a hell of an empty spot. He contacted Everin and told her, *Now I know what you went through.*

Everin said, *What happened?*

Alerton sent her a mental flash of his last thirty-six hours. He felt her deep remorse and empathy for him.

I need to see you, he said.

Everin asked, *Are you going back to New York?*

I will be there within twenty-four hours.

I will see you in New York then.

<hr/>

Six months later, Alerton began to have nightmares, and Hamens did not have nightmares. But there he was, in a cold, wet, and dark place. That was all there was. He would wake up, and that was all he would know. Some nights, he would totally wreck the big bed. But that did not matter; he was rich beyond belief. No one person knew the full extent of his riches. He had accounts in twenty-seven different names in twenty-one countries. He had started rich, and in five hundred years, his wealth had increased exponentially. But what did it matter? Marie was gone. Six golden anniversaries gone in that terrible plane crash.

He had spent a large chunk of his useless fortune to get the crash report—not the one given to the public but the real one. One executive had made a decision that kept a certain pilot flying. Alerton could imagine falling into that rough, cold spot where the plane had crashed, but that did not bother him, so what was causing his nightmares?

Finally, two weeks later, he said, *To hell with it*, and he called his secretary, Gail, and told her the name of the group of islands and told her to go there, buy him a large catamaran, hire an expert crew, and stock the boat well.

Alerton said, "You know what I like."

Yes, she did know his taste. It was usually Italian, though she wasn't sure why, as he was not Italian and, as far as she knew, had never lived there. But today he was in one of his moods.

Alerton said, "Go straight to the airport. Marge in transport already has a first-class seat for you. My helicopter will take you to Kennedy. Hurry—you can put clothes and things on your company card."

Soon Gail was on the express elevator, and as she stepped out onto the private helipad and hangar, the Augusta's blades were already turning. As soon as she buckled up, they were in the air. In a few minutes, she was being rushed through express lanes to a waiting jumbo jet. The other passengers wondered who this person was that an airline would hold up a jet for her. Again, as soon as she was in her seat, they were rolling. The steward helped her buckle up and asked, "Do you want your drink?"

Gail asked, "What do you mean?"

The steward said, "Well, your boss bought everyone a drink, and that includes you too."

Her phone vibrated. They had just lifted off. She looked at the steward, and he nodded. It was Alerton. He said, "I will be there in about twenty-four hours. I want that catamaran bought and ready when I get there." He ended the call. He did not do that often, but when he did, she knew to stay out of his way.

She liked Alerton, and she knew he'd had a hard time accepting Marie's death. He paid his close employees well and seemed to care about them. Sometimes he had surprises for them, and they would wonder how he had known.

When Alerton got to south Cocos, Gail, as usual, had done her job. He was not crazy about the paint job, but the catamaran was large, with new engines and sails. After looking the boat and the crew over, he thanked Gail, told her she had done a good job, and gave her a hug, which was unusual. He said, "We are sailing, but why don't you do a little vacation here in the Cocos or on Christmas Island?"

Then Alerton was off. He looked back at her as they sailed away. Because he could read her mind, he knew she wanted more with him. She was an attractive, proficient woman, but right now, Marie was the only woman on his mind.

Five hours later, they made their first island. Alerton did not know what he was doing or why he was doing it; it was just instinct. If there was a road, they drove it, and if there was just a trail, they walked it.

Two days later, Alerton came to the captain and said, "Caleb, this is not the island. Let us go."

Caleb replied, "Pardon me, sir, but what is the right island?"

"I do not know, my friend, but we will keep looking until I do know."

Fourteen days later, having given up on their sixth island, Alerton and Caleb sat in the shade of a restaurant, talking and looking out onto the street. A group of young women, obviously poor, walked by, and one of them, an underfed blonde girl of fifteen, turned and looked at Alerton and said, "Alerton!"

Alerton nearly had a heart attack, but before he could recover, she was gone, and he could not find her. In a state of shock, he walked back to the restaurant. He ordered them two more drinks, and when the owner brought them, Alerton asked, "Do you know who that slim blonde girl was?"

The bar owner said, "Of course. She is the orphan."

Shocked, Alerton asked, "Why is she called the orphan?"

The owner said, "You haven't heard the story?"

Alerton was getting impatient. "Tell me."

The owner said, "Well, her parents owned a catamaran just like yours, and they rented it out to tourists, but one day, it was just the girl and her parents out sailing. They were out for three days."

Alerton interrupted. "What happened?"

"Well," the restaurant owner said, "a large piece of an airplane fell onto the boat and destroyed the boat and killed both her parents."

Alerton sat there stunned. He did not know what to make of the story or how to put the pieces together. Did it mean something, or was the whole thing crazy? He had to pursue it. He asked, "Where does she live?"

The owner said, "She lives with some poor folks up on the north side of the hill."

Alerton turned to Caleb and said, "I have to go up there."

"I know," Caleb said, "and I am going with you."

"First," Alerton said, "I want all the details I can get from the restaurant owner."

"Of course," said Caleb. He motioned to get the owner's attention and said, "Bring three drinks."

The owner sat down with them, and Alerton said, "Tell me everything you know about the girl and the accident."

"Well," the owner said, and then he stopped.

Alerton laid a note in front of him.

"It's been spooky," he said, and he stopped again.

Alerton laid two more large notes in front of him, looked him straight in the eye, and said, "Talk."

The owner said, "Well, the family did not live here. We don't know where they lived."

"Did you try to find out?"

"We inquired, but we could not find out. They were just freelancing boaters taking people fishing, on boat rides, and whatever anybody wanted to get money to live on. They were sort of like hippies."

"OK, then what is spooky?"

"The whole thing—the mysterious plane crash. They can't find it because the water is too deep, and whoever was flying it had turned off all the transmitters."

"Continue."

"Word is it came apart in the air, and pieces and people were falling everywhere."

Those words tore at Alerton's heart, because Marie's last words were still written on his heart.

The owner continued. "Well, it must have been a big piece, or more than one, that hit the boat, for they say the couple were killed, and the boat sank right away."

"The girl?"

"Well, she was wearing a life preserver, and it kept her afloat for three days till they found her."

"Three days?" Alerton said, incredulous.

"Yes," the owner said. "No one knew where the plane crashed. They were looking everywhere for it."

"Tell me about the girl."

"Doctors said they did not see how she survived as bad as she was injured. In fact, the people who found her said it looked like she had been torn apart and then put back together. But then the doctors, when they got to see her, said they had exaggerated."

Oh, Alerton thought, *could Marie have helped her in some way?*

The owner said, "Well, the girl acts a little funny sometimes or says words that don't make sense, but we don't think that is too unusual, as much as she has been through."

"Of course," Alerton said. "I am going up to see her. Will you drive us?"

Soon they were in owner's old car, riding along on a bumpy road. Alerton had never been so nervous in his life. They pulled up in front of a run-down house on a gravel road. The whole family came out: a couple and their four children. Then the lithe blonde girl came out of the house.

Alerton went to the couple, and after a small amount of stiff conversation, he asked, "Can I talk to the girl?"

They said yes, and he turned to the girl, who was apprehensive of this stranger but was polite.

Then he nearly fainted as he got a mental message: *Alerton, most of my mind and memories are in here.*

In shock, Alerton sent a mental message back to her loaded with emotion: *Oh, Marie, I love you. I have missed you so.*

And I love you, she said. *But you must be careful; she does not know I am here. She thinks she has a guardian angel who talks to her.*

Alerton said, *She does. I am going to take her back to New York. But I have so many questions and so little time. Why haven't you contacted me?*

Are you a prisoner? Alerton then said, *They say I am upsetting her, and we must go.*

Yes, Marie said, *my range is very short, and I am a prisoner of a sort. I have all her senses to experience, but I do not control her. I can see, but I can't tell her where to look. I can hear whatever she hears; I taste whatever she tastes; and if she is cold, I am cold.*

Alerton said, *I have to leave, but I am going to adopt her and give her a great life. I will try to free you, but you will be with me.*

Marie said, *I know you will. I have known you for three hundred years. And I love you too. By the way, she has nearly all Hamen blood.*

As they rode back to the village in the run-down car, Caleb turned to Alerton and said, "They said her survival was spooky. Well, what I have seen tonight was pretty damn spooky. You were talking to someone, and it wasn't the girl."

Back at the restaurant, standing outside in privacy, Alerton said, "Caleb, you have been a good friend on this search."

Once they were back on the boat, Alerton had Caleb recline in an easy chair and said, "Think of me as a hypnotist or magician," and soon Caleb was in a trance. Scanning, Alerton saw he had lost a son as a young man and never had gotten to say goodbye to him. Pulling memories from Caleb's mind, he created a goodbye conversation.

Caleb, upon waking up, broke down crying and said, "Yes, you are a devil or something, but thank you."

The next eight days were a nightmare for Alerton. First, he gave a large amount of money to the couple with whom the girl, named Dana, had been living, which felt fitting, as they were poor and had taken Dana in as family. But then every petty official on the island had a paper he had to sign. It wasn't that much trouble, but Alerton just wanted to get Marie, a.k.a. Dana, back to New York. When he got her to Cocos, reporters were there, and Gail was still there to chaperone Dana. The rag papers printed wild stories about "one of the world's richest men," as they called him. Was the girl a love child he had come to claim? Was she going to be the fifty-first shade of Grey? He had been compared to the character Christian Grey before.

Even Gail, his trusty secretary, said to Alerton, "Are you sure you know what you, a single man, are doing in adopting a pretty fifteen-year-old girl?"

He grinned and said, "Then it would be OK if she was fat and ugly?"

She hollered, "You are impossible! This is serious."

He said, "Gail, you do not know the whole story, and you may never know the whole story. But know this: I am doing what is right."

Gail looked at Alerton and said, "Until you prove me wrong, I will believe you."

Strangely, a tabloid reporter Alerton disgraced came closest to the truth. He said the girl was an alien, and that was how she had survived.

Finally, Alerton, Gail, and Dana were in their cozy seats on Alerton's 37, on their first leg back to New York. Alerton got with Gail and said, "I want you to hire about ten good maids. One will be the boss of the rest."

"Why so many?" Gail asked.

Alerton did not answer her question. He said, "The boss's job will be to ensure two maids are there all the time." Then he pushed the button to make his seat recline. It appeared he was relaxing.

Dana was in the fancy seat across from him. Mentally, he sent a message to Marie: *I've been missing you.* It was a phrase they had used for more than two hundred years.

Marie replied, *And I have been missing you.* Then there was a torrent of words and emotions.

Within two weeks, Alerton had Dana settled in. Gail had hired twelve maids, picked a boss, and set up their schedule. Alerton had used his influence to put Dana in a very private school.

David Davidson, the disgraced reporter, came to see Dana at her school, and after several tries, he got to talk to her. When her chauffeur brought her home from her exclusive private school, she went straight to Alerton.

Dana said, "David Davidson talked to me today."

Alerton braced himself for the worst. He clearly remembered the day Davidson had rolled his boxlike container on wheels into his office. Davidson had been trying to get an appointment with him for a long time. Davidson, at the time, had been a well-respected reporter. Reporters were dangerous to people like Alerton. Alerton finally had given in, curious because Davidson said he had evidence. It had turned out Davidson had traveled the world and gathered every photo and painting of Alerton, showing that Alerton, by different names, was at least four hundred years old.

Alerton had said, "All right, Mr. Davidson, how much do you want for them and your silence?"

Davidson had said, "Money? I do not want your money. I want to be the most famous reporter on the planet. This is larger than King Tut."

"Mr. Davidson, I cannot let you do that."

"How can you stop me? A news crew filmed me coming into this building."

Alerton had gone into his mind and shown him. Davidson had stumbled out with a burning desire to write a wild book about spacemen. He'd left his evidence box, and Alerton had kept one painting and destroyed the rest. He could not destroy a Van Gogh of Marie at Arles, even if it was unsigned.

Alerton asked Dana, "What did he tell you?"

Dana said, "That you are an alien from outer space and that you put a curse on him so that he can write only silly stuff no one will believe."

Alerton asked, "Do you believe him?"

Dana said, "He says you want to experiment on me and take me to your planet."

Alerton said, "I asked you if you believed him."

Dana hesitated. She took too long to answer, so Alerton lightly probed her to see what she really thought.

Dana said, "You are probing my mind right now. You must be an alien; Earth people can't do that."

"You do it," Alerton said. "I've seen you with your girlfriends. You know what they want before they tell you. Are you an alien?"

Dana turned red. She stammered, and tears came to her eyes. "When I came back to the island after the accident and people started giving me sympathy, I could tell what was real and what was not."

Alerton said, "You feel things that other people don't."

"At first, I thought everyone could do that, but then I learned I could do things they could not. Last month, when I wanted to run the hundred-yard dash at school, you told me not to, and I threw a fit, so you took me to a private track and timed me."

"And what was your best time?"

"Eight seconds flat. I set a new world record, but I can't tell anyone."

"And what does all this mean?"

"I am different. You are different. I do not know where we came from, but I know we are different."

Alerton used his mind to scan Dana lightly to find out how she really felt about things. He was pleasantly surprised to see she had developed a deep affection for him, even though she seldom showed it. He saw she was deeply loyal to him, and he saw there was a lot of Hamen in her.

Marie came into his mind then and said, *You are all she has, and she is at least half Hamen. I had to use a lot of myself to put her back together.*

"Who else is here?" Dana asked. "Who else is always here?"

Alerton said, "My wife."

"What?" Dana asked. "What are you saying?"

"The airplane that killed your parents and tore you apart—well, my wife was a passenger on it."

"So she is a ghost, and we are being haunted?"

"No. She was in a part of the plane that was somewhat protected as the dive went nearly sonic, and most people were shredded. My wife was protected and wound up in pieces like you."

"I was in pieces?"

"Yes, just like your parents."

Dana moaned. "But then we would be dead."

"My people," Alerton said, "have remarkable healing powers. Remember when I was watching your softball game, and you got hit in the mouth and busted a lip and broke a tooth?"

"I wanted a doctor."

"I told the chauffeur to take us home. And you kept wanting to go to a doctor. But when we got home, your lip was well, and by the next morning, your tooth was well."

"So," Dana asked, "what happened at the crash?"

Alerton took a deep breath. "Even though my wife's healing powers are great, she could not save both of you."

"And you mean she saved me?"

"Yes, she did."

"Pop," she said, using the familiar term, "this is pretty darn hard to accept."

"And you don't?" Alerton asked.

"No, darn it." She stomped her foot. "I do believe all of it because I have been around you for a while, but this is crazy."

Yes, Marie said to Dana. *Yes, even for us, as far as we know, it has never been done before.*

"Oh my God, where are you?" Dana asked.

I am in your mind. I have been there ever since I put you back together.

In a serious moment, Dana asked, "Are you going to take over my body and get rid of me?"

No, Marie said, *we have plans to rescue me, and if they do not work, I will cease to exist, and you will be free of me. I did not want you to die; you have only lived a short life, and I have lived a long one.*

"How old are you?" Dana asked.

Three hundred forty-one years.

"No," Dana said. "No one lives that long."

Alerton spoke up. "I am six hundred ninety-seven years old."

Dana practically went into shock. Scanning Dana, Alerton saw she would be true to the three of them, and he put an engram into her mind to keep her from slipping accidentally.

Marie worked on their list of requirements for their project: between thirty and fifty-five years old, no husband, preferably no children, memory 95 percent gone, and no chance of normal recovery. Marie asked, *When will you tell Dana the whole story?*

Soon, Alerton said. *You created a wonderful person.*

I am jealous, Marie said.

I know, Alerton said, *but I love only you.*

Under orders from the boss, Mark was driving a plain car. He was driving to an apartment building on the east side. The boss had not told him why, and Mark had not asked. The car did not look plain like a police car; it just looked ordinary, so people would not look at it twice. The boss had told him to park in the parking garage across the street. Mark had expected him to get out of the car, but he did not. He simply sat in the backseat with eyes closed, concentrating on something, for about twenty minutes.

Finally, Alerton opened his eyes, smiled, and said, "I think that problem is over. Take me back to my apartment, Mark."

Across the street, in the apartment building, a man at a desk with a laptop was struggling to stand up. He grabbed at an old-fashioned phone, but it fell to the floor. He let himself drop to the floor. He barely managed to bring the phone to his lips, but no words would come out. He knew he was having a transient ischemic attack, or TIA—like a ministroke. He knew someone who had had one. He found the pendant hanging around his neck and, with numb fingers, pressed the button. Help would be there soon. His mind was getting fuzzy. *Oh, hurry. Please hurry.*

As Davidson's heart had pumped blood through his lungs, some lung tissue had broken loose and floated in the blood up to his brain. It blocked two vital blood vessels. Without blood flow, the brain cells could be damaged quickly and permanently.

Alerton had just sat back to relax, when, in his mind, he heard Dana scream. Then Marie told him, *Someone has wrecked us on purpose.*

Stay in the car with the doors locked, Alerton told Marie.

Because Alerton had wanted to use Mark on his errand, a different driver had driven Dana to school. Marie gave Alerton their exact location. The driver had made the mistake of opening the door. He had been shot and killed.

Two men grabbed Dana and rushed her to a van with another man driving. Marie gave Alerton second-to-second updates. A large man was holding Dana in a crushing restraint with a hand over her mouth. Alerton reached deep into his history and sent a message to Dana: *Do not resist this message: Hamen martial arts.*

Dana bit the man's hand, and he screamed, waving the bloody hand in the air. While the thug was still reacting to the bite, Dana drove a flat, rigid hand into his throat, destroying his windpipe. As she spit out the piece of hand in her mouth, the second thug tried to grab her, and she threw him to the back of the van. He ran at her and received a flat, rigid hand to the side of his neck. The blow broke his neck, and he fell dead at her feet. She spun and grabbed both of the driver's shoulders, shouting in the voice of a warrior of a thousand years ago, "Stop the van!"

As soon as the van stopped, Alerton said to Marie and Dana, *Get out of the van. Now walk west; do not run. I am nearly there.*

Within minutes, Dana was in Alerton's car, overwhelmed. Alerton said, "I will explain everything later, but this is what happened: the bad guys stopped your limo and shot your driver, and you ran away. You know zero about any van, no matter what anyone says."

Dana looked deeply at Alerton and said, "Pop, you have a hell of a lot to tell me."

Several hours later, Alerton was in his business office, and Gail, his secretary, buzzed him and said, "There are two detectives here to see you."

Alerton thought for a moment and then said, "Wait five minutes, and then show them in."

When the two detectives came in, they were polite, but their first question surprised him: "Do you have a ninja watching over Dana?"

"First," Alerton said, "I would prefer you refer to the young lady as my daughter, not Dana."

"All right," one officer said, "same question of your daughter."

"No, gentlemen, I don't but why would you ask such a strange question?"

"Because the attackers killed your driver, and somehow, your daughter ran away, but someone jumped into the van and took two large men apart. The driver never saw them, but the person's loud, strange voice sounded oriental."

"No, gentlemen, other than my four bodyguards licensed by you, I have no one guarding me or my daughter. And after my departed bodyguard has a proper burial, I will be hiring another. Do you have any evidence of this alleged ninja?"

"We have some DNA from the piece of hand the ninja bit off—you know, the perp who choked to death. The lab said the DNA was unlike any they had ever seen and must have been contaminated."

Alerton then asked, "What about teeth impressions?"

"Well, we shouldn't tell you this, but the piece was torn out of his hand and then chewed up. That is one reason we know it was a professional ninja—they cover their tracks."

Alerton asked, "What about the driver?"

"The driver confessed. He does not want bail; he just wants a quick trial and then jail. He is scared to death."

"Gentlemen," Alerton said, "it looks like you might have a vigilante on your hands."

"We hope not," one officer said. "They can be a lot of trouble."

"Well," Alerton said, "I have no ninja on my payroll."

They thanked him for his time, offered condolences for the fallen guard, and left. After a few minutes of collecting his thoughts, Alerton, nearly laughing, contacted Marie and said, *The police think Dana was a ninja.*

God, Marie said, *she was. I have never seen anyone transform like that. She is a hybrid, Alerton; she is different from any Hamen or earthling you have ever known.*

I know, Alerton said. *I hope this turns out well.*

<hr />

Alerton had programs on all his computers to scan medical facilities for mental patients, head injuries, TIAs, strokes, comas, and more. Every night, he went over any new cases added to his selective list, but so far, none had even come close to fitting what they needed. He was getting frustrated, and Marie was getting frustrated.

Sometimes living with a teenager could be interesting, and at other times, it could be boring as hell. Dana had her eighteenth birthday party with a dozen close friends and most of their parents at a high-dollar restaurant. Then they went to a club, and it went on and on. Dana was inexhaustible, and her friends tried to match her.

The next night, Alerton was back at the computer. As usual, he saw nothing at first—but then one case popped out. A young female had gone to the dentist, and the flow meters on his gases had failed, so he'd given her the wrong gases. The brain was washed. It was probably healthy, but there was no activity. She was technically brain-dead.

The family was being asked to harvest her. *No, no, no,* Alerton thought. The blood type was right, the Rh was right, and the cranium capacity was right, and she was five foot seven and 140 pounds. Then Alerton saw the killer and wanted to scream, *No! Why? Why did it have to be this way? She had parents and a brother.* She had no children, of course, because she was only eighteen.

Marie must have been watching him, because she spoke up and said, *You know this may be the best match, the best chance I ever have.*

I know, Alerton said, feeling beaten. *But if I save you, I lose you.*

No, you would not, Marie said. *We couldn't get married at first, but we could eventually.*

You do not understand about Hamens. You would look like you were eighteen for two hundred years. We do not age like earthlings. Do I look six hundred ninety-seven years old?

Alerton, I love you, and I always will, but I want this chance.

What if it fails? What if you are worse than you are now?

You know what I want: I want to be alive and normal. If it fails, I ask you with all my heart to terminate me. We had three hundred wonderful years, and we have the chance for me to live on and still love you. Even if it must be as a daughter, it would still be me and still be love. You could marry someone else.

Now Alerton was doing something Hamens rarely did: crying. *Yes*, he said, *I owe it to you. You have been wonderful for me, and I will pursue this with everything I have.*

At five o'clock in the morning, three of Alerton's men knocked on the doors of three scientists. Because of who Alerton was and how his donations influenced research, the scientists were at his office at six o'clock. He already had scanned them, and he trusted them. He told them he wanted the girl's body, untouched. "Tell what you must tell, and pay what you must pay. I want that body now, untouched."

Dr. Starret said, "We will do it. We trust you."

Alerton looked intently at all three and said, "Believe me, this is a noble cause. When you learn everything, you will be proud of acquiring the body, and it will be in your facility."

Over the next two days, Alerton, electronically, mentally, and by private detective, kept track of the three scientists and their assistants. Finally, the call he had been waiting for came. Dr. Starret said, "The body is here."

In the past two days, Alerton had spent about three hours each day talking to Dana, telling her who she was and what she was.

"So," Dana said, "technically, the crash killed Dana."

Alerton said, "What was left of you was not survivable."

"And this Earth wife you had created could not survive either, so she created a new Dana."

"Basically, that is it."

"And now the new Dana is smarter, faster, and better than the old Dana."

"Whether you are better is up to how you live your life."

"And now you want this spirit who has been living inside me to go into that brain-dead girl's body."

"This being you call a spirit was my wife for a long time."

"Then I totally agree. I will go with you to the clinic and help you with this project. Because yes, I understand the crash killed me, and Marie brought me back to life."

"Thank you."

Dana looked at Alerton and asked, "Do I have another space relative on Earth?"

Alerton replied, "A couple. Everin, whom you have met, is my sister. Metrool is my brother, and Margaux is his hybrid wife."

Everin chimed in and said, *Hello, Dana. Welcome to the family. I am very close to my brother; we have been family for a long time.*

Alerton's phone rang with a special ringtone that told him it was Dr. Starret. Dr. Starret told Alerton the body had been delivered to his research hospital, and temporarily, Dr. Starret had total possession of it.

"Did you get the type of room and equipment I asked for?"

"Everything is either in the hospital suite or in the anteroom next to it."

"Very good," Alerton said. "Call me back in twenty minutes." He turned to Dana. "Are you willing to go to the research hospital and take part in this?"

She said, "Of course. I owe my life to Marie."

Marie chimed in and said, *Thank you, Dana.*

It was twenty-five miles to the hospital, but they did not take a helicopter, because Alerton did not want to draw attention. Their trip had to be secret. Mark drove the large, heavy, quiet limo, and the ride was silent. All were thinking about what the night would mean to them. Dana would be alone, with no angel to advise her. It was the critical night for

Marie. Would she be alive, dead, or totally scrambled? If something went wrong, Alerton would have to terminate her, as he had promised. It could be the last night of her existence.

Alerton's emotions were torn in several ways. He had never joined with a woman on Hamen, and on Earth, for the first two hundred years, he had had physical relations with a few but nothing serious. Then he had met Marie. Now, after three hundred wonderful years, he was losing her. Even if the experiment worked perfectly, he was going to lose her. If it went perfectly, she would become an eighteen-year-old young woman. She would have forty-three- and forty-four-year-old parents and a twenty-year-old brother. She would cover for not knowing them or remembering them by being an amnesia victim. They would be so happy to get her back that they would enjoy telling her everything they had ever done. She, of course, could have no contact with Alerton.

The family was middle class; they did not have a lot of money but were good people. Alerton had had them investigated, and the whole family had only one traffic ticket, and it belonged to Marie. Alerton had arranged for the research facility to check Marie over and give her $100,000. But tomorrow she might not exist. Dana lately had begun scanning now that she knew what it was.

Alerton said, *Marie, you do not have to do this.*

I know, Marie said. *I know you would support any decision I made.*

Mentally, Dana told Marie, *You could live with me as long as I live if you wanted.*

I know, Marie replied, *but I want to live. I want to feel the wind on my face and the sun on my skin.*

Soon they were in Starret's office.

Alerton asked, "Is this person healthy and free of disease?"

"Yes," Starret said. "Except for no brain activity, she is normal. There is no brain activity, none of the experts could induce any, and you, a businessman, think you can?"

Alerton took Starret into another office and said, "You know I put a lot of funds into your facility and into several others. You do not know everything they give me. You promised me twenty-four hours of total security and privacy."

"Yes," Starret said, "that is all I can legally cover. I cannot risk losing my license and my position. Your area of the hospital will be sealed off and guarded. No one will disturb you. But you cannot take her out of the area."

"What if she walks out?"

"That is impossible."

Starret led them into the hospital suite, and Dana gasped. The woman in the bed could have been her sister. She was young, pretty, and pale.

Starret said, "Do you need anything that was not on your equipment list?"

"No," Alerton said, "that is all we need."

Alerton escorted Starret out, locked the door, and talked to Marie. Then he wiped a vein with cotton and alcohol, picked up a syringe, and filled it with his blood. Then, using the patient's PICC line, Alerton injected his blood into her.

Soon her vital signs improved slightly, but they had not been bad before. They continued to watch the woman, but nothing changed. An hour after the first injection, they gave her one from Dana. Two hours later, there was still practically no brain-wave activity.

Alerton and Mark rolled in a second hospital bed, and Mark transferred the equipment in the anteroom to the suite.

In the days before that night, Alerton had instructed Mark on setting up the equipment. Mark was one of the few people Alerton trusted totally. He let Alerton scan him anytime he wanted to; he had nothing to hide. His wife had deserted him when he came back from military duty as an invalid. Alerton had given him a job, and when he had learned Mark's true virtues, he had given Mark a cc of Hamen blood three times. It was not enough to change him, just enough to repair him. Mark worked out and was fit now, but he had no family. Alerton's family was his family.

Alerton had Dana lie down on the second bed and asked, "Are you ready?" She said yes.

There were two computers—they were the fastest computers on Earth. They had been made by the self-modified Hamen creator. Their storage capacity was unlimited. They had special modules and headgear. Twenty-seven days ago, the creator had informed Alerton that the equipment was ready.

Alerton had asked the creator what technology it had used, and it had informed him that the Purgon was most suitable.

"Oh," Alerton had replied, "the corrective device on Hamen."

"Yes," creator had said. "If it can take information out, it can put information in."

Now Dana and the patient were in the headgear. Alerton asked Dana and Marie if they were ready, and both said yes. Mark turned the program on, and the computers and headgear began to make strange sounds.

"Currently," Alerton said, "the computers are mapping your brains."

Forty-seven minutes after the computers started, they stopped.

Alerton read the report. "Ninety-six percent match. That is great."

Mentally, Marie said, *Let's do it.*

Alerton said, "You know this still may not work."

Marie said, *I know, but do it now.*

Alerton gave Mark the signal, and the noise and lights began again.

One hour and fourteen minutes later, Dana's computer shut down, and a robotic voice said, "Dana may remove her headgear."

Alerton helped her remove it, and Dana sat up shakily. "Wow," she said, "that was a heck of an experience. It felt like you had bugs in there."

Alerton asked if Marie was there inside her, and Dana said, "She is not here."

The computer on the body continued for another hour and a half, and then it shut down. The robot voice said, "You may remove the headgear."

Dana and Alerton removed it, but nothing happened. The young woman just lay there. However, an hour later, the patient let out a long moan, and Alerton and Dana became excited—but nothing happened.

Thirty-seven minutes after that, a strange voice said, "I am here." The words were garbled, but they understood.

The strange, stumbling voice spoke again. "I am here, but everything is not arranged right."

"Are you OK?" Alerton asked.

"Yes, darling, I am here, and I will be," Marie said. "The transfer was a little rough, but I am happy with it. I believe I will be viable, and I have already seen that Hamen brainpower works here. I can rearrange things."

Alerton again swabbed his arm and then filled a syringe about halfway and injected it into the PICC line. He said, "I love you."

Marie replied, "And I love you," as the patient mumbled.

Alerton said, "You know what happens now."

The patient, with the stumbling voice, said, "Yes, I will be a patient waking from a coma with total amnesia. I will not know anyone; I will not remember anything we have done together. They will have to tell me and show me pictures."

Alerton then asked Dana, "Can I be alone with the patient?"

"Of course," Dana said, and she went into the anteroom.

Alerton took the patient in his arms and crushed her to him. It was like holding a dying person.

Her voice was uneven and ragged. "Kiss me," she said. "I am Marie, and it will be a long time before we can kiss again." They kissed fiercely several times.

"I will wait for you," Alerton said.

"No," Marie said, "you are a famous, respected elder businessman, and I will not destroy that. We had three hundred wonderful years. Never forget me, and never forget how much I love you; I love you enough to give you up. You must go on. You know we already have large targets on our backs."

"Yes," Alerton said, "but I would just as soon meet my demise as lose you."

"You must go get Starret, and we must part."

After two more kisses, Alerton broke away and told Mark, "Quickly pack up everything, and load it up. Leave nothing."

With eyes full of tears and not looking back, Alerton left the suite. He called Starret, who said sarcastically, "Are you finished with your voodoo?"

"Yes," Alerton said, "and the patient is awake."

"Impossible!" Starret practically yelled.

"Then come see."

Twenty minutes later, Starret arrived with four other doctors. They were all over the patient, scheduling forty more tests. From across the room, Alerton talked to Marie. His last words were *Goodbye for now*.

⊷❦⊶

Dana walked up to the door of Alerton's business office, which was on the upper floor of Alerton's two-story complex. Dana said, "Open," and the door opened. There were only two voices that would open the door. Dana went into the vast room of dark wood, leather, and subdued lighting meant to enhance Alerton at his large desk. Dana walked up to his desk, and when Alerton looked up from his computer, she said, "You gave Marie some of your blood, didn't you?"

"Yes," Alerton said, "five different times. Why do you ask?"

"Well then, she had your blood in her, and she used part of herself to make me. So I really am your and Marie's child."

"Dana, believe me, I totally think of you as my child. Also, I am very proud of you."

"Thank you," she said. "I was wary of you, but I have been around you for three years now, and I know I can trust you."

Alerton replied, "Is that why you scan me?"

She blushed. "I am just being nosy. Your losing Marie—I know how large that was."

"You know, you, Everin, and Met are the only ones I let scan me."

"Thank you. I will not betray your trust."

"I know I have done many things you do not approve of, but I have only done what I thought was necessary to protect the ones I care about."

"Do you think Hamen ever tried to find you?"

"I don't think they knew what happened to us."

"Do you think they ever came looking?"

"Not for us," Alerton said.

"But you think they may have come here?"

"Yes."

"When?" Dana asked.

"In the 1950s and '60s," Alerton said.

"Why do you think they came then?"

"The people of Earth had become nuclear."

"Why would they want to check on that?"

Alerton hesitated and then said, "Because of our visits, Earth's people have not advanced in a normal manner."

"What do you mean?" Dana asked.

"Your advancement has been erratic. Your mental and physical conditions are about where they should be."

"I hear doubt," Dana said.

"Yes, your music, science, and weapons are much further advanced than they should be. Your science and weapons are about fifteen to twenty thousand years ahead of where you should be."

"Are you serious?"

"Yes. We have had to interfere a few times."

"You three?"

"Yes. It was just mental, but we have had to help leaders make the right decisions. Sometimes they can't get information that we can."

"Like what?"

"What another leader really wants. What he will settle for. That is hard for a spy to find out."

"So you have prevented a war?"

"No, I would not say that, but we have prevented some incidents."

"Would you tell me what they were?"

Alerton smiled and said, "You do not need to know."

Dana laughed. "Yeah, if you told me, you would have to kill me."

Alerton smiled again and thought, *That is nearly true.*

———— ›❄‹ ————

In a small town fifty miles away, Marie, now known as Hannah, was in a quandary. Marie was rich, but she could not get any of her money to her new family. Hannah could not walk into a bank with one of her many accounts and say, "Hello. I am Marie, and I want to draw my money out." She hated to contact Alerton, but she saw no other way. It would bring up love and hurt in both, but her new family were in dire straits, when they could have been well off.

Alerton? Marie sent a mental message.

Yes, Marie? he replied.

I need your help.

Are you all right?

Yes, it isn't like that. I have this wonderful family who are providing for me wonderfully, and they are flat broke. In trying to save this girl, they begged and borrowed every dollar they could. Now those bills are coming due. Her grandparents even mortgaged their home for her. And I have this huge fortune I can't touch. I would like for you to figure out a way to get a large part of it to the family.

274

I will get back to you when I have a way.

Thank you, sailor, Marie said, using a term of affection she had used for many years. Alerton broke contact, and she wondered, *Should I have said that?*

Two days later, Alerton messaged her: *Marie?*

Yes, I am here.

You need to get someone in your new family to buy you a lottery ticket in the big lottery.

Irritated, Marie asked, *Alerton, is this a joke?*

Alerton said, *No, Marie, I am serious. You need to get hold of a ticket for the big lottery and get the number to me as soon as you get it.*

Two hours later, Hannah talked Sarah, her mother, into going to a convenience store to buy a ticket. Before going, Sarah said, "I don't know why you want this thing, but OK."

As soon as she got the ticket, Marie relayed the numbers to Alerton.

Three days later, at 10:20 at night, Hannah was in her bedroom. She heard her brother, James, making noise in the living room. With her wobbly walk, which was improving, she went toward the noise. When she got there, James had the ticket in his hand.

James said, "We won! We won the damn lottery!"

The rest of the family heard the commotion and came into the living room. Hannah's father, Harry, said, "This may be real, but it may not be."

Two days later, in the lottery office, Hannah, James, and Harry were informed they really had won. If they took the cash option, the amount would be $26 million. A few minutes later, the whole family was in a conference room provided by the lottery.

Sarah, Hannah's mother, said, "Honey, you practically forced me to buy that ticket. So, Hannah, this is your money."

"No," Hannah said, "you and Dad sign and put this into your accounts. I totally trust you and Dad to do the right thing."

Sarah said, "Oh, honey, you are still the same sweet girl you always were."

No, Marie thought, *but from everything I have learned, she was a wonderful person.*

Three days later, Marie received a message from Alerton, and she said, *Yes, I am here.*

Alerton said, *Hannah is becoming a very rich young woman.*

Yes, thank you for the lottery.

I don't mean just that. She now has a large account in a local bank and a much larger account in a national bank. The paperwork will be sent to me for now, but gradually, all your fortune will be put in Hannah A. Williams's name.

Thank you, Alerton. She almost automatically said, *I love you*, but stopped herself.

But he read her mind and said, *I do you too. Goodbye.*

Two young women, Dana and Hannah—what would their futures be?

36

2017

Three years later

ALERTON WAS AT HIS DESK IN THE ALERTON ELECTRONICS TOWER IN Manhattan, when his secretary rang his phone. Alerton picked up the old-style desk phone and said, "Yes?"

The secretary said, "There is a Uriel de Vinci here who wants to see you."

Alerton thought, *No, it cannot be. It has been four hundred years since I have heard from this happy farmer.* He pushed a button, a screen popped up, and there was Uriel on the screen. He was a tall, good-looking man of sixty—older, of course, since it had been 570 years since they had helped him. Alerton thought he was at least six hundred years old. Alerton told his secretary to send him in.

Alerton stood up as Uriel came in, and they embraced for two or three minutes with thoughts passing back and forth between them. Then Alerton invited him to sit, and they began to talk.

Uriel told Alerton, "I need your help."

Alerton said, "Of course. How can I help?"

Uriel shocked him by saying, "Andromeda is dying, and regular doctors cannot help her."

Alerton asked, "How can I help?"

"I think the same treatments you gave me would save her."

"What is her illness?"

"You knew she was older than me, and you probably knew she was a higher percentage earthling than me. She has aged faster than I. She got you to help me, and she has been a good sister to me all these years. I have to help her if I can."

Alerton thought back eighty years to the time they'd saved Talaron and said, "Maybe we can."

They talked for a while—Uriel was fluent in English—and then Alerton made a phone call to Everin. He asked her to have dinner with him. She said, "Of course."

Alerton said, "Oh, I will be bringing our old friend Uriel with me."

Everin replied, "Wow, I will love it."

Alerton rang his secretary and told her, "Call my pilots, and tell them to have the 737 ready to fly to Italy at eight in the morning."

Uriel asked, "Are you married?"

Alerton said, "That is a long story. She was in a plane crash, and I do not have her anymore." The memories were rough on Alerton. In return, he asked Uriel if he was married.

Uriel replied, "Not now, but I have been married five times."

Alerton asked, "Do you have children?"

"No, I saw what happened to me, so I did not let that happen."

"Did you stay in Vinci?"

"We stayed there for thirty years the first time. We loved the place, so we have gone back and stayed for a time many times. You gave us a start financially; you paid for the farm and put money in the bank. Andromeda and I worked, and we were successful. We rented that farm out and bought others as we moved around the country. Andromeda is smart, and we have been quite successful."

Alerton took Uriel down one floor to floor 109, which was his home. Alerton knew by sensing that his twenty-one-year-old daughter was home.

Alerton introduced Uriel to her, and she said, "Whoa, Pop, there is a lot here you have to tell me."

Uriel, who was a mix of earthling, Engel, and Hamen and had strong senses, looked at Alerton and said, "You have a lot to tell me."

Dana looked at Uriel and then at Alerton and asked, "You knew him five hundred seventy years ago?"

Uriel said, "Yes, they saved my life. I was ready to terminate myself."

Dana asked, "Why would you want to do that?"

Uriel replied, "I was a monster."

Alerton said, "He was not a monster, but he looked very bad, and people judge by looks."

As Alerton and Uriel were about to leave to meet Everin, Dana asked, "Will you come back and talk to me?"

Uriel said, "Of course I will."

Once they were in a taxi, Uriel said, "You have a lot to tell me about your daughter."

Alerton said, "I will, but it will take a while."

In a few minutes, they were at a well-known restaurant two blocks from Everin's Central Park apartment. Everin already had a table for them.

Everin embraced Uriel, kissed him on the cheek, and said, "You are as handsome as ever."

Uriel looked at Everin and said, "You are sad." He hesitated. "You lost Doc."

Tears came to her eyes, and she used mental power to push them away. "Yes, I lost the love of my life."

Uriel said, "I was at your wedding; I know what you two had. It was wonderful." His comment brought a smile to her face.

Everin said, "That was the happiest day of my life. Doc never let me down or disappointed me."

A waiter took their drink order, and Uriel ordered a bottle of Uriel 1999 vintage. Alerton knew of the wine, but he had not associated it with their Uriel. They began to discuss Andromeda.

Uriel said, "She has always been a big sister to me. She has taken care of me and my wives and helped me run the businesses." Uriel saw a look of surprise on Everin and said, "Oh yes, after you gave us a start, we went on to other farms. We started pressing and bottling the olive oil. Then we went into making wine from our grapes. When it came time to move on, we would buy another farm, say, eighty miles away but rent the old one out. We own a lot of Italian real estate."

Everin asked, "Andromeda never married?"

"No, but she had many companions over the years, and they enjoyed each other. Like me, she was afraid to have a child and did not know if she could have one or not."

They discussed what they could do for Andromeda, but it was not scientific. Alerton and Everin told Uriel how close Talaron had come to dying. The wine came, and it was excellent and reminded them of Tuscany.

Suddenly, Alerton received a message from Metrool: *Hey, Alerton, I am getting all kinds of stray waves from you. What is going on?*

Alerton answered, *Our old friend Uriel is here, asking for our help. We are flying to Florence tomorrow.*

After a moment's hesitation, Metrool asked, *Can you stop in England and let Margaux and I go with you?*

Yes, we can. We will be at Gatwick.

We will meet you there.

After dinner, Everin went home to her longtime Central Park apartment. She could almost feel Mavis's presence. Mavis had lived with Everin for a long time, right up to the time she'd passed away.

Alerton and Uriel took a taxi back to the tower so Uriel could keep his promise to Dana. Alerton let them talk alone. He was proud of Dana. She worked for Alerton Electronics, and in his opinion, she was his most brilliant engineer.

Eventually, Uriel came from the living room to the den, where Alerton was, and said, "Now you have to give me that story."

"All right," Alerton said. "I told you Marie was in a plane crash."

"Yes, you said she died in a plane crash."

"No, I said I lost her in a plane crash."

"Then you have a story to tell me."

An hour later, Uriel said, "So Marie is in a new life, and Dana really is Marie's and your daughter."

"Yes," Alerton said, "that is the only way I think of her."

The next morning, Alerton and Uriel rose early, ate, and then got in Alerton's limo. They picked up Everin and were on their way to the airport.

In thirty minutes, they were about to board the new version of the 737. The two crews were checking it out, as they always did. Alerton nearly always had two crews so there would not be any holdups. They entered the plane at the front, just behind the relief crew's quarters. The plane had a small kitchen; two bathrooms, one with a shower; and sixteen business-class-type seats. One of the two stewards was the chef. The flight was long but smooth.

They landed at Gatwick Airport, and Margaux and Metrool were there waiting for them. The plane was quickly refueled, and they boarded. The takeoff was smooth, and soon they were busy talking.

Two hours later, they landed at Amerigo Vespucci Airport in Florence. Uriel had called ahead and had two cars and drivers waiting on them.

Alerton had been back to Florence many times on visits. It was always an amazing city to him.

Forty minutes later, they arrived at the farm. Although it obviously had been rebuilt and modernized, the farm had the same aura. They were all quiet for a while. Uriel's cook had a continental breakfast for them. It was approaching dawn.

When they had passed enough time, Uriel took them in to Andromeda. The once tall, strong woman sat crumpled in a wheelchair. The difference was a shock. They all went to her, embracing her and talking to her. It was evident this pale, withered lady was glad to see them. The talking and exchanges went on until she had to rest. Then the group gathered and talked about what they could do for her.

The next morning, after breakfast, they gathered with Andromeda to discuss what they could do for her.

After a while, she said, "Thank you for coming to help me. You came to help me once before, five hundred seventy years ago. I vividly recall I was tied to a stake, and they were about to burn me, but you saved me. Uriel feels he has to save me now, but I have lived a wonderful life. I have spent years with many wonderful companions. I have done everything I ever wanted to do. I have always had a very strong brother to protect me. I know the Hamen tradition, and I am ready to cross over."

They were shocked and silent; some had tears in their eyes.

Metrool spoke up. "Of course we will honor your wishes. If you change your mind, that is all right also." The conversation ended, and the group dispersed.

After a while, out in the vineyard, Uriel got with Alerton and asked, "What if I can get her to change her mind?"

Alerton said, "If it becomes something she wants to do, we will do it."

Uriel, with tears in his eyes, said, "I do not want to lose her."

Alerton said, "I know. I did not want to lose Marie, but some decisions are not ours to make."

The next few days were confusing. The Hamens were glad to see one another, but it was a stressful situation. Andromeda was not fighting her crossover, but she was not rushing it. She was enjoying having old friends around, and they would not deny her that.

Alerton knew Uriel had talked to Andromeda twice about their helping her, but she had not changed her mind. Alerton and Metrool visited one of Uriel's wineries, and Metrool showed Margaux where they had lived a long time ago.

Later, Everin, taking them all with her for support, went to her and Doc's former home. It was still there, and while touring the empty home, Everin collapsed. Alerton carried her back to the van.

They started to drive away, but Everin grabbed Alerton's arm and said, "Not yet, please."

Alerton had the driver stop in front of the home. It was as if Everin were in a trance for a few minutes. Then she sat up, and Metrool asked, "What was it, Everin?"

Everin said, "It was as if Doc were talking to me, and I saw him just as he was when we lived here."

Uriel thought for a moment and then said, "Sometimes emotion can be embedded in a location."

Everin said, "I do not know what it was, but it was real." Looking toward the home, she said out loud, "I love you, Doc." She then said, "We can go now."

They drove to other places they knew in Florence. They noticed Everin was calm now.

Alerton had the driver drive by where their first bank had been. A tall, shiny building had replaced it.

Back at the farm, as was their custom, they spent a lot of time with Andromeda. They wanted no pressure on her either way.

Then it was obvious that her condition worsened. Again, Uriel appealed to her to let them treat her. Again, she turned him down. Then Uriel did a strange thing: he went to Margaux and asked her to tell Andromeda the story of how Metrool had saved her life.

Margaux went to Everin and Alerton and asked, "What should I do?" They were neutral. Margaux was in a tight spot.

She went to Andromeda and said only, "I was severely injured, and Metrool saved my life. Uriel wants me to tell you about it." Then she went to another part of the home.

Later, Uriel was with Andromeda, and she told him, "Tell Margaux I would like to hear her story."

They all became aware that Margaux was going to talk to Andromeda. They were both hopeful and fearful.

After the dinner meal, Andromeda invited Margaux into her bedroom to talk to her. Margaux told her the story.

Afterward, Andromeda said, "It is a wonderful story, and I will think about it."

Margaux left her room, and a few minutes later, Uriel went in and hugged Andromeda good night. Then the group gathered in the living room to have a glass of wine and talk before they retired.

At approximately three thirty in the morning, they all were awakened by strong brain waves. Uriel immediately ran to Andromeda and saw she was gone. They all gathered in her room and did a formal Hamen remembrance. The look on her face was tranquil, with a hint of a smile. It was not a sad or painful face. Uriel rushed out of the home and into the vineyard.

They could all feel his storm of emotions. They did not bother him. At one point, Alerton opened his senses and saw him chopping wood to work off his emotions. Later, Uriel came in and headed for the shower and clean clothes. Then, looking and acting normal, Uriel called the proper authorities, and he obviously had connections.

The authorities came out to the farm, did a cursory exam, filled out some papers, and left. Within an hour after that, funeral people arrived with a beautiful casket and burial clothes for Andromeda.

The Hamens were all sent outside. After an hour, they were invited back in. The casket was on a stand in the large living room. The funeral director said, "We will open the top half of the lid for fifteen minutes, and then we will close it."

They all came close one by one and silently said their goodbyes. When Uriel stood beside the casket, Alerton felt his message: *You should have let us treat you.* The casket was closed, and the morticians were about to leave.

Alerton heard one of them tell Uriel, "We will be here tomorrow at two o'clock."

After the morticians were gone, Alerton asked Uriel, "What is at two o'clock?"

Uriel took a deep breath and said, "In the southeast part of Florence is an old cemetery. It has many beautiful monuments and many large tombs."

Alerton said, "Yes, I have been to it."

"A long time ago, someone built a large tomb, but it was never used. I have acquired ownership of it, and tomorrow we will take Andromeda there."

"That is wonderful."

"That is also where I would prefer to be after my demise."

The next day, the funeral home brought a hearse and two limos to the farm. They loaded the casket into the hearse, and the people got into the limos. It was about a twenty-mile drive through country and city to the graveyard. It was quiet during the drive.

The group watched the six pallbearers carry Andromeda on the long walk across the old cemetery. When they reached the tomb, another person from the mortuary set up a stand, and the pallbearers set the casket down on it. Clergy were already there, and soon they had done the burial ceremony. The tomb was opened, and Andromeda was carried into it and placed on a stone bench on the right. The tomb was closed, and the clergy said a few more words.

When the funeral was over, the Hamens felt flat as they walked back across the large cemetery. They boarded the limos, and they were nearly to the farm, when Alerton got a call from Dana.

She said, "Pop, are you sitting down?"

"Yes, I am," Alerton said. "What is this about?"

"I have some bad news. A truck went out of control and rammed a taxi."

"Who was in it? One of my friends or one of my employees?"

"Brace yourself, Pop."

"Dammit, Dana, tell me who."

"It was Marie."

Alerton caught his breath and could not breathe for a minute. Finally, he asked, "Is she alive?"

Dana said, "Yes, she is. She is in critical condition at the Presby Hospital."

Alerton said, "Go see if you can do anything for her. I will be there as quickly as I can."

Alerton then called Terry, one of his pilots, and said, "Get the 37 ready for immediate takeoff. Plot the quickest route to New York."

Terry asked, "Are we going to Gatwick?"

Alerton answered, "No, just the quickest way to New York."

Alerton then told the others about Marie and said, "I have to go."

Everin said, "I am going with you." She told Metrool and Margaux, "You should stay with Uriel for a while."

Margaux replied, "We are going to stay at least a month."

One of Uriel's limos rushed them to the airport, and a few minutes after they arrived, the jet engines were running. Quickly, the jet was rushing down the runway and climbing into the air. Alerton pushed a button on his personal chair and told the captain, "Fly as fast as is safe."

The captain replied, "Yes, sir."

Alerton and Everin talked some about what he knew. Everin suggested he put himself out for a while, and he did. She put her mind to work to see how she could help.

Everin realized they had two problems: saving Marie's life and keeping the hospital from finding out she was an alien. Everin got the plane's satellite phone and made a call to Roy Jones.

"Dr. Jones, this is Everin. Do you remember me?"

The doctor answered, "How could I possibly forget? I spent so much time with my grandmother in your apartment."

"I loved your grandmother Mavis," Everin said.

Roy replied, "Believe me, she knew you did."

"Roy, do you have doctor and surgeon privileges at Presby?"

"Yes, I do."

"I have a huge favor to ask of you."

"If I can do it, I will do it."

"Roy, there is a patient at Presby who was terribly injured in a taxi accident. We want all her tests seen only by you."

"I believe I can do that."

"Please take over her care quickly. She does not take drugs, and she does not even take medicine, but some of her tests may look strange."

"I will go now and do what I can."

After a few hours, Everin woke Alerton and told him what she had done.

Alerton said, "Oh, thank you, Everin. I was only thinking of saving her life."

Everin replied, "Well, she does not need to be on the front page of the tabloids."

As soon as they landed, they got a taxi to the Presby. When Alerton got there, he found Hannah's parents were sitting with her, so there was no reason for him to go in. Instead, he messaged Marie and said, *I am here, and I will take care of you.* He felt the emotion in the thank-you she sent back.

Dr. Roy Jones cornered Alerton and took him to a private room. He had a whole armful of x-rays and papers. He said, "Alerton, you have some talking to do."

Alerton tried to stall him, but he pushed. Roy said, "I have known Everin for forty-five years, and she looks exactly the same now as she did then." He pointed to the x-rays. "I am taking x-rays of Hannah's broken bones every two hours, and her bones are healing faster than anyone's ever have."

Alerton said, "I guess you would like a good answer."

Roy said, "Yes, I would. I know you own major pharmaceutical companies. Are you giving her medicine that is not on the market?"

Alerton calmly replied, "No, we are from another planet."

Roy scoffed and said, "Now you are trying to be funny."

"No, I am being honest because I need you." There was a book lying on the table, and Alerton made it float above the table.

Roy said, "A magician's trick."

Alerton made Roy's right arm go up and down and then both arms, and after, Roy was a believer.

Alerton said, "That young girl is a wonderful person, and I do not want her in the newspapers because of a few weird tests."

Roy said, "I understand, and I will keep it quiet, but you have a lot to tell me. I have seen Everin learn a new language in three afternoons, and I have seen her lift furniture that a man could not lift."

Alerton promised to tell him things, and he put engrams in his mind so he could not reveal them.

A few minutes later, Alerton happened to be passing by when Sarah Williams went out for a cup of coffee. She saw him and loudly said, "You!"

Alerton paused and said, "Yes, lady?"

"You were there when they revived my Hannah."

"Yes."

"I always felt that you were part of waking her."

Alerton said, "Maybe a little, ma'am."

Sarah went back into Hannah's room.

Alerton messaged Marie and said, *I have made friends with your doctor, and he is going to keep your secret. You are healing fast.*

Marie said, *Thank you for everything, Al. I still love you, sailor.*

Alerton left the hospital with tears in his eyes.

Printed in the United States
by Baker & Taylor Publisher Services

Havoc, Thy Name Is Twenty-First Century!

Thermodynamic Isolation and the New World Order

Peter Pogany

Havoc, Thy Name Is Twenty-First Century!
Thermodynamic Isolation and the New World Order

iUniverse books may be ordered through booksellers or by contacting:

iUniverse
1663 Liberty Drive
Bloomington, IN 47403
www.iuniverse.com
1-800-Authors (1-800-288-4677)

ISBN: 978-1-4917-3900-6 (sc)
ISBN: 978-1-4917-3899-3 (e)

Library of Congress Control Number: 2014944297

Print information available on the last page.

iUniverse rev. date: 10/14/2015

Contents

Summary vii
Introduction xi

Chapter One
    Basics of thermodynamic reality 1
Chapter Two
    Analytical approach to the Drawdown 11
Chapter Three
    Grand illusions of anthropocentrism 27
Chapter Four
    The thermodynamic view of universal history 51
Chapter Five
    Diachronic momenta of consciousness 71

Concluding remarks 101
Appendix A
    Difference between problem and predicament 103
Appendix B
    World history as the synoptic narrative
    of a thermodynamic unfolding 121
References 131

Summary

The world at large does not see physical obstacles to endless economic expansion. Few ever think that what appears to be an acceptable rate of growth of their respective national economies adds up to an untenable acceleration at the global level. A 3-percent average annual growth across the planet would double world output (Gross World Product) in two dozen years and would quadruple it in half a century. The growth vehicle will run out of economically accessible resources long before such peaks of absurdity could be reached, wrecking the environment along the way. Yet, given the Earth's increasing population, the three percent is required to keep average per capita incomes from falling. Global society has reached a critical stage. The organization of its productive activities will collapse without exponential growth but the era of unbridled exponentiation is over.

We are being bombarded around the clock with good news about resource abundance and epochal breakthroughs in nanotech, fusion energy, algae, and the cornucopian blessings of digitalization just around the corner. Indeed, it is in the vital interest of the expiring world order to accentuate these positive developments and keep each on its discreet plane of marginal comprehension, discouraging their analysis in an integral context.

Granted, there is plenty of oil left in the Earth's crust, but it is strictly of two kinds: "expensive" and "too expensive." This circumstance, by itself, dampens growth prospects; but that's not all. The size of the global economy already far exceeds what renewable resources could support, and the current form of economic organization is systemically unfit to lead to an optimal "maximum renewable (green)/minimum nonrenewable" mix. The "new machine age," no doubt a great promise, threatens to curtail demand for labor; a problem that neither the market nor public authority can solve.

Contemporary economic thinking is locked into two boxes. The outer one is called "a-physicality." The inner one is "a-historicity." The time has come to make economics think outside these boxes.

As the nexus between *Homo sapiens* and its ecological constraints ripens, science needs to address the "global scale issue" in thermodynamic terms. The material entity that the human biomass and produced objects represent may be a good starting point. This entity (called "global population plus its economy," GLOPPE, throughout the text) is seen as a spontaneous thermodynamic process with two fundamental characteristics: it is dissipative and it entails a *"steady state/ chaotic transition/steady state"* pulsation.

Dissipation follows from the second law of thermodynamics. Economics will eventually have to absorb apodictically that regardless of scientific-technical developments and the intensity of entrepreneurial drive, the aggregate, long-run supply of telluric substance-borne free energy is on a path of declining elasticity. To hasten recognition, it would be helpful to consider the planet an isolated, rather than a closed thermodynamic system. From the perspective of its evolutionary potential, the world is indeed *Under the Dome*. Universal history is the human face of GLOPPE's thermodynamic ("*steady state/chaotic transition/steady state*") periodization that has an *a priori* direction.

Specifically, it will be argued that (a) the emergence of classical capitalism in the nineteenth century answered the need for comprehensive, homogenous self-organization; (b) this *steady state*, interrupted by World War I, was replaced after World War II (i.e., "1914-1945" was a *chaotic transition* that led to a new *steady state* as represented by the postwar and current world order); (c) the implied transformation has been accompanied by a nonarbitrary, causally determined, irreversible socialization (growth in multilayered interdependence) of intranational and international economic relations; and (d) global society is drifting toward a new form of self-organization that will recognize limits to demographic-economic expansion.

What will it take to go from considering tightened modes of *multilateral* governance a monstrous dystopia to people around the world on their knees begging for a planetary *Magna Carta* that is more detailed, focused and enforceable than the United Nations Charter of 1945? It will take nothing less than a mutation in consciousness, as outlined by the Swiss thinker, Jean Gebser (1905-1973). But a mutation of the implied magnitude amounts to nothing less than a break with centuries of ingrained habits, values, and expectations. It is simply inconceivable without the hard fate of macrohistoric turmoil.

The world lives suspended over an abyss. To appreciate its depth one must recognize that whereas "1914-1945" was the price paid for a mere historic adaptation, the impending turbulence must yield a transformation of evolutionary significance. The argument that the potentially disruptive violence of such a difficult mutation may be diffused by an arbitrary lengthening of its time falters on the already binding physical constraints to economic weight gain.

The new *chaotic transition* will start between now and the 2030s; and, barring a miracle, it will turn the world into a charnel house on a scale that will make the destruction, gore, and horrific imbecilities of "1914-1945" look like a mere prologue. But the will to live must triumph in the fullness of time. Once this defining, dark chapter is closed and the world discovers itself, there are many reasons to believe in the rebirth of an all-embracing, well-founded Hegelian optimism.

Introduction

Orthodox economics assumes a self-adjusting, facile harmony between the economic process and its material resources. This credo of ecological independence, which is logically consistent with existing institutions, social life, politics, culture, and ethics, now faces the censorship of reality.

Predictions that the global economy will double its size in 18 or 24 years (based on the widely used 4- and 3-percent annual growth rates of the Gross World Product, respectively) are dead in the water. The fanciful dream about turning the world into a shopping center for 10 billion people with ample parking for their 2.5 billion motor vehicles by mid-century is clearly in the realm of Fairyland.[1]

If the planet's economy operated at the full employment of its currently available resources, or if it would make significant strides toward it, the phenomenon of Nature applying the brakes on the human enterprise would be

---

[1]   Meadows, Meadows, Randers, and Behrens (1972) planted and Meadows, Meadows, and Randers (1992) rekindled the scale limit problematic. The immune system of established economic ideology rejected both publications with vexatious derision.

quite obvious. Only relative sluggishness dulls and slows the already unfolding clash between our civilization and its physical constraints. But reckoning with a historic no-exit situation is clearly on the horizon. The prevalent form of economic organization, which cannot survive without accelerating output levels, tends to activate its inhibiting antidotes: rise in the cost of nonrenewable resources[2]

---

2   James D. Hamilton's econometric work has convincingly demonstrated the significant role oil price hikes must have played in triggering worldwide economic setbacks in the wake of Middle Eastern crises and OPEC embargoes. The plasma role image of crude oil in the global economy was made even clearer by evidence that skyrocketing oil prices (explainable by excess demand) played a major role in the recession of 2007-2008, as well:

http://www.voxeu.org/article/did-rising-oil-prices-trigger-current-recession

"Oil Prices, Exhaustible Resources, and Economic Growth" (a chapter prepared for the *Handbook of Energy and Climate Change*) by the same author details the reasons why the economic (and hence geopolitical) consequences of the inevitably approaching stagnation and decline in oil production are likely to be severe:

http://dss.ucsd.edu/~jhamilto/handbook_climate.pdf

Keith Sill elaborated on the evidence that oil price increases lead to economic slowdown:

http://www.philadelphiafed.org/research-and-data/publications/business-review/2007/q1/br_q1-2007-3_oil-shocks.pdf

The UK-based New Economics Foundation (NEF) equated the upward-trending marginal cost of oil production with a glass ceiling on economic growth:

http://dnwssx4l7gl7s.cloudfront.net/nefoundation/default/page/-/files/Glass_ceiling_webReady_.pdf

Two IMF working papers bolster the conviction that the world faces an oil predicament:

http://www.imf.org/external/pubs/cat/longres.cfm?sk=25884.0

http://www.imf.org/external/pubs/cat/longres.aspx?sk=40066.0

Kurt Cobb poignantly commented on the two papers:

http://www.resilience.org/stories/2012-11-11/

and in the likelihood of punishing environmental mishaps.[3] To assess the future without Pollyannaish subterfuge, the planet's thermodynamic isolation ought to be considered a self-evident axiom. (Stephen E. King's symbolic energy field that came down on a single locality in his novel, *Under the Dome*, envelopes the entire world -- menacingly as well as protectively, like the trusted walls of a *Domus*.[4]) Supporting arguments are summed up in Chapter One.

Chapter Two presents a rudimentary, quantitative platform for the proposition that the sum of free (available) energy contained in earthly matter undergoes an accelerated qualitative degradation. Indeed, it is a complex sponge of gradients that can be squeezed only once. The global community's downhill movement on the free energy hyperplane is referred to as the *Drawdown*. The aside on Saint

---

does-the-imf-believe-we-have-a-peak-oil-problem

The marginal cost of the following metals threatens to escalate in the foreseeable future: "Precious metals," i.e., Silver, Gold, and the platinum group (Ruthenium, Rhodium, Palladium, Osmium, Iridium, in addition to Platinum); "minor metals" Gallium, Germanium, Indium, and Thallium; the "tungsten group" (i.e., Tantalum, Zirconium, Niobium, and Molybdenum, in addition to Tungsten) and the 15 Lanthanides ("rare earth elements"). The economic significance of this list can hardly be overestimated. As alloys, catalysts, and components, these elements are indispensable in the production of structural materials, computers, a wide range of industrial goods, household appliances, medical and optical products, transportation, space-engineering, and defense equipment. For details on the depletion of industrial metals in the broad context of limits to economic expansion, see Diederen (2010).

[3] Gore (2013) demonstrates the imminence of experiencing the consequences of environmental abuse.

[4] The enigmatic, lynx-eyed sight with which a consummate artist can transcend the world's disorderly, confusing progression is a reassuringly perennial trait of human intelligence.

Anselm was motivated by the idea that even the best cause needs propaganda: To associate the entropy law with the ethical imperatives of a new, long-run-equilibrium-seeking *Weltanschauung*, it needs to be adjudicated thoroughly and repeatedly.

Chapter Three intends to demonstrate how wrong-headed modernity's intrinsic assumption is; namely, that thanks to man's engineering genius and entrepreneurship, the enormous amounts of energy the sun radiates to the planet, and the indestructibility of matter and energy, the global economy does not have a scale limit. It can grow forever as if propelled by an invisible *deus ex machina*. The deep root of this conviction is an unrecognized fallacy of composition: Average consciousness (i.e., the world at large) implicitly extends the individual's thermodynamic openness (a biological necessity) to the entire global population.

Chapter Four spells out that meta-history (or universal sociological history) is an epiphenomenon of the thermodynamically dissipative process represented by the combined demographic-economic expansion. The *"steady state/chaotic transition/steady state"* sequence characteristic of such processes may be recognized by considering "1914-1945" the *chaotic transition* that led from the first *global system, laissez faire/zero multilateralism/metal money* (GS1) to the second and current one, *mixed economy/weak multilateralism/fractional reserve money* (GS2). Examples illustrate how widespread chaotic transitions are in Nature. The reason for this special emphasis is that the world is in the prodromal phase of another nonlinear macrohistoric episode as it strains toward a third, hypothetical *global system* (GS3): *two-level economy/strong multilateralism/mostly government money* (*maximum reserve banking*).

Given the insolvability of the aggregate scale problem within the parameters of the extant socioeconomic order; and that the system with a truly macroscopic, empirical approach capable of solving it is abhorred on sight, one can reasonably predict the coming of a universal crisis of consciousness. This is the subject of Chapter Five. It centers on the teachings of Jean Gebser (1905-1973).

Appendix A, "Difference between problem and predicament," elaborates on the historical inevitability of *chaotic transitions* and illustrates it by demonstrating the current *global system*'s unfitness to minimize dependence on nonrenewable resources.

Appendix B, "World history as the synoptic narrative of a thermodynamic unfolding," recaps and expands the thermodynamic theory of universal history.

Chapter One

Basics of thermodynamic reality

GLOPPE

The *global population plus its economy* (GLOPPE) is the combined substance of the human biomass, other life-forms in human service, and objects created through the economic process. Although at first glance it may seem demeaning to generalize to the point where the difference between *Homo sapiens*, a goat, and a toaster vanishes, without making this gigantic, restless organized lump of matter the center of analysis, the world as a biological and socioeconomic phenomenon, with a powerful and (as it will be argued) unstoppable momentum, is reduced to a multiplicity of meaningless perspectives gained by staring through knotholes.

GLOPPE is a life phenomenon. Thus, it is not "unnatural" in the sense Rudolf Clausius (1822-1888) used the expression to characterize the transformation of heat into work by combustion engines. *Au contraire*! Like electricity, life appears whenever its physico-chemical conditions come together. The close proximity of zinc, carbon, and acid will make electrons flow; that of atmosphere, liquid water, certain elements and physicochemical stability will create a natural flux of energy we call life. Since life subsumes the urge to improve the quality of living, GLOPPE may be considered to be thermodynamically spontaneous even if it is manifest in innumerable nonspontaneous activities, as the multiplication of individuals and the fabrication of use values make it abundantly obvious.

Physics attributes spontaneous processes to the eternal thermal agitation of molecules, atoms, and subatomic particles. The question as to how this technical definition could apply to purpose- and rationality-suffused GLOPPE may be answered this way: Chance fluctuations in the brain would like to make cerebral matter and the rest of the body spread out in space, thereby increasing disorder in accordance with the second law of thermodynamics (*second law*). However, the solid contours that define the organism force Nature's primordial entropic drive to follow a complex, indirect strategy. The pockets of order, created by the conscious, willful bustle of an ever larger and better organized human community, will be exceeded by the disorder this phenomenon generates in its surroundings. ("Does intelligent life throughout the cosmos represent an effective strategy of Nature to hasten the restoration of thermodynamic equilibrium in the universe?" Who would dare to answer this question with a claim of credible objectivity? But it seems that *la promesse de bonheur* is the entelechy-carrot and *la joie de vivre* the weekly compensation for an existence that we cannot "rationalize" without committing "philosophical suicide" -- to use Albert Camus' expression. Life and Reason will never sit at the same table.)

To comprehend the practical consequences of GLOPPE's thermodynamic spontaneity, it is essential to have a realistic idea about the medium in which the demographic-economic expansion unfolds.

Terrestrial Sphere

The distance between the Earth's center and its surface at the equator is 3,963 miles. This is the longer way. Going poleward to the surface, the distance is 3,950 miles. If we continued along this radius 6,000 miles straight up, we would be well into the exosphere, where the veil of gases surrounding the planet begins to fade into the interplanetary vacuum. The radius of this sphere is 9,950 miles, roughly 10,000 miles. We can call this imaginary spatial figure, which has a diameter of 20,000 miles, the *Terrestrial Sphere* (*Sphere*). Some stray atoms of hydrogen and other light gases escape from its area into outer space, and meteors and cosmic dust enter it. However, the weight of the mass leaving and entering is negligible compared to the total weight of mass contained in it.[5] With regard to matter, the *Sphere* is virtually closed. The atoms it contains can be broken down into elements or ensembles of elements, such as metals, semimetals, and nonmetals, or minerals and nonminerals. Oxygen is the predominant element. In volume, it is followed from a great distance by potassium, sodium, and calcium. In weight, it is followed somewhat more closely by silicon, aluminum, and iron. For all intents and purposes, the *Sphere*'s inventory of atoms is constant.

What kind of thermodynamic system is the *Sphere*?

---

[5]   The mass of the Earth is estimated to be 5.97×10^{18} tons. Since this calculation was based on the Earth's radius, the *Sphere*'s mass must be greater than this figure.

Modern thermodynamics distinguishes among three kinds of systems: Open, closed, and isolated (Kondepundi and Prigogine, 1998, pp. 3-7). An open system exchanges both energy and matter, the isolated system exchanges none of the two; and the closed system exchanges one of the two with its surroundings. According to these definitions, the *Sphere* is a closed system. It exchanges energy with the exterior (solar radiation, re-radiation) but not matter. Whatever we do with earthbound substances, incorporating them into our bodies, using them as raw material; discarding the bodies, throwing away or reusing matter over and over again, the weight and composition of atoms remain unchanged in the *Sphere*.

GLOPPE's energy comes from absorbing solar radiation and sucking free energy from material structures found in the *Sphere*. Material is the tight constraint. A closer examination of this proposition begins by accepting that GLOPPE is subject to the laws of thermodynamics.

The first law of thermodynamics (*first law*) guarantees that matter in the *Sphere*, whatever happens to it, will not be destroyed. The *second law* is much less reassuring. It informs us that GLOPPE is dissipative. The two main interpretations of the *second law* are "inevitable waste" and "increasing disorder." The first refers to the fact that heat gained from the internal energy of matter cannot be transformed into mechanical energy with one hundred percent efficiency (work output/heat input is always smaller than one). The second interpretation states that disorder in an isolated system tends to increase. It is exactly this second interpretation that allows conventional economics to wipe "entropy" from its list of preoccupations: "Entropy increases in an isolated system, but not in a closed one."[6]

---

[6]   Rudolf Clausius invented the word "entropy." He took "trope," which

Samuelson (1948), the quintessential background study of GS2's *text*,[7] sets the limits of according consideration to thermodynamics in postwar economic ideology. It invokes *Le Chatelier's Principle* as Nature's physical approximation of a self-equilibrating market economy (*op cit.* pp. 36, 38 n. 81, and 168).

In perfect harmony with the dogma of open-ended acceleration as *the* equilibrium, economics textbooks generally avoid the *second law*, although adhering to this "party line" has become next to impossible when teaching courses in natural resource/ environmental and ecological economics. References to entropy in this domain vary from stating the issue correctly without dwelling on its monumental significance (Daly and Farley, 2004); or describing it with succinct accuracy and then forgetting about it (Pearce and Turner, 1990); to presenting a formal argument against irreversible entropic accumulation based on a vague thermodynamic characterization of the *Sphere* (Common and Stagle, 2005).[8] Nevertheless, proofs and demonstrations of the *second law*'s relevance continue to emerge in general economic literature (e.g., Krysiak, 2006, and Jing Chen, 2005).

The world's *de facto* isolation

Given the uniformity of the Earth's solar-lunar environment, the *Sphere* ought to be considered an isolated thermodynamic

---

is Greek for transformation, the core of the concept, and sandwiched it between the prefix "en" and the suffix "y" (cf. Cropper, 2001, p. 101).

[7]   *Text* is the catechism-like summary of a *global system*'s economic blueprint. See Chapter Four.

[8]   See more on the subject of falsifying global thermo-dynamicity in Chapter Three.

system in order to put structure-borne free energy into the relief it deserves.

This apophantic proposition ought not to be shocking. Isolation is never perfect (e.g., gravity and electromagnetic forces penetrate even thermoses). Declaring a system to be sealed off always rests on factors deemed to be relevant from some empirical vantage point. Since GLOPPE is a function of a diminishing terrestrial and a constant extraterrestrial (solar-lunar) flow of energy (and importantly, the second kind cannot be used without drawing from the first kind), the dynamics of our world is better analyzed by focusing on the time-dependent variable. The international scientific community needs to acknowledge perspicuously that, as a mirror process to GLOPPE's growth, the *Sphere*'s totality of *res extensa* (its corporeal substance with chemical potential) has a quantitatively expressible quality that tends to diminish over time. A corollary of this acknowledgment reveals humanity's true thermodynamic condition: The expansion of metabolic exchanges within an isolated system is endogenously constrained and eventually quenched.

The "macro" perspective

The Earth, the Moon, and the Sun together form an isolated thermodynamic system. Although it is, in fact, more isolated than the best thermos, the great distances between these heavenly bodies prevent the formation of the mental image of isolation. Therefore, to see with greater clarity, it may be suitable to consider the Sun's presence on Earth, as well as the Moon's gravitational bounty, as if they appeared on the *Sphere*'s imaginary enveloping surface, i.e., on the *Dome*.

According to this perception, solar radiation does not travel 93 million miles in 8.3 minutes but it is here permanently with the same strength. The average perpendicular radiation per unit of time and surface at the mean distance between the Sun and the Earth, the so-called "solar constant," is indeed a stable, geological fixture of life on Earth, allowing the flow of sunshine to be regarded as a fund-service with the characteristics of being inexhaustible, non-stockpilable, non-materially incorporated, non-excludable, and contingent on a non-arbitrary rate of use.

Visualizing the circumference of the *Sphere* as the loci from which solar rays originate (along with the Moon's gravitational effect) and where the remainder of returned infrared radiation sinks into oblivion, helps the mind to accept the simple fact that GLOPPE expands in a thermodynamically isolated niche. For the price of taking our optical illusion of solar and lunar nearness at face value we purchase thermodynamic reality.

The "micro" perspective

The free energy endowment of the *Sphere* (Ω) may be seen as an exhaustive trichotomy: Category I (Ω_1) is solar radiation; Category II (Ω_2) is matter that depends operatively and continuously on a dynamic with Ω_1; e.g., the atmosphere, land and water surfaces that facilitate and drive the water, nitrogen and carbon cycles. Category III (Ω_3) is matter in the maintenance of which the Sun's presence plays a passive role. Most substances labeled as "nonrenewable resources" (e.g., metals and fossils) belong to this category. Without the Sun these resources would not exist but their endurance over geological eons shows that they are independent of the Earth-Sun dynamics as observed over historical timescales.

Theoretically, weightless Ω_1 may be converted into mass ($e = m\, c^2$) but there is no technique available to put this equivalence into practice. Until extraterrestrial matter is captured, the world's working substance is "$\Omega_2 + \Omega_3$" -- *punctum.*

Transformations occur between these two categories but their sum is constant at a given moment. Viz. the *Sphere* is isolated from contact with any other system that contains free energy and GLOPPE is moving the *Sphere* toward thermodynamic equilibrium. To repeat, Ω is the sum of two constants. The continuous interaction between Ω_1 and the ensemble of free energy enclosed in substances $(\Omega_2 + \Omega_3)$ signifies an openness that is strictly internal to the *Sphere.*

***

Thinking about the *Sphere* as a closed system leaves the world's thermodynamicity open to dispute, engendering disconnected (isolated) views about the future. Considering the *Sphere* isolated ends the controversy, allowing global society to comprehend its true condition integrally: *Since the weight of the Sphere is constant, any swelling of GLOPPE compresses the rest of the Sphere* (defined as the *Surroundings* in the next chapter).

The paradigmatic acceptance of the *Sphere's* isolation may indeed be considered the *pons asinorum* of a new, meaningful economics -- with consequences, of course. David Ricardo is waiting on the other side of the bridge with folded arms. When generalizing his land-oriented differential ground rent theory to free-energy-containing structured matter (which, in contrast to "Ricardian land," is destructible and is being destructed, but just as surface it has a limited supply), his fears about unmet long-term expansionist resource needs become justified.

As the *Drawdown* depletes the generally beneficial rent bonanza; i.e., the so-far persistent productivity difference attributable to using the easiest accessible chemical energy instead of marginal (best rent-free) molecules for the same purpose (presuming identical capital inputs as Ricardo did), the trend toward impoverishment appears on the horizon.[9]

Subsistence living promises to become the margin of output; ridden with conflicts because resource-owning nations want to maximize their rent collection, and because a stagnating economy is civil discontent waiting to happen -- especially at a time when government spending must be curbed. (It cannot be left unmentioned that doctrinaire GS2 economists do not see danger in creating mountains of debt because they cannot accept the idea that the global economic organism is already embroiled in a hostile confrontation with Nature's police cordon.)

---

[9]   GS2's *text* reproaches Ricardo for ignoring technological development, but the analysis it has inspired fails to recognize the critical dependence of the "Green Revolution" on oil; GLOPPE's best-known, already active, universal tight constraint.

Chapter Two

Analytical approach
to the *Drawdown*

If we define GLOPPE as the "system," the *Sphere* minus GLOPPE's matter the *Surroundings*, and consider the manifold activities in which the system engages the *Surroundings* purely mechanical work,[10] the *first law* says:

(1) ΔU (*Sphere*) + ΔW (GLOPPE) + ΔW (*Surroundings*) = 0

where ΔU (*Sphere*) is the change in the *Sphere*'s internal energy (potential energy contained in the chemical bonds of its molecules, equivalent *in toto* to the energy required to create the *Sphere*); ΔW(GLOPPE) is the amount of work GLOPPE performs on itself during the same period (e.g., reproduction of humans and animals in human service; simple replacement of used up capital goods), and ΔW(*Surroundings*) is the work GLOPPE completes on the medium against which it expands (e.g., adding to the human

---

[10]   GLOPPE may be thought of as giving new forms to matter, a characterization that fits the concept of work.

biomass, making barren lands arable, extracting petroleum and natural gas).

Remembering that an exact correspondence exists among measures of energy, heat and work (all expressible in joules), the *first law* may be applied to the thermodynamic interactions that result in GLOPPE's existence and expansion in the following way:

(2) $\Delta Q = \Delta U \text{ (GLOPPE)} + \Sigma \Delta W$

where ΔQ is the heat added to GLOPPE (by solar radiation and by sucking free energy from the *Surroundings*); ΔU (GLOPPE) -- henceforth ΔU -- denotes change in GLOPPE's internal energy (e.g., starch accumulates in corn kernels, photosynthesis); and $\Sigma \Delta W$ is the work GLOPPE does, once again on itself and on the *Surroundings* combined.

So far, the application of the *first law* did not take the thermodynamic isolation of the *Sphere* into account. Without such consideration equations (1) and (2) appear to be solely the expressions of the "no-free-lunch" principle.

The full appreciation of the *first law* requires the conservation principle; i.e., that in an isolated system neither energy nor matter (as a form of energy) can vanish. Indeed, the number of atoms in the *Sphere* remains the same regardless of GLOPPE's fate. The sum of free and bound energy is constant. But whereas the *first law* reminds us that not even the enormity of solar and substance-contained free energy may be translated into a *perpetuum mobile*, the *second law* conveys an additional, profoundly important warning: *The ratio of bound energy within the total (i.e., the sum of bound and free energy) grows irreversibly.*

Let us shine a beam of light on thermodynamic reality by comparing GLOPPE to the rusting of iron.[11]

Iron symbolizes the preconditions of life (including photosynthesis[12]) in this analog and the dispersed oxygen molecules in the surroundings stand for the totality of terrestrial matter. The reaction between dispersed oxygen gas and solid iron molecules reduces entropy since the resultant iron oxide (rust) has a relatively solid structure. This is possible only by an increase in the surroundings' entropy through heat release, to an extent that exceeds the entropy reduction caused by rusting. The process is spontaneous and, accordingly, exothermic. But unlike for GLOPPE, entropy reduction and the overall greater increase in entropy in the immediate space are measurable along the macro-coordinates of pressure and temperature.

Since the free energy feeding GLOPPE may be regarded as heat transfer under constant atmospheric pressure, the examination of the *second law*'s effect may proceed by leaning on the concept of enthalpy (H).

H is a state variable indicative of a system's thermal energy, its thermodynamic potential. It is the sum of the system's internal energy and the energy required to allow it to exist by exerting pressure (P) to maintain volume (V):

---

[11] The example closely follows Gillespie, Humphreys, Baird, and Robinson (1986), pp. 880 and 881.

[12] In compliance with the *first law*, plants convert solar to chemical energy, and the amount of energy included in the matter used by plants remains unchanged as the seasons pass. The *second law* may be recognized in the qualitative degradation of the matter involved; in the inefficiency of energy conversion as well as in the loss of energy plants give off as heat.

(3) $H = U + P.V$

Given that assigning numerical values to a system's energy contents is an unsolved problem, actual calculations aim at estimating changes in enthalpy under constant pressure:

(4) $\Delta H = \Delta U + P. \Delta V$

Increases in the entropy of the *Surroundings* may be expressed with the help of alterations in GLOPPE's enthalpy as follows:

(5) ΔS (*Surroundings*) $= - \Delta H$ (GLOPPE) / T

where T is the absolute temperature (Kelvin scale) at which the process takes place.

Since theoretically, alteration in GLOPPE's enthalpy is the sum of enthalpies contained in GLOPPE's components minus the sum obtained by adding up the enthalpies of material inputs ("products" and "reactants" in thermochemistry), ΔH (GLOPPE) may be expressed in the following way:

(6) ΔH (GLOPPE) $= \sum H$ (GLOPPE components) $- \sum H$ (Material inputs)

As a manifestation of the *second law*, the absolute value of the first term must be smaller than that of the second; that is, GLOPPE releases more bound energy into the *Surroundings* than the amount of free energy it sucks from there during a given period: ΔH (GLOPPE) < 0.

GLOPPE performs work by pushing back, compressing the *Surroundings*. The negative sign of ΔH (GLOPPE) implies an exothermic (heat releasing) process. More precisely, GLOPPE exhibits net exothermicity. While it is also endothermic by taking heat (free energy) from the

Surroundings, it releases more heat into it (bound energy). Nonetheless, global warming, a well-documented side effect of human expansion, indicates that some of the bound energy GLOPPE releases is, in fact, heat.

Over a short period, GLOPPE's expansion is isothermal. In this case, the work performed (W) in the process of increasing its volume from v to V, under pressure P, may be conceptualized with the help of the following equation:

(7) $W = \int_v^V P \, dGLOPPE$

This is, of course, a major simplification. GLOPPE is endothermic also by living on solar radiation and this fact does not allow global warming to be considered the sole result of rendering material structures useless through the metabolic interaction between GLOPPE and the *Surroundings.* GLOPPE augments the greenhouse effect as a result of pollution (extruded heat in material form; i.e., bound energy remaining in the *Sphere*) by lowering the "albedo;" the ratio of solar heat the *Sphere* reradiates into the *Surroundings.*

The *second law* states that the reduction of entropy via creating structures contained in GLOPPE will be exceeded by an increase in the entropy of the *Surroundings*:

(8) ΔS (*Sphere*) = ΔS (GLOPPE) + ΔS (*Surroundings*) > 0

The absolute value of the first (negative) term is smaller than that of the second (positive) one. Note that ΔS (GLOPPE) is the sum of a positive measure, indicating the tendency of any created structure to come apart the second it has been created (the result of thermal agitation everywhere across the universe, including the human brain), and (a larger in absolute value) negative one that stands for the creation of structures, in a temporary defiance of the *second law*.

Fusing various interpretations of the *second law*, it may be said that entropy inescapably and irreversibly increases in the *Sphere* as the matter contained in it drifts toward states of higher probability.

Simple algebraic manipulation of (5) and (8) yields

(9) $-\text{T} . \Delta\text{S}$ (*Sphere*) = ΔH (GLOPPE) $-\text{T} . \Delta\text{S}$ (GLOPPE)

The left-hand side of the above equation is defined as change in "Gibbs free energy;" that is:

(10) ΔG (*Sphere*) = ΔH (GLOPPE) $- \text{T} . \Delta\text{S}$ (GLOPPE)

"Gibbs free energy" is a concise state function that includes those state functions and variables which command interest in the present context. It helps visualize the total, chemically free energy in the *Sphere* because G can be equated with the dot product of two vectors: one containing the quantity of each substance in moles (G) and the other the "Gibbs free energy" content of the corresponding mole (M):

(11)   G = G. M

Given that ΔH (GLOPPE) is negative and ΔS (GLOPPE) is positive, ΔG (*Sphere*) is negative.

ΔG (*Sphere*) being smaller than zero is the result of the global loss that exceeds in absolute value the sum of billions of dispersed gains ($\Delta\text{G} > 0$) which result from the nonspontaneous (endergonic) creation and maintenance of humans and extrasomatic objects.

All this is not intended to prove that GLOPPE is depleting the *Sphere*'s stock of free energy enclosed in structured matter. The contrary would be a sorry exercise in "question begging" because the conclusion reached via enthalpy and "Gibbs free energy" already presumed the hypothesis about the way the *second law* affects the mutually enforced demographic-economic expansion. Growth in the *Sphere*'s entropy was ensured by the continuous negative change in GLOPPE's enthalpy, which in turn, was based on the entropic argument encapsulated by equation (5).

To answer the question "then why not simply state these propositions," no lesser authority than that of Saint Anselm of Canterbury (1033-1109) needs to be invoked: "... unless I first believe," said the father of scholastic philosophy, "I shall not understand." Belief in humanity's thermodynamic reality does not, of course, come from revelation; it is not testimony-grounded wisdom to be imparted through the pastoral leadership of inspired ministry.

The problem of recognizing GLOPPE's entropic nature (as witnessed by the disparagement with which conventional economics defers such recognition) resides not so much in the difficulty of comprehending the basic argument as in a lack of willingness to clear the passage toward its acceptance: Belief in practically infinite resource abundance -- using the conservation law and the bounty of solar radiation as uncritically regurgitated arguments -- is the taproot through which upbeat business psychology, *a priori* confidence in permanently accelerating growth can be sustained in GS2's Keynesian economies.

Under these circumstances, a laconic affirmation that the *second law* bears down on humanity's ecological niche, sagacious as it may be, is next to useless in enlightening the public. It flies in one ear and out the other. Aphoristic brevity effectively turns the proposition into futile dust by depriving it of its nourishment -- appropriate mindfulness.

When the purpose is to develop an easily blocked-out flash of insight into a firmly held conviction that penetrates the quotidian; stirs curiosity, breeds theoretical skills and moral capital, grunt work is needed. As demonstrated, even a limited examination of GLOPPE's interaction with its tellurian constraints has hammered home that GLOPPE is a spontaneous process (i.e., it will not stop until the energy potential for its continuation forces it to do so through social means rather than by physically running out of free energy congealed in matter); helped to digest the enormous significance of the qualitative distinction between free and bounded energy, and to think about work, heat, and energy as varied aspects of the same phenomenon.

In the present context, Saint Anselm's sequence relies on the following dialectic: Understanding, which presumes absorption of details; and belief, which hinges on pithy, supra-theoric maxims ("sound bites") reinforce one another until belief becomes strong enough to sustain ecological realism in individual consciousness. Such dialectic is immanent to collective thinking.

Of course, words by themselves will never substitute for the trauma that separates being stoned on cornucopian ends and principles from entropy-consciousness. But preparatory self-edification by expanding the field, exposing its hidden dimensions, penetrating into its layers through analysis and discussion may be expected to reduce its length and intensity.

To continue in this spirit, let us sum up in continuous terms, the consequences of GLOPPE's spontaneity. When T is later than t;

(12)   S (*Sphere*, T) > S (*Sphere*, t)

I.e., entropy accumulation in the *Sphere* from t to T (denoted as S^*) is positive:

$$S^* (\textit{Sphere}) = - \int_t^T S(\text{GLOPPE}) \, dt + \int_t^T S(\text{Surroundings}) \, dt > 0$$

The absolute value of the second term exceeds that of the first one, the result of anti-chance (negentropic) structure-forming activities implied by GLOPPE.

Alternatively, using Fermi's equation, (Fermi, 1936, p. 46), the "exchange of heat" between a system and its surroundings will be negative:

(14) $\sum_i Q_i / T_i < 0$

where positive Qs indicate heat (low entropy energy) received by GLOPPE from the *Surroundings* and negative Qs stand for the heat surrendered to them (in the form of higher entropy energy). T_i stands for the Kelvin-scale temperature at which Q_i is transacted. T_i may also be defined as the average temperature in the area that environmentalists designate as the biosphere. This approach allows for the recognition of global warming, a nonissue until the 1960s, but an exponentially increasing one since then. (Cf. Gore, 2006, 2009, and 2013.)

Current economic fundamentalism, which ignores GLOPPE's diminishing potential to do work (transform heat to work), regards equation (14) as an equality; i.e.,

$\sum_i Q_i / T_i = 0$; pretending that GLOPPE is a reversible process; and that the *Surroundings* act as a heat bath; i.e., an infinitely large and unchanging thermal reservoir regardless of GLOPPE's scale and dynamism.

The likely slowing of entropy accumulation over equal periods based on (12) is consistent with the famous Boltzmann formula:

(15) $S = k.\log W$

where entropy associated with the macrostate of a given system (S) is the multiple of the Boltzmann constant (k) and the natural logarithm of the level of disorder (W) as it is measured combinatorially by the number of microstates conceivable in a given macrostate. Equation (15) suggests that the entropy generation of GLOPPE will necessarily slow down.

This projection is also implied by the general characteristics of the equation showing the time evolution of "Gibbs free energy" in an isolated system. The first derivative of this equation is negative at constant pressure and temperature (conditions that do not interfere with our basic propositions); while the second derivative is positive, implying a decelerating convergence to the minimum. (Cf. Kolesnikov, Vinokurov, and Kolesnikov, 2001, pp. 135 and 136.)

The build-up of entropy may be considered in a different way (following Fermi's "second example;" Fermi, 1936, p. 56): GLOPPE (assumed momentarily to have a fixed scale) "works" on the *Surroundings*, heating them up by friction. Thus, not even "zero population/zero economic growth" would save the world from running down its ecological potential. Georgescu-Roegen (1976) made a strong point of this.

The continuous loss of "Gibbs free energy" is consistent with GLOPPE's spontaneous, irreversible (exergonic) nature. Moreover, in conformity with basic thermochemistry, GLOPPE could never use up the entire stock of "Gibbs free energy" theoretically at its disposal. Indeed, there is no conceivable socioeconomic organization under which humanity could extract the last drop of enthalpy from the planet's material structures. Thus, GLOPPE-caused entropy accumulation straining toward the equalization of chemical energy potentials is not expected to eradicate matter in the *Sphere*. As long as the cosmos does not suffer "heat death" -- the cessation of all subatomic vibrations and related chance fluctuations -- this obviously cannot happen. Put differently, GLOPPE cannot become so big that it would wipe out free energy, turning the *Surroundings* into a homogenously inert (chaotic) system relative to itself.[13]

But this is hardly a solace. GLOPPE can increase randomness in the distribution of terrestrial molecules relative to its biological and economic-technical needs to a point where free-energy containing structures no longer accommodate a large population of well-living individuals. The range of human-specific enzymes restricts the pathways of metabolic conversion. Our creaturely limitations exclude the assimilation of nourishment from paper or dirt, and matter can be used for extrasomatic purposes only as long as the free energy required to access it does not exceed the free energy it contains. Making metal from metal ashes and

---

[13] The conclusion of Takuro Uehara's model (Takuro Uehara, 2013) that an "ecological economic threshold" is likely to precede the "ecological threshold" is correct and highly relevant.

gasoline from fumes does not promise a brilliant future. And counting on technology to prevent or reverse the general degradation of matter is a defective theoretical orientation. It is equivalent to claiming to have discovered a perpetual motion machine (cf. *infra*).

Approach to lethally high entropy levels for the species is unlikely to be monotonous. As mentioned before, a smooth approach is conceivable only for nonspontaneous processes. Given, however, that GLOPPE is spontaneous, a major, historical collision (or a series of such collisions) with its constraints looms on the horizon of universal history.

The following assertion lends further support to this hypothesis. Individuals can exist only in an open thermodynamic relationship with their surroundings but socioeconomic institutions and perceived norms of stability tacitly presume that the same openness exists between groupings of individuals (e.g., business firms and nations) and their surroundings; and consequently, between human civilization and the *Sphere* (cf. *infra*).

In purely abstract terms, events corresponding to a "forcing algebra" (containing a set of forcing equations) will induce GLOPPE to follow a dynamic path of decelerating dissipation. However, for the moment there are no convincing signs that a cure for the emerging disease is developing *in tandem*. Given the extreme dynamism of the resource demand structure and technological progress, the absolute size of molecularly contained free energy is an unquantifiable, metastable constraint (the ultimate "moving target"). But these complications ought not to make the world lose sight of its central problem: the *Drawdown* inevitably raises the cost of a given rate of free energy flow from the *Surroundings* into GLOPPE.

How much effort has been exerted to catalyze the needed enlightenment with negligible results is illustrated by the fact that none of such relatively new concepts as exergy, anergy, ektropy, enstrophy, and emergy (all intended to direct public attention to the world's most basic long-run problem) has won appreciable notice.[14] None of them has acquired *meme* status; that is, "a node in semantic memory" (to adopt Edward O. Wilson's expression; cf. Wilson, 1999, p. 148) with cultural significance.

$$***$$

To conclude this chapter, let us underscore that GLOPPE's engagement of the *Surroundings* cannot be viewed as a purely physical phenomenon; i.e., a process of equalization that targets mechanical, thermal, and chemical nonuniformities between two compartments of an isolated system. Movement toward thermodynamic equilibrium (maximum entropy) proceeds through what, from Nature's perspective, appears to be the anti-entropic effort of life. Indeed, GLOPPE's existence and dynamism reveal the six characteristics of living systems:

(i) Humans (without whom their extrasomatic extensions would obviously not exist) are composed of cells; (ii)

---

[14] The term exergy is attributed to Zoran Rant (1904-1972). It combines the energy and entropy balances of a closed or isolated system; i.e., its distance from thermodynamic equilibrium; or equivalently, the maximum work it is capable of performing. Anergy is its complement. Thus, Energy = Exergy + Anergy. Exergy has been used in several publications. (See, for example, Diederen, 2010.) Ektropy is the negentropy living structures need (cf. Georgescu-Roegen, 1971, pp.190 and 204). Enstrophy refers to energy decay (dissipation). It comes from fluid dynamics. Emergy denotes the amount of exergy deployed in realizing qualitative transformations. (H. T. Odum used this concept in his pioneering work on integrative environmental accounting; cf. Hall, 1995.)

GLOPPE is an organization (in the age of *global systems*) that turns simple substances into complex ones while maintaining internal equilibrium (homeostasis); (iii) it uses energy to survive; (iv) it grows; (v) it reproduces (also in the extended "Lamarckian" sense by maintaining the evolving institutions as well as matching behavior-conditioning legal, cultural, ethical fixtures required for stability in inter-subjective relations); and (vi) it responds to the environment (including its self-created socioeconomic environment) in adaptive ways as it grows and its relationship with the *Surroundings* changes.

To relate the spontaneous thermodynamic essence of the world's demographic-economic self-amplification to an active portion of our semantic force field, picture GLOPPE as a bubble. Nonrenewable resource production and activities based on it constitute the contiguous sectors of its sphere. GLOPPE has surged beyond what its proportions relative to substantive fundamentals could support, yet it continues to dilate (as if blown larger and larger by the consolidated lung capacity of expatiating masses). The financial cosmos is an appendix that creates bubbles on this bubble. But whereas the bursting of financial bubbles is a data-generating process translatable to economic history (i.e., connectible to the past); the bursting of GLOPPE will likely come in a series of frustrated surges, adding up to a singularity of evolutionary significance.

Finally, a note to the margin of the "climate change" debate: GLOPPE generates entropy and thereby moves the *Sphere*'s macrostate toward equilibrium (i.e., the number of possible microstates increases). This process is equivalent to an augmentation in the cost of information required to know where exactly dispersed matter is and what it is "up to." The growing elusiveness of the *Sphere*'s microstate (that is, our decreasing ability to characterize the detailed conditions of the physical environment through selected, coarse criteria) also diminishes the capability to assess environmental threats. Conflicting predictions of climate models and the associated clash of expert opinions, each referring to the other as completely false (if not a hoax or paid advocacy) is a vivid illustration that "ecological information entropy" is on the rise. (See the "island example" in Pogany, 2006, pp. 110-115.)

Chapter Three

Grand illusions
of anthropocentrism

Considering the *Sphere* an isolated instead of a closed thermodynamic system and GLOPPE a spontaneous rather than a nonspontaneous process has powerful implications for the future. Whereas a nonspontaneous process in a closed system decelerates as it approaches equilibrium, this is not the case for a spontaneous process in an isolated system (Kolesnikov, Vinokurov, and Kolesnikov, 2001, p.135). That is, GLOPPE is programmed to collide with its constraints.

With a naiveté that will be the wonder of later generations, contemporary, thermodynamically ingénue economics celebrates the small fractions that energy and material resources represent in the national accounts of advanced countries.[15] It flatly ignores that the increasing volumes of

---

[15]   Given the inelasticity of demand for energy and material resources (and the unrealistic expectation that science and technology will always find equally low price substitutes within the mass of material that enters the economic process) price increases are matched by increases in spending

free energy that stand behind the relatively small percentages are irreversibly growing subtractions from a fixed stock.[16] Science, in general and in the long run, cannot reverse this process because its economically feasible applications through technology are a function of the average condition of matter in the *Sphere*.

Neoclassical market fundamentalists prefer to dispense with the *second law* by making false references to the *first law*[17] and by calling the *Sphere* a thermodynamically open system because of abundant solar radiation. Let us start with the second way and deal with the abuse of the *first law* under the section entitled "Falling for the perpetual motion fallacy" *et passim*.

Worshipping the Sun God

---

shares. Once the price rises significantly for a key resource; e.g., oil, the dynamics of aggregate demand spells danger for economic expansion, eliminating incentives for substitution.

[16] Former U.S. Treasury Secretary, Larry Summers, drew a big laugh at the IMF Economic Forum (November 8, 2013) when he conjured up the image of economists writing papers on the economic consequences of cutbacks in electricity. Since the starting point is that electricity generation represents a small percentage of the GDP, models would indicate a correspondingly small effect -- then, all of a sudden, the lights go out. Accepting the *Sphere's* thermodynamic isolation as a *datum* is the quintessential precondition for seeing the devaluation of primary material and energy resources based on their puny ratios in national accounts as analogously nonsensical. The long and short of it is that contemporary economic analysis functions in a universe of profound misunderstandings.

[17] "Assuming a small and exhaustible supply of resources is nonsense. This defies the law of conservation of mass-energy and denies the fact that in the earth's crust beneath the sea and further toward the core there are vast supplies of mineral resources, some located and charted and others known to exist in a general way." (Lipsey and Steiner, 1975, p. 860.)

Economists wax eloquent about the sun reflexively to protect their beliefs from that darn, red herring of entropy: "It is appropriate to conclude that, as long as the sun shines brightly on our fair planet, the appropriate estimate for the drag from increasing entropy is zero" (Nordhouse, 1992, p. 34).

The quoted work is certainly *la pièce de résistance* in tarring the applicability of the entropy principle in economics with a neoclassical brush. Observe the double sleight of hand when Nordhouse quotes Georgescu-Roegen's statement: "the entire stock of natural resources is not worth more than a few days of sunlight" (Nordhaus, 1992, p. 34). By mistakenly claiming that Georgescu-Roegen considered solar radiation "negentropy income," Nordhouse made Georgescu-Roegen negate his own thesis.

Georgescu-Roegen referred to negentropy as a concept of dubious value that somehow managed to become current in denoting information as the exact opposite to disorder (a "throwing the baby out with the bath water" kind of overly sweeping criticism on his part with which the present author respectfully disagrees). But by characterizing solar radiation as negentropy, a lot can be gained to make the world safe for eternal economic expansion. Namely, negentropy so used brings solar radiation and material resources under a common aegis, implying substitutability between them.

Two factors help maintain this illusion: First, both solar energy and free energy enclosed in material structures can be expressed in calories (or in some other measure of energy); second, there is a theoretic equivalence between energy and matter since Einstein discovered a fixed exchange rate between the two; i.e., the speed of light squared. It is a huge number, but a constant one. Matter is energy and energy is matter. But we need to think a little further!

The substitutability between solar radiation and matter is one way: Matter is used to generate energy but there is no technology to produce economically significant quantities of matter from energy.

It is the relatively high concentration of energy compared to the ambient environment that renders an energy carrier precious. Calories that the sun pours on the Earth are diluted compared to the concentration of free energy contained in fossil fuels (Diederen, 2010, p. 28). All forms of (fund-service type) solar energy need free energy contained in material structures to be harvested. Thus, ultimately it is the internal energy (the sum of kinetic and potential energy) contained in the fixed number of terrestrial corpuscles that limits GLOPPE. The much-heard bleating about the long-term tendency of natural resource prices to decline originates in an optical illusion that sees the pastures of the future as a mirror image of the past. Natural resource prices do not reflect entropic reality simply because economic thinking is oblivious of a deeply ingrained fallacy of composition.

Believing that openness of the parts is also a property of the whole

All carriers of life exist in open thermodynamic systems as energy and matter flow in and out through their boundaries. Nourishing low entropy (ordered structures) enters the individual and after being used for growth and/or maintenance, it is extruded into the environment as higher entropy (more disordered) structures and body heat. The local reduction of entropy (manifest in anabolism), with its inevitable consequence of increasing entropy in its surroundings (through catabolism), appears as the right-to-life steady state for the individual; in fact, so much so that the organism's thermodynamic openness (henceforth *openness*) has been extended to group behavior.

The question "What will it take for global society to recognize that inconsiderate and contentious *openness* is the most obtrusive adversary of a dignified, commonly shared future?" cannot be answered. Yet even a cursory glance at universal history encourages the requisite induction.

Resource issues caused the exodus from Africa during the waning ten thousand years of the Middle Paleolithic and, much later, from Asia during the Upper Paleolithic and Mesolithic periods. Europe was colonized (displacing the Neanderthals); Paleo-Indians migrated from Central Asia to the Americas; and, radiating along the south-east coast of Asia, human genes reached Australia.

Nomadic groups migrated when their expanding ranks depleted the area, where they sustained themselves through hunting, fishing, and gathering, or when demand for the same resources by rival groups pushed them toward new horizons. Later, when animal husbandry was added to the roster of economic activities, the exhaustion of (or competition for) grazing soil added to the push.

Problems with extrusion of high entropy (henceforth *extrusion*) must have been insignificant relative to finding food and shelter. In due time, the pressure exerted by rendering the intake of low entropy (henceforth *intake*) sparse, along with the psychological strain caused by permanent commotion, insecurity, danger, and occasional starvation, inspired efforts to use land more intensively. The Neolithic Revolution (beginning ca. 10,000 BCE) marked the dawn of agriculture and the creation of fixed settlements on each continent.

Leaning heavily on livestock production (primarily sheep and cattle farming), tillage-by-hoe agriculture was extensive. Military conquest compensated for the decline in crop yields and for the wholesale generation of fallow land. But intensification through crop rotation, irrigation, the use of fertilizers, and ever more advanced tools did not bring world peace. Population growth outstripped productivity growth, catalyzing the motivation to build empires.

As a by-product of early urbanization (in the Nile Valley, the Fertile Crescent, and later in China) the problem of *extrusion* appeared in the form of epidemics, caused by fecal contamination and the consumption of infected animal meat. Spontaneously developing transitional zones between adjacent communities (so-called ecotones) became common sources of infection and primitive, high-density settlements were hotbeds for host-to-host transmissions. Bubonic plague, smallpox, typhus, and tuberculosis appeared long before the Christian era.[18]

Industrialization had set into motion a rapacious quest for *openness*. This historic process began most markedly in China at the outset of the second millennium (CE); and, after establishing footholds during the late medieval period in Western Europe (with the British Isles in the lead), it embarked on its ever more pronounced acceleration after 1500 -- the symbolic year that marks the attainment of geological globalization. The *intake* was rabid and brutally competitive at every level. Nations grabbed as much land as they could through conquest and colonization; the

---

[18] Cf. Despommier, D., Ellis, B.R., and Wilcox, B.A., "The Role of Ecotones in Emerging Infectious Diseases:"

http://www.hawaii.edu/publichealth/ecohealth/si/course-ecohealth/readings/Despommier_etal-2006.pdf accumulation of extrasomatic structures as personal property and in the ownership of production units assumed the norm of rational conduct. The road for the democratization of this overwhelming objective became ever wider and unobstructed as the bourgeoisie struggled with increasing success for the creation of markets in labor, commodities, and money.

The conflict between unconstrained *extrusion* and GLOPPE's growth exploded during the 14ᵗʰ century with the bubonic plague ("Black Death"). While the expanding urban centers of Asia and Europe lacked the most elementary infrastructures and measures of public sanitation, the intensification of commerce between the continents guaranteed the spread and lack of effective control of *Yersinia pestis* (the bacterium generally held responsible for the devastation).

The learning process had been halting and painful. Even after the danger of total extinction subsided, bubonic plague returned in later centuries along with smallpox, cholera, typhus, and influenza.[19] It took many generations to recognize that larger volumes and more varied masses of waste widen the ecological niche for rodents, fleas, lice, and bacteria, multiplying the fecal-oral pathways of infection.

En gros, epidemics may be considered a symptom of inadequate adjustment in *openness* to changed conditions in a community's relationship to its environment. Population growth increases *intake* and *extrusion*; and higher density, in the context of intensified geographic connectedness, demands new communal equipment (e.g., sewers), hygienic standards (e.g., rules regarding food and water safety), and

---

[19]   For a list of major epidemics through history, see the following site: http://en.wikipedia.org/wiki/List_of_epidemics

practices (e.g., burial protocols and waste disposal) coupled with matching stringency in individual self-care and interpersonal relations. The evident difficulty of such evolutionary adaptation lies in the complexity of going from one structure of *openness* to the next, where the word "structure" intends to convey the mutual interdependence of technical, social, and individual factors. In retrospect, the world's adaptation to the conditions its expanding ranks and productive activities have created appears as a victory of its *vis viva*. But the ultimate accomplishment is not at hand. The age of *global systems* has not given birth to the recognition that the materialized aggregate of human aspirations (GLOPPE), conceived through the actualization of ever greater measures of *openness*, is filling up a thermodynamic system that is not open.

GS1 did register significant successes in preventing and containing epidemics but it may be better characterized as providing socioeconomic incentives for a ruthless pursuit of *openness* at all (i.e., individual, business firm, and national) levels. The burst of demographic and economic growth during the system's most successful, Victorian-Edwardian period stifled early clarion calls about resource depletion and environmental degradation.

GS2 has brought a major but not a critical change. Since the late 1950s preoccupation with conservation and environmental protection has become a permanent and often passionate dimension of social discourse. But despite laudable efforts, respectable partial results in policies and technical fixes, the typical consciousness cannot reconcile the world's growth dependency on its material welfare (i.e., individual income derived from economic activities) and the ever worsening disequilibrium between GLOPPE and its physical possibilities. If it could, then GLOPPE would not be a spontaneous thermodynamic phenomenon and reason could guide it to a smooth landing.

Regarding *intake*, most of the planet's inhabitants continue to welter in the illusion that material abundance can grow forever. Most people could not care less about the unsustainable resource demands their actual level of living generates or what their aspired level would entail. Firms are even less sensitive and for a good reason. Private business cannot survive without expansion (a basic fact that zero-growth advocates tend to overlook) and expansion means more material and energy. Jubilation over the historically recent structural evolution of highly developed economies -- the coming to dominance of the service sector and specialization in relatively low-natural-resource-dependent high-tech products -- is an astonishing example of narrow-minded, fragmentary reasoning.

There is no ameliorative slowing in the *Drawdown* when a nation imports material and energy-intensive manufactures from China instead of producing them domestically! Moreover, only one-fifth of the planet's population possesses the fixed assets necessary for a civilized life (as the concept is interpreted today); and even in the implied ensemble of the developed countries, infrastructures need to be replaced from time to time. The idea that GLOPPE's *Drawdown* can assume a viably slow pace through an agreement reached among the three blocks; the developing world (defined by the *The World Bank* as "Lower middle and low income economies"); emerging economies, and the richest nations, is about as realistic as "Goldilocks and the Three Bears."

Peter Pogany

Confrontation-laden Post-Cold War[20] geopolitics has revolved around access to natural resources, oil chief among them. An extensive study (commissioned by the Swiss National Science Foundation) at Columbia University[21]confirmed that asymmetry in resource endowments has been a *casus belli* in international relations since the end of World War II. The study has also revealed that the closeness of oil fields to a sovereign state's administrative borders tends to invite strong-arm showdowns.

On the *extrusion* side, the GS2 era has ushered in many admirable public initiatives and welcome adjustments in individual thinking and behavior. But here again environmental concerns are trumped by the dependency of general welfare on the expansion-demanding profitability of economic activities.

Most firms acted as uninhibited, devil-may-care polluters as long as they could. The pulp and paper industry had to be told that its activities caused deforestation and pollution. The designation "smokestack industry" (e.g., iron and steel works and the chemical industry) came into vogue during the 60s. Toward the end of the last century, public pressure in industrialized democracies had finally resulted in fairly comprehensive regulations both upstream (e.g., via "dirty input limits") and downstream (e.g., "emission controls"); that is, at both the in-taking aperture and the extruding cloaca of man's extrasomatic

---

[20]   The four decades of world-conflagration-threatening standoff (known as the Cold War) was about global systems. Communists, led by the Soviet Union, wanted to replace GS2 with their own system. (See Pogany, 2006).

[21]   Caselli, F., Morelli, M., and Rohner, D.; "The Geography of Inter-State Resource Wars:"

http://econ.columbia.edu/files/econ/camoro_2013_4.pdf

(industrial) "digestion." Certainly, but then large businesses began to pass on environmental harm to poorer countries.

Data on international waste trade shows that residues of production and consumption, too dangerous or uneconomical to recycle (either because of their quality, composition, material nature, or lack of demand) tend to end up in the world's poorer regions. Shipments of refuse from the rich to less-well-to-do countries increased markedly since the 1980s as governments in the former category imposed restrictions and higher costs on domestic waste disposal (cf. Tiemann, 1998). An especially sharp increase has been noted in transporting "dead electronics" (so-called "e-waste") to developing nations. The 1989 "Basel Convention for Controlling Transboundary Movements of Hazardous Wastes and their Disposal" attempted to impose "global environmental justice," but not surprisingly, entrepreneurial interests have been finding ways to play out these good intentions (cf. Clapp, 2001). Similar concerns plague the long-term disposal of high-level (non-recyclable) radioactive waste. While governments in the developed world struggle for the public acceptance of "deep-mined geologic depositories" within their respective borders, Central Asia is on the way to becoming the world's radioactive waste dump.[22]

Whereas in the past, disequilibrium between *extrusion* and the world's self-organization was manifest primarily in the person-to-person transmission of epidemics, the range of postwar environmental problems has become incomparably

---

[22]   See, for example, Biggar, H., "Radioactive Waste Threatens Central Asia," published in the *Europe and Central Asia Newsletter* of the United Nation Development Programme:

http://europeandcis.undp.org/news/show/3162BB7C-F203-1EE9-BF11E0BCB6B5DBA4.

wider. Leaning on well-founded scientific evidence and forward thinking, the environmental agenda now includes heightened concerns about global warming and pollution. The first one is tied to extreme weather, malnutrition as a result of droughts, and an increase in the frequency of natural disasters. Air, soil, and water pollution, on the other hand, is expected to multiply the potential of vector-borne diseases (e.g., malaria) and threaten the individual's breathing and digestive systems. It could be held responsible for birth defects and it may even prompt harmful mutations in the human gene pool.

Wallowing in *openness* has indeed become a menace to *Homo faber*. William Rees' "ecological footprint" analysis (see, for example, Rees, 2006) is an excellent start to examine this universal phenomenon numerically.

"Ecological footprint" converts into a synthetic surface measure ("global hectare") the resources that a certain level of living and associated life-style commands. Calculations allow for comparisons among nations; even among individuals. If the results, pointing to a serious "ecological deficit"[23] for the world as a whole, were not alarming enough, the actual situation is far worse. Simultaneously -- and as a clear consequence of -- the prolonged ecological overshoot, the planet's capacity to supply renewable resources on a sustainable basis is declining. What is more; the approach ignores nonrenewable resources; thus, the unavoidable depletion of structure-borne free energy; the qualitative (thermodynamic) degradation of the *Sphere* in accordance with the *second law*.

---

[23]   Fifty percent is perhaps the most frequently quoted number, meaning that it takes one and a half years to regenerate the renewable resource bundle demanded by the human biomass during one year.

Even with these limitations, "ecological footprint" analysis shows worsening ecological conditions; and differences among nations are becoming more accentuated. Judging from GDP growth forecasts, fast-developing economic giants, China and India, are slated to increase their "footprints" dramatically, playing catch-up with the ecological intensity of developed economies.[24] By and large, developed and fast-developing nations tend to escalate their *openness* more blatantly than the rest of the world. If one also takes into account increasing income inequalities within countries (as noted, for example, by Gore, 2013) as an indicator of widening footprint differences within national communities, it becomes apparent that the world is oblivious of its thermodynamic fallacy of composition.

The sober conclusion is that thinking about *openness* has not changed all that much. It is still true that *Homo homini lupus* when it comes to claiming low entropy and vindicating the right to dispose freely of the feast's useless and harmful remnants.[25]

---

[24]   Dietz, T., Rosa, E.A., and York, R. introduce a technique for projecting future levels of ecological footprint and make some interesting international comparisons:

http://faculty.washington.edu/timbillo/Readings%20and%20 documents/SUGGESTED%20READINGS/dietz_etal_2007.pdf

[25]   A detailed survey of households in the Netherlands showed a low level of "energy literacy and awareness" in the population (Brounen, Kok, and Quigley, 2013). Based on the questions asked in the survey and on the country's high living standards (coupled with its significant ecological footprint), one may justly conclude that, on the average, even relatively wealthy individuals remain unconcerned about the planet's growing resource problems. The contrarian view, expressed through the Environmental Kuznets Curve (EKC), is GS2 ideology under an analytical carapace. (Wagner, 2008, compellingly criticizes the econometric methodology deployed in support of EKC.)

Falling for the perpetual motion fallacy

Nonecological economics imputes a prohibitive marginal cost to restricting the transfer of free energy from the *Surroundings*. Its fundamental message is that growth is equilibrium and equilibrium is growth. So had it been in the past, so it is now and so it shall be in the future.[26]

"AK" models, the most primitive form of endogenous growth theory, lock out diminishing returns. By enlarging the concept of capital to include human capital, this feat could be accomplished even without technical progress. More advanced elaborations (e.g., "innovation-based growth theory") appeal to technological advancement, superseding Robert Solow's "manna from heaven" no-explanation needed explanation of technical progress (cf. Solow, 1957). But it does not take much to discover that technical progress (production technology, increase in the number and quality of products), as par for the course of endless endogenous growth, still remains a kind of never-ending supply of gold nuggets. True, they don't fall from heaven. They are handed out by the Invisible Hand of Maxwell's Demon.

With incisive clarity, Romer (1990) defined technical progress (the inexhaustible driving force of economic growth) as "improvement in the instructions for mixing together raw materials." We can recognize Maxwell's Demon despite the Adam Smith wig tied in a bag with ribbons that he now wears.

To remind the reader, Maxwell's poignant thought experiment featured a Demon who miraculously flouts the

---

[26]   For an authoritative and comprehensive survey of growth theories, see Barro and Sala-i-Martin (1995).

second law by operating a trap door that separates a relatively energy-rich and a relatively energy-poor compartment within an isolated system. Using his magic wand, he opens the door only for high-energy molecules from the low-energy compartment and for low-energy molecules from the high-energy compartment. Instead of evening out energy levels (as Nature has taught man invariably happens), the "rich becomes richer and the poor becomes poorer."

Traditional economics makes an analogous claim. Relying on his growing stock of information, the Demon directs high energy from the *Surroundings* into GLOPPE and it releases ashes and fumes; low-energy content particles or bound energy (economically inaccessible heat) into the former, without increasing overall entropy in the *Sphere*.

This demonic *legerdemain* falters on the information-entropy tradeoff: Increase of information at the Demon's disposal is a reduction in entropy only within a sharply delineated part of the system (the sum of the two variables is always zero within its bounds). We cannot outfox the *second law*. Increase in the entropy of the entire system (i.e., in the *Sphere*) must exceed the reduction of entropy (by way of more technological-scientific knowledge being translated into goods) within any part of the system (i.e., in GLOPPE).[27] In short, information is not free. It has an entropy cost imposed on the whole of the isolated system. The Demon pretends to be ethereal when we observe him but he wolfs down pizza off stage.

Endogenous growth theory makes it clear that technical knowledge (information containing instructions on how to

---

[27] For an accessible and entertaining description of the information-entropy liaison, see Chapter One in Loewenstein, 1999.

work with raw materials) is inherently different from other economic goods, most importantly because such instructions can be used over and over again. This conceptual separation helps to see the parallel between the endogenous growth theory's notion of technical development and Maxwell's Demon.[28]

Economics coldly asserts that there is no free lunch: "positive" production is nonsense without inputs; e.g., $Y_j \cap R^r_{++} = \emptyset$ (Ginnsburgh and Keyzer, 1997, p. 39). Then, with abstractions so remote from real life that they would make the Sage of Königsberg shake his head, transformation functions focus on constrained maximization. The magic occurs through the illusion created around the constraints: GLOPPE prestidigitates them away as it grows.

To safeguard the holy grail of eternal exponentiation, traditional economics flashes its deputy's badge already at the city limits. A not overly derisive way of sending the *bête noire* back to where it came from (i.e., to the Columbus of thermodynamic meaningfulness, Georgescu-Roegen) entails the trump argument that comes so naturally to quantity-obsessed rational consciousness: whatever cannot be subjected to mensuration is irrational. Or, equivalently, if there is such a thing as entropy accumulation at all, market prices already reflect it because they reflect everything.[29]

---

[28] Endogenous growth models distinguish among physical, human, and intellectual capital. The first grows as a result of savings, the second via education, and the third through monopoly-rent-motivated R&D (with public support here and there).

[29] Nordhouse, for example, puts "negentropy drawdown" on the back of the venerable neoclassical production function workhorse by way of a clean-as-a-whistle dynamic term, and then he takes it off stating that prices already reflect it (Nordhouse, 1992, p. 33).

(See Chapter Five for an explanation on how a-historic objectification of market prices blindfolds analysis.)

Although wholly unidentified, the Economic-Entrepreneurial Demon who perpetually pushes out GLOPPE's growth possibility frontier is alive and well in the dogmatic certainty of present day economics. In a "min"-prefaced aggregate production function that combines labor, land, capital, natural resources, and technology, this last term includes an endogenous process that assures natural resources will never be the narrow constraint. This is more than just free lunch. It is free meals forever and anon.

The Demon is indeed manna from heaven for bored patent clerks who can hardly wait for the next "perpetual motion inventor" to send the office into roars of laughter (once the crank is safely out of the building).

The secure horizon of endless growth already hints that the economy is a *Perpetuum Mobile*, running on the virtually infinite duration of sunshine. But, of course, it has a more respectable name: It is called "market-incentive-driven, technology-facilitated unceasing growth guaranteed by eternal, seamless substitution."

In more detail, *Perpetuum Mobile of the First Kind* (the one that violates the *first law*) assumes that one can get out more energy from a process than one puts into it; or, equivalently, that work can be done from bootlegged surplus energy. The concept of endogenous growth does something like that. From the alchemy of competitive search for monopoly rents, coupled with institutional assurances to diffuse knowledge, it secretes technology-generating ideas; quanta of motive power that are additional to energy (including material) inputs accounted for by economic data.

But endogenous growth is more ingenuous than your usual "something for nothing" contrivance. It has also discovered a *Perpetuum Mobile of the Second Kind* (the one that violates the *second law*): GLOPPE expands without dissipation. It is implying even a *Perpetuum Mobile of the Third Kind.*[30] This magnificent dream assumes a mechanism so free of friction and heat loss that it becomes one hundred percent efficient; i.e., GLOPPE of any scale can run indefinitely on the *Sphere*'s limited material resources.

The party of techno-drunkenness continues

Rejection of the *second law* is rooted in mankind's nostalgia for timelessness; or, if that cannot be granted, at least for the continual increase in comfort and convenience as compensation. This entrenched impulse is as understandable as wishing for permanent blue skies.

C2C

The exaggerated optimism reflected by the "Cradle to Cradle" principle, which began with the publication of Braungart and McDonough (2002) comes dangerously close to implying that human-built mechanisms may be perfected to a point where they imitate Nature's eternal self-equilibration in the broadest sense. Many suggestions that arose from the C2C movement are, of course, commendable from the environmental and conservation standpoints but its cornerstone is not less quixotic than a perpetual motion contraption. It lives on the false premise that the old cliché "Nature is always in equilibrium" can be made net of matter's qualitative degradation.

---

[30] Not related to the third law of thermodynamics.

Giga-gushing about "nanotech"

The fast expansion of nanotechnologies, including spin-transport electronics ("sprintronics"), is doubtlessly a significant development with potentially vast effects on the future. But a fair warning is in order. Nano-engineered materials used in various devices, coatings, cosmetics, and golf balls have not kicked the depletion of nonrenewable resources off the field of human concerns; i.e., the *perpetuum mobile* is not at hand. Since scanning and funneling at the atomic level is frightfully evocative of Maxwell's Demon, it is so much more important to remember Maxwell's rejection of the possibility of violating the entropy law, along with other cogent arguments that disprove the latent existence of the Demon.[31]

Sober preliminary assessments underscore that the spread of nanotechnology will demand vast amounts of energy, water, and various polluting chemicals. The impact on the global environment will remain unknown for decades but is presumed to be negative.[32]

To put the new technique in perspective, let us not lose sight of at least three general, unchangeable conditions of the world we live in: (i) nanotechnology will not reduce overall

---

[31]   Cf. Norbert Wiener's frequently quoted argument (Wiener, 1961, p. 58).

[32]   See, for example, the study of the *International POPs Elimination Network's Nanotechnology Working Group*:

http://nano.gov/sites/default/files/dsti_stp_nano201212.pdf

To appreciate how little governments know about the extent of use and impact of nanotechnologies, consult the report of *OECD's Directorate for Science, Technology and Industry, Committee for Scientific and Technological Policy, Working Party on Nanotechnology*:

http://www.eeb.org/documents/090713-OECD-environmental-Brief.pdf

need for structured matter. Regardless of how a product is manufactured, it must remain at the human scale to have use value. (Ceramics may be produced through manipulating molecules but who wants a Procrustean loo?); (ii) to the extent material is saved via an actual increase in productive efficiency, the economic system's growth dependence will claim the savings (Jevon's paradox!); (iii) regardless of how production technology evolves, the associated reconstitution of matter will not change the *Sphere*'s inventory of atoms. It will only push it toward a greater disorder; reducing information about where they are and what they are up to.

Ode to fusion and algae; 1D-thinking about 3D-printers

Nuclear fusion power offers a game-changing vista. It is widely regarded as environmental-friendly and it runs on superabundant Deuterium and Tritium. But do not be taken in by the ceaseless pelt of celebratory press reports about limitless power being at hand. Commercial use is decades away and, if electricity were to become dirt cheap, the chains of the *second law* would bite painfully into our flesh and the current form of pathologically growth dependent economic organization would capsize.

An exorbitant increase in the demand for electricity would, in all likelihood, accelerate the dilapidation of material resources. The rationale to substitute electrical cars for fossil-driven ones would certainly take hold, but (as argued in Appendix A) this substitution process cannot be a continuous one that converges toward and then crosses the tipping point under GS2's watch.

The perpetual motion phantasm also lingers around algal (cellular) oil. It seems inexhaustible indeed if it is tied mentally to solar radiation alone, abstracting away from its nonrenewable material/environmental costs. The pioneering multidisciplinary approach involved in its development merits congratulations. But let us remember what financial huckstering around this great promise wants investors to forget: Commercial-scale motoring on the "green muck" is at least one generation away. And it is impossible to tell what the relative significance of this form of bio-energy will be once "green" energy reaches the critical level, defined as the moment when the renewable energy and material base's "own use" (as interpreted in input-output analysis) embarks on a path of irreversible expansion.

The hubris surrounding 3D printers; the creation of self-multiplying machines that will put production on automatic pilot, as it were, lends acute topicality to Goethe's cautionary tale about the Sorcerer's Apprentice. Besides its physical impossibility, an autonomous global machine (a single, aggregate-use object) that would produce everything the world ever wanted would obviate Labor and Capital, and free enterprise, along with economics, pretty much as Rosa Luxemburg envisioned the end of this field of inquiry through central planning.

Digital manifestos galore

Among the many signs of our chaos-bound times, one peculiar phenomenon is worth dwelling on for a minute. Thoughtful people publish books about how and why digital science and technology portend a brilliant future; then go on to enumerate the problems the new age entails without recognizing that our economic organization cannot handle them. Since solutions must be suggested (and they better be upbeat, practical, and thoroughly consonant with standard expectations and recognized academic authority) the authors invariably sing the popular hymn: "growth, growth, growth;

jobs, jobs, jobs!" Given that mixed-economy governments have already over-prescribed their fiscal-monetary stimulants, the healing incantation "growth and jobs" is, in essence, a piously whispered doxology addressed to the "Market."

Brynjolfsson and McAffe (2014) is the apotheosis of a scholarly *pas de deux* to this theme. The starry-eyed logorrhea begins by quoting an extraordinary royal *wirrkopf*: "Technology is a gift of God," the famed savant said. (This dreadful silliness ranks with his eloquent disparagements of environmental concerns.) Side by side with a helpful enumeration of the blessings that "The Second Machine Age" will bring to the world, Brynjolfsson and McAffe more or less put their digits on the main threat: Digital technology is suspected of being a serial job killer. What to do with the potential masses of incomeless people and the (consequently) unsold bounty of commodities those ever-more-intelligent forerunners of androids drone-deliver to department stores and supermarkets -- short, of course, of producing also some consumer robots? Why, read introductory economics, the catechism; the *text*. (The catechetical nature of introductory college economics is explained in the next chapter). Absorb its wisdom and everything will be alright (op cit. 206-208). The authors' cognitive dissonance is underscored by their recognition of the worsening income distribution, which may be both a subsidiary consequence and an emerging disabler of digitally-mastered productivity growth. The chatty tome even offers some career counseling on the order of "Plastics" -- the laugh-inducing word of advice uttered in the 1967 movie, "The Graduate."

"The Second Machine Age" was a roaring success. There is no reason why it should not have been. It contains useful information, it is entertaining; and who would not like to hear serious scholars confirm the cherished belief that technology, like a miraculous interloper, will solve all our problems. This is providentially ordained, isn't it? (The same thrice holy "Invisible Hand" that created equilibrium in Adam Smith's village markets just keeps on giving.) The flaws brought to light here glisten only in the fissures of modernity's decaying walls. Good salesmanship can easily divert attention from them.

***

Accepting the *Sphere*'s thermodynamic isolation (and, consequently, the relevance of the *second law*) when weighing the prospects of long-term economic expansion removes the guilt of sacrilege from admitting that the historically increasing returns to scale to technological progress are destined to expire. Regardless of scientific brilliance and efforts expanded, Nature's limit to any materially expressed growth is unyieldingly hard under these circumstances. Forget about "and yet." The *Drawdown* demotes all other processes, even the accumulation of information in the service of producing skills, to lower, subsidiary, and therefore, bounded phenomena.

Recognizing the general decline of returns to "R and D" from spatially dispersed, sectorially isolated incidents is a long, uphill road. The suggested world view demythologizes the landscape and provides a shortcut to understanding.

Chapter Four

The thermodynamic view of universal history

GLOPPE is what physicists call a "far-from-equilibrium, dissipative structure" (FFEDS) that evolves unidirectionally, irreversibly and has emergent properties.[33] Ilya Prigonine, Nobel Laureate chemist (1917- 2003), is credited for establishing this school of thought.[34]

The time evolution of a FFEDS is marked by relative steady states separated by chaotic transitions (or bifurcations).[35] Evolutionary theories also characterize this pulsatile sequence as order/disorder, equilibrium/coordination disequilibrium; discontinuous transformation, "evolution by

---

[33] "Far-from-equilibrium" refers to systems/structures that are separated by a considerable distance from "equilibrium," which, for the physicist, means the homogenous dispersion of matter.

[34] Prigogine (1997) provides an overview; Pogany (2006) describes the theory's application to history.

[35] Rosser (1991) surveys the use of "chaos" and the closely related concept of bifurcation in economic literature.

jerks" (as opposed to "evolution by creeps"), and punctuated equilibrium.

Descriptive world history traces the thermodynamically-rooted process: Three centuries of GLOPPE's steady growth preceded the Industrial Revolution during the second half of the 18th century (with Great Britain as its center) and the social revolution that began in France with the storming of the Bastille in 1789. A *chaotic transition* that subsided only in the 1830s led to the genesis of the first *global system*, GS1, characterized as *laissez faire/zero multilateralism/metal money*. GS1 fell apart with the outbreak of World War I. A new *chaotic transition*, which lasted until the end of World War II, ushered in the second and current *global system*; *mixed economy/weak multilateralism/fractional reserve money*.

One is not mistaken by designating the first *global system* as "classical" and the second one as "reformed" capitalism. There are significant differences between the two. Whereas Capital enjoyed nearly absolute power over Labor under GS1, GS2 is based on a compromise between the two. Labor can bargain collectively, workers enjoy unconditional legal and political enfranchisement in industrial democracies (GS2's *vanguard*); respect and dignity in all spheres of life. From being a mere watchman of private property under GS1, the role of the state has increased to that of a responsible director of economic and social development. The international community had no framework of cooperation under GS1. As of the second half of the 20th century, it has the United Nations with its many charter organizations.[36]

Social science does recognize the difference between classical and reformed capitalism but only with a shoulder-shrugging

---

[36]   See Appendix B for a more detailed description.

indifference. It misses the significance of this historic transformation; namely, that it is the result of an ardent struggle; that it is irreversible, and that it is the human face of a physical (thermodynamic) process.[37]

Connecting the thermodynamic process with the emergence and history of *global systems* may seem arbitrary at first. But there is no viable alternative once we accept that the phases associated with the growth and complexification of a material entity in a thermodynamically isolated space must have a recognizable historical version, a narrative aligned with known forms of socioeconomic organization and world events. Since thermodynamic complexification (as it is proposed for interpretation) is global in its scope, its corresponding historical categories must also be global. And indeed, GS1 and GS2, and the world-transforming interludes that led to GS1, and from it to GS2, are the most far-reaching historical categories.

Each *global system* has its *text*.[38]

The basic operating principles of a unified world economy, as elaborated in David Hume's price-specie flow and Adam Smith's *The Wealth of Nations,* may be considered GS1's *text*. GS2's *text* is the introductory economics college textbook,

---

[37] For the sake of illustration, let us compare GS1 to the *Matrix* in the like-titled motion picture, and GS2 to *Matrix Reloaded*. Of course, the analog has its limitations. Most importantly, whereas the cineastes' conceptualization suggested extra-terrestrial domination over life on Earth, the proposed theory maintains that the control is exerted by anthropogenic abstractions that became embodied in institutions and guidelines for adaptive behavior. The control exerted by a *global system* is certainly extra-individual. Moreover, given that the history of global self-organization is enveloped in (or is the manifestation of) a dissipative thermodynamic process, it may also be considered extra-human, thus validating artistic insight to a large extent.

[38] Cf. Pogany (2012).

the prototype of which, authored by Nobel Laureate Paul A. Samuelson (1915-2009), first saw the light in 1948. To use a religious metaphor, the "General Theory" (Keynes, 1965), published in 1936, was the synoptic gospel, based on which Samuelson penned both the Roman catechism, the "Foundations" (Samuelson, 1948), containing the hieratically expressed cornerstones of faith for mitered men of the cloth; and the Baltimore catechism ("Economics") for use in classrooms around the world. The latter work has served as the boilerplate for numerous other primary tools of university-level economic education as well as the canonical source for "penny catechisms" (the simplified and brief "Q and A" approach) to enlighten the general public as to why common sense leads to GS2 and why it radiates the glory of eternal salvation.[39]

GS2's *vade mecum* promotes the will-o'-the wisp of limitless growth. Citing the secular rise of real wages during the industrial age, technical progress offsetting the law of diminishing returns in the aggregate and over the long run; the small percentage that land and material inputs represent in total output, it dismisses classical predictions about global output running out of steam.[40]

---

[39] The suggested doctrinal parallel connects GS1 with the *Old Testament*. However, given the state of communication technology during the first *global system*'s lifetime, the prophetic insights of Hume and Smith never made it into a *text* comparable to Samuelson's "Economics." One may venture to say that the "General Theory" (Keynes, 1965) provided the first historically valid assessment of GS1's organizational foundations.

[40] Did Keynes suspect that the system he inspired would not last forever? Probably he did. Rereading "General Theory" (Keynes, 1965) now in GS2's end times, its author comes across as the genius in a hurry who throws a sketch of his ideas on the table with "try something like this, it might work for a while," then leaves.

The second half of the 20th century was the time to celebrate the analytical apparatus that crystallized around GS2's *text*. It disproved Marxian prophecy about the unquestionable collapse of capitalism through anarchy. Communist ideologues overlooked that Marx talked about a different *global system* than mixed economies being linked through *multilateralism*. The founder of scientific socialism analyzed GS1 and not GS2. Interestingly, most economists in the West also overlook that the second world order's arrangements between Labor and Capital, between the public domain and the private sector, and among nation states, represent an irreversible historic change, a thermodynamic transformation in an isolated system. Barring an annihilation-caliber catastrophe, such a transformation is physically determined to proceed from the simpler toward a more complex system. The oversight is not a peccadillo. It flows from a regrettably uniformed and antipathic nostalgia for GS1.

Since 1968, *la crème de la crème* was annually emblazoned with the "prize in economic sciences in memory of Alfred Nobel." It used to bring unsurpassable eminence and admiration far beyond the confines of economic sciences. How well the economy is understood is a make-or-break issue for everybody, after all. But now, when the chill of historical inevitability sends shudders through the second *global system*'s tired flesh, the award's lack of connection with living reality is painfully clear.

The 2013 Prize was shared by Eugene Fama, Robert Shiller, and Lars Peter Hansen. While the first laureate showed that rationality rules security markets but we cannot put our finger on it; the second demonstrated that irrationality dominates them with pockets of rationality. The third one was recognized for his unprecedented econometric deep drilling to quantify systemic risks (also connected to security markets). And would anyone care to argue that what is quantifiable is also subject to rational control?

Some commentators got hung up on awarding conflicting schools of thought. But there is no real controversy. Upon closer inspection, the meta-message may be descried: Our lives and fortunes, our social safety net, the direction of the thumb given to the job performance of the President; the disposition to consume and to borrow, to invest or not to invest -- in short, whether we smile or cry -- all depends on what happens in the markets where second-hand securities are traded. Not only do economists look for true rationality (that is, in the signifier's broadest sense, inclusive of historical connections) in all the wrong places, the system jazzes them up for misreading it. (With the guileless candor peculiar to the humanistic wealthy, Peter Nobel, a great-grandnephew of Alfred Nobel, has politely expressed his disgust at the whole exercise.)

Well into the 21st century, the time has come to deal with the consequences of the species' frenetic demographic and economic expansion. With a population over seven billion and an annual economic output pushing toward the $90 trillion mark (on a PPP basis, at present writing), GS2 no longer works and no emetic in the form of policies, programs, or reforms can purge it of its ecologically indifferent parameters and dotard maxims. A new global social contract is needed, one that takes into account the relationship between the planet's occupancy and its physical constraints.

Yet awakening remains lackadaisical and fragmentary. The *text* goes on living as if it were business as usual: Thanks to man's entrepreneurial and technical genius; the infallibility of the price system, combined perhaps with some limited public guidance, all existing and potential environmental and resource problems are as good as solved. Growth can go on forever. It is equilibrium, after all!

No one can be blamed for this. The *text* cannot adapt in major ways because it is an organic constituent of the firm alignment among all levels of organization (from the local to the global), incentives, exhortations, coercions, and expectations. The relentless augmentation of output is the bedrock of profit-maximization through decentralized business decisions, the core principle of both GS1 and GS2. Competition as the main driving force under both systems implies capital accumulation because of the simple fact that cost reduction is its main method; and because its workings are inextricably linked to the endogenous reciprocity between the surging human soma and the accumulation of produced extrasomatic low entropy.[41] Economic expansion that occurs roughly at the clip of the real rate of return (sum of population and productivity growth) remains a central propositional category for economists. Nonetheless, trying to apply the *text* to never-before-seen phenomena,

---

[41] Satisfaction of a ceaselessly increasing demand for capital goods through private markets is linked to the growth of manpower, the availability of wage goods, and the private-debt based money supply, which must grow faster than debt is extinguished; otherwise economic growth slows and stops. The integrality of GS2's spontaneously coordinated demographic, economic, financial, and monetary processes reveals the system's Achilles' heel -- accelerate or collapse! It is worth noting that even centrally planned, "nonmarket" economies would decelerate if they attempted "simple reproduction." Marx already saw this. (Cf. Luxemburg, 1968, pp. 89-92. Joan Robinson's remarks in the introduction of the quoted work are helpful to clear up this issue.) Of course, "expanded reproduction," the only feasible alternative, means geometric progression with a greater than one common ratio. Human experience to date is simply not conducive to imagining a world of zero economic/population growth.

traditional thought faces growing criticism from outside the mainstream.[42] Reality's much more severe judgment cannot be far.

The *text* hides the impossibility of interminable acceleration by making annual GDP growth appear like walking on a flat plateau of ordinary socio-political-economic existence. As mentioned before, the "business as postwar usual" 3-4 percent *per annum* global growth till mid-century would mean a doubling of the world economy every 24 or 18 years, respectively.[43] Rising energy and material input prices at full employment (or appreciable movement toward it), in association with the increased fragility of the world's tangled and twisted monetary-financial system; and ever more likely environmental calamities, guarantee a totally different horizon.

Looking at GS2's credo from outside the fool's paradise of *ad infinitum* growth, one finds it riddled with internal inconsistencies. For example, while it adamantly opposes the labor theory of value and the sustainability of increasing returns at the micro scale, it inadvertently embraces both in a macroeconomic, macro-historical and broad technical sense. Viz. abstracting away from extrasomatic factors is equivalent to a somatic energy theory of value (i.e., labor theory of value, if we bring all categories of subjective efforts to a common denominator, regardless of their utility, mental-physical mix, and form of compensation); and the hope that the system can coax out an annual pace of output

---

[42]   Fullbrook (2012) is an excellent example.

[43]   Economic consultants making these upbeat (time-symmetrical) projections have developed a devilishly clever language game. They use words such as "risks," "challenges," and "opportunities" to erase the specter of insurmountable limits to growth.

expansion that exceeds the rate of demographic surge in the moving feast of "foreseeable future" proxies the belief that decreasing long-run average costs represent an eternally valid economic norm. Consequently, economists who were fed in their infancy with the mother's milk of "Economics" will see a luring *terra firma* ahead when, alas, they should sense a dangerous, forlorn, swamp-infected landscape.

The bottom-line: Long-term planetary sustainability cannot be carved out from GS2's wood. Global self-organization will have to be restructured. A new world order (GS3) is needed. It may be characterized as *two-level economy/strong multilateralism/mostly government money* (*maximum reserve banking*).[44]

This brave new world where the global community has become a political society is clearly out of reach. It is, in fact, literally repulsive! Who wants governments getting so deeply involved in economic management; who wants a global currency and a global central bank? No one! -- Except perhaps the *Illuminati* and some secret groups wielding enormous authority, according to the conspiratorial fringes of the Internet. No, no, and no again! In light of the eventual need for a system that does not collapse without compounding economic activities along the line of a radically divergent geometric series, the only possible answer to the question "What will it take to go from opprobrium to acceptance?" is "a new *chaotic transition*;" that is, an *ex ante* impenetrably *extempore* search for a new global steady state.

One of the most fascinating and mystifying aspects of *chaotic transition* is what scientists and philosophers call "emergence;" qualities in the newly emerged system could

---

[44]   See Appendix B for details.

not be deduced by investigating the individual components that made up the original system. Who would have thought in 1914 when the world declared war on itself that out of seemingly endless hecatombs and unimaginable suffering; hopeless efforts to restore GS1 and huge false starts (communism and brutal attempts by two industrialized countries to subjugate the rest of the world) a global order of consumer capitalism organized along the principles of the American New Deal, side by side with the comforting presence of the United Nations, would appear in 1945?

We can recognize in "1914-1945" the three general phases of a successful bifurcation: spontaneous symmetry breaking, experimentation, and resolution. Thus, world history reflects the general principles of discontinuous transformations with emergent properties. Such transformations have been observed in the inorganic world, in biology, and in social organizations (on a lesser than global scale). A few examples follow.

Snowflakes: In the conversion of low temperature vapor to snowflake crystal (a stronger, more structured material organization with six-pointed symmetry), chance vibration at the molecular and atomic levels frustrates predictions of the three phases of chaotic transition, even when control parameters (such as temperature and humidity) are well known and precisely measured.

Magnetization: Similarly, human insight is limited in foreseeing the emergence of higher order in a piece of iron that is being cooled. Above the *Curie point* the atoms vibrate wildly; below it they calm down. As the shuffling subsides, internal forces of negative and positive poles find an arrangement resembling a latent magnet along the North-South axis. But before this happens, they have to sort out their own attractions and repulsions. For a fraction of a second, all the tiny domains must be confused. They do the inorganic equivalent of "which way should/could I turn?" as they try to settle into a collectively more comfortable energy state. If individual atoms involved in mass action are programmed by Nature to assume positions and angles so as to be latent magnets, ready to respond to external magnetic attractions, the actual programs elude us. The size of the iron, its external conditions, the speed of heating, the level of purity and variety of concentration all influence the modality of coming to a new, stable internal arrangement. As far as the human mind is concerned, the information allowing order to be established develops through a spontaneous, experiential tumult -- trial and error.

Slime mold (Dictyostelium discoideum): It hangs around as a carefree, highly individualistic heap of single-celled units until the physical environment becomes less hospitable and low entropy turns scarce. At that point the ranks seem to be confused, but an extreme social cohesion soon emerges in the form of a single organism that crawls across garden floors, gobbling up rotting leaves and wood in its path.[45]

Fetus: Thirty-eight weeks following fertilization, the inner mass of identical cells begins the radical elaboration of future organs. Of course, we know by now that the information required to create structural and functional subsystems resides in the DNA. However, heredity's aperiodic code must overcome an unsurveyable opulence of atomic-molecular disorder. From a profusion of chance and fragmented micro-endeavors emerges the grand design of human organism and consciousness.

---

[45] For details, see the study of Garfinkel, A., "The Slime Mold Dictyostelium as a Model of Self-Organization in Social Systems," in Yates (1987).

Hawaiian Creole: As described by Talbot (1988), "Creole" is the generic name given to a language that develops when dominant and subordinate groups speaking different pidgins live in prolonged contact. In 1875, when the United Sates signed an agreement with the Hawaiian monarchy, the sugar industry in the islands began to boom and labor poured in to work on the plantations. Attempts at simplified communication in rudimentary Hawaiian, Korean, Japanese, and Spanish mingled with the overseers' English. Sometime during the turn of the last century, the first generation of native children began to speak an entirely new language, complete with its own grammar and syntax. Although it borrowed words from all the tongues represented in the original Babelian melee, it was incomprehensible to immigrant adults, including the English-speaking plantation owners. Even more surprisingly, the Hawaiian Creole's grammar and syntax are similar to those of hundreds of other Creole languages around the world, even though their vocabularies are entirely different (ibid).

Organizations: Modern management science has connected discontinuous transformations in business firms (e.g., as a result of facing bankruptcy) to chaos theory. In such models, bifurcation is manifest in discontinuity, the working ground from which a new stable configuration transpires after an indeterminate period of clashes among proposed solutions, internal power groups, and influential individuals.[46]

---

[46] Cf. DeShon and Svyantek (1993); Dooley and Johnson (1995); as well as Leifer, R., "Understanding Organizational Transformation Using a Dissipative Structure Model:"

http://hum.sagepub.com/content/42/10/899.short

See also Thiétart, R.A. and Forgues, B., "Chaos Theory and Organization:" http://orgsci.journal.informs.org/content/6/1/19. abstract?ijkey=57e74557b452783ee20f31b767bfff3abb8b5ecf&

Chaotic transition on the global scale is just as natural and inevitable as in the above-quoted examples. But it is a case apart for two major reasons.

First, the world's transmutation is comprehensive without a residue (i.e., there is no subject that would not also be an object of the process).

When Rodin turned a block of bronze into an aesthetic marvel, the separation between subject (creative prodigy) and object (lifeless matter) was unequivocally complete. In the sharpest conceivable contrast, the emergence of a new *global system* is the work of an inextricably fused subject and object: The world is both the sculptor and the sculpted. The thinking thing (cogito) can create a "Thinker," but the global community as a whole, driven by nothing more than billions of individually-anchored inchoate impulses to live and to live better, must "rethink itself" -- and as history has shown at a cruel price -- in order to re-emerge from the womb of its defunct self.

Second, as demonstrated by historical experience (i.e., 1789-1830s and 1914-1945), *chaotic transitions* are measured in decades. This circumstance further contributes to the analytical and moral difficulty of accepting that descriptive history, with its leading personalities and fateful events, is simply the verbal distillation of a thermodynamic (physical) dictum: Chaos separates steady states.

Chaotic transition is near when the established order becomes prone to disruption through stochastic developments. This characterization corresponds to the "butterfly effect" as initial condition sensitivity has been nicknamed in the

---

keytype2=tf_ipsecsha

study of nonlinear dynamics. How an innocuous and totally unpredictable small event on the molecular/atomic level escalates in significance may be illustrated by the assassination of Archduke Francis Ferdinand, heir apparent to the Hapsburg throne, in Sarajevo, on June 28, 1914.

Through tragicomic events, the conspiracy of young Serbian nationalists came very close to a ridiculous failure.[47] But just when the whole thing looked like a youthful blunder, randomness came to the aid of Big History.

One of the conspirators, Gavrilo Princip, who skipped dinner the night before, got hungry and decided to sample the offerings of Moritz Schiller's delicatessen downtown. In the meantime, the Archduke insisted on going through with the originally scheduled program, even extending it with the PR gesture of visiting the military hospital where the victims of the earlier bomb explosion were treated. General Potiorek, the governor of Bosnia-Herzegovina, decided to speed up the convoy by taking the unencumbered, freeway-like "Appel Quay" along the river. He informed everyone about the route change except the chauffeur of the car in which he sat with the royal visitors. The conveyance ended up alone in the narrow downtown street where Schiller's establishment was located.

The General yelled, the chauffeur stopped and began to back up as a crowd of onlookers gathered. Gavrilo, now in the

---

[47] One of the conspirators threw his bomb. Hearing the explosion, he dutifully bit into his cyanide capsule and jumped into the nearby Miljacka River. What he did not know was that the bomb bounced off the Archduke's car and exploded under the next one; that the cyanide was years past its "expiration" date, and the river that was expected to swallow him was about three inches deep at that time of the year. The rest of the conspirators did not act. They either thought that the deed was done or became paralyzed in the critical moment.

front of the restaurant, found himself face to face with his targets. He pulled out his pistol and killed the Archduke and his wife. As is well known, the ensuing chain of diplomatic events led to the thundering "Guns of August." The curtain fell on GS1 and the world found itself in the raging forge of global transformation.

It is hard to see the "from insignificant to significant" paradigm of escalation in this event. In order to find the real innocuous, totally unforeseeable occurrence (inviting even the notion of being external to human affairs as these are presumed to be observable by the naked eye), we must enter the brain, the neurophysics of forming thoughts, making determinations, and instructing the body to carry them out.

Superficially, it may appear that the nearly infinitesimal material conditions that led to GS1's demise resided in the random coincidence between two electrochemical events: One that signaled hunger for the assassin (especially for the offerings of Herr Schiller) and the momentary forgetfulness of the General to instruct his driver about the change of route. Of course, the proposed explanation is more complex and comprehensive: When GLOPPE's scheme of self-organization becomes obsolete, the minute probabilities of random, insignificant events (each capable of starting a fatal chain reaction) accumulate to a level where system failure becomes a physical inevitability or, using the customary sociological term; a historical necessity. To put it crudely, something will set the ball rolling *perforce*. This view of the world connects irregularities with regularities, the chance variations in the subatomic universe (the infinite number of Brownian movements of particles in GLOPPE) with causalities that become comprehendible *ex post*.

Since the thermodynamic take of history tells us that a critical transformation in the *global system* must occur in order to rectify GLOPPE's antiquated relationship with its ecological constraints, our world is pregnant with a new *chaotic transition.*

The socially destabilizing effects of stagnation, combined with widening income differences within nations, the insane expansion of credit (implying enhanced bubble risks);[48] the euro crisis (Boyer, 2013), the U.S. debt crisis (Pollin, 2012), and sharpening conflicts over resources, represents thousands of catalysts to make the famed butterfly flap its wings. While it is clearly impossible to foretell time, location, and the modality of the GS2-disrupting chain reaction, the certainty of its nearness weighs heavily on our generation.

GS2 --> GS3 will be much more difficult than GS1 --> GS2 was. It presupposes the generalized transformation of national, racial, and religious out-groups into in-groups on the way to the *cosmopolis.* Since this process is not conceivable through unilateral gestures, it presumes the simultaneous appearance of bilateral reciprocities, hence becoming a multilateral phenomenon, most likely as the result of a global-scale moral catharsis at the concluding phase of the impending *chaotic transition.*

---

[48]   The stock of global credit increased from $57 trillion in 2000 to $109 trillion in 2009 and (excluding a global *Krach*) it is expected to reach $210 trillion by 2020:

http://www3.weforum.org/docs/WEF_NR_More_credit_fewer _crises_2011.pdf

Vasco and Gabaix (2013) have found that the expansion of the financial sector has been a major factor in the recent rise of macroeconomic volatility.

The recognition that the difference between GS1 and GS2 was much smaller than between GS2 and GS3 gives one pause. If it took "1914-1945" to accomplish a relatively small transformation, what will it take to develop a working consensus on the institutional parameters and correlate personal behavior for a drastically different form of global self-organization?

Only the proffered intensity of the need to find a solution brightens the horizon.

Seventeenth-century philosopher Thomas Hobbes argued for the importance of the state. Without its power to tame interpersonal competition, he said, life would be "solitary, poore, nasty, brutish, and short." (Hobbes, 1952 reprint, p. 97.) We may add a vital corollary to his insight: The state can remain effective only if its scope and methods change with GLOPPE's growth, which is obviously not a mere swelling but also a progression to ever higher modes of self-organization. Unless the state reappears in a new, updated form on the stage of universal history as the *global res publica*, sometime later in this century, the law of the jungle will grab the world by its throat.

***

Let us sum up what has been said so far.

A spontaneous thermodynamic process in an isolated system is not inclined to soft landing. GLOPPE must collide with its terrestrial limitations. What we experience in the world of economic relations does not simply mirror this physical fact. It is identical with it. Allegorically, the *Sphere's* thermodynamic isolation may ring the doorbell around the clock; GS2's mindset will not answer it. It cannot face the fact that we live in a prison, whose once spacious walls are becoming less so as a result of the Leviathan prisoner's (GLOPPE's) galloping weight gain.

Sooner or later natural resources will be seen in a different light. Economic thinking, rigidified around the low percentages of matter and energy in the GDP, will relent and the idea that the human community exists in a rapidly deteriorating ecological relationship will gain practical significance. Awakening will include the explicit acknowledgement that the level of competition associated with GS2 dictates a dangerous pace of the *Drawdown*; that self-interest in its current form and intensity is turning into a pervasive "external diseconomy" (a Moloch) from the standpoint of global society as a viable collective subject.

In the course of the impending *chaotic transition*, it will be a great temptation to see a problem where there is, in fact, a physically-determined macrohistoric predicament.[49]

Public pressure may put government in charge, but any tax/subsidy scheme -- the first to come out from GS2's toolbox -- would only make things worse. Taxing incomes, corporations or consumption in order to increase the flow of low entropy into GLOPPE obviously cannot stand. Nor could the virtuous idea of contriving scarcity through environmental and resource taxes gain space, at least not decisively. Witness how agreements on controlling climate change are swept

---

[49] Appendix A elaborates on the difference between problem and predicament, and demonstrates that transition to a "green-resource-based" world economy is bound to flop. This potential failure is one particular way to demonstrate the general crisis of the *global system*. GS2 treats the transition as a problem (solvable through clever policies, long-run programs, and moral suasion) when in reality the world faces a predicament (i.e., a "simultaneous transpolitical and transboundary problem") solvable only through *chaotic transition*.

out of the way by the GLOPPE's spontaneous dynamism; the demographic momentum and the profit motive, upon the fulfillment of which income and employment depends.

Man's cultural evolution is a tale that could be told by the rise and fall of the global "energy returned on energy invested" (EROEI)[50] generalized for aggregate molecularly stored free energy (AMSFE); or, alternatively, by the incline and decline of the global shadow price (Λ) of AMSFE; i.e., "d GWP /d AMSFE."

First, the scarcity rent collected on a unit of structured matter (a possible interpretation of Λ) will increase as the supply of molecularly stored free energy becomes less elastic, but demand for it continues to rise.[51] Competition will determine the distribution of the total rent, but the growth of this total is thermodynamically guaranteed. In due time, Λ must fall (despite reduction in the stock of economically extractable free energy). The turnaround is a way to characterize and describe the crisis that an expansion-dependent system cannot avoid.

How will the associated lower marginal utility and marginal cost of drafting the next least-cost unit of free energy from the *Surroundings* into GLOPPE (alternative interpretations of Λ) decline without the stock of molecularly-stored energy becoming more abundant is the 21st century's great puzzle.

---

[50]   See more on EROEI under "What is wrong with rationality" in Chapter Five.

[51]   Rent is the price of a unit of free-energy-containing structured matter as it is found and taken possession of *in situ* in the *Surroundings*. It may be viewed as the difference between the same unit's market price and the cost of making it part of GLOPPE.

The current generation will not be able to solve it. Our consciousness is simply unfit for the task.

Further investigation is premised upon a link between universal history (including social and economic history) and the temporal succession of consciousness structures.

Chapter Five

Diachronic momenta
of consciousness

Consciousness as "differential totality"

In a narrow sense, when it is directly connected with cerebral activities or conditions; that is, when it has a demonstrable physical basis, consciousness could be called "differential totality." It contains all the information necessary to deal with the most burning problems that the physical-social-cultural-economic environment presents for the individual. The adjective "differential" is meant to draw attention to the circumstance that consciousness is made up of active and passive components. The first category comprises those perceptions and memories that have an immediate bearing on adaptation, on the quest of rewards; as well as on information about feasible alternatives to carry out related activities. The second category contains all other information pertaining to individual existence. The separation is not rigid. Consciousness is best visualized as a continuous spectrum that stretches from intensely active components, engaged when dealing with a crisis in the family, at the workplace, or in the environs otherwise delineated; to the body's biological processes, which remain passive unless attention is explicitly drawn to them (e.g., in the doctor's office).[52]

In the age of global self-organization, the second category includes neuro-chemical imprints of the *global-system*-specific "rules of the game:" the local application of internationally comparable institutions along with the principles and modalities governing intersubjective relations. During a *chaotic transition*, the world is split into antagonistic subfields; viz. the conflict-ridden difference in the "rules of the game" based upon which the individual had to seek survival or differential success in the United States, the USSR, or in Nazi Germany during the 1930s.

The passivity of our knowledge about enduring socioeconomic conditions is tantamount to the objectification of human relations, to the provenance of what Georg Lukacs called man's "second nature;" an extension of eternally valid laws of being (e.g., the circadian rhythm, the way waves break on the seashore) to reified institutions. What people living under a stable *global system* consider "true assertions" about history, society, and the economy presupposes a scaffolding of the conceptual universe that the mind tends to conflate with the laws and regularities of the natural world ("first nature").

No "second nature" can be eternal. Cultural evolution is, in fact, a story about creating, maintaining, and getting rid of "second natures."

Stated differently, "objectivity" is a historical category. It shifts over time, not only in the natural sciences but

---

[52]   Schrödinger (1967, pp. 99-109) inspired this paragraph.

also in socioeconomic relations. We can say with Hegel that the real is rational and the rational is real. Behavior, free of moods, impulses, and passions, will be adaptive; or, by the contiguity of signification, will be considered rational when individuals and their groupings (e.g., firms and nations) reap practical advantage from obeying the rules and logical schemes associated with the objective expediencies of a socioeconomic framework (reality). Of course, reality changes, while it is human nature to believe in the immutability of the day's rationality. One can readily recognize the need for chaotic interludes to lead from one relative steady state to the next in a spontaneous, far-from-equilibrium, dissipative process such as GLOPPE.

The wide acceptance that individual consciousness is inseparable from its socioeconomic substratum did not come easily. Ever since the 17th century, when René Descartes fathered modern dualism by drawing a sharp dividing line between *res cogitans* and *res extensa*, philosophers have struggled to reunite the two. "Mind and society are two aspects of the same evolutionary process" argued Giambattista Vico already in the first half of the 18th century (Schumpeter, 1954, p. 137). Much more was to follow through the contributions of Kant, Hegel, Marx, Husserl, the psycholinguists, the existentialists, the structuralists and the postmoderns.[53] Yet, you can peruse contemporary economic literature without finding an admission that, to a large extent, we see economic life not as it is but as we are; complex products of a world order. But impending drastic changes and requisite adaptation are

---

[53] Edmund Husserl (1859-1938) is credited for the explicit break with Cartesian dualism and for the overflow of positivism it inspired. By directing attention to the "subject" and "consciousness," Husserl exerted a crucial influence on 20th century philosophy. Cf. Stewart and Mickunas (1990).

bound to rekindle the "historical school," which disintegrated after the collapse of GS1.

Gebser

The importance of Jean Gebser regarding the philosophical schism that separates dualism from a complete inseparability between the individual's internal and external worlds (i.e., the self with its "thinking thing" and the surrounding socioeconomic milieu) resides in advancing the notion of *integral-arational* consciousness.

Gebser's archeology of consciousness identifies five patterns, structures or mutations: The *archaic* (the first one to emerge from the "origin" was marked by instinct and presentiment); the *magical* (characterized by a pre-conceptual; pre-symbolic, vital life-feel); the *mythical* (cohesive apprehension through pre-egoic polar thinking); the *mental* (spatial, dualistic, conceptual, system-building, synthesizing, abstract comprehension); and the *integral-arational*, which transcends, unites, and balances all previous structures.

Gebser argued that the structures remain co-present over time. Thus, a subsequent phase "overdetermines" rather than replaces the previous one; thereby creating a cumulative complexification that will become transparent only when the typical individual (i.e., global society) embraces *integral-arational* consciousness.[54]

---

54 For more complete descriptions of Gebser, see Combs (1996) and Feuerstein (1987). The ultimate source is, of course, Gebser (1975 and 1984). The second date refers to *The Ever-Present Origin* as rendered brilliantly into English by Noel Barstad and Algis Mickunas. Although the subject is not relevant in the current context, it needs to be strongly underscored that consciousness meant a great deal more for Gebser than what physicalist "brain science" can tell us.

Only states of mind that arise from *integral-arational* consciousness are capable of accommodating the seemingly antithetical convictions that (a) an individual, or a group of identically thinking and motivated individuals (i.e., a socially defined *genus*), may make an independent and objectively relevant assessment about society and history; and (b) that all such assessments are stamped by the prevalent *global system* and, in case they point beyond it, i.e., represent blueprints for the next world order, they could not be implemented through transformations commonly associated with reforms and political programs. (Just remember what it took for GS2 to be born!)

How right F. Scott Fitzgerald was when he said that intelligence is the ability to accept two contradictory ideas and still function. The intelligence he referred to is not a high IQ or some remarkable analytical or artistic talent; it is the faculty of leaving certain competing ideas, whether they are scientific propositions or articles of faith, nonconflated and unbrokered. It is the readiness to tolerate a conundrum without dialectical resolution or relegation of the whole problem to the waste basket -- it is *integral-arational* consciousness in practice.

But let us return to the socio-historical perspective to see for what other reasons (besides striking a mental-psychological balance between voluntarism and fatalism) *integral-arational* consciousness is humanity's teleological attractor.

Each consciousness structure coincided with distinctive socioeconomic conditions:

The *archaic*, with primitive hunting, fishing, and gathering; the *magical*, with more advanced versions of the same activities within increasingly complex social schemes centering on the horde; the *mythical* was characterized by agriculture; and the *mental* by industry coming to dominance. The *mental* structure can be traced to ancient Greek philosophy in an era marked by a spurt in the development of handicrafts, shipbuilding and the geographic expansion of trade.[55]

Consciousness structures go through an efficient and a deficient phase, according to Gebser. He considered rationality (with its offspring of vulgar materialism) the deficient form of mental consciousness, dating from the second half of the 18th century when, propelled by the English industrial and the French social revolutions, the world's first *chaotic transition* began, settling in GS1. Time "broke forth," Gebser argued, meaning both an increasing preoccupation with time and its spatialization (e.g., the positive-feedback-loop-like, self-multiplicative spread of flowcharts, schedules, and plans, turning time into a divisible quantity marked off along an axis) to the detriment of individual wholeness.

Mental-rational consciousness evolved during the past two centuries. GS1 required masses of parsimonious, placidly obedient, beaten-down philistines. Hašek's "good soldier" Schwejk and Büchner's Woyzeck illustrate the absurdity and tragedy of the resultant deformation of individual consciousness. But as soon as the system became ensconced, rebellion was born, growing in intensity; from Melville's "scrivener" Bartleby to Stone's Eugene Debs, the socialist labor organizer ("Adversary in the House"). The GS1-typical persona was straining toward its GS2 avatar; the insatiable consumer with a mortgage and assorted credit cards. The implied transformation makes perfect sense.

---

[55]   The often quoted gem of Protegoras: "man is the measure of all things" (uttered two-and-a-half millennia ago) was one of the first documented manifestations of mental consciousness (Gebser, 1984, p. 77).

GS2's dependence on permanent economic proliferation requires a personality that displays "The better I live, the more I demand!" as its permanent marquee.

From a Gebserian standpoint, the worsening deficiency of mental-rational consciousness (expressed through imputing a quasi-divine status to the ratio) is organically tied to the historic breaking forth of integral-arational consciousness.

What is wrong with rationality?

The public at large, unfamiliar with Gebser, is taken aback upon hearing criticism of rationality.[56] It sounds like a blanket rejection of analytical matter-of-factness in diagnosing personal, business, or social problems. "What is the alternative: irrationality?"

Gebser was aware of this reaction and made it absolutely clear that he did not equate *ratio* with understanding or common sense (Gebser, 1984 -- henceforth EPO -- p. 95). Rather, he used the concept in accordance with the word's original Latin meaning: to reason by comparing magnitudes. He criticized rationality (the general practice and adulation of the *ratio*) for its proclivity to subdivide complex phenomena into partitioned sectors; to view the world through narrow perspectival slits with an exaggeratedly

---

[56]   Gebser focused on rationality as a method, a way of thinking; an attitude, rather than on rationalism as a philosophical viewpoint in opposition to empiricism. Since Kant's synthesis (his "Copernican revolution"), philosophers have been guided by a compelling need to balance the two radically opposing schools of epistemology. Although this subject is of no concern here, one may take what follows as a deposition against neoclassical synthesis (the traditional economics of our day) for favoring rationalism (splendid mathematics with soothing, GS2-germane ratios) at the expense of some worrisome ratios that reveal the empirical significance of hitherto unidentified developments.

quantitative emphasis (EPO, p. 93). Since the 18th century, this orientation has nurtured a fervent belief in primitive dualism; that humanity, amidst its dramatic *tâtonnement* through time, may be split into an objectively thinking subject that could analyze, counsel, and chaperone the rest of totality as if it were an object. Syntheses built on this approach result in rigid, disconnected systems that have little to do with the fullness of reality.

Gebser argued that the progressive strengthening of this method is destructive (EPO, pp. 96 and 97) as it reduces comprehension to "amorphous nullity" (EPO, p. 180), leading to "rational chaos" (EPO, p. 303). The sequel to the implied systemic irrationality is intensified consciousness, integral comprehension (EPO, p. 480).

Building on Gebser's thought; the current project apostrophizes rationality as it is being generally used; i.e., signifying reason, logic, and pragmatism. "Rationality" so interpreted concords with the concept's elaborations in economics, where it broadly refers to the application of these attributes in the representative agent's genetically-programmed pursuit of self-interest, based on the maximum amount of information available for the next move in the market place. What is wrong with that? The conflation of "rational" assessments with their source, their form-giving *prius*, to begin with!

Truth, as it is believed to be at the core of rational thought, is a child of the Present. Or, as Hegel explained, we consider rational what is real. Of course, he knew (as we also do upon a moment of reflection) that the real is the portrait of sovereign time. This premise leads to the proposition that "rationality" is the offspring of GS2 and, therefore, it needs to be distinguished from integral rationality; i.e., rationality in a broader sense.

Whereas rationality in the context of thermodynamic realism imparts the caveat that exponential growth under the conditions that characterize existence in the *Sphere* cannot be but transitory; the "rationality-infused" economic mind pretends that the actual socioeconomic context is the final, ideal, unsurpassable phase of socioeconomic evolution; i.e., that the composition of economic agency, the interpretation of self-interest, and the structure of information upon which economic actors base their decisions are all timeless. "Rationality" makes the economist consider Nature as if it were bundled in the global self-organization, behaving as just another pliable production factor that man's entrepreneurial-engineering genius has already forced into diminishing significance. Integral rationality sees the bundling exactly the other way around.

Contemplation of integral totality (uninhibited by the compartmentalization of scholarship and free from the childish notion that socioeconomic evolution is over) raises analytical thinking above the sound and fury of daily politics; it becomes trans-ideological. Its fundamental thesis bears repetition: The harmony between growth and demand for growth is not timeless; "rationality" is a transient and expiring version of rationality.

The realm of understanding that breeds a continuum of GS2-canonical ratios.

The *text* defines economics as the science that builds conceptual and practical bridges between the supply of and demand for resources, given that the first always falls short of the second. When "Econ 10" relates "finite resources" to "infinite wants," it presents the emperor naked without the clever tergiversations that top-carat textbook authors (including, of course, the first and original one, Professor Samuelson) use to cover up the fact that GS2's *text* is strictly a "period piece".

"Infinite wants" is pure GS2 philosophy since, according to its credo; neither the resources nor the demand for them ever stops expanding. Why? Because the insatiable desire of utility-maximizers to accumulate wealth will always be satisfied by insatiable profit-maximizers, whose magic wands just keep waving "outward" that compliant production-possibility frontier!

This framework has proved to be conducive to abstracting the human into *Homo oeconomicus*; a software code with the intelligence level, emotional universe, and primitive intentionality of an internet search engine. (For more on *Homo oeconomicus* see Dopfer, 2005, pp. 21, 22, 27, 28, 29, 33, 41, 371, *et passim*.)

The description of consumer and producer behavior through elasticities, margins, derivatives, and prices; the state of the economy, that of a firm or of the representative agent; their expectations via changes (described by growth rates, indices, and present values) all hinge on calculating ratios. Of course, there is no economic analysis without ratios. The complaint here is that GS2's "rationality" claims universal cogency *in perpetuum* when broader rationality suggests that it belongs to a bounded, system-specific ideology in the socioeconomic-evolutionary phase space.

The tendentious, "rationality-" motivated simplification of economic phenomena has dilated into a dazzling variety of extravagant lucubrations to depict the economy as a super-temporic, self-perpetuating circular-motion mechanism that expands, as measured *summa summarum* by the world output (GWP).

Let us add with emphasis that GS2 economics -- being a time-dependent applied philosophy -- is not responsible for the state of the world. It has been caught up in the process that has led to it. In no way does contemporary economic thought deserve to be put in the dock for its central position that the acquisition of material goods (or their money equivalents) occupies in the GS2-typical individual's self-projection. GS2 is an inevitable thermodynamic phase and during its reign there is indeed a stylized resemblance between the average persona and *Homo oeconomicus.* Since the corresponding "rational" psyche shows a tendency to degrade others to mere means, perceiving actions in the economic sphere as automatisms generated by a web of objectively calculable quantitative relationships is no intellectual hallucination.

Thermodynamically-determined historical forces bring to the fore supra-personal organizational principles, which, after becoming embodied in a temporally abiding *global system*, "phenomenolize" themselves in a multiplicity of protean substrata. These, in turn, allow system-specific instrumental rationality to be deployed in the pursuit of system-consecrated goals; i.e., maximizing satisfaction derived from the sensuous immediacy of material goods or that of money; potent freedom in search of direction. This has been the life form of capitalistic sociality under both GS1 and GS2.

Nonetheless, such exoneration can hardly be extended to the brassy support that some of the most iconic figures of postwar economics have provided for legislative measures and policies that exaggerate the social service potential of unchecked financial hooliganism (inclusive of subsidized speculation, colossal moral hazards, and the ruthless exploitation of *weak multilateralism*).

Under the guise of opening the arena for the "rationality" of market forces, domestic and international finances have been deregulated with the simultaneous instauration of jaw-dropping bonuses to capital market operators. The fact that such a combination has the rational consequence of releasing criminal energies, spreading fraud through the economy and the political system can hardly be a *kudo* for "rationality."

The "rational expectations" and the "efficient-market" hypotheses certainly comprise "Exhibit A" of both the mental habit of chopping and slicing reality, then building blind syntheses on the lifeless residual of inorganic monads; and economics providing the platform from where paeans about the cure-all effects of unfettered hunger for wealth could be vociferated. Both formulations are unerringly intra-GS2 constructs. They say nothing more than GS2-generated information will be used according to GS2's ways of thinking and behavior, and that will throttle GS2 forward.

The hefty criticism directed at these theories[57] may, to a large extent, be attributed to disgust with their suitability to support arguments in favor of bringing back 19th century *laissez faire*. Although the neoclassic methodological model of applied mathematics hides uninstructed political passions well, such a historic regression is plainly impossible.

A thermodynamic unfolding; e.g., GLOPPE, proceeds from the simpler form of organization toward the more

---

[57]   Syll (2012) puts REH in its place.

complex one. Irreversible changes in institutions, values and expectations as well as the metamorphosis of "human nature" (to maximize generality) are expressions of this complexification. Propositions to return to a less complex framework of socioeconomic existence; to a lesser degree of socialization (i.e. to weakened forms of interconnections among economic actors, between these and public authority, and among nations) are stillborn no-goes.

We live in the century when in the sober morning light of day, the famed exclamation of Jean Sismondi (1773-1842) -- "What on Earth! Wealth is to be everything and the human absolutely nothing?"[58] -- will viscerally resonate across the world. Then "rationality" with its dehumanized representative mamluks will move from the throne it currently occupies in the province of social theory to a chapter in the history of economic thought.

The following reflex-like manifestations of "rationality" are meant to demonstrate how insufficient GS2's principles and reasoning have become.

Keep inconvenient ratios off discourse!

The age of *global systems* (beginning with the second half of the 18th century when the world went into labor with its first-born system) is what Gebser identified as the era of the *ratio*'s increasing dominance within mental consciousness. GLOPPE's mass accelerated during modernity and GS1 gave way to GS2 to facilitate this process. Economics, as a

---

58   "Quoi donc! La richesse est tout, les hommes ne sont absolument rien? " Cf. Jean Sismondi, "Nouveaux Principes d'Economie Politique," p. 330: http://fr.wikisource.org/wiki/ Livre:Sismondi_-_Nouveaux_Principes_d%E2%80%99%C3% A9conomie_politique.djvu

science, an ideology, and best source of advice on social and economic policies, became both a catalyst and a faithful mirror of humanity's somatic/extrasomatic expansion in full swing.

Growth, unconstrained by physical factors, generated growth-indicating, growth- justifying ratios. "Rationality," as a companion attitude of the world's "Sturm und Drang," could be fair and balanced. When it excluded *global-system* critical *ratios* from the mainstream; e.g., Marx's "rate of exploitation," it acted on behalf of rationality. However, with the *Boyg* of resource constraints looming on the horizon, "rationality" has split with rationality. Today, it blindly embraces ratios that promise the continuation of the hectic storm and stress that GLOPPE imposes on the *Surroundings* and upstages quantitative relationships that rationality wants to present.

As the symbolic spokesman of man's inevitable progress through the mastery of natural forces, "rationality" has already declared victory over the world's energy problem. Public officials and representatives of the media, made dizzy by information about hundreds of years of supplies of natural gas and unconventional oil, have dispersed angst over "peak oil." It seems to be only a question of detail to secure a constant and growing flow of energy that is (a) cheap enough to operate the expanding real global capital; (b) so as to replace every unit of used up nonrenewable energy carrier by the discovery of new reserves; i.e., seeing discoveries accelerate *in tandem* with depletion, and (c) accomplish all this without turning Mother Nature into our worst enemy.

To make this nonsense believable, cornucopian ideologues, disguised as energy consultants, are pushing irrelevant ratios. The promotion of natural gas in the U.S. is a case in point. Total reserves at the 2010 level of domestic use would indeed last for 100 years. But total reserves comprise probable and possible in addition to proven reserves; i.e., not all the identified resources may be economically accessible. And then, how could the projected worldwide increase in demand for the rest of the century leave U.S. output at the 2010 level? The same "rationalistic" deficiency echoes from upbeat talk about unconventional oil.

Let us bring a ratio called "energy returned on energy invested" (EROEI) to center stage. As its name indicates, EROEI nets out energy production's own demand. When it is high, the real price of energy is expected to be low, and *vice versa*. It is perhaps the most compact temporal indicator of GLOPPE's career.

The past two hundred years' dramatic growth was made possible, in effect, by switching the extrasomatic energy base from wood, which had an EROEI of approximately 30:1, to coal and then to oil (with 80:1 and 100:1 EROEIs, respectively.[59]) But sometime during the last century, oil production began to experience increasing average costs. This is clearly illustrated by the evolution of EROEI in U.S. oil production:[60]

1930s, EROEI = 100:1
1970s, EROEI = 25:1
1990s, EROEI = 11–18:1

---

[59]   See page 7 in the New Economics Foundation's study:
   http://dnwssx4l7gl7s.cloudfront.net/nefoundation/default/page/
   -/files/Glass_ceiling_webReady_.pdf

[60]   Ibid

According to the quoted work, if the current trend of increasing demand for oil continues, the prevalent 20:1 global average of EROEI for oil will descend to 1:1 in the next 20–30 years. Given that energy is needed to process downstream the calories sucked from the *Surroundings*, the practical limit to economically feasible production may be approximately 2:1.

It is not true that superabundant unconventional oil (i.e., oil obtained through methods other than extraction from conventional wells) has made the world safe for happy motoring and cheap consumer goods at an accelerated rate for generations to come. Since price is determined on the margin and unconventional oil production involves an estimated EROEI of 3:1, the price of the barrel remains relatively high. And therein lies the mechanism of secular economic stagnation -- the "new normal."

Output wants to grow when the price of oil is low but then investment aimed at expanding supplies is weak. When the price heads North, capital becomes interested, but then the danger of a new recession provoked by the rising exchange value of the economy's plasma begins to linger. GS2's inability to free the world from this devilish macro-seesaw by providing autonomous incentives for ravaging non-conventional oil reserves may well be a blessing in disguise. The economic system is actually broadcasting that the Earth is fed up with GLOPPE's ecologically inconsiderate inflation. Unfortunately, zombie-like doctrinaire economics has stuffed up ears with a thick wax of "irrationally exuberant" ratios.

The long-run decline of EROEI means diminishing returns to scale; a trend of rising (relative) marginal cost of energy, unpreventable by the deployment of any amount of entrepreneurial genius and general technical progress (growth in total factor productivity). Supposing that technical advances will nullify this global trend rests upon the innocent assumption that energy invested could be valued at a lower price than energy returned; viz. not noticing that money cancels out in EROEI.

The fall of EROEI over time is the best indication that market fundamentalism is wrong about secular price rises augmenting supplies and triggering substitutions while allowing the world to keep its foot on the accelerator.

The related, much used argument that high energy prices will curb demand for energy (again, while allowing global output to soar toward the skies) is yet another pitiful instance of "rationalistic perspectivism." It incorrectly generalizes the moderation of energy costs in the most developed industrialized countries, missing two relevant points.

First, the buildup of industry in the "South" has made (and continues to make) possible the buildup of the service sector in the "North." Of course, hair salons for dolls in New York and Paris use less energy than doll manufacturing plants in China. If you compare the hourly dollar wage of an American or French doll hairdresser with that of a worker somewhere in Guangdong, you will see why the service sector has twice the weight of industry in world statistics. (According to U.S. Government data, global output is 63 percent services, 31 percent industry, and 6 percent agriculture.)

Second, assuming that economic development in the "South" will further increase the portion of services in global output is the wrong way to assess potential demand for energy. (The number of hours the "South" would have to spend in industry to live at "Nordic" levels would be a much better starting point.) Four-fifths of the planet's souls living in the "South" cannot leapfrog over metallurgy, chemical industry, and manufacturing into a post-industrial service economy, which itself depends on physical capital for its existence and expansion.

The inescapable fact is that the world, as it has evolved technically and as it is now in terms of production organization, property relations, micro- and macroeconomic management, simply cannot curb its appetite for crude oil and continue to grow at its customary postwar rate.

EROEI is a glaring example, but certainly not the only ratio GS2 prefers to de-emphasize. Muddled by their crude optimism, advisers of "Dig-baby-dig!" prefer not to relate the rate of depletion of oil reserves (production) to the discovery of new reserves. This ratio shows a conspicuous increase.[61] Apropos natural resources, in general, citing the increase of coal production since the second half of the 19th century when W. S. Jevons mistakenly predicted the depletion of coal supplies; and analyses demonstrating the tendency of the real price of oil to return to an equilibrium level during the past century are much more in the spirit of GS2.

If it had a stamp, GS2 would mark "debt growth to economic growth" and "aggregate debt to GDP" ratios as "naughty," and the proportion of the budget deficit in the GDP as "nice" (since the latter is small, even as the world keeps drifting toward inevitable bankruptcy; and its ups and downs imply

---

[61] See Kurt Cobb's article and the California-based *Post Carbon Institute*'s primer on "peak oil" at the following sites, respectively:

http://www.resilience.org/stories/2013-03-17/depletion-the-one-word-oil-optimists-refuse-to-utter

http://www.resilience.org/primer

the possibility of rational control). In general, index numbers and growth rates showing unidirectional evolvements do not receive the "scholium and corollary" they would merit. A closer look at these would reveal that the self-equilibration of world trade and government spending through market forces are GS2-disgest-perpetrated fabulations.

Say after me: There is nothing new under the sun!

"Rationality" has deformed historical hermeneutics by the diachronic imposition of today's analytically interpreted (synchronic) structure; that is, forcing quantitative characterizations of the lived moment on qualitatively different, long superseded or projected future structures of totality. History has become the history of how primordial market forces have accommodated the timeless human expediency to maximize profits and consumption.

GS2 historiology denies the temporal relativity of socioeconomic arrangements; its votaries see present society and its antecedents through neoclassical utility and production functions. Accordingly, the past is best described by recognizing the proto-variants and primitive manifestations of today's market-oriented behavior, social interactions, and legal-institutional framework. The favored approach to economic history resonates with the French adage: *plus ça change, plus c'est la même chose.*

"This Time is Different; Eight Centuries of Financial Folly" (Reinhart and Rogoff, 2009) is a fair specimen of this overwhelming tendency. It is openly motivated by a kindred mantra: "We have been here before." Lauded for being thoroughly researched and wonderfully presented, the book is not unlike the veterinary school's anatomical model horse that displays all the equine diseases to be studied.

Indeed, it exhibits the three basic deficiencies attributable to "rationality:" (i) perspectivism with exaggerated quantitative emphasis; (ii) simplistic dualism; and (iii) sweeping advocacy of corrective, "rational" measures.

(i) The authors use the accumulation of debt (always a ratio, either in relation to some measure of the ability to pay or to its temporal self) as the central criterion to marshal a large variety of sovereign and banking crises since the infancy of capitalism to a central collection point, where they lose their qualitative identity. History becomes a color-neutral arrangement of bare skeletons -- comparable numbers (tables and figures) -- linked through standard "money and banking" concepts, and modeling tropes.

(ii) Society is split into a cognizant subject -- sober observer (the authors) and a potentially responsible government (provided it heeds their admonition and advice) -- and the rest; the messy progression out there (the object) personified as an incorrigible dumbo who keeps falling into the same error time and again.

(iii) After eight centuries of madness; i.e., doing the same thing and expecting different results, the lesson is clear. RX: "macro-prudential supervision." That's what the world needs now, "rational" control through "rational" comprehension. And it can be done, provided that policymakers "do not become too drunk with their credit bubble-fueled success..." (As if policymakers were not captives of their times, caught in the configuration of economic, social, political, and cultural imperatives.)

If the concrete motives for speculation differed over the centuries, if the incidents studied were embedded in drastically different environments in terms of scale and intensity of economic activity, institutions and geography;

if they differed in their modalities and in their economic and broader social impact, then how can one generalize beyond confirming that excessive greed, corporate miscalculation, and political survivorship, combined with manipulation, gullibility, and inertia in mass behavior, tend to make fitful overreaches go haywire at great expense to the general public?[62] All that pedantic disquisition just to say that (as of this writing) new bubbles are on their way! Of course they are and they will burst. That's what bubbles do. We need neither an oversized data base nor a Delphic tripod to see that far into the future. The bubbles currently expanding threaten the entire system and, like all others before them, are not inclined to just fade away.[63]

If it is only the thought that counts; that is, if we overlook that the practical value of general advice derived from

---

[62] Treating the eras of pre-global systems, GS1, "1914-1945," and GS2 as qualitatively separate force fields would be the first step in periodizing the career of speculation over the past eight centuries. And further subdivisions are strongly recommended. For example, the six decades of GS2 could hardly be considered homogenous. Indeed, what did Wall Street know in the 1950s about "too big to fail" banks, derivatives, "HFT," and the need for financial intermediaries (e.g., pension funds) to engage in speculation in order to survive; about persistently growing internal and external imbalances? Modern time series analysis, now literally on line, might be applied to discern whether an instance of going overboard could be considered a short-term disequilibrium shock or an economic explanation-defying "innovative residual" in a non-stationary, time-dependent process. There is no reason why historic analysis and econometrics could not get married.

[63] As observed above, GLOPPE itself is a spontaneously developing bubble, and financial bubbles are mere spontaneous epiphenomena of this big, out-of-control process. Exhortations to control and mitigate the effects of bursting disequilibria in banking, public finance, and in international economic relations are reminiscent of tiny Red Cross flags being waved amidst the patriotic crowds of European capitals, celebrating the outbreak of the "Great War" in 1914.

guiles generalizations is zero, the authors of "This Time is Different" appear to be more GS2-esque than GS2 can ever be. They suggest nothing less than that insufficient "rationality" hampers the relentless exponentiation of productive forces. In the end, GS2 hears what it wants to hear: "I shall always be because I have always been!"

A-historicity as an epistemological ideal reduces life to a stationary system with a time scale. It negates the fundamental dynamism of evolutionary struggle: the crucible of finding, maintaining, and renewing order amidst the unabated multiplication of actors and activities. It overlooks the most obvious aspect of history; namely that the proliferation of life and economic activity across the planet has been and remains a relentless novelty producer.

The world changes beyond the control of mind and will, sweeping along personal lives and reasoned judgment. The *cogito* is inundated with so much new information that believing that "this time is different" is par for the course because in so many different ways it really is. In other words, objectivity transcends and renews itself under different guises. In each experience of boomeranging immoderation, the *personae dramatis* (banker, policymaker, impostor, and victim) saw different, historically specific zones of potentialities and contingencies light up in the enduring restlessness of radical presence. In this optic, one may discover that, in many instances, crises may have prompted the accumulation of debt and not *vice versa*.

A-historicity is the fountainhead for the continuous flow of ludicrous propositions to bring back the institutions (or perhaps more accurately, the lack of institutions) of GS1; to condemn Keynes in favor of Adam Smith; or, to argue with equal futility for "Keynes" in the false belief that GS2's reified global order could be declared null and void through coercive grandstanding. A-historic insensitivity may also be detected in using "we" as the almighty voluntarist decision maker capable of stamping out pollution, making electrical cars dominate the highways (thereby ending our "addiction" to oil). Such "we"-predicated motions tacitly assume an *ad libitum* political control over the *global system*'s parameters or they do not recognize the existence of these parameters at all.

The world has an energy problem? No sweat. Here is the solution!

"Rationality" is complete with an ax-grinding advocacy of whatever limited angle of observation the individual represents.

An example: Two eminent energy experts, M.Z. Jacobson and M.A. Delucci, estimated that a comprehensive strategy to shift the world's energy basis toward renewable sources would require about 3.8 million wind turbines. (See "A Plan to Power 100 Percent of the Planet with Renewables" in the November 2009 issue of the *Scientific American Magazine*.) But, according to André Diederen (senior scientist at the Netherlands-based research institute, *TNO Defense, Security and Safety*) the manufacture of that many large (5 MW) wind turbines would demand roughly three million tons of Neodymium. The current annual production is 18,000 tons and Lenntech, an associate organization of the Technical University of Delft in the Netherlands, puts global reserves of Neodymium at eight million tons.[64]

---

[64]   From André Diederen's presentation, entitled "Materials Scarcity and the Elements of Hope," at the *Bioneers Global Conference*, May 31- June 1, 2010, Driebergen, the Netherlands.

As already mentioned, total reserve figures do not reveal what proportion of them is economically recoverable, since they are the sum of proven, probable and possible deposits, a circumstance aggravated by the fact that this "rare earth" element is hardly found in pure form, implying that a good chunk of the eight million is too expensive to access. Moreover, unlike the commons (the oceans and the atmosphere), metal reserves are national property. China happens to be the country richest in Neodymium and it has recently imposed controls on the exportation of "rare earth" elements. Even in the extremely unlikely case that three million tons could be produced, how about replacing wind turbines? They don't last forever.

The obstinate pushing of nuclear, geothermic, hydroelectric, and solar power; natural gas, bio-fuels; and, as mentioned above, nanotechnology, reeks of a similar relegation of vital factors and angles of analysis to a fictitious, automatic problem-solving black box. *Pro domo* trumping *pro omnis* must play a major role in this phenomenon.

Concerning the reversal of environmental degradation, neither the demonstrated ineffectiveness of the parochial, national (or even subnational) approach, nor the hopelessness of dealing with the world's environmental problems by leaning on the profit motive, provokes a tocsin in "rationality"-ruled mental consciousness. The piecemeal approach to emission controls will not generate planet-wide virtuous circles and private business will always choose profit over reducing pollution as long as the regulatory vacuum permits it.[65] As Professor Nicholas Stern stated, "Climate

---

[65] Niven and Rausch (2013) concluded that supply elasticities for fossil fuels would have to be infinite (or nearly infinite) to generate net negative emission leakage. (Of course, infinite supply elasticity for

change is global in its origins and in its impacts. An effective response must therefore be organized globally and must involve international understanding and collaboration" (Stern, 2008, p. 26). This is certainly true, but global-scale inductive synthesis will have to wait until GS3 transposes GS2's "rationality."[66]

If it is not in the market prices it does not exist.

The unwillingness to see GLOPPE as a spontaneous bio-social configuration explains why market prices do not account for the entropic process that mercilessly shadows the world. The valuation of commodities simply cannot reflect the *Drawdown* if the average mind ignores it. Claiming the contrary is rooted in the drastic overreach of "rationality"-dominated social science that blows out of proportion the empirically undeniable, but ultimately limited subject-object dualism; the range of influence any individual may exert upon the robust, institutionally-embodied, coordinative structure of interpersonal relations.

---

an omnipresent input is an absurd condition. It implies that even a Planck-length displacement of the price would disrupt the economy.) The investigation's main conclusion seems to be absolutely correct: "Leakage estimates from CGE models are unlikely to be negative." Examining the effectiveness of methods to improve air quality in California, Auffhammer and Kellogg (2011) confirmed that the no-nonsense, strong ("inflexible") approach is superior to leaving the choice of compliance mechanism in the hands of private business (refineries in the article's context) in order to minimize interference with profit maximization.

[66] Using a global CGE model, Timilsina and Mevel (2013) showed that unless forest lands are spared in efforts to achieve national biofuel production targets by 2020, greenhouse gas emissions owing to land-use change would exceed the reduction attributable to substituting biofuels for gasoline and diesel. This result supports the argument that a stronger global approach than what GS2 can deliver will be needed to address issues of sustainability on the planetary scale.

The equal validity of supply/demand relations to every economic agent does not mean that prices have an independent ("objective") existence outside our consciousness. Prices may well account for all the factors that billions of linked consciousnesses consider relevant in our era, but for nothing more.[67] And when this web evolves as a result of the anticipated wide-scale recognition of the Earth's *de facto* thermodynamic condition, the resource cost-core of prices[68] (especially of large, expensive durable goods) will likely include an explicitly articulated awareness of the entropic principle, although right now it is hard to imagine

---

[67] The ecological economic model of Takuro Uehara (2013) demonstrated that market prices do not reflect the boundaries of an ecological system.

[68] That is, prices that abstract away from supply and demand; or, alternatively, a quantitative remainder when their interplay is negligible. GS2 economics does not believe in the existence of such a quantity. Its assumptions and postulates claim that prices arise from dynamic, equilibrium-seeking interactions among ratios. Samuelson considered prices "Langrangean multipliers" (Samuelson, 1948, p. 231); evidently needing a comprehensive equation system to be calculated. Debreu emphasized that prices are void of any intrinsic appurtenance (Debreu, 1959, p. 33). Eugene Fama's "intrinsic asset values" do not refer to material and energy inputs.

The implied residual cannot be a labor input in the Marxian sense. Marx himself drifted from his original labor theory of value, which stipulated absolute numbers, toward embracing ratios. (Joan Robinson effectively summarized this contradiction between volumes I and III of *Das Kapital*. Cf. Robinson, 1962, p. 39.) Thus, the above expression "quantitative remainder" is "undoctrinaire" as it implicitly refers to a theory of value yet to be invented. This proposition is less vague than it first appears if one is mindful that the "rationality" of consumers and producers, which is invoked in determining prices in current economic theory, is based on the world's fallacy of composition regarding thermodynamic openness, a collective illusion perpetrated by the rosy glasses of unfounded bounteousness that thermodynamic irrationality has welded to seven billion heads. Wanted: a total (somatic plus extrasomatic) energy theory of value that heeds the *second law*!

seeing a "calories per Kelvin" coordinate in economics textbooks.

Refusal to see the whole

An integral assessment of the world economy (in combination with the thermodynamic perception of history) may sound like this:

"The continued expansion of GLOPPE inevitably aggravates resource and environmental problems. The marginal cost of nonrenewable resources will show a long-run tendency to increase;[69] global pollution and world output are positively correlated. Instead of stimulating growth to a significant extent, measures to boost market confidence in GS2's current ruptured state only enhance banking power. The lid on growth forces entrepreneurial talent and energies to flow increasingly toward idle (gambling-type) speculations, assorted tricks, frauds and depredations. Governments face the unpalatable choice between fiscal default and losing their sole tool to ameliorate the consequences of income differentiation, which become progressively worse as a result of stagnation. Given the role of the U.S. dollar as the source of international liquidity, the *lingua franca* of cross-border economic relations, the size of U.S. debt and the size of the world economy are also positively correlated. This is an unrecognized aberration in the relationship between the *pivot* and the rest of the world. The political turmoil and deadlock surrounding fiscal deficits across GS2's *vanguard* is the only logical response to this systemic no-exit situation."

---

[69]   Renewable substitutes will not eliminate this problem. For example, "green" electricity is clearly more costly than electricity generated from traditional (nonrenewable) sources. Cf. Borenstein (2012).

"Rationality" (as a philosophical doctrine *cum* methodology) inspires the separate investigation of the above-mentioned issues, denying their organic totality. But its critique ought not to stop at simply negating the validity of this orientation, as if positing an antithesis. The integral approach demands the recognition that the enormous volume of high quality, varied economic analysis performed in subfields helps lay the foundations for a future, *truly* global approach to global problems.

In this context, one would be delinquent not to feel grateful to the liberal-democratic society we live in. Beyond what is being said about the prevailing global order's historic merits in Appendix B, GS2's "Weimarian" spirit has also allowed the critics of its crony economics to fear nothing but criticism itself.

Consciousness and the new world order

What will the parameters of a warranted new *global system* be? Regardless of how rightly or wrongly "GS3" may characterize it; any consistent attempt to answer that question must imply a radically new social, economic, and political organization.

"Ay, there's the rub..."

The difference in institutional terms between GS3 and GS2 is so significant that bridging it is impossible without envisaging a major transformation of individual consciousness; yet, the average individual would not -- could not! -- be inwardly transformed as long as socioeconomic institutions characteristic of GS2 prevail. Patterns of behavior, thoughts and feelings ("BTF," as psychologists refer to it) have become crystallized around GS2. The transformation-disabling circle is complete and strictly closed.

Through their mutual cogency, the average individual's internal and external worlds keep each other in check. GS2 does not allow the emancipation of freely chosen artistic, scientific, athletic, and spiritual preoccupations (all of which spring from the inclinations of integral consciousness) among other elements of life on a massive, society-wide scale. And the adaptive necessity to mud-wrestle for survival prevents the genesis of a potent force that could surmount "rationality's" dominion over the consciousness. This paralysis leaves the perception of national interests unchanged, thereby also preventing the increasingly needed mutation in the conduct of national polities.

The unfolding collision between the elemental force of man's volition and its ecological constraints, along with a historic crisis of epic proportions, may be regarded as the struggle of integral consciousness to deprive "rationality" of its current dominance. The immanence of thermodynamic reality and integral consciousness, straining to become empirical life, is one and the same process. The dissonance that will have to be resolved is manifest in a faintly recognized, innermost nostalgia of the individual for wholeness and in the deficient conduct of organizational groupings at all levels; e.g., firms, nations, *multilateral* agencies. The structure of dissonance is devoid of hierarchy. Each of its components is an equally profound part of the whole; and the form-giving intentionality of transcendent physical power will target it as if it were a single organic unit. The factual presence of new, transparent and controllable institutions will mark the end of the watershed, eliminating the historically persistent feud between self (interiority) and outside reality.

But who can say what it will take to turn today's world into a newly enlightened one of enhanced global solidarity; with societies that favor cooperation over exaggerated, competitive self-assertion; responsible sociability over alienation; integrative open-mindedness over stubborn, perspectival dogmatism, altruism over extrasomatic hedonism?[70]

Chaotic transition is not our best friend but there seems to be no other solution than to wait for the broom of history to sweep away the world's unsolvable and growing disharmonies, making space for the experiential spasms that *perforce* develop in the wake of clashing ideas, interests, and passions.

"The germinal phase is the crux," said "I Ching," the Chinese book of changes, a long time ago.

The *second law*'s forward pointing arrow (time) is the most profound autonomous variable. It will prove that self-augmentation-infused, war-to-the-knife-ready modernity cannot be the "end of history," after all; only the end of mankind's "new prehistory" -- if we are lucky. If not, it will be remembered as the end of "pre-bona-fide-sapiens" beginnings.

---

[70] Altruism of individual organisms directed at a group (in the animal kingdom, in general) can evolve by natural selection, according to Edward O. Wilson (Wilson, 2000, p. 87). In the concluding chapter of the quoted work, Wilson convincingly argues that humanity's ecological steady state may well favor altruistic genes.

Concluding remarks

(1) During the past hundred years the world learned that the state cannot plan economic growth to satisfy individual wants. In the current century, it will have to learn that sustainability and the limitless growth of consumption are antinomic. For most firms (i.e., for the foundation of the global economy), movement toward a renewable resource base and pollution control will not prove to be good business.

(2) The acknowledgment that the totality of activities has a scale limit is understandably slow because economic developments are evaluated in the conceptual and quantitative terms of a system that does not recognize the existence of such limits. Nonetheless, a trickle of information about binding resource constraints and the system's doctrinaire incapacity to pay attention to them has begun to seep into public discourse.

For example, the proposition that skyrocketing oil prices triggered the Great Recession (rather than, as is widely believed, the bursting of the housing bubble for the sheer reason of over-extending credit) has gained some traction. It is indeed highly plausible that the fuse of the turmoil-provoking explosion was lit at a gas station/grocery store somewhere along the interminable commuting route between a North American city, where the jobs are, and exurbia, where the zero-down-payment houses were built and sold on the assumption that the costs of transportation and food would never interfere with the perpetual climb of real estate values.

The trickle is bound to become an eddy and then a cascading maelstrom; as it is discovered that real growth has slipped under Nature's control. It is telling that instead of restarting significant acceleration, the continued buildup of public debt and digital money only makes asset bubbles blossom like mushrooms after the monsoon. To paraphrase Bertolt Brecht, the bitch that bore the monster of rising oil prices causing economic dislocation via financial havoc "is in heat again."

(3) Unless humanity can break out from its sublunary cradle, it will find itself in an evolutionary blind alley, uglified by featureless Gorgon heads. Sending mining robots to the Moon and terraforming Mars (i.e., making the Red Planet more earthlike through modifying its ecology) are the most frequently quoted ways to capture extraterrestrial matter/space. This is the only type of permanent, unlimited expansionism capable of preserving man's Faustian will in the gloriously rugged spirit of seafaring discoverers.

Appendix A

Difference between problem and predicament

To highlight the difference between problem and predicament, it might be helpful to think of a *global system* as a temporal phenomenon with a reasonably bounded topological space and distinct algebra. Communication and other forms of interaction (production, exchange, financial-monetary mechanisms, etc.) allow for an effective, operative connectedness among the points of a system-specific topological space (T_i); that is, among individuals, firms, and nations. The axioms and algorithms of the related algebra (A_i) imply logical interrelationships among both nonmathematical and quantitatively expressed concepts that guarantee the continuity of economic processes and other supra-individual patterns along with convergent (system-conforming, system-preserving) solutions of related problems. "T_i/A_i" is a symbolic expression of the fact that the global organization as a cerebral network of billions of nodes reproduces itself.

If we live in the time of "T_1/A_1"and a crucial problem arises, the solution of which demands "T_2/A_2," we are faced with a predicament. Chaos separates two consecutive, relatively stable periods precisely because, for a given generation living under a *global system*, the predicament remains incognito, hiding behind the mask of a problem. It takes bitter economic and (in a broader sense) socio-historic experience to find out that a major, irreversible change in conditions demands the transformation of average consciousness, which is inseparable from a new socioeconomic order, a new economics.

A little "Monday morning quarterbacking" on the 19th century's "Great Depression" (1873-1896)[71]should make things clearer. Looking at that extended crisis from today's perspective, one might say: "If national governments under GS1 had been equipped with GS2-type fiscal and monetary tools (and policymakers had been thinking the same way as they do today); had national societies been endowed with GS2-typical safety nets; had the United Nations been in existence, the intense suffering of a generation could have been avoided."

But it is exactly the difference in "T/A" that distinguishes *global systems*. GS1 did not have GS2's topology. Individuals, firms, and nations were not the same as they are today and they interacted differently. GS1 lacked GS2's problem-solving algorithms; it had a different algebra. Embowered by the classics' pious myth about *laissez faire* being equal with full employment, the world waited for Santa Claus while tens of millions unreached by private charity sank into abject poverty. In the international arena, the "Scramble for Africa" tortured

---

[71]   "1873-1879" in the bulk of American literature.

and humiliated the population of an entire continent while pushing European empires toward all-out war.[72]

GS1 faced a predicament, not a problem. The world came out of it temporarily but not through economic policies designed to revive business. It is very likely that the arms race (a kind of unintended, aboriginal Keynesianism), which the "Scramble for Africa" kicked into high gear, pulled the global economy out of the quagmire.

If Napoleon had two machine guns, he would have won Waterloo. Had he a few tanks and a single B-17 "Flying Fortress," his battle would have been a walk in the park. Such anachronous substitutions seem trivial, yet they are used *sans gêne* by economists; both forward and backward: Forward when a long-dead system's component is placed in the present context, for example, when advocating the restoration of the gold standard. And backward, when policymakers of another era are criticized for not thinking the way present ones do. Blaming central banks for the Great Depression is a notable example.[73]

---

[72] The unsavory subordination of less developed economies to creditors from the industrialized world is a great flaw in international economic relations. It became prominent during the mature decades of GS1 and has remained so since World War II. Evidently, in this domain, not even the substitution of GS2's "T/A" for that of GS1 would help flush out the difference between the two *global systems*. Characterizing GS2's *multilateralism* as "weak" seems appropriate for this reason as well.

[73] Milton Friedman excoriated the Fed's tight money policies during the 1930s, while others blasted its easy money policies in the years leading up to "1929." This is an inherently false exegesis. Saying that policymakers during the *chaotic transition* should have known what they know now is as much of an anachronism as putting a Kalashnikov into the hands of Napoleon. During "1914-1945," the contents of consciousness regarding supra-individual legal-institutional liens that bind national societies and the community of nations together,

Why do educated, talented people err in such a primitive fashion? Because postwar generations have become inured to the mental habit of a-historicity.

If counterfactual substitutions have any scientific legitimacy, it may be found in pondering the historical forces that drive the transformation of global self-organization; the mass clamor and relentless pressure -- articulated through system-transcending political will -- to solve problems insolvable under prevalent conditions.

"T/A" may be called the *global system*'s structure. It has a clean bill of health as long as it ensures (or at least holds out the hope for) economic expansion in excess of population growth in most parts of the world, without endangering social peace by crossing a certain threshold of inequality, which, of course, varies significantly among nations. A *global system* is in a predicament when its structural problems become global. The border region of GS2's predicament is recognizable from the convergent conditions of "structurers" and "structurees" in the *multilateral* context.

When a developing country or a "transition economy" experiences severe external imbalances (typically chronic trade deficits), the IMF is there to help on the condition that the beneficiary government performs structural adjustments. These intend to repair the "structuree's" "T/A," deemed to be out of line with its unblemished perfection as observed in the most-developed industrial nations, GS2's vanguard -- the "structurers."

"Structurees" undertake the reduction of unemployment, national debt, and income differences, according to the recipes of those who know it better.

---

lingered in a post-GS1, pre-GS2 no-man's-land. "T/A" was in limbo.

"Structural adjustment programs" have been severely criticized for doing more harm than good. They are not only anachronistically *laissez faire*-nostalgic, pointing back toward GS1; and therefore, bound to dissatisfy the affected societies, but they are also unlikely to produce the hoped for results given the world economy's miserable prospects for vigorous snowballing. As the problems associated with debt, unemployment, and inequalities worsen in the economies of the "structurers," the day will come when the "structurees" will simply tell them: "Now look, who's talking!" From that moment on, the need to search for a new "T/A" should become much clearer.

One way to formulate the world's current predicament is to assert that GS2's "T/A" is not suited for shifting the resource base from predominantly nonrenewable to predominantly renewable sources. Public discourse treats the transition to a "green economy" (henceforth *transition*) as a challenge, surmountable within the *global system*'s topological space (i.e., while GS2-typical individuals, firms, and nations interact within the organizational texture of the mixed economy, *weak multilateralism* and minimum reserve banking); using mainly tax/subsidy schemes (GS2's most characteristic algorithm to solve social and economic problems).

While being critical of policies designed to foster "sustainability" and factually sound in their analysis, the most respected government and academic authorities never raise any doubt about the fitness of the extant world order to complete the passage.[74] They are sold, in effect,

---

[74] The periodic reports released by the International Energy Administration (IEA) of the U.S. Department of Energy; the International Energy Administration (IEA); and other prestigious sources such as the "Frankfurt School UNEP Collaborating Centre for Climate & Sustainable Energy Finance" give a reliable, comprehensive picture of contemporary thinking

on "gradualism," the endless supply of aces that economic orthodoxy hides up its sleeves, and confirm day after day that the world has "only" a problem.

The overarching obstacle *transition* faces is directly tied to the basic argument that has motivated the present project. Energy condensed in matter is the planet's scarce natural agency. Not only can we not produce one gram of matter from the practically infinite amount of energy that surrounds us, but we also cannot generate a single calorie of energy without material inputs, most of which come from nonrenewable sources.

Oil is the tightest component among substances that contain easily accessible free energy. The creation and operation of all "green-energy"-generating facilities require refined oil products -- and not only as the primary source of energy to transport manpower, material and equipment. There are no adequate renewable (biological) substitutes for plastics in manufacturing pipes, valves, fittings, railings, and thousands of other applications in construction, including machinery, at the current level of economic activities. In a broader sense, civilized life, as we know it, is inconceivable without petrochemical products, from food to pharmaceuticals, from asphalt to plumbing fixtures, from computers to clothing and daily hygiene.

It is not possible to replace plastic at the present (let alone projected) levels of use with products derived from agriculture and forestry.[75] *Transition* is being pursued

---

about the advancement of "green energy." From the last quoted source, see, for example: "Global Trends in Renewable Energy Investment:"

http://www.unep.org/pdf/GTR-UNEP-FS-BNEF2.pdf

[75] A decisive move toward substituting corn-based pellets for those gained from oil (via naphtha) would create a global food crisis. The rush to

without the slightest thought of this latent scale limit. Yet it represents an insurmountable obstacle.

Symbols might help here to state the case unambiguously. If GWP_{cal} stood for the global economy's annual "calorie demand" (combining energy used *qua* energy with the energy contents of material inputs) and we denoted the maximum amount of renewing and renewable calories for the same year (again combining the two subcategories) as $\max R_{green\ cal}$ then clearly, $\max R_{green\ cal} \ll GWP_{cal}$. The actual size of the predominantly nonrenewable-input-driven world economy far exceeds the limit set by the "green base."

Consequently, even if efforts to substitute away from fossil resources as the crucial source of non-energy (i.e., material) inputs paralleled those aimed at effecting passage to a global "green energy" base, the joint process would be arrested by the insufficiency of "green material." The aggregate of resources the Earth can reproduce on an ongoing basis might well be a nebulous quantity, an unassignable limit; nonetheless, it is an indomitable troll. One ought not to press against it.[76]

Nor can some ideal situation be reached in which "green energy" dominates all aspects of life (from productive activities to personal transportation) while the "green

---

ethanol a few years ago was a good illustration of elementary economics. The opportunity cost of corn ethanol is the food not produced using the same area of corn land. Apropos plastic, the food container made from corn (even if it is biodegradable) reduces food supplies -- and not only in the "short run." It requires only a modicum of integral thinking to acknowledge that thoroughgoing measures to substitute energy and material inputs of biological origin for those obtained through refining oil would create a tragedy of unimaginable proportions.

[76] Please note, the critical aspect here is "scale," not "technology."

material" base expands (along with a simultaneously shrinking reliance on fossils) as far as it is possible without reducing global output. The free market cannot lead society there and the scope of government involvement on the level that would make a decisive difference is incompatible with our economic organization.[77] Short of war, government authority in resource allocation is strictly curbed under GS2.

As stated above, the world economy already exceeds the planet's "green" support capacity. The potential danger residing in this chasm is accentuated (made more "dynamic") by the discrepant relationship between strengthening intentions to "green" the resource base and GS2's dependence on permanent output exponentiation. In the long run, either the push for a "green economy" or inertia about it spells lethal disruption: The "push" by reducing the totality of available resources;[78] "inertia" by allowing certain key nonrenewable inputs to become prohibitively expensive; while prompting the ghost of massive environmental disasters to step out from the shadows of oblivion.

To rephrase the premise, GLOPPE's size, in combination with the postwar form of global self-organization, has created

---

[77]   To cite a technical detail, crude oil refining (fractionation) is geared toward turning heavier components into gasoline and other transportation fuels. What it would take to adjust technology once "green energy" replaces oil products in propelling 4-wheelers and shifting the distillation system in the opposite direction is not a current topic. However, there is no doubt that a considerable increase in obtaining naphtha (suitable for making plastic) from the present-day roughly ten percent of the oil used for the purpose on average, constitutes a major technical and economic challenge that would require significant public intervention.

[78]   Raised above a certain point, government intervention by itself destabilizes a market economy.

a hothouse-like environment for explosive demographic-economic growth. But by now, physical obstacles are blocking the interminable compounding of scales, without which domestic and international socioeconomic institutions fall apart. There is no feasible policy or program that could shepherd the world through the *transition* gently while also seeing to a ceaseless rise of plenitude.

As described in the text, GS2 is unfit to exist under growth-inhibiting physical obstacles and it has come face to face with a major one: the disappearance of cheap oil. Owing to the irreversible decline in the "energy returned on energy invested" (EROEI), associated with oil production, the price of "black gold" must hover at relatively high levels even when the economy remains sluggish. If policy measures designed to reinvigorate expansion actually worked, oil prices would rise to recession-inducing heights. As a consequence, the totality of global activities is inclined to trace out a saw-tooth graph; slow recovery goes into a spurt to be recessed shortly by skyrocketing oil prices. Growth goes back into hibernation and the barrel falls -- *reprise*. Mother Nature has condemned mixed economies to Sisyphean travail.

There are, of course, several other indications that history's *global system*-forming force is no longer in sync with GS2's principles. The financial-monetary order is on deathwatch; the absence of vigorous growth has turned the lopsided distribution of wealth into a ticking social-political time bomb. What is worse, the mechanism of further aggravating income inequalities continues to function even when (as at present) average per capita incomes stagnate.[79] And it is only

---

[79] Constraints to expansion cause chronic unemployment; and, consequently, incomes fall in some segments of society (also as a result of excess labor exerting a downward pressure on wages). Since the

a question of time before the subtle elbowing for resources among nations assumes more radical forms of competition.

Complete this picture with wobbling banks, ethically ruined investment houses, sovereigns barely breathing under growing mounds of debt, and it becomes glaringly plain that the macroeconomic stability required for the *transition* is a pipe dream.

Market fundamentalists see things differently. Thinking without the slightest hunch of the historical relativity of socioeconomic institutions, they often express their conviction in this fashion: "When fossil-based energy becomes too expensive, profit hungry investors will pour capital into renewable energy. The tried and trusted interplay between demand and supply will take care of this problem (if there is indeed one). And, this above all: Leave government out of it. It only distorts the market, since it cannot do anything right. As Milton Friedman said, 'If you put the federal government in charge of the Sahara Desert, in five years there'd be a shortage of sand.'"

Putting GS1's dozing *laissez faire* state (that used to wake up with a menacing snort only when it heard whispers about labor organizations) into the life structure of the post-World War II era is a prime example of anachronistic substitution. Such disoriented yearning for a bygone system has no valid intellectual content. It is in fact a cunning falsehood that paved the way to turning the financial world into a theater of the absurd.

---

average per capita income is presumed to hover in a standstill, decline in one part of the social spectrum must be balanced by a rise in another.

The market has remained powerful under GS2, but it cannot free *transition* from its troubled destiny. Private-gain motivated, decentralized decisions work well when the task is to reallocate resources so as to substitute one product for another, one service for another, even one resource for another. But it cannot possibly work when what is substituted for is also a perfect complement of the substitute.

When oil is simply "expensive" and the world dallies in a near recessionary (roughly zero per capita income growth) condition, while governments strain their resources and central bankers their imagination to kick expansion back into gear; instead of rushing into the "green base," capital searches for a cheaper mix among fossils; e.g., shifting toward coal and natural gas. And instead of stimulating the *transition,* a "too expensive" barrel shuts down growth altogether.

As far as wishing government away from any and all fields of economic activity, anti-state zealots ignore the extent to which suppliers of nonrenewable energy depend on public budgets to expand their scale of operations against the increasingly binding constraint of declining EROEIs. They also forget that renewables would never have reached their current stage of development without significant subsidization.[80]Solar and wind potency have to be extracted from the ambient environment; that is, from diluted sources, as opposed to scooping up easily accessible free energy concentrated in fossils. "Green power" has needed (still needs and probably will need forever) a great deal of research, development, and

---

[80]   Although nonrenewable energy has received the bulk of government support in the new century, renewable energy has moved into the lead as far as subsidy per unit of energy is concerned.

demonstration that the private sector is not in the position to provide.[81]

---

[81]   Three strategies to *transition* stand out: government involvement, which although substantial, does not amount to long-term autonomous investment (U.S.); government involvement that does (Germany); and China -- a case apart, since the world's most populous country does not have a genuine mixed economy.

The United States aims to satisfy 20 percent of its energy needs from renewable sources by 2030, but efforts to foster the *transition* do not add to a consistent, long-term policy. Cf. a study by E. Donald Elliott:

http://www.cov.com/files/Publication/ce0ce0e2-1d8b-4ef4-8dd9-5bffa4af86f8/Presentation/PublicationAttachment/5b91deeb-1583-46b7-a048-624472b2d90f/Why_the_United_States_Does_Not_Have_a_Renewable_Energy_Policy.pdf

Federal help does not go beyond temporary (not necessarily renewable) inducements for private profit/private risk allocations. This makes investors think long and hard before signing up and many shy away from the possibility of being sent off with a "see-you-later, allocator" pat on the shoulder.

By featuring guaranteed, long-term (15-20 years) inducements, the German approach does approximate autonomous investment in renewable energy. "Feed-in tariffs" grid operators pay to generators of "green electricity" are largely recovered through higher rates to consumers, while the federal government is ready to step in with budget allocations to fill gaps; support the strategy whenever, wherever it is needed. By 2030, the country expects to generate ca. 45 percent of its electricity from renewable (mainly wind and solar) sources. At present, this pioneering, ambitious endeavor is embroiled in an awful technological, economic, social, and political mess.

Two thirds of German executives active in the energy field gave a "miserable" grade to the country's *transition* policies (*Energiewende*), according to a 2013 survey. Most of them consider a market-led integration of renewable energy into the grid unlikely:

http://www.presseportal.de/pm/100382/2549686/umfrage-energiemanager-kritisieren-deutsche-energiepolitik-scharf

By combining central planning with market-oriented elements, China's grand design of *transition* clearly illustrates the two-leveled nature of its economic organization. State energy companies (for which profit

The unsuitability of GS2 to lead the world to an intermediary "max green base/min nonrenewable base" mix, which would give global society a decent interval to rethink, regroup, and adapt, may be recognized by looking at the built-in limits to government spending and at some formidable "chicken-egg" obstacles that flicker in *transition*'s abstruse destiny.

EROEI's declining long-run trajectory (mirrored in the rising marginal cost of energy generation) represents an annealing barrier to expansion that the system is inclined to soften through state support. But the transposition of natural restraints to the ability of governments to anodize these can only be temporary.

Public debt is already a major concern around the world and national governments and authorities in charge of regional

---

is of secondary importance) act as flexible intermediaries between long-term budget allocations to renewable energy projects of all kinds and the activities of profit-maximizing firms. The goals are lofty. By 2030, wind and solar sources are supposed to satisfy 100 percent of the country's demand for electricity.

But the future in the East is just as somber as in the West. *Transition*'s forced march is bound to create major structural imbalances, which never fail to accompany central planning; and these will have to be dealt with amidst the mega-challenge of trying to raise the per capita income (currently one-fifth of the U.S. level) of 1.4 billion, luxury-hungry, restive consumers. Failure to deliver would result in wrecking communist party headquarters city by city, province by province. But a fiasco is assured also because the country is embedded in a systemically half-debilitated global economy that runs on and is governed by oil. The allure of happy motoring has already turned China into the world's largest oil importer and passenger vehicles in the Middle Kingdom number still fewer than half of U.S. registrations. It is not unreasonable to assume that if per capita income doubled in China, the country would claim the entirety of oil traded in international markets. Without any doubt, the Chinese experience with the *transition* will contribute in major ways to making the world's predicament explicit.

integration frameworks and *multilateral* institutions do not shrink from drastic steps aimed at slowing (perhaps even reversing) its accumulation.[82] But even if all budgets were balanced, government spending is not a free variable. It is circumscribed by the threat of oppressive taxation.

Support extended to businesses also has *multilateral* limits. If a subsidy program alters the "terms of trade," it faces immediate institutional challenge via complaints by the affected nation(s) at WTO.[83]

In addition to the financial limit on pumping affordable energy into the economy, the "green base" also has a mighty rival for budgetary allocations: fossils. People living in industrial democracies want their respective governments to exercise leadership; look into the future, set socially desirable goals and make their realization effective. But once control over spending is established (voluntarily or involuntarily) and the distribution of available funds becomes a much sharper issue, "green" is bound to lose. When the representatives of traditional energy interests cry out: "What!? The government is picking winners and losers while endangering overall economic performance?"

---

[82] GS2's *multilateral* institutions demand structural adjustments in countries where fiscal imbalances are deemed to be excessive. EU member states (especially in the euro-zone) are subject to severe administrative pressure to control their deficits. While as the provider of the world's major reserve currency, the United States escapes such punitive measures, the country's policymakers are aware of the danger and, encouraged by the international community, they are committed to bringing the federal deficit under control. Evidently, the operators of the *system* do not recognize the predicament. Cutting the deficit causes immediate damage to economic performance. The *text* is quite clear about this.

[83] The EU and China have mutually accused one another at the WTO for violating the rules of fair trade regarding the exportation of solar energy-related equipment.

the public (believing that the government interferes with market forces only when it aids the *transition*) will line up behind hydrocarbons and coal.

Aided by worries about employment, income, and immediate growth prospects, the *status quo* has a built-in potential to defuse attempts "to rock the boat." And movement toward a "green economy" is fraught with economic calamities that both Labor and Capital dread. Even the much-chided short-term focus of big business, manifest in straining every nerve to maintain net profit margins and share values from quarter to quarter, is congruent with immediate social interests.

There is even more to GS2's unfitness to manage the *transition*. If the process has managed somehow to reach the point where "green" is ready to unburden oil from powering transportation, a vicious "chicken-egg" obstacle would pop up: What profit-dependent entity wants to mass-produce electrically propelled cars without matching filling stations and what private business wants to build such filling stations without the mass-production of cited conveyances? The scale of expense and level of organizational involvement that would be required to remove such obstacles are not in GS2's repertoire.

In short, there is a mismatch between GS2's "T/A" and the mastery of *transition*. By now, having no other choice, GS2 governance has grossly distorted market prices in the energy field. As a consequence, society will learn that the energy has turned into a growth-limiting resource not from a supply and demand graph but from governments admitting bankruptcy, proposing new ways to govern.

A key statistic underscores the predicament. The world's reliance on fossil fuels for roughly four-fifths of its energy needs today is the same as it was 25 years ago when "green energy" became a social issue. The relentless flow of victory reports about "game-changing technological breakthroughs" and "enhanced competitiveness" have evidently applied to "nonrenewable energy" as well. And now, in light of stunted growth conditions and the *global system*'s related proneness to chaotic dissolution, all those ambitious projections about "green" gaining the upper hand 20 to 30 years down the line, while per capita income keeps soaring toward the Sun on five continents, seem like exercises in surrealism.

Analytical vision suffers from a general impairment. Most people, perhaps also the majority of scholars, live under the impression that, whereas nonrenewable resources are limited, the renewable ones are unlimited. Reality is tragically at odds with this perception. The practical exploitation of renewable and renewing energy and material resources -- the "green base" -- requires the same nonrenewable resources whose short supply and/or polluting characteristics have motivated the *transition* in the first place. What is more, the "green base" claims agricultural land. So much about its infinite supply and implied zero opportunity cost.

The *transition* cannot reach the tipping point without a fundamental disruption. Going from a predominantly nonrenewable-based to a predominantly "green"-based global economy (i.e., crossing the tipping point) entails a reduction in the scale of activities, negative aggregate output growth. This clearly does not mesh with a "grow or die" economic organization. And, as argued above, *transition* cannot make its way to an optimal intermediary position (max green base/ min nonrenewable base). As shown above, there are two interrelated reasons for this: The world economy's actual conjuncture and the *global system*'s unsuitability for the task.

The threat of resource shortages and mounting dangers of environmental degradation -- "ecological constraints" -- have forced the world to adopt *transition* as a collective, long-term goal. However, the historical significance of this turning point is obscured by intermittent growth suffocation. When growth is lethargic, oil prices are not excessively high. Prospects seem like "old times" and *transition* slips to the back burner. But in a decade or less, the renewed stirring of expansive potency raises the price of oil. While *transition* appears to be urgent under these circumstances, the increase in overall energy costs has raised its price tag too.

The energy sector's heavy dependence on public support reveals that raw market forces cannot secrete an ideal price ratio between fossil and "green energy," which, through automatic self-adjustment, would guide the *transition* while maintaining long-term macroeconomic stability, meaning growth.

Without government help, the private sector has no special appetite for augmenting the "green base" and GLOPPE has entered the phase when even traditional energy, generated from nonrenewable sources, demands increasing amounts of public assistance. Patching up the income-differentiating tendency of the global socioeconomic order and subsidizing growth through the expansion of energy production add up to a "lose-lose" choice: Augment debt until the system breaks or force austerity measures on national communities until they break the system.

The predicament may be summed up by asserting that mixed-economy governments do not have the tools to put an end to this malignant situation. Their toolbox contains only a limited ability to spend (on projects and subsidies) and to by-pass revenues (through tax easements) when nothing short of drastic, operative transformation of the economic structure would be needed. Reverting to medical symbolism, a GS2-typical government, as a physician, may hand out prescriptions but it is not allowed to operate. China has a rudimentary two-level, experimentally post-GS2 form of economic organization. This enables its government to practice surgery on the body economic under its control, but operation *transition* cannot succeed, given the patient's precarious condition and the operating theater -- the ramshackle *global system*.

In the complex symbiosis between economic élan (fueled by a virtually unfettered depletion of resources and an evidently unstoppable destruction of the environment) and the incessantly reproduced communality of short-term preoccupations across societies and national boundaries, we can recognize GLOPPE's thermodynamically spontaneous nature.

The *transition* must stall. Sometime between now and the 2030s, the world will find that the capacity of reasonably-priced "green" resources it managed to create cannot fill the gap left by "much too expensive" oil, waning natural gas, and closed coal mines. The associated historical experience will surely remove the cataract from the eyes, giving global society a new chance to look at itself in the mirror.

Indeed, our civilization does not have a problem. It is the problem.

Appendix B

World history as the synoptic narrative of a thermodynamic unfolding[84]

The thermodynamic process that characterizes the human story (cultural evolution, universal history) is ecologically dissipative, hence irreversible, by the *second law of thermodynamics*. The requirement of growing degrees of self-organization renders it *pulsatile*.[85] The dissipative expansion of self-organized physical entities must go through dynamic steady states (*global systems*) interrupted by bifurcations (*chaotic transitions*), episodes during which parameters for the next dynamic steady state are selected and introduced.

The *global system* is the planet's broadest and most comprehensive framework for socioeconomic institutions and

---

[84]   For full length exposition, see Pogany (2006).

[85]   This theory is based on the work of Nobel Laureate chemist Ilya Prigogine (Prigogine, 1997). It was first applied to world history by Ervin Laszlo (Laszlo, 1992).

behavior. It is the result of implicit collaboration at the species' level. *In strictly physical terms, it may be viewed as a dynamic steady state of billions of interconnected neuroanatomical states.*

During 1500-1789 (GS0), the world underwent sweeping changes as preparations for the age of *global systems* accelerated. European explorations and colonization completed geographic globalization. Modern scientific thinking emerged and vital discoveries were made in physics, chemistry, biology, medicine, and astronomy. The ideas of all-embracing individual liberty and freedom of conscience, along with the legal concept of "nation" as a form of sovereign territorial organization were born. The *Enlightenment* has gone a long way in prying the frozen fingers of dogmatic thinking from the human mind and identifying the project of social progress. The epoch produced unmatched achievements in the arts.

As the ensemble of particles (human cells plus all human-crafted objects) grew, its size had to reach the point where it required global-scale organization in order to grow further. *Laissez faire/metal money/zero multilateralism* was the first *global system* (GS1), with Great Britain as its *pivot*. It lasted from the 1830s until World War I.

Despite its well-known success in raising per capita output for a growing population, GS1 became increasingly unable to accommodate further economic development. Its main limitations may be summarized under four points.

(1) Dependence on gold limited the supply of money; (2) while industrialization reached the level at which national economies were prone to accelerate and decelerate, system parameters did not include instruments; i.e., fiscal and monetary policies, to counter this phenomenon; (3) the

system skewed distribution too much in favor of Capital at the expense of Labor, thereby constraining the development of mass consumption/mass production; and (4) it was unfit to accommodate schemes for international cooperation while the growing interdependence among national economies began ever more forcefully to demand an institutionally determined, comprehensive ("multilateral") framework.

By 1914, initial-condition sensitivity hid in the incongruity between system parameters and the state of the world. The "Guns of August" blew GS1 to smithereens.

The period 1914-1945 was the *chaotic transition* that led to the introduction of the second and current *global system, mixed economy/fractional reserve money/weak multilateralism* (GS2). As observed in thermodynamic processes via bifurcation, diverse and intensely conflicting approaches emerged to reestablish order; i.e., a dynamic steady state.

These were the alternatives: (1) Restoration of GS1 by attempting to bring back the gold standard; (2) Communism: A new form of socioeconomic self-organization; (3) Fascism: Territorial conquest through military aggression, winner takes all (semi-colonial or colonial status for the rest of the world); and (4) Mixed economy: A new relationship between public authority and the market as well as between Labor and Capital.

Mixed economy triumphed.

The critical transformation realized during the New Deal in the United States spread quickly to industrial democracies following World War II, becoming the backbone of GS2's domestic economic organization. It implies a private-ownership-based market economy with important roles assigned to the state in securing economic prosperity and social peace.

The United Nations and its charter organizations represent *weak multilateralism*. Its flagship agencies in the economic and financial sphere are The World Bank, the International Monetary Fund (IMF), and the General Agreement on Tariffs and Trade (GATT), which became the World Trade Organization (WTO) in 1995. The United States took the role of *pivot* from Great Britain, upgraded with system administrator-like functions.

GS2's *multilateralism* is labeled "weak" for three reasons: (1) Compartmentalized nation states lack the ability and *multilateral* agencies lack the authority to prevent multinational giants, including banking houses, from engaging in international operations that the world at large may find underhanded and harmful; (2) in certain areas; e.g., health and environmental protection, there is no dependable (strongly goal-oriented, result-guaranteeing) *multilateral* oversight. National governments can manipulate the representative agencies by feigning compliance; (3) in some other areas, most notably in financial affairs, *multilateral* organizations have become overbearing. With its stubbornly pursued neoliberal approach to globalization, the IMF is the poster child for strong action on weakly relevant (hence, potentially detrimental) principles.[86]

---

[86] No other criticism in this area has yet matched the significance and convincing power of the analysis provided by Joseph Stiglitz, former vice-president and chief economist at The World Bank. See, for example, the April 17, 2000 issue of *The New Republic*.

Nonetheless, GS2 outshined and outperformed GS1. It brought material welfare within the reach of billions. During the threescore years from 1950 to 2010, despite an increase in world population from 2.5 billion to 6.9 billion, per capita global output (income) grew more than four-fold.[87]

Thus, the proposed archeology of the current world order:

GS0 (1500-1789) → GS1 (1834-1914) → GS2 (1945-present)

Communism: Less than a global system but more than a footnote to history.

Recognition of the above-presented perspective had to wait for the collapse of Communism. During the Cold War, global society accepted the notion that there were two parallel, competing *global systems* vying for domination. Planet-wide self-organization appeared to be bi-systemic. In retrospect, Communism was not and could not have become a *global system*:

(1) To avoid isolation, communist-controlled countries had to deal with the rest of the world through GS2's *multilateral* institutions dominated by industrial democracies;

(2) The Soviet Bloc, representing the "developed socialist world" during the Cold War, accounted for 5 percent or less of global trade;

(3) The communistic social order appealed only to a small minority of the world population and this circumstance

---

[87]   Estimates based on historical data published on line by The World Bank, and the IMF.

disqualified it from becoming the foundation of a new global order;

(4) Socialist societies did not develop distinct socioeconomic personal traits. They only suppressed and deformed GS2-typical behavior. (Populations formerly under communist rule snapped out from socialist institutions and immediately adopted multiparty, private entrepreneurship-based economic organizations, roughly at their respective pre-communist levels of social development.)

This is not to deny or even belittle the historic significance of Communism. Its early economic growth performance and proclaimed idealism presented the rest of the world with a major economic and political challenge. As a balance wheel, the communist threat helped define the respective weights ("the mix") of private and public expenditures in the mixed economy. It pushed the balance in favor of public expenditures (e.g., military spending in the United States, social programs in Western Europe and Japan). During its existence, the communist sphere provided the socio-psychological, philosophical prop needed to prevent the real hegemonic world order (GS2) from acquiring ontological status; i.e., its attributes becoming confused with natural laws.

We can acknowledge this by observing that a restriction of public authority followed the catastrophic demise of socialist statehood. The era since 1991 has witnessed a forceful wave of deregulations and privatizations; only the environmental/conservation and anti-globalization movements demonstrate that GS2 is a historic form of self-organization.

Given that communism was not a *global system*, we may conclude that, thus far, the sequence "GS0àGS1àGS2à" best describes thermodynamically interpreted universal history. The following synaptic table summarizes the main characteristics of these organizational stages.

Stages of Evolving Global Self-Organization

	Distinguishing economic feature (1)	International trade (2)	Labor/Capital relations (3)	International cooperation among governments (4)	Game-theoretical classification (5)	Organizational complexity (6)
GS0	Agrarian	Agrarian products, metals, and primitive manufactures; employment level does not depend on international trade	Feudalistic hierarchy; collective bargaining is not a known concept	Nonexistent	Zero-sum game	Absence of global self-organization
GS1	Large-scale industrial	Add inter-industry commodity exchange; employment moderately depends on trade	No framework for collective bargaining; legal system unequivocally favors Capital	Implicit	Positive-sum game without cooperation	Low level of global self-organization
GS2	Mass production, consumption	Add intra-industry commodity exchange; employment strongly depends on trade	Framework for collective bargaining; legal system creates balance between Labor and Capital	Explicit	Positive-sum game with cooperation	Higher level of global self-organization

What is next?

The ticking of the evolutionary time machine now heralds the onset of a new transition. The reason is not, as Marx thought, that capitalism (now in its modern or reformed version) could not provide prosperity for the masses, or that capitalist economies suffered from incurable limitations to grow. The reason is the exact opposite: GS2 cannot stop growing. Its existence is contingent on maximizing growth and, therefore, it is incompatible with a predominantly renewable-resource-based global society in agreement about the use of scarce, nonrenewable resources and the environment. The *Sphere*'s ability to support economic growth is limited and the limits have begun to talk back.

The thermodynamic interpretation of global history predicts a halt to population and economic expansion for purely physical reasons. This general condition requires a new *global system*: GS3 -- *two-level economy/strong multilateralism/ mostly government money (maximum reserve banking).*

Legally binding international agreements on the use of nonrenewable energy and material resources, as well as on harmful emissions, would enlarge the government's role in economic affairs since administrative methods would be needed to ensure national compliance with globally determined goals. The implied *strong multilateralism* would split national economies (hence, the world economy) into a free-market and a public authority-dominated sector. While carrying on the best traditions of constructive entrepreneurship, businesses in the first domain would bid for resources and emission rights; joint private-public ownership would prevail in the second one. The state's substantial holding of private shares would eliminate most, if not all, income taxation.

The monetary system would be based on a global currency issued by the global central bank.

Maximum bank reserves would restrict the ability of banks to extend loans. Just as under the prevailing minimum reserve system, some banks in some instances may keep no reserves at all; under the maximum reserve system some banks in some instances might be required to keep 100 percent reserves. While such an arrangement may not eliminate the creation of money through debt, it would certainly change its nature. The consent of depositors would be required to make loans, making financial intermediation once again the modest helper that draws together scattered household savings in order to place them into the hands of *bona fide* entrepreneurs. "Enterprise," in the Keynesian sense, would squeeze out "speculation."

The economic role of grass roots communities would increase significantly.

A remark about China is in order. It is a *sui generis*. Its socioeconomic organization is not GS2-typical. Its economy is not a mixed one in the sense that emerged during the American New Deal and was subsequently applied throughout the industrialized world (and then again in the wave of socioeconomic transformations following the collapse of communism in Europe). In an intriguing way, China points beyond GS2. The country's approach to "greening" its resource base is a clear example of its economy's two-leveled nature.

The unbreakable interdependence between the mutation of average consciousness to its integral structure and the transformation of the world from a biomass driven by spontaneous appetition to one capable of globally shared apperception has profound implications for man's biological evolution. The altered relationship between Life and Nature (technically, between GLOPPE and the *Sphere*) is equivalent to a major modification in humanity's hermeneutically isolated (biotic-abiotic) environment. It will demand adaptation on the genetic level. That being said, one must humbly return to silence. Not unlike Kant's *Ding an sich*, the species' evolutionary potential is beyond the realm of intelligible phenomena, beyond knowledge gained through rationally expandable objective experience. GS3 seems to be the optimal solution but it should not be considered a historical inevitability, a cosmic necessity. As David Hume taught us, "Nature is always too strong for principle."

***

The thermodynamic conceptualization of socioeconomic evolution is a form of physiocracy. Although it ought not to be considered a sequel to the like-named 18th century school of economics, there are some similarities, even beyond considering nature the underlying force of economic activity, which, abundant as it is, has a population-controlling fixed factor -- agricultural land for François Quesnay et al. Simply financed strong central authority protecting economic liberalism is perhaps the most relevant, additional parallel, with qualifications, of course.

For the original physiocrats, the absolute monarch embodied the degree of central authority deemed vital for widely shared economic prosperity within a nation. From the thermodynamic perspective, *strong multilateralism*, implying a consciously self-regulative democratic world, is regarded as indispensable for the dignified future of all.

It is worth mentioning that Quesnay showed a remarkable interest in China, seeing a great promise in the fusion of central authority with Confucian philosophy. The focus gravitates toward China also in the thermodynamic framework of universal history. The most populous country's two-level economic organization seems to anticipate what the planet will eventually need, but with Confucianism, not communism, in the background.

References[88]

Auffhammer, M. and Kellogg, R. (2011), "Clearing the Air? The Effects of Gasoline Content Regulation on Air Quality," *The American Economic Review*, vol. 101, no. 6, pp. 2687-2722.

Barro, R.J. and Sala-i-Martin, X. (1995), <u>Economic Growth</u>, McGraw-Hill, Inc., New York, NY.

Borenstein, S. (2012), "The Private and Public Economics of Renewable Electricity Generation," *Journal of Economic Perspectives*, vol. 26, issue no.1, pp. 67-92.

Boyer, R. (2013), "The Euro Crisis: Undetected by Conventional Economics, Favored by Nationally Focused Polity," *Cambridge Journal of Economics*, vol. 37, issue no. 3, pp. 533-569.

---

[88] Only print and online library items.

Brounen, D., Kok, N., and Quigley, J.M. (2013), "Energy Literacy, Awareness, and Conservation Behavior of Residential Households," *Energy Economics*, vol. 38 (July), pp. 42-50.

Braungart, M. and McDonough, W. (2002), Cradle to Cradle: Remaking the Way We Make Things, North Point Press (Division of Farrar, Straus and Giroux), New York, NY.

Brynjolfsson, E. and McAffe, A. (2014), The Second Machine Age, Work, Progress, and Prosperity in a Time of Brilliant Technologies, W.W. Norton & Company, Inc., New York, NY.

Clapp, J. (2001), Toxic Exports, the Transfer of Hazardous Wastes from Rich to Poor Countries, Cornell University Press, Ithaca, NY.

Combs, A. (1996), Radiance of Being: Complexity, Chaos, and the Evolution of Consciousness, Paragon House, St. Paul, MN.

Common, M. and Stagle, S. (2005), Ecological Economics, An Introduction, Cambridge University Press, New York, NY.

Cropper, H. W. (2001), Great Physicists, Oxford University Press, New York, NY.

Daly, H. and Farley, J. (2004), Ecological Economics, Principles and Applications, Pearson and Longman, Delhi, India.

Debreu, G. (1959), Theory of Value, Yale University Press, New Haven, CT.

DeShon, R. and Svyantek, D. J. (1993), "Organizational Attractors: A Chaos Theory Explanation of Why Cultural Change Efforts Often Fail." *Public Administration Quarterly*, vol. 17, no. 3, pp. 339-355.

Diederen, A. (2010), <u>Global Resource Depletion, Managed Austerity and the Elements of Hope</u>, Eburon Academic Publishers, Delft, the Netherlands.

Dooley, K. and Johnson, L. (1995), "TQM, Chaos, and Complexity," *Human Systems Management*, vol. 14, no. 4, pp. 1-16.

Dopfer, K. (ed.) (2005), <u>The Evolutionary Foundation of Economics</u>, Cambridge University Press, Cambridge, UK.

Fermi, E. (1936), <u>Thermodynamics</u>, Dover Publications, Inc., New York, NY.

Feuerstein, G. (1987), <u>Structures of Consciousness, The Genius of Jean Gebser -- An Introduction and Critique</u>, Integral Publishing, Lower Lake, CA.

Fullbrook, E. (2012), "To Observe or Not to Observe: Complementary Pluralism in Physics and Economics," *Real-World Economics Review*, issue no. 62, pp. 20-28.

Gebser, J. (1984), <u>The Ever-Present Origin</u>, Ohio University Press, Athens, OH.

Gebser, J. (1975), <u>Transformation of the West</u>, (in German), Novalis Verlag AG, Schaffhausen, Switzerland.

Georgescu-Roegen, N. (1976), "Energy and Economic Myths" in <u>Energy and Economic Myths: Institutional and Analytical Essays</u>," Pergamon Press, New York, NY.

Georgescu-Roegen, N. (1971), <u>The Entropy Law and the Economic Process</u>, Harvard University Press, Cambridge, MA.

Gillespie, R.J., Humphreys, D.A., Baird, N.C., and Robinson, E.A. (1986), <u>Chemistry</u>, Allyn and Bacon, Inc., Boston, MA.

Ginsburgh, V. and Keyzer, M. (1997), <u>The Structure of Applied General Equilibrium Models</u>, The MIT Press, Cambridge, MA.

Gore, A. (2013), <u>The Future, Six Drivers of Global Change</u>, Random House, Inc., New York, NY.

Gore, A. (2009), <u>Our Choice, A Plan to Survive the Climate Crisis</u>, Rodale and Melcher Media, New York, NY.

Gore, A. (2006), <u>An Inconvenient Truth, The Planetary Emergence of Global Warming and What We Can Do About It</u>, Rodale and Melcher Media, New York, NY.

Hall, C.A.S. (ed.) (1995), <u>Maximum Power, The Ideas and Applications of H.T. Odum</u>, University Press of Colorado, Niwot, CO.

Hobbes, T. (1952 reprint), <u>Hobbes's Leviathan</u>, Oxford University Press, Glasgow, UK.

Jing Chen (2005), <u>The Physical Foundation of Economics</u>, World Scientific Publishing Co. Pte. Ltd., Singapore.

Keynes, J.M. (1965), <u>The General Theory of Employment, Interest, and Money</u>, A Harbinger Book, Harcourt, Brace & World, Inc., New York, NY.

Kolesnikov, I.M., Vinokurov, V.A., and Kolesnikov, S.I. (2001), <u>Thermodynamics of Spontaneous and Non-spontaneous Processes</u>, Nova Science Publishers, Hauppauge, NY.

Kondepundi, D. and Prigogine, I. (1998), <u>Modern Thermodynamics, From Heat Engines to Dissipative Structures</u>, John Wiley & Sons, New York, NY.

Krysiak, F.C. (2006), "Entropy, Limits to Growth, and the Prospects for Weak Sustainability," *Ecological Economics*, vol. 58, issue no.1, pp.182-191.

Laszlo, E. (1992), <u>The Age of Bifurcation: The Key to Understanding the Changing World</u>, Gordon and Breach Publishing Group, New York, NY.

Lipsey, R.G. and Steiner, P.O. (1975), <u>Economics</u> (fourth edition), Harper & Row Publishers, New York, NY.

Loewenstein, W. R. (1999), <u>The Touchstone of Life; Molecular Information, Cell Communication, and the Foundations of Life</u>, Oxford University Press, New York, NY.

Luxemburg, R. (1968), <u>The Accumulation of Capital</u>, Modern Reader Paperbacks, New York, NY.

Meadows, D. H., Meadows, D.L., and Randers, J. (1992), <u>Beyond the Limits</u>, Chelsea Green Publishing Co., White River Junction, VT.

Meadows, D. H., Meadows, D.L., Randers J., and Behrens III, W.W. (1972), The Limits to Growth, Potomac Associates, New American Library, Times Mirror, New York, NY.

Niven, W. and Rausch, S. (2013), "A Numerical Investigation of the Potential for Negative Emissions Leakage," *The American Economic Review*, vol.103, no. 3, pp. 320-325.

Nordhause, W. D. (1992), Lethal Model 2: The Limits to Growth Revisited, Cowles Foundation Paper 831; Brookings Papers on Economic Activity, 2; Yale University, New Haven, CT.

Pearce, D.W. and Turner, R.K. (1990), Economics of Natural Resources and the Environment, Johns Hopkins University Press, Baltimore, MA.

Pogany, P. (2012), "Gebser's Relevance to the Global Crisis" in Filling the Credibility Gap, Mickunas, A. and Murphy, J. (eds.), Nova Science Publishers, Inc., Hauppauge, NY.

Pogany, P. (2006), Rethinking the World, Shenandoah Valley Research Press/iUniverse, Lincoln, NE.

Pollin, R. (2012), "U.S. Government Deficits and Debt Amid the Great Recession: What the Evidence Shows," *Cambridge Journal of Economics*, vol. 36, issue no.1, pp.161-187.

Prigogine, I. (1997), The End of Certainty, The Free Press, New York, NY.

Rees, W.E. (2006), "Ecological Footprints and Biocapacity: Essential Elements in Sustainability Assessment" in Renewables-Based Technology: Sustainability Assessment, Dewulf, J and Van Langenhove, H. (eds.), Wiley Online Library.

Reinhart, C.M. and Rogoff, K. (2009), <u>This Time Is Different: Eight Centuries of Financial Folly</u>, Princeton University Press, Princeton, NJ.

Robinson, J. (1962), <u>Economic Philosophy</u>, Doubleday & Company, Inc., Garden City, NY.

Romer, P.M. (1990), "Endogenous Technological Change," *The Journal of Political Economy*, vol. 98, no. 5, Part 2, pp. S71-S102.

Rosser, J.B. Jr. (1991), <u>A General Theory of Economic Discontinuities</u>, Kluwer Academic Publishers, Boston, MA.

Samuelson, P.A. (1948), <u>Foundations of Economic Analysis</u>, Harvard University Press, Cambridge, MA.

Schrödinger, E (1967), <u>What is Life? Mind and Matter</u>, Cambridge University Press, New York, NY.

Schumpeter, J.A. (1954), <u>History of Economic Analysis</u>, Oxford University Press, New York, NY.

Solow, R.M. (1957), "Technical Change and the Aggregate Production Function," *The Review of Economics and Statistics*, vol. 39, no. 3, pp. 312-320.

Stern, N. (2008), "The Economics of Climate Change," *The American Economic Review: Papers and Proceedings*, vol. 98, no. 2, pp. 1-37.

Stewart, D. and Mickunas, A. (1990), <u>Exploring Phenomenology, Guide to the Field and its Literature</u>, Ohio University Press, Athens, OH.

Syll, L. (2012), "Rational Expectations -- A Fallacious Foundation for Macroeconomics in a Non-Ergodic World," *Real-World Economics Review*, issue no. 62, pp. 34-50.

Takuro Uehara (2013), "Ecological Threshold and Ecological Economic Threshold: Implications from an Ecological Economic Model with Adaptation," *Ecological Economics*, vol. 93 (September), pp. 374-384.

Talbot, M. (1988), <u>Beyond the Quantum</u>, Bantam New Age Books, Inc., New York, NY.

Tiemann, M. (1998), *Waste Trade and the Basel Convention: Background and Update*, U.S. Congressional Research Service, Pub. No. 98-638 ENR, Washington, DC.

Timilsina, G.R. and Mevel, S. (2013), "Biofuels and Climate Change Mitigation: A CGE Analysis Incorporating Land-Use Change," *Environmental and Resource Economics*, vol. 55, issue no.1, pp.1-19.

Vasco, C. and Gabaix, X. (2013), "The Great Diversification and its Undoing," *The American Economic Review*, vol. 103, no. 5, pp. 1697-1727.

Wagner, M. (2008), "The Carbon Kuznets Curve: A Cloudy Picture Emitted by Bad Econometrics?," *Resource and Energy Economics*, vol. 30, issue no.3, pp. 388-408.

Wiener, N. (1961), <u>Cybernetics</u>, The M.I.T. Press, Cambridge, MA.

Wilson, E.O. (2000), <u>Sociobiology, The New Synthesis</u>, The Belknap Press of Harvard University Press, Cambridge, MA.

Wilson, E.O. (1999), <u>Consilience</u>, Vintage Books, A Division of Random House, Inc., New York, NY.

Yates, E.Y. (ed.) (1987), <u>Self-Organizing Systems, The Emergence of Order</u>, Plenum Press, New York, NY.

Printed in the United States
By Bookmasters